A GAME OF LIES

Clare Mackintosh is a police officer turned crime writer, and the multi-award winning author of seven *Sunday Times* bestselling novels. Translated into forty languages, her books have sold more than two million copies worldwide, and have spent a combined total of sixty-eight weeks in the *Sunday Times* bestseller chart. Clare lives in North Wales with her husband and their three children.

For more information visit Clare's website claremackintosh. com or find her at facebook.com/ClareMackWrites or on Twitter @ClareMackint0sh

Also by Clare Mackintosh

DC Ffion Morgan
The Last Party

I Let You Go
I See You
Let Me Lie
After the End
Hostage

Non-fiction
A Cotswold Family Life
I Promise It Won't Always Hurt Like This

Clare Mackintosh

A GAME OF LIES

SPHERE

SPHERE

First published in Great Britain in 2023 by Sphere
This paperback edition published in 2024 by Sphere

1 3 5 7 9 10 8 6 4 2

A CIP catalogue record for this book is available from the British Library.

ISBN 9-781-4087-2599-3

Typeset in Sabon by Palimpsest Book Production Limited, Falkirk, Stirlingshire
Printed and bound in Great Britain by Clays Ltd, Elcograf S.p.A.

Papers used by Sphere are from well-managed forests and other responsible sources.

MIX
Supporting
responsible forestry
FSC® C104740

Sphere
An imprint of
Little, Brown Book Group
Carmelite House
50 Victoria Embankment
London EC4Y 0DZ

An Hachette UK Company
www.hachette.co.uk

www.littlebrown.co.uk

For Sarah Clayton, Lynda Tunnicliffe and Huw McKee

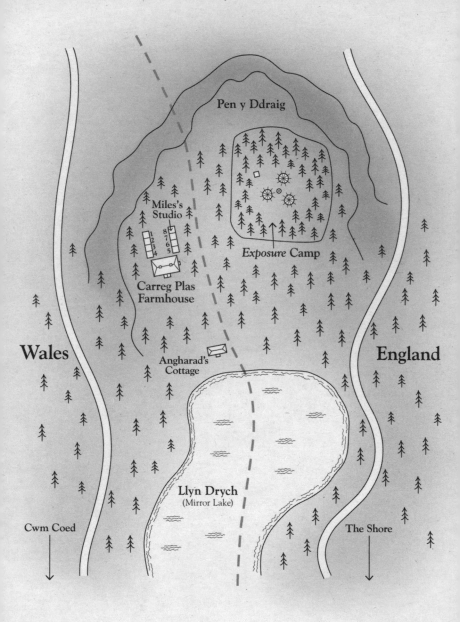

Pen y Ddraig

Miles's
Studio

Exposure Camp

Carreg Plas
Farmhouse

Wales

Angharad's
Cottage

England

Llyn Drych
(Mirror Lake)

Cwm Coed

The Shore

Contestants living in the *Exposure* Camp
Pam Butler   Ceri Jones
Jason Shenton   Henry Moore
Aliyah Brown   Ryan Francis
Lucas Taylor

STATEMENT

In light of today's tragic events, this evening's episode of Exposure *will not be broadcast. All filming has now ceased, and the remaining contestants and crew are being supported. The matter is in the hands of the police, and we will be making no further comment at this time.*

Young Productions

PART ONE

ONE

MONDAY | DC FFION MORGAN

The smell is sour and sweet at the same time, like fruit left to rot. Ffion breathes through her mouth but the stink's so bad, she can almost taste it.

'Was that you?' DC Alun Whitaker speaks without looking up from his paperwork. He's too vain to wear reading glasses, and deep grooves form at the corners of his eyes as he squints at the file.

'No, it bloody well wasn't.' Ffion shuts down the witness state-ment she's been reading and opens Rightmove. She needs the calming influence only five minutes of property porn can bring.

'Women aren't supposed to fart.' Alun looks across the bank of desks and raises his voice. 'I bet Georgina doesn't.'

Georgina shrugs back at him, pointing to the noise-cancelling headphones she wears over her dark, cropped hair. *Just a podcast*, she always says, if anyone asks. Ffion has long suspected that Georgina isn't listening to anything at all – the woman's quick enough to say yes to a *paned* when the kettle goes on – but is selective about what she wants to hear.

'I couldn't be with a woman who farts,' says Alun. As though he had a choice in the matter. Alun's last foray into the dating world had resulted in a bank transfer to an untraceable account and a computer virus that emailed out the last ten photos from Alun's camera roll, three of which had made Ffion want to bleach her eyes.

'Farting's for blokes,' he adds. 'It's not ladylike.'

Ffion contemplates trying to squeeze one out, just to be contrary.

Alun spins his chair to face her. He has long, thin limbs, and when he rests his hands on his knees, as he's doing now, he puts Ffion in mind of some kind of insect. 'Do you know where the case summary is for the Proctor GBH? I can't find it on the central drive.'

'That's because it's on my laptop.'

'Your personal laptop?' Alun raises an eyebrow and folds his arms. Ffion tries to remember if it's crickets that rub their legs together, or grasshoppers. 'You're supposed to save them directly on to the shared drive.'

Ffion doesn't know what sound Alun's arms would make if he rubbed them together, but it would no doubt be fucking annoying. She frowns at her screen, as though she's trying to solve a complex formula, instead of expanding her Rightmove search by another ten miles. 'I'll save it on to the drive when it's finished.'

'Imagine if all my files were on my personal laptop. What would you do if I got hit by a bus?'

'Throw a party?' Ffion clicks on a two-bedroomed apartment, five miles from Cwm Coed. Her rented cottage is perfect – and a blessed relief after a year living at home with Mam and Seren – but now her landlord wants it back. *Sorry, Ffion, but I can get twice as much for it as a holiday let, and times are hard . . .*

No shit, Ffion thought, when she started looking for a new place, discovering that prices had practically doubled in the past year. Living outside the village would mean no more easy strolls back from the pub after a lock-in, or popping round to Ceri's for

4

a coffee. On the other hand, it would be nice to leave the house without having her every move reported back to Mam. *Your Ffion's looking tired . . . did I see her at the doctor last week? I did wonder if she was pregnant . . .*

This apartment looks perfect, though. Brand new, affordable——and for over-sixties only.

'Fuck's sake.' Ffion clicks away from the bedroom balcony with views over the river. She wrinkles her nose as the noxious smell wafts her way with renewed vigour.

'And if *you're* hit by a bus, we won't know what's happening in the case.' Alun is refusing to let it go. 'We could lose crucial evidence.'

'When you make sergeant,' Ffion says, 'you can tell me what to do. Till then, back off. You're not my boss.'

'Quite right,' comes a cheerful voice from the door. 'I am.'

Detective Inspector Malik is resolutely jovial. Even when issuing a dressing-down – something of which Ffion has been on the receiving end a number of times – there's an avuncular tone to his voice, as though the subject of his lecture has been caught scrumping apples, instead of taking a riot van to collect a sofa from IKEA.

Malik takes a step forward, then sniffs the air. 'It smells like someone died in here.'

'It's Ffion,' Alun says.

'It's horrific. Open a window.' The DI is wearing his favourite waistcoat – a chessboard, complete with game in play. Ffion imagines there's a subliminal message in the checkmate or stale-mate or whatever is happening by the top button.

Georgina's already jumped to her feet to do the DI's bidding. Ffion narrows her eyes. Heard that alright, didn't she? Georgina Kent is what bosses call *diligent* and Ffion calls a try-hard. First to arrive, last to leave, and treats social invitations as though she's robotically programmed to decline. Neither Georgina nor Ffion wear much make-up, but Ffion imagines this is an intentional decision on Georgina's part, and not – as it is in Ffion's case – because she can't be arsed. Georgina has the sort of olive skin that tans in five minutes, whereas Ffion's skin is the colour of skimmed milk.

Malik holds up a printout. 'I need someone to check out some bones in Cwm Coed. Could be a moody one.'

'Sounds like someone I know.' Alun grins at Ffion. She's about to throw something at him when an audible fart erupts from her corner of the office.

Malik glares at her. 'Is that what I think it is?'

Ffion abdicates responsibility with a raised palm. 'This is what happens when you make me come in to the office every day.'

'You're telling me that stink is my fault?'

Ffion had been perfectly happy working out of her cubbyhole office in Cwm Coed, or writing statements in her car by the edge of the lake, reporting in as infrequently as she could get away with. Seventeen months ago, a murder investigation at luxury lakeside resort The Shore had turned the spotlight well and truly on to Cwm Coed – and on to Ffion. Her last appraisal – *not a team player; struggles with authority* – landed her with a fifty-minute commute to Bryndare and a scowl it would take more than Botox to shift.

'Ffion, I'm sorry to be the bearer of bad news, but coming to work is literally what you get paid for.' Malik crosses the office. 'It certainly doesn't give you *carte blanche* to do *this*.' He jerks Ffion's chair, rolling it backwards to reveal a large, hairy heap beneath Ffion's desk.

To call Dave a dog would be simplistic. Cursed with the neuroses of the Prozac generation, Dave jumps at loud noises, barks at prolonged silences, and is only truly happy when pressed against Ffion's legs or – ideally – on top of her. Given that Dave is the same height as a seated adult, this is particularly challenging at traffic lights, when he takes the brief pause as a sign that their journey is over and he can climb into Ffion's lap like a forty-kilo cat.

'How many times have I told you?'

Ffion wonders if Malik is addressing Dave, but then the DI turns to her, and she realises he's waiting for an answer. Dave's tail thumps slowly on the carpet.

'At least six,' Alun chips in. Arsehole.

'I can't leave him at home. He howls. The neighbours have complained.'

'So get a dog-walker. Leave him with your mum. Sign him up to the bloody circus. I don't care, Ffion – just stop bringing him to work!'

Dave unfolds himself from beneath the desk and Ffion makes a grab for his collar. 'What if he's my emotional support dog? Being with animals is proven to relieve stress.'

'The only thing being relieved around here is that dog's bowels. Take him home. Now.'

Reluctantly, Ffion gets to her feet. 'I might as well go and look at those bones, then. Since I'm going that way.'

'Oh, no.' Malik waggles a finger. 'I'm not having you swanning around at home with no one to keep an eye on you. Either Alun or Georgina can take it.' He turns to them. 'There's some kind of reality TV show being filmed on the mountain by Cwm Coed.'

'*Exposure.*' Ffion pulls on her coat. It's May, but this is North Wales, which means it's still practically winter.

'Never heard of it,' Georgina says. 'Sorry, sir.'

'I wish I could say the same.' Malik grimaces. 'It sounds ghastly. Seven "ordinary men and women", the trailer says, but what ordinary person wants to be filmed eating fish eyes and bulls' test—'

'I think you might be thinking of *I'm a Celebrity*, sir.' Alun looks faintly queasy.

'Anyway, the producer called in the bones this morning and—'

'Did they find them at the *Exposure* camp, or at the farmhouse where the crew are staying?' Ffion says. 'The house is ours, but the camp is just across the border into Cheshire.'

'I don't know where—' Malik stops. 'How do you know so much about this?'

'I know one of the contestants. Ceri Jones. She's the postie in Cwm Coed.' Ffion shuts down her computer. 'See you tomorrow, then.'

'Tomorrow? Ffion, it's only three—'

'No point in coming back only to go home again, is there? I'll work remotely for the last couple of hours.' Ffion smiles guilelessly. 'Oh, and don't rely on SatNav for the farm – it'll dump you in a field. You want to take the single-track road past Felingwm Isaf and hang a right at the big oak tree.'

'*Velin-goom Ee-sav*,' Malik repeats slowly. On paper, the DI possessed the minimum level of Welsh required of him to transfer from Surrey police to North Wales. In practice, he's still mastering pronunciation. He sighs, as though what he's about to do pains him. He holds out the printout to Ffion, keeping a firm grip on it for a few seconds after she takes it. 'Don't piss about.'

'Of course not, sir.'

'And take someone with you.'

'Honestly, boss, I work better on my—'

'You work with someone else or you don't go. Simple as that.'

Ffion looks first at Alun, then at Georgina, neither of whom look wildly enthusiastic about the prospect of teaming up with her. 'Talk about a rock and a hard place,' she mutters.

Alun chortles. 'I've got a hard—'

'Georgina,' Ffion says firmly.

Malik fixes Alun with an unforgiving stare. 'The 1980s called. They want their inappropriate banter back.'

'Sorry, sir, won't happen again.' Alun's cheeks blaze and Ffion suppresses a snort.

'Are you ready?' Georgina stands with her coat over one arm, as though Ffion's the one keeping her waiting.

'I was born ready.' Ffion opens the door. 'Come on, Dave.'

TWO

MONDAY | FFION

Ffion's Triumph Stag is parked in the section reserved for motor-bikes. She finishes the roll-up she smoked in six long drags as they crossed the rear yard, and holds out Dave's lead to Georgina.

Georgina eyes the dog with trepidation. 'Can't he go in the back?'

'He gets car sick. He'll be alright with you.'

'It's not him I'm worried about.' Georgina gets gingerly into the passenger seat, holding the lead as though it might explode. Dave squeezes himself into the footwell, his head almost level with Georgina's. Ffion pulls back her hair into a ponytail. This morning, after another of Alun's 'hilarious' asides, she'd tightened it with such force that her hairband had snapped, leaving her hair a tangle of red frizz that could only politely be called curls.

Ffion tugs a spare band from the stash she keeps on the Triumph's gearstick. She bought the car with the money her dad left her, and she has since spent ten times that amount keeping the russet-brown rust bucket on the road.

'Is this car legal?' Georgina is eyeing the – ingenious, to Ffion's mind – piece of cardboard wedged into the passenger door to stop the window from dropping open.

'It was serviced last month, as it happens,' Ffion says, omitting the fact that Trefor *Garej* told her it was a *bloody death trap* and

10

he was only letting her have it back because his cousin was married to Ffion's dad's nephew's wife, and she'd give him a row if he didn't.

The road that runs from Bryndare to the other side of Pen y Ddraig mountain is narrow and twisty, with a sheer drop on the passenger side. Georgina doesn't flinch. She's more preoccupied with keeping Dave – and his motion-sickness drool – confined to the footwell. Despite her best efforts, by the time they drop towards Cwm Coed the dog is on Georgina's lap, his head brushing Ffion's shoulder. Every few minutes a mournful whine cuts across the noise of the car's ancient engine and he paws at Ffion's lap, as though she might have forgotten he was there. Fat chance.

Ffion took on Dave in a rare moment of weakness, after attending an arson at a rescue shelter where Dave was several years into what was turning out to be a whole-life sentence. *He'll be put to sleep next week*, a shelter volunteer told Ffion. *It's so sad – he's got so much love to give.* They saw her coming, Huw said afterwards. *They make out all the dogs are on death row, you wally. Twenty quid says you end up giving it back to them.*

It isn't the twenty quid, Ffion thinks grimly, as she wipes drool from her shoulder, it's the principle. However much she regrets her impulsive decision to take Dave, losing a bet to her ex-husband is out of the question. Besides, beneath the bad breath and the flatulence Dave has some redeeming qualities, she's sure of it. She just hasn't found them yet.

The sky is a vibrant blue, but drifts of mist lie in the pockets of space beside the mountain. They blur the edges of the road, but Ffion knows the twists and turns as surely as she knows her own body. Far below them, Llyn Drych snakes along the valley. The lake is as narrow as a river in some parts, and Ffion spent her

11

childhood summers swimming from one side to the other. She would pause in the middle, treading water on the unseen border between England and Wales, feeling – for that instant – as though she belonged to neither place. The hamlet of Felingwm Isaf, which roughly translates into English as Lower Mill Valley, lies at the northern tip of Llyn Drych – or Mirror Lake, as the incomers call it. Ffion slows, looking for the turning that will take them up to Carreg Plas, the farmhouse currently being used by the *Exposure* crew. The single-track road climbs steeply and Ffion hopes they don't meet anyone; Trefor *Garej* had had a few choice words to say about her brakes.

'What's the score with this *Exposure*, then?' Georgina says.

Ffion navigates around a sheep which is reclining on the warm tarmac. 'Don't you watch telly? The ads have been on every five minutes.'

'I only use streaming channels really. There's never anything decent on terrestrial.'

Ffion begs to differ. At least, she would, if she could be bothered, which she can't. Terrestrial TV (or, as Ffion calls it, normal telly) is comfort TV. It makes Ffion think of bringing Mam a cuppa when *EastEnders* is starting; of teenage negotiations over watching *Hollyoaks* instead of S4C. It makes her think of highlighting the films in the *Radio Times*, the Christmas before Dad died; of Mam asking Ffion to play with baby Seren till *Teletubbies* came on. Plus normal telly has *Homes Under the Hammer*, Ffion's guilty pleasure.

Ffion glances at Georgina, who is attempting to rotate her face, owl-like, away from Dave's hairy snout. 'Like the boss said, it's a reality TV show. Seven contestants living on Pen y Ddraig mountain for a fortnight. The usual challenges, a public vote – you know the sort of thing.'

'Not really.'

Ffion looks at her. 'You've never watched *Big Brother*?'

'No.'

'*Love Island*?'

'No.'

'*Married at First Sight*?'

'Tell me that's not as horrific as it sounds.'

'It's worse.' Ffion turns through an open gateway on to a gravel drive. 'That's what makes it so brilliant.'

She parks the Triumph in front of Carreg Plas, a solid, stone-built farmhouse to which someone has added a small wooden porch. Two bay trees in square pots stand sentry by the front door. As they wait for someone to answer the door, Georgina looks down at Dave.

'Why don't you just leave him in the car?'

'Because he'll eat it.' Ffion bangs the knocker again, then gives up and walks around the side of the house. The garden gate is open, and they find themselves in a cobbled courtyard. If the view from the front of the house, looking down on to Llyn Drych, was spectacular, the back is nothing short of breathtaking. Dense woodland slopes up from the farmhouse, giving way to the rocky landscape of Pen y Ddraig, its summit swirled in mist.

On either side of the courtyard are two rows of red-brick outbuildings with slate roofs. The numbers one to eight are painted on to stable doors.

'Horses?' Georgina says.

'I said, I'm not doing it!' comes a woman's voice from number eight.

'Bloody argumentative horses.' Ffion walks towards the open door, just as a dark-haired woman with a full face of make-up storms out and heads for the farmhouse.

13

'Sorry about that. The talent can be a little temperamental.' A man steps forward, hand outstretched. 'Miles Young, Young Productions. Young by name, less so by nature nowadays.' He gives a rueful grin, then laughs, pushing a hand through thick white-blond hair. He's in his late forties, with pale blue eyes and eyelashes so fine they're almost invisible. High cheekbones give him a pinched, rather anxious look, despite his broad smile.

'The talent?' Georgina shakes his hand. 'Detective Constable Georgina Kent, Bryndare CID.'

'My presenter, Roxy Wilde. Such charisma – the camera loves her.' Miles offers his hand to Ffion. 'And you are?'

'DC Morgan. I understand you've found some bones?' As Ffion says his favourite word, Dave sits bolt upright, his tail sweeping an arc on the cobbles.

'I called hours ago. Where have—' Miles stops himself, screwing up his face in self-admonishment. 'Sorry, I don't mean to sound . . . You must have a million more important things to do. It's just that we're on such a tight schedule. Most reality TV programmes show footage recorded the day before, or even earlier, but we're breaking new ground. What you'll see tonight will have been recorded today. Fortunately we've got a lot in the can already – the contestants stayed at the farmhouse last night, you see, so this delay isn't as disastrous as—'

Ffion cuts in. 'Could we see the bones, Mr Young?'

Miles glances back at his desk, which boasts two computers and a tangle of leads, then tears himself away. 'Of course.' He reaches for his jacket. In addition to the desk, the room has a double bed and a slim wardrobe. Ffion spots a tea tray, and the door to what she assumes is a bathroom. A large casement window at the back of the room looks on to the woods in the foothills of the mountain.

'It's a cracking spot, isn't it?' Miles locks the door behind them. 'Our location scout did a good job. Camp's about twenty minutes up the mountain.'

'Who stays at the farm?' Georgina asks.

'I'm in the main house, along with Owen – that's our cameraman – and Roxy, who you've encountered. Number eight's my studio, and the rest of the stable rooms are for the contestants, for when they're evicted.' Miles takes them through a gate at the rear of the courtyard, which leads on to the mountain.

'They come back here?' Ffion says.

'It's a condition of their contract. Two nights back at the farm for interviews. Once that's done and dusted, they get their participation fee.'

'Which is how much?' A gorse bush snags at Ffion's legs.

'Ten grand.'

Georgina whistles. 'Nice.'

'Not as nice as the hundred grand the winner – or winners – will get.'

'Bl—imey.' Ffion manages to divert the expletive. Malik says she needs to *temper her language*, whatever the fuck that means. People have complained, apparently.

'I imagined there'd be more of you,' Georgina says. 'Big lighting rigs, catering wagons, a vast crew.'

'I like to keep things tight when we're filming,' Miles says. 'It's been bedlam while we were building the camp, but now we're rolling I've stripped it back to the bare minimum. We've got a runner who comes each day, a security guard, and for anything else I need I call the production office.'

'What are the contestants doing now?' Despite the impression she gave DI Malik, Ffion knows very little about *Exposure*, beyond the fact that a bunch of wannabe survivalists getting pissed off with each other on a North Wales mountain has to be worth a watch.

'Well, not a lot, thanks to these bones,' Miles says drily. 'One of them suggested they dig out the fire pit, and as soon as I saw what they'd uncovered – I was watching from the studio, of course – I sent our runner up to call a halt to proceedings.'

They keep walking for several more minutes, then, ahead of them, Ffion sees a high wire fence. 'Is that it?'

'Yes. It belongs to a neighbouring farm. Erected for pheasants, I believe, so it's not the most rigorous of barriers, but it marks the boundary nicely.' He raises his voice. 'Everything alright, Dario?'

'Right as rain, boss.' Dario has the sort of square frame you don't mess with, and a head like a polished egg. He wears a high-visibility jacket which extends almost to his knees, with SECURITY on his left breast in shiny blue letters. He eyes Dave with interest. 'That one of them cadaver dogs, is it?'

Georgina makes a noise which Ffion might have taken for a laugh, were it not for the fact that Georgina Kent never, ever laughs.

'Not exactly,' Ffion says.

'That Zee's been back,' Dario tells Miles.

'You'd have thought she'd have got the message by now.' Miles turns to Georgina and Ffion. 'There's this girl. Woman, I suppose. Her name's Zee Hart, and she's got some godawful YouTube channel called *Hart Breaks*. She applied to be on the show, then, when she was knocked back, she had the audacity to put herself forward as a presenter for a TV segment she wanted to call *Extra Exposure*. Wanted to interview contestants as they got knocked out, that sort of thing.'

'She's put up a tent,' Dario says.

16

'A tent?' Miles's voice – already high-pitched – goes up an octave. 'That's not allowed, surely?'

'Where is it?' Ffion says.

'About twenty metres from the perimeter fence, on the other side of camp.' Dario points.

Ffion shrugs. 'Nothing to stop people wild camping on the mountain.'

'Monitor her,' Miles says. 'Let me know if she moves.'

'Will do, boss.'

'And no one's to go beyond this fence without my say-so, okay?'

'Got it.'

'The show airs at seven –' Miles clasps his hands together in prayer '– and then . . . well, don't be surprised if the tabloids swing by.'

He gives a knowing chuckle and Ffion blows out her cheeks. What would it be like to possess such extraordinary levels of self-confidence? Okay, so *Exposure* sounds like good telly, but it's just another reality show, when all's said and done. A tabloid hack would only trek out to Snowdonia if the cast were wall-to-wall celebrities.

Unless, of course, the bones turn out to be interesting . . .

They follow Miles through a metal gate, which Dario padlocks behind them with a *click*. Ffion feels instantly too hot, despite the wind which, up on the mountain, feels anything but summery. She couldn't do *Exposure*. Not in a million years. Quite apart from having to live with six strangers for a fortnight, she couldn't handle being locked inside what is effectively a cage. Like wild cats in a safari park, she thinks, and she imagines stalking the boundary, looking for an escape.

'How big is the enclosure?' Georgina asks, as they weave their way through narrow-trunked, densely planted trees. Ffion glances at her, wondering if she's feeling as claustrophobic as Ffion, but her face is its usual impassive mask.

'Pretty big.' Dario gestures to the trees. 'It was all woodland, but Miles had a section cleared in the middle for the camp.'

Sure enough, a few minutes later the woodland opens out and they're standing in the clearing. The trees shield the fence from view, giving the impression of total isolation. They could be in the middle of dense forest, Ffion thinks. They could be in another country, another time.

Three large cream bell tents stand in a line at the back of the clearing. A short distance away is a wood-fired hot tub, logs neatly stacked against its side, and on the opposite side is what Ffion assumes – from the spade leaning against the door – to be a compost loo.

In the centre of the camp is a rudimentary kitchen, built in the same expertly rustic fashion as the loo, plus a vast table – seemingly hewn from a single piece of wood – and seven seats. Above the table, metal lanterns sway on a thick rope suspended between two poles. Aside from the rustle of leaves in the breeze, it's eerily quiet.

Ffion points to a small windowless structure clad in horizontal planks, the width of a phone box, but half the height. Steps have been cut into the ground, in order to access the door. 'What's that? Another loo?'

'The . . . er . . . diary room,' Miles says, but there are two spots of colour on his cheeks. Ffion wants to ask more, but Miles is directing their attention to the rest of the camp. 'Boys are on the left, girls on the right. The third bell tent is the chill-out zone. There are cameras in the tents and in this communal camp area, but not in the woods – any filming there will be with Owen and Roxy.' He points to the fire pit. 'Here are the bones.'

They walk towards the kitchen area, where another spade lies

18

abandoned next to a pile of dirt. A couple of metres away is a tall tree stump with a padlock bolted to the surface.

Ffion is about to ask what the lock is for when Dave yanks his lead so hard she almost falls over. 'Oi!' She yanks back, before remembering what the *Perfect Puppy* book says. 'I mean, *off*.' She can do without Dave running away with a murder victim's meta-tarsal. She's about to make a *how humerus* joke, but decides Georgina wouldn't appreciate it.

The three of them look down at the shallow grave, in which lies an assortment of dirt-encrusted bones.

'You've done the right thing by stopping filming,' Georgina says.

'The thing is, if we don't get going again soon—'

'We'll need to get an anthropologist out from Bangor University. They'll tell us whether the bones are animal or human. If they're human, they'll date them, then establish if the site's of archaeo-logical importance.' Georgina takes out her phone. 'We should notify Cheshire Constabulary – we're on their side of the border.'

'You won't get any reception up here,' Miles says. 'It's why we use radios.'

Ffion feels eyes on the nape of her neck. She turns to see a brown-skinned woman watching them from the entrance to the women's bell tent. She's young and slim, and she's wearing what Ffion assumes is the camp uniform: khaki combat trousers and an orange fleece. Dark hair falls in two thick plaits over her shoulders.

'What are you doing?' Miles has followed Ffion's gaze and is striding towards the bell tent. 'I told you to stay out of the way!' He practically shoves the woman back inside, and Ffion catches a glimpse of the name *Aliyah* on the reverse of the woman's fleece, before Miles sweeps the canvas door across the entrance.

'This is batshit,' Ffion mutters, crouching to get a closer look at the bones.

'Sorry about that.' When Miles returns, he's all smiles again. '*Exposure* is sponsored by a major gambling operator. It's crucial the contestants aren't influenced by the outside world, which means keeping them away from visitors – even upright citizens like yourselves!' He laughs, then looks at the bones and sighs. 'Do you have any idea how long this is going to take? We're expecting record viewing figures – the hype's been incredible. Thousands of people applied for *Exposure*. Some of the rejected ones tracked me down, begged me to reconsider – threatened me, in a few cases. This show is a big deal.'

Miles's speech has little effect on Georgina. 'These bones could belong to a murder victim, Mr Young. I'd say that's a pretty big deal too, wouldn't you?'

'We air in three hours and we still have the contestants' briefing to shoot, not to mention prepping the live segment—'

'The bones aren't human.' Ffion looks up from the fire pit. 'You can crack on.'

Miles exhales. 'That's excellent news, thank you, officer.'

'Hang on a minute, we can't just . . .' Georgina glares at Ffion. 'The Standard Operating Procedure clearly states—'

'They're animal bones.' Ffion stands, wincing as her knee clicks. Is it normal for your body to start clicking in your early thirties? Lately, Ffion has caught herself making a tiny *aah* sound when she sits down. It's a short step from there to having prunes every morning and watching ITV dramas with the subtitles on because *actors all mumble nowadays*.

'I had no idea you'd done an anthropology degree.' Georgina's voice is laced with sarcasm.

'I haven't.' Ffion reaches into the grave and fishes out a small metal tag, trailing the remnants of what might once have been a collar. 'But I've yet to encounter a human corpse tagged with the number of a veterinary practice.'

That evening, after work, Ffion opens her fridge. She last looked inside approximately three and a half minutes ago, and there is no more in it now than there was then. Ffion picks up Dave's lead. 'Come on, mate, we'll eat *Chez Morgan* tonight.'

It's just before seven when she opens the back door of her childhood home. The kitchen is Elen Morgan's natural habitat, and Ffion's surprised to find it empty. Laundry hangs on the airer above the range, and Mam's notebook lies open on the table, neat ticks against the items on her to-do list. *Change towels in holiday let. Buy teabags. Return library books.*

'Mam?' Ffion opens the fridge and her stomach rumbles in anticipation of the cold meat pie she finds there. She rootles in the salad drawer for tomatoes and lettuce.

'In here,' comes the response from the lounge. 'Turn it up, Seren, I can't hear a thing.'

'It's the adverts, Mam. And I thought you didn't want to watch it, anyway?'

'Watch what?' Ffion carries her spoils through to the lounge. 'Alright, Caleb?'

Seren's boyfriend is sprawling on the floor. He's bulked out lately and his jawline has lost the softness of adolescence. Only the floppy fringe still marks him out as a teenager. He sits bolt upright. 'Yeah, good. You alright?' he adds, as an afterthought. Seren says Ffion makes Caleb feel uncomfortable, as though he has to watch his step.

'I will be, once I've eaten this,' Ffion says. 'Budge up.' She kicks Seren's feet off the sofa so she can sit down.

'It's a restaurant I'm running now, is it?' Mam says. She's wearing a red apron with the word YES in bold white letters – the logo for Yes Cymru, the movement for Welsh independence.

'Three stars. Limited menu. Customer service needs work.' Ffion takes a bite of meat pie and nods towards the telly. 'Right. What are we watching?'

THREE

MONDAY | ELEN MORGAN | EPISODE ONE

'Er, *Exposure*?' Seren says, as though Ffion is stupid.

Elen tuts. The problem with teenagers is they think they know everything. Ffion was the same at that age. Too big to send to the naughty step; too young to have had the corners bashed off them out in the real world.

'How was your day?' she asks Ffion. 'Anything interesting?'

'Not really.'

'I had an Amazon parcel stolen off the doorstep today.' Elen tries to get everything she needs from Cwm Coed's high street, but she needed printer ink and it couldn't wait till her next trip to town.

Seren shushes her. 'It's starting.'

On screen, violent colours clash into each other, exploding into graphics that make Elen's head hurt. To think she's missing *Heno* for this. A vivid blue circle stretches taut as an elastic band, only to *ping* back into what Elen now sees is a garish interpretation of the town's lake. Above it, a lurid green triangle slams into place amid fireworks of purple and orange. In perfect synchronicity, a clashing, urgent soundtrack builds to a crescendo, as letters drop from the sky and crash on to the mountain.

E X P O S U R E

Seren squeals with excitement.

'Ffi?' Elen prompts.

Ffion tears herself away from the screen. 'What?'

'My parcel.'

'It's probably next door.'

'No, I checked.'

'Ah, well.'

'Oh, that's lovely, that is. My own daughter, a high-flying police officer—'

'I'm a constable, Mam.'

'—and she can't be bothered to investigate when her own mam's been the victim of a hate crime. *Ah, well*, said the police spokeswoman.'

'It's not a hate crime, Mam.'

'Well, *I* hate it.'

'That's not—'

'Remember all those thefts last year, and no one was ever caught? We've got a serial offender on our hands. Or a copycat.'

'Shh!' Seren turns up the volume.

Elen peers at the screen. 'I don't recognise any of them.'

'They're not celebrities, Mam, you're not supposed to recognise them.' Lately, Seren has taken to speaking to her as though Elen is demented, instead of simply menopausal. 'They're just normal people.'

'Except for Ceri,' Ffion says, through a mouthful of pie.

'Ceri's not normal? That's not a very kind thing to say, Ffion Morgan.'

'I mean you'll recognise her.'

'See that pile of logs by the hot tub?' Caleb leaps to his feet, pointing at the screen, which shows what awaits the contestants in camp. 'I stacked those!'

'You did really good,' Seren says loyally.

Ffion sets her plate on the floor for Dave to wash. 'Why were you stacking logs in the *Exposure* camp?'

'I'm working there,' Caleb says, not taking his eyes off the screen, where the seven contestants are walking up Pen y Ddraig towards the camp.

'You're the *Exposure* runner?'

'I did tell you,' Elen says.

'Mam, you told me Caleb was *running*.'

Elen flaps a hand at Ffion. Runner, running, what of it? On screen, the camera focuses on each contestant in turn, their name and occupation appearing in a banner beneath them.

'*Pam Butler*,' Seren reads. 'Head teacher. She looks like my old PE teacher.'

Elen frowns at her. 'Your PE teacher was a man.'

'Exactly.'

'Well, I think she looks very capable,' Elen says, feeling the need to defend Pam, who really doesn't look anything like a man, except that her hair is cut in a practical short back and sides. Like all the contestants, she wears khaki trousers with side pockets, and a bright orange fleece with her name printed on the back. Pam's trousers have been rolled up at the ankles, Elen notes. They could at least have found a pair to fit her, poor thing.

'What's a "childcare practitioner" when it's at home?' Ffion says, as *Aliyah Brown* appears on their screen, flashing perfect teeth at the other contestants.

'She works in a nursery,' Caleb says.

'Then why don't they just say so?' Ffion says. 'I suppose they'd call me a "crime practitioner", would they?'

Caleb gives a sly grin. 'Actually, Miles called you a—'

'*Jason Shenton*,' Elen reads loudly. '*Firefighter*.' Jason has a beard – one of those small, neat ones that look as though they've been drawn on with pen and ink – and Elen wonders what the contestants are allowed in the way of toiletries. She wouldn't call herself high-maintenance, but you don't get skin like hers in your early sixties without a bit of retinol, and she wouldn't want to be parted from it.

'He'll win,' Seren says. 'Look at the size of those biceps.'

Elen glances at Caleb, but he's either secure enough not to mind his girlfriend leching over another man, or too engrossed in the show to notice. Elen suspects the latter – the lad was cock-a-hoop to land this running job, and fair play, he's working hard at it. Seren's hardly seen him recently which is no bad thing, what with A-levels this month.

The next two contestants are both men. *Henry Moore* is an accountant with the accent of someone who's moved around a lot. He's tall with dark hair, and although not Elen's type – he's twenty years too young, for a start – it's clear he'll be competition for Jason when it comes to the female vote.

'Imagine being stuck in a camp with an accountant.' Ffion yawns.

'You can't write off an entire profession,' Elen says. 'You'll never find a husband with an attitude like that.'

'Are you auditioning for *Pride and Prejudice*? I don't want a husband. I had one of those and I got a refund.'

'A boyfriend, then,' Elen says, but Ffion doesn't respond. Elen sighs. All any parent wants is for their children to be happy, isn't it? And Ffion might think she's happier on her own, but Elen's not convinced.

'I'd rather be stuck with an accountant than a vicar,' Seren says, as *The Reverend Lucas Taylor* waves to the cameras. His pink cheeks give him a cherubic air, although Elen imagines he must be in his fifties.

'He's really nice, actually,' Caleb says. 'I made him a coffee yesterday, when he arrived. White, no sugar. He said it was perfect.'

'You do make good coffee,' Seren says.

Five minutes into the programme and Elen is already bored. She thinks of all the things she should be doing (laundry, an online shop, the accounts for the holiday let) and all the things she'd *rather* be doing (anything but this), and sighs loudly.

'Mam, no one's forcing you to watch it,' Seren says.

'Just showing my support for Caleb, *cariad*.'

Elen hadn't been sure about Caleb at first. He's English, for starters, and that isn't her being racist, just that a Welsh one would have been better. But for all his London street smarts, and the wisecracks Elen's not sure she always understands, Caleb Northcote is a good lad, and he and Seren have been inseparable for the past year.

'I can't wait to see your name in the credits, babe.' Seren leans over and kisses Caleb. A wave of emotion washes over Elen: like being homesick even though you're having a lovely time on holiday. Elen has watched Ffion grow up (although there are times when that progression is debatable), and now it's Seren's turn. Elen glances at Ffion and realises she is watching Seren too, and that her expression says everything Elen's feeling. The two girls are cut from the same cloth – right down to the untameable hair and the stubborn set of their mouths. *Resting bitch face*, Seren calls it. Elen refrains from commenting that it can be remarkably mobile, too, in her experience.

'So strange to see someone you know on the telly,' Ffion says, as *Ceri Jones* comes into shot. Elen half expects to see Ceri in her usual postal worker shorts, but she's wearing the camp uniform, the bright orange top making her pale skin look sallow.

'More strange to want to be on it,' replies Elen, who sees no appeal in becoming a performing monkey in front of a public vote. She's surprised to see Ceri – who was bullied dreadfully when she was a teenager – putting herself through something like this, when she's usually so private. Elen has always found it ironic that they know so little about Ceri Jones, when the postwoman knows so much of everyone else's business.

The people of Cwm Coed had discovered Ceri was going to be on *Exposure* the same way the rest of the nation did: in a splashy online story about the 'hot' new reality TV show. The story was accompanied by a sidebar headed 'Five Facts about North Wales', three of which were incorrect. 'I gather you're going to be famous,' Elen had said the next morning, as she took her post.

Ceri had reddened. 'I wasn't allowed to say anything. Not till the announcement.'

'What made you apply?'

'Dunno, really. Bit of fun, isn't it?' Ceri had said, but the flush was darkening, and she hadn't hung around to ask after Seren, or for Elen to fish for what Ceri and Ffion had got up to when they went to Liverpool the other weekend.

'Don't you think it's a bit out of character for her?' Elen says now, as they watch Ceri join the other contestants. 'Doing this, I mean?'

'She thinks she can win.' Ffion shrugs. 'And if she does, she's quids in.'

Seren slides on to the floor to join Caleb, who has shuffled closer to the television. 'I thought she had a Sugar Momma?'

'Seren!' Elen chastises, even though Seren is almost eighteen and will soon be leaving home.

'They broke up.' Ffion nods towards the screen. 'Can we actually watch this now, please?'

'That's Ryan,' Caleb says, a split second before the man's name and occupation appears at the bottom of the screen. *Ryan Francis, software engineer.*

'He doesn't look like he'll present much competition.' Ryan is walking with Ceri, picking his way gingerly across the rocky terrain. He has the look of a man who spends too much time indoors, Elen concludes. His features are rounded, and long lashes frame soft blue eyes. When he catches his foot in a rabbit hole and stumbles, Ceri snorts with laughter. The camera zooms in on Ryan, blinking away tears.

'That's not like Ceri,' Ffion says.

But Ceri's not usually playing for a hundred grand, thinks Elen, and money does strange things to people.

Ryan scrubs at his face.

'Twitter's going to destroy him.' Seren speaks with the resigned insight of her generation. 'I might have to give him a pity vote.'

'For one pound twenty plus network rates? You can use your own phone if you do.' Elen won't be casting a vote, although, if she did, it would be for the head teacher, who is a woman after Elen's own heart. No sooner have the contestants arrived in camp than Pam Butler is swiftly organising their chores.

'Henry and Jason, you get a fire going; Aliyah, sweetheart, are you okay to make the beds up with Lucas?' She plants both hands on her ample hips and surveys their surroundings. 'See that cupboard marked "food", Ryan? Go and see what we might be able to rustle up for lunch.'

'Notice she's getting everyone else to do the work,' Ffion says archly. 'Typical teacher.'

A loud scream makes everyone jump – both on screen and in Elen's lounge. Aliyah comes haring out of the women's tent and throws herself at the nearest man: the accountant, Henry Moore.

'There's a massive spider!' She shudders, brushing herself down as though she were teeming with bugs. 'Get it out, please! I can't sleep in that tent if there are going to be spiders there.'

Seren snorts. 'She's not going to last long.'

Henry puts an arm around Aliyah and gives her a squeeze. 'I'll sort it.'

The camera cuts to an interior shot, as Henry enters the women's tent and looks around. Three beds are positioned in a fan shape, their pillows almost touching the canvas walls. A wooden locker sits at the foot of each bed, and in the centre of the tent is a pile of giant bean bags.

'Shows like this would normally have dozens of editors,' says Caleb, with the experience of a fortnight in the industry. 'But the way Miles has done it is really clever. He and another editor spent weeks on the template for the show, so Miles can drop footage in as quickly as possible. Storyboarding, it's called. Miles works insane hours. He goes for a run every morning, but otherwise he's at his desk from like six a.m. till after the show goes out.'

On screen, Henry is shaking out bedding. He stoops and cups something in his hands.

'People say Miles is a control freak, but I think he's a genius. And he's sound, too, you know? Like, giving me my first TV credit – that's huge. It's really going to open doors.'

Back in camp, Henry has disposed of the spider and received a hero's hug from Aliyah.

'I know it's pathetic,' she says. 'But it's the way their legs are all . . .' She lets out a squeal at the thought of it.

Henry laughs gently. 'Everyone's scared of something. Don't sweat it.'

'What are you scared of?' Aliyah asks.

'Me? Water.' Henry looks embarrassed. 'I almost drowned when I was a kid.'

'Oh, my God.' Aliyah puts a hand to her chest. She looks as though she's about to ask more, but the pair of them are summoned by Jason, who has found a spade and decided they need to dig out the fire pit for a better result.

'They found bones. Right there,' Caleb says, and it's clear he's been bursting to share this news.

'Bones?' Elen looks at Ffion. 'Do you know about this? It could be a crime scene.'

'Thanks for the advice, Mam.'

They're interrupted by a glamorous brunette striding on to screen. At first glance she's in the same combat trousers as the contestants, but Elen notes that the tailoring is better, and that the utilitarian buttons have been switched for glittering silver ones. In place of the orange fleece is a black gilet, unzipped to reveal a hint of cleavage.

'Welcome –' the presenter gives a dramatic pause '– to Dragon Mountain!'

The contestants' cheers are drowned out by the chorus of *It's Pen y Ddraig!* from Elen's lounge, almost certainly echoed in every house in Cwm Coed, Elen thinks. Dragon Mountain indeed. *Bobl bach!*

'They were going to use the Welsh name,' Caleb says. 'But Roxy couldn't say it properly.'

'If people can't say it, they shouldn't be on it,' Elen says tartly.

'Ladies and gentlemen.' Roxy Wilde has a twinkle in her eye. 'You think you're here for a survival show, don't you?' There are shouts of *Yes!* from some of the contestants. Pam and Ryan exchange uneasy glances. Roxy delivers her punchline with panache. 'You're wrong.'

'What does she mean?' Elen waits for Caleb to explain, but the lad looks as confused as the rest of them.

31

'All of you have a secret,' Roxy says. 'Something you've worked hard to conceal from your friends and family.' The camera closes in as she smiles wickedly at the seven contestants. 'You're not only competing for cash. You're competing to keep your secret. You're competing to avoid *Exposure*.'

'Holy fuck,' Ffion says.

Seren gives a short, shocked laugh. She turns to Caleb. 'You kept that quiet.'

'I – I wasn't allowed to say anything,' Caleb says, but Elen sees he's flustered. He turns away from them, clearly upset that the 'creative genius' he so reveres hasn't let him in on the show's own big secret.

'Your objective,' Roxy is saying, 'is to finish the fourteen days with your secret intact. Whoever's still standing after the final episode receives an incredible hundred thousand pounds each!'

'They can't do this, Ffion *bach*, surely?'

'I think they are doing it, Mam.'

Roxy has produced a metal box which she's padlocking on to a wooden plinth close to where Jason and Henry were digging the fire pit. She turns and addresses the camera. 'This box contains all the contestants' secrets, and *you* can vote for the contestant you want to expose.'

'Oh, my God, let's vote to expose Lucas!' Seren says. 'I bet he's a pervert – vicars always are, aren't they?'

Elen feels nauseous. Who came up with such a twisted idea? How did it ever get approved? She wants to leave the room, but she's unable to move, gripped by the awfulness of what she's watching.

'Voting will be open continuously, and at any point when we decide to, we'll send the viewers' least favourite contestant to the confession pod.' Roxy grins. 'And let's just say we have a few

tricks up our sleeves to encourage those revelations . . .' There
follows an abrupt, dizzying montage of a tiny windowless space
containing nothing but a throne-like chair fixed to the ground.
In the first shot, water pours into the room; in the second, rats
swarm over the seat. There are spiders next, then snakes, then
cockroaches. A sudden flurry of wings, then the crimson splash
of blood. The next shot shows the pod from the outside, and Elen
sees that the structure is narrow as a coffin and submerged into
the ground. She shudders at the thought of being trapped inside
it.

Roxy Wilde is rattling through the rules. Contestants can try
to win a day's immunity by exposing someone else, but if the
accuser's guess is wrong, it's they who will enter the confession
pod to face three minutes of their own personal hell.

'This is brutal,' Seren breathes, and yet, on screen, the contestants are giving whoops of excitement.

'Bring it on!' cries Jason.

'I am *so* up for this!' Aliyah says.

Roxy turns to the camera. 'What do our contestants have to
hide? Join us tomorrow evening to find out!'

As the credits roll, Elen, Seren and Ffion look at each other in
stunned silence.

Ffion whistles. 'Poor Ceri. Do you think she had any idea?'

'I doubt it,' Elen says. 'I get the impression no one knew. Is that
right, Caleb?'

But Caleb is intent on the screen, looking for the credit that
will kickstart his career in television. He blinks rapidly as the
music finishes, then turns to Seren in confusion. 'It wasn't there.
My name wasn't there.'

Seren's mouth drops open. 'The bastard.'

Elen doesn't admonish her. She looks at Ffion, and she knows they're both thinking the same thing. They're thinking about how they'd feel if their own secrets were exposed; they're imagining how those men and women on Pen y Ddraig feel at the prospect of public humiliation.

'He promised me.' Caleb is almost in tears. 'He said there wasn't a budget to put me on the payroll, but I'd be in the credits as production assistant.'

'Absolute c—'

'*Diolch yn fawr*, Seren Morgan, that's quite enough.' Elen crosses the room and snaps off the TV. 'Well, no one will be tuning in to watch *that* drivel tomorrow, if they've got a shred of decency about them—'

Ffion gives a bark of laughter. 'But they haven't, Mam. Reality TV is the modern-day equivalent of taking your knitting to an execution. Half the UK will be watching this tomorrow, desperate to see someone's life torn apart.' She shakes herself, as though the thought makes her feel dirty. 'I'll tell you one thing: finding a pile of old bones is going to be the least of their troubles.'

FOUR

TUESDAY | FFION

Sure enough, DI Malik calls Ffion at ten-thirty the following morning. 'Where the hell are you?'

'At home.'

'Please tell me you're not still in bed.'

Ffion looks at Dave, who is sprawled at her feet across her duvet. 'I'm not still in bed.' Being *on* the bed, she reasons, is not at all the same thing. 'I'm finishing up the case summary on the Proctor job. I thought I'd do a better job on it if I worked without interruptions.' She does, in fact, have the summary on her screen; right behind the email she's drafting to her landlord, offering to meet him halfway between her current monthly rent, and what he'd get renting to holidaymakers.

'I need you back at the farmhouse. Georgina's already on her way.'

'Boss, if those bones are human, I'll eat my—'

'An *Exposure* contestant is missing.'

A few drops of rain hit Ffion's windscreen as she drives to Felingwm Isaf, and as she turns on to the single track road leading to Carreg Plas it begins to drizzle. Georgina is waiting on the drive with a takeaway coffee in one hand and Ffion looks in vain for a second one. She and Leo had established an unwritten rule when they were working on the Rhys Lloyd murder investigation last year: first on scene brings the brews.'

Georgina clearly works to a different set of rules.

Dammit – now she's thinking about Leo. Ffion tries very hard not to think about Leo Brady. It had all been going so well, till she messed things up. Ffion doesn't believe in 'The One' – how can there only be one perfect match, in a world with eight billion people? – but she and Leo had fitted together in a way Ffion hadn't thought possible. It had scared her. It'd felt so big, so important that she didn't fuck up. When the job was over, Leo had messaged to say Will you have dinner with me? and she'd stared at it for so long her vision blurred. She knew what she wanted, but she couldn't say it, and the longer she didn't say it, the harder it became to say anything at all. He never messaged her again. That was it, her one-shot chance. And she blew it.

'The MisPer is Ryan Francis,' Georgina says, walking towards the house.

'Morning,' Ffion says pointedly.

Georgina had landed in Ffion's department three months ago, tight-lipped about her reasons for leaving a busy Major Crime office for the relative quiet of Bryndare Criminal Investigation Department.

'What's her story, then?' Ffion asked DI Malik, after he'd told her about the incoming team member.

'Not everyone has a *story*, Ffion,' Malik said. Ffion didn't buy it. Everyone had a story, and, if Malik wouldn't share it, Ffion would have to go straight to the horse's mouth.

'How come you left Major Crime, then?' She'd planned to soften her interrogation by shouting the new girl lunch in the canteen, but Georgina had brought a sandwich from home and was eating at her desk.

'Just fancied a change.'

'Hell of a commute.'

'I moved house, too.'

'Got family here? Friends?' People moved away from Bryndare, not to it.

'No,' Georgina said, with such coldness that even Ffion didn't dare try again. One thing she was certain of, though: Georgina Kent definitely had a story.

Roxy Wilde is wearing jeans and a white vest top, with an oversized cardigan she pulls around her midriff when she opens the door. Without the glossy curls and make-up she's barely recognisable as the glamorous presenter on the inaugural episode of *Exposure*.

'That was quite the plot twist last night,' Ffion says.

'That's reality TV for you.' Roxy gives a smile that doesn't reach her eyes. 'You never know what's coming.'

She takes Ffion and Georgina into the kitchen, which is dominated by a vast pine table surrounded by heavy wooden chairs. In the centre is a plastic-covered tray of pastries and one of sandwiches. 'Breakfast and lunch,' Roxy explains. 'They're delivered each morning. Help yourself. There's coffee over there, if you want some.'

Ffion doesn't need asking twice. She slots an espresso pod into the shiny machine on the counter.

'How's Ceri doing? She delivers my mail,' she adds, seeing Roxy's questioning expression and deciding it was the easiest explanation. Ffion had never hung out with Ceri before the Rhys Lloyd murder investigation, which had uncovered a side to Ceri – and to several others in the village – Ffion had never seen. She and Ceri had toasted the trial with a swift half in Y Llew Coch – which had turned into several pints, a lock-in and a kebab on the way home – and agreed they could do worse than to do the same again some time.

'Will she win, do you mean?' Roxy flicks her gaze to the door. 'Because I'm not supposed to—'

'No, I mean, how is she? Did she take the news okay?' Ffion lifts the plastic lid from the tray of pastries and eeny-meeny-miney-mos between a chocolate twist and a *pain au raisin*. She lands on the twist, lets her hand hover for a second, then takes both.

'I guess.' Roxy tugs the cardigan tighter around her stomach.

Ffion bites into the *pain au raisin* and the pastry melts into her tongue. God, that's good. Mam had wondered if Ffion was upset that Ceri hadn't told her she was going on *Exposure*, but Ffion hasn't given it a second thought. They're drinking buddies, not BFFs; adults, not stress-head teens angsting about messages left unread. Ceri's easy company. She deflects personal questions with a snippet of gossip from her round, only occasionally touching on what's happening in her life. 'We broke up,' was all she said, when Ffion had asked when she was next seeing the woman she'd met online. The unspoken boundaries suit Ffion, who has heard enough gossip from Ceri about the lives of people in Cwm Coed not to pass on any details from her own.

'Have you texted him back, then?' Ceri said, a few weeks after Leo had suggested dinner.

'How did you—' Ffion screwed her eyes shut. Bloody Seren, shouting her mouth off. 'Your round, is it?' she said instead. Leo Brady was off-limits.

The kitchen door opens, and Miles comes in, sporting a wide smile wholly incongruous with the day's events. He's wearing a bright yellow running jacket and a beanie, and he's accompanied by a man in Gore-Tex trousers.

'This is Owen,' Roxy says, 'our cameraman. Miles, the catering woman wanted paying – where's the petty cash tin?'

'It's upstairs, on my chest of drawers. Make sure you get a receipt.' Miles turns to Ffion and Georgina. 'Well, did you see the show?'

'Yes,' says Ffion, just as Georgina says *No*.

'It was trending on Twitter all evening, and the papers are all over it. Tonight's ratings are going to be epic. It's marvellous!'

'Less marvellous for Ryan Francis, it seems,' Ffion says.

Miles is instantly sombre. 'Yes, I suppose so.'

'The bloke obviously couldn't hack it.' Owen shrugs and helps himself to a *pain au chocolat*, scattering pastry flakes over his chest as he demolishes it.

'Do you blame him?' Roxy's sharpness is a world away from the mischievous tone she adopted for last night's programme. 'Would *you* want your innermost secrets exposed on national television?'

'Wouldn't worry me,' Owen says. 'I've got nothing to hide.'

'You didn't know, did you?' Ffion looks at Roxy. 'That's what you were arguing with Miles about when we came yesterday. He'd just told you, and you weren't happy about it.'

'I told him it was cruel,' Roxy says quietly.

Owen raises an eyebrow. 'Still here, though, aren't you?'

'I'm a professional. I wouldn't walk out halfway through a job.'

'Wouldn't walk out on a pay cheque, more like.'

'Minor artistic differences,' Miles says, flashing Ffion and Georgina a smile. 'Roxy took a while to understand my vision, that's all. There's nothing cruel about encouraging honesty, is there? We're holding a mirror up to society, with all its filters and fake news. We're saying: be true to yourself.'

'It's a genius concept.' Owen grins. 'And not too shabby on the old CV. I've had two production companies on the phone already, asking for my availability.'

'You're not going anywhere, mate.' Miles puts an arm around

Owen's shoulders. 'This is just the start – wait till you hear about the next show I'm planning.'

Ffion wonders if Miles's plans include Roxy, who has turned away and is washing up her coffee cup. 'When did Ryan Francis leave the show?'

There's a split-second pause. 'Around three o'clock this morning, we think,' Miles says.

'And you waited till now to report him missing?' Ffion raises an eyebrow.

'I expected him to turn up, to be honest, not least because he's contractually obliged to return to the farmhouse after leaving camp. Heaven knows what I'm going to tell the media if he doesn't show up.' Miles sees Ffion's face. He clears his throat. 'Although obviously all that matters is finding him safe.'

'Quite.'

'When did you realise he'd gone?' Georgina asks.

'The contestants started getting up around seven o'clock, but several of them were still in bed at ten. I went for my run, and when I got back to my desk they'd discovered that Ryan had stuffed a pillow and a couple of jumpers under his blankets. The man himself was nowhere to be seen.'

'We reviewed the footage,' Roxy says. 'There are night vision cameras in the tents, but it can be quite hard to make out what's happening. It looked as though Ryan was just turning over in bed, but when we watched it again we saw he'd dropped out of it, on the side furthest from the camera.'

'A few minutes later,' Miles says, 'you can just make out a move-ment in the fabric of the tent as he slips underneath it and out into the woods behind the camp.'

'Where does he live?'

'Staffordshire,' Miles says. 'I tried calling his wife, Jessica – she's listed as his emergency contact number – but she isn't picking up.'

'Any medical issues?' Georgina's taking notes.

'Nothing current.' Miles's wording is careful. Too careful, Ffion thinks.

'Something historic, though?'

Miles hesitates. 'Ryan disclosed on his application form that he'd suffered from depression,' he says quickly. 'But that was all behind him. He was fit and well, and he passed a medical with flying colours. We take a very robust approach to mental health, don't we?' He looks at the others to back him up, and Owen nods vigorously. Roxy, Ffion notes, says nothing.

Ffion looks at Georgina. 'Get Control Room to check psych wards as well as A&E. Minor injury units too. And we need a Staffordshire unit despatched to his home address. Even if he hasn't gone home, we should inform his wife and see what additional information she can give us.'

'His mobile phone and wallet are still in his bag in his stable room.' Roxy looks anxious. 'I thought it would be okay to look through it. In the circumstances.'

Ffion gives a tight nod. Ryan's been gone for around eight hours, and it doesn't take a mastermind to work out why. 'What's his secret?'

Miles frowns. 'I beg your pardon?'

'If Ryan left of his own accord, it's a fair assumption he did it to protect his privacy. So what was he hiding?'

'I can't tell you that.'

'This is a missing person investigation, Mr Young. You have a responsibility to—'

'You don't understand – there have been hundreds of thousands of bets placed since the first episode went out last night. Bet247 are taking wagers on who's leaving first, who sleeps with who, what everyone's secret is . . . They're making a fortune.' Miles sighs. 'My hands are tied.'

'I'll get a description circulated.' Georgina has her radio in one hand, a list of actions in the other. 'And request search-and-rescue?'

Ffion nods, and as Georgina updates Control she dials Huw's number and steps outside into the courtyard. 'There's a job on its way to you,' she says, when her ex-husband answers. The drizzle is still light, a silvery mist that rests on Ffion's jacket as though it doesn't have the energy to carry on. Higher up, around the summit of Pen y Ddraig, the sky is still periwinkle blue, wisps of cloud drifting eastwards with no apparent urgency. Ffion is used to the vagaries of Cwm Coed's weather; to the discrepancies from one village to the next. There are times when one end of Llyn Drych is bathed in sunlight, the other fighting squalls coming off the mountain.

'A search-and-rescue job?' Huw says. 'Or are you wanting a loft conversion?'

'I'd need a loft to convert first.'

'Still no joy on the house-hunting, then?'

'Nope.' There was a time – even a few months ago – when Huw would have taken this as an opportunity to remind Ffion she had a perfectly good home back with him. Even as the divorce went through, Huw was telling Ffion that it wasn't too late, that it wouldn't ever be too late. She could still change her mind. He doesn't say it today, and Ffion feels at once relieved and sad to realise that chapter of her life has finally closed.

'What's the job?' Huw says.

Ffion walks along the stable rooms on one side of the courtyard. 'High-risk MisPer on Pen y Ddraig. White male, brown hair, five eleven. The request'll come through Control Room, but I thought

42

you'd appreciate the heads-up.' Ffion tries the handle of number eight – Miles's studio – and finds it locked.

'Can I help you?'

Miles's voice is hard, but when Ffion turns around the producer is smiling. It unsettles her; makes her doubt her own instincts.

'Huw, I've gotta go.' Ffion hangs up.

'Were you looking for something, DC Morgan?'

'How did Ryan get out of camp?'

'We found a section of fence where the wire's been bent up at the bottom.'

'I'd like to see it.'

'You can't talk to the other contestants.'

'Don't tell me what I can and can't do, Mr Young.' Ffion holds his gaze. 'Are you going to show me where it is?'

Miles says nothing.

'Maybe I'll take a wander up there myself. Get one of the contestants to show me?'

'Fine.' Miles's eyes narrow. 'I'll get the runner to take you.'

Caleb says nothing while Miles briefs him, only nodding earnestly as Miles impresses on him the importance of keeping the contestants in their tents. Georgina and Ffion – who has no intention of abiding by Miles's 'conditions' – start walking. The drizzle has slowed and as the morning slips into afternoon, a rainbow arcs over Llyn Drych.

'Do you think something bad's happened to Ryan?' Caleb says, catching up with her.

'Hopefully not,' Georgina says, which is barely an answer at all. Ffion hates non-answers. *We're doing all we can*, or *The investigation is ongoing*, or *Early indications are encouraging*. They're insulting to members of the public who are, for the most part, perfectly capable of reading between the lines. They deserve more.

43

'Most missing people turn up within the first twenty-four hours,' Ffion tells Caleb. 'He could be trying to get home, or he might be lost on the mountain. He could have been injured.'

'By a bear or something, you mean?'

Ffion stops. 'Caleb, mate, I know you're a city boy, but how many bears have you seen since you moved to Wales?' She taps his head. 'Engage brain then speak, yeah?'

They follow the perimeter eastwards, looking for the section of damaged fence. A short distance away, half hidden in the trees, is a dark blue tent. Ffion stops walking.

'Who's that?'

'Zee Hart. She's alright.'

The YouTuber Miles was so derisive about. In unspoken agreement, Ffion and Georgina walk towards the small clearing. As they draw near, a voice calls out from inside the tent. 'Who goes there?' A striking young woman with blonde hair, shaved on one side, emerges from the tent sporting a fierce grimace. 'Friend or foe?'

'She always does that,' Caleb says.

Zee laughs and jumps up to greet them, the movement displacing a faint waft of marijuana. 'Didn't you ever read *Swallows and Amazons*? My dad got me into it, even though we lived like a million miles from the sea.'

'Police.' Georgina ignores the question, flashing her ID and casting an eye over Zee's belongings.

'Police?' Zee says, in a markedly less friendly tone.

'We're looking for a missing person – a white man in his thirties. Have you seen anyone matching that description?'

'I haven't seen anyone.'

Ms Hart doesn't like the police, Ffion thinks. Older than Seren, although not by much, Zee wears dungarees the colour of an overripe plum. Her wrists are covered in silver bangles that clatter into each other as she pulls her hair over one shoulder.

'You're the YouTuber, right?' Ffion asks.

'That's me! *Hart Breaks*. You know, like "breaking stories"? I'm doing a series now called *Extra Exposure, with Zee Hart*. I get quite a few glimpses of the contestants when they come near the fence, and I overlay that with my commentary on each episode and—'

'Is it your job, then?' Ffion interrupts before Zee gets into full flow. 'Your YouTube channel?'

'Yes.' Zee flushes. 'Well, I work in McDonald's too. But YouTube's going to be my full-time job; I just need to get my subscribers up. That's what this is about.' She waves a hand towards the *Exposure* camp. 'Although it would be a million times easier if I had the cooperation of the production team.' This last is directed towards Caleb.

'Hey, don't shoot the messenger. It's not my fault Miles isn't up for it.'

'You could give me an interview, though.'

'I'd lose my job,' Caleb says, and it's clear from his tone that he and Zee have had this conversation before.

Zee gives him a sly look. 'I'm not sure you can call it a job when you're not being paid and the producer misses you off the credits.'

Caleb's face fills with rage. 'You b—'

'Okay!' Ffion steps between them. 'Zee, if you see a man who looks lost, please call 101.'

'What's his name?'

'Sorry, that's strictly on a need-to-know basis.'

'Oh, my God, is it a contestant?' Zee's eyes light up. 'Is it Jason? No, hang on, you said brown hair. It's not Henry, is it? He's my favourite.'

Ffion starts walking.

'It's Ryan, isn't it?' Zee shouts after them. 'Is it Ryan?'

The point where Ryan escaped from camp is on the northern side. The ground beneath the fence section has been scraped out, the bottom of the wire bent up enough to allow him to wriggle underneath.

Caleb picks a scrap of orange fleece from the wire. 'Like a prisoner-of-war.'

Ffion pictures Ryan, crawling through the dirt like an animal, and imagines how desperate he must have felt. Escaping meant he didn't have to face anyone: not Miles, not the journalists, not his family. But with no money and no possessions, where was he planning to go?

'They're not actually prisoners though.' The security guard, Dario, comes up behind them. 'They can leave; they just won't get the participation fee. I know Miles is pissed at me for Ryan going, but he hired me to prevent people breaking into camp, not stop them leaving it.'

'On that note,' Ffion says, 'can you open the gate for us? We need to speak with the other contestants.'

Dario looks uncomfortable. 'I don't think Miles would—'

'I don't give a shit what Miles would like. Open it, please.'

When Seren turned ten, Mam and Ffion took her to the Harry Potter studios for a birthday treat. Ffion walked down Diagon Alley and half expected to meet Hagrid coming the other way. Now, she feels the same weird sense of otherworldliness as she steps into the camp. Yesterday, it was simply the site of some dug-up bones, but now Ffion feels as though she's stepping into her TV. The fire pit has been finished and a pile of logs is smouldering in the centre.

As Ffion and Georgina approach, one of the logs falls to the side, sending ash flying into the air like confetti. The six contestants stand. Dario and Caleb keep their distance, no doubt fearful of Miles's reaction. Ffion sees Dario glance at the trees. She follows his gaze and sees a camera, mounted high on a trunk. She looks around. Now she knows what she's looking for, the others are easy to spot.

'He'll be watching,' she says to Georgina, as quietly as she can. 'We'd better make this quick.' She addresses the group. 'Who was the last person to see or speak to Ryan?'

Ceri meets Ffion's eyes and they exchange the briefest of smiles. If you didn't know Ceri, Ffion thinks, you'd assume she was okay – that she was enjoying herself, even. But the bags under her eyes are never usually so pronounced, and her pale face looks haunted and anxious. Ffion doesn't ask her how she's doing. She doesn't give a shit about Miles's sponsors, but she won't drag Ceri into it. She can't help but wonder, though: what is Ceri's secret?

'That was us.' Henry points to Jason and then himself. 'We're in the same tent as Ryan, but to be honest he didn't say much, did he?'

Jason shakes his head. 'Henners and I were talking about what the hell was going on – you saw the show, right? I mean, it's fucking nuts – but Ryan wasn't joining in. I figured he was tired, or working some shit out, you know?'

'I gave him a lip salve.' Aliyah sounds close to tears. 'I brought one in as my luxury item? I thought it might cheer him up, but he just put it in his pocket – didn't even hardly say thank you.' She pushes her bottom lip out. 'It was strawberry, too – my favourite.'

Pam raises a hand, as though she's in class.

'Yes?' Ffion says.

'I spoke to him after supper. He was very upset.'

47

'What about?'

'What do you think? I can't speak for everyone, but I'm an upstanding member of the community and I'm sure Ryan is too. Being accused of concealing something, it's . . . well, it's slander. Isn't it?' She looks around. 'Even if we get out of here unscathed, people will assume there's no smoke without fire. We could lose our friends, our jobs.'

'Absolutely.' The Reverend Lucas nods fervently.

'Did Ryan give any indication he was planning to leave?' Georgina asks.

Everyone shakes their head.

'He was scared of the interviews,' Aliyah says. 'You know: what the newspapers would say about him.'

'What they'd make up, you mean,' Pam says darkly.

An engine revs, and Ffion is just thinking how odd it is to hear a car on the mountain when a quad bike roars into camp with Owen at the helm.

'Everyone in the chill-out tent,' Owen says. 'Now!'

A few of the contestants – Jason, Pam, Ceri – demur, but the others turn meekly towards the largest bell tent and follow Roxy inside.

'Truth or lie,' Owen says.

'I beg your pardon.' Georgina raises an eyebrow.

'Today's activity.' Owen looks at the three remaining contestants. 'Chop chop. I want to set up some shots now, while Roxy's getting ready.'

'Do you have any more questions, officers?' Pam turns pointedly to Ffion.

'Not right now.'

'You'll let us know when you find him, won't you?' Ceri says, as they walk towards the bell tent.

'Of course,' Ffion says, but the contestants have already been herded inside.

'We need to let Cheshire know they've got a MisPer.' Georgina is looking at a map on her phone.

Ffion had thought she and Leo might run into each other. There would be some multi-agency meeting or another cross-border job, she'd thought.

But there hadn't been.

Until now.

'They might ask us to keep it – I don't know what their resourcing's like, over this way – but we need to notify them, at least.' Georgina takes out her radio. 'I'll get control to call their duty inspector.'

'I'll do it.' Ffion speaks quickly, before she can change her mind. 'I've got a contact there – it'll be quicker.' She looks at her phone, but there's no signal. 'I'll be back in a bit,' she tells Georgina. 'Have a look at Ryan's belongings. See what he left behind.'

She scrolls through her contacts as she walks through the camp and back towards the farmhouse. Her heart's beating wildly and she doesn't want to call, but she does want to, because now she can speak to Leo without losing face. And if he mentions the text she can say she never received it, because of course she'd have answered if she'd received it . . . *Of course I'd have answered! I'd have said sure, let's go for dinner. So, you know, if you want to, we could . . .*

A single bar of signal appears at the top of Ffion's screen, followed by another. Her pulse races as she presses the call button.

They can pick up where they left off.

FIVE

TUESDAY | DS LEO BRADY

When a detective sergeant job came up in Cheshire's Criminal Investigation Department, Leo jumped ship from Major Crime. He missed the cut-and-thrust of a murder incident room, but he was working with great people, and he no longer had to face the obnoxious DI Crouch every day. Leo's strategy had been to pretend the detective inspector's constant jibes didn't matter – he'd even laughed along when he could bring himself to – but, inside, it had hurt. It was Ffion who had changed everything. 'Maybe it doesn't bother *you*,' she'd said. 'But what about the next poor sod Crouch picks on?' So Leo had stood up to Crouch, and kept standing up to him until the bigoted jokes had stopped. For a while, the two men had co-existed on Major Crime, but even if Simon Crouch no longer said what he was thinking, Leo had known he was still thinking it. When he saw the job advert for CID, it felt like a fresh start. The clincher was the final line of the ad.

Flexible working requests welcomed.

Twice a week, Leo leaves work early. He picks up Harris from school, together with an overnight bag and whatever instructions Allie has included (the most recent note reminded Leo to wash out Harris's lunchbox before repacking it for the morning – *it smelled distinctly fishy last time*) before heading home for what has become their favourite activity. Leo and Harris are learning to cook.

Leo can manage the basics – he's not a complete idiot – but he spent married life being shooed out of the kitchen (later, in the divorce, this was reframed as *refuses to contribute to domestic duties*) and never progressed much beyond spaghetti bolognese and chilli con carne, which even Leo knows is just mince in different outfits.

Each week, Leo and Harris pick a different country, and Leo downloads a recipe from the internet. They've had varying degrees of success (their Andorran stew resulted in an emergency Deliveroo), but both agree they've nailed jollof rice.

This week it's Italy, and, since Leo can already rustle up a spag bol, they're making pizza. Leo did the base yesterday and left it chilling in the fridge, and now Harris has stretched it into something resembling a circle and has spread tomato sauce in a careful circle. He throws on handfuls of grated cheese, scattering a liberal helping on the floor.

Leo turns up the music. 'Great job, mate. Ham or chicken?'

'I'm vegetarian now.'

'Oh, are you?' Leo contemplates his son, who wolfed down a roast dinner at the weekend, and whose sandwich crusts from lunch carried traces of tuna. 'No worries. How about tomato?'

Leo's phone buzzes, and he checks the screen then lets the call go to voicemail. For the past month, Leo has been seeing a woman he met online. To be more accurate, he has had three dates, and isn't entirely certain he'd like a fourth. Gayle's LinkedIn declares her to be a *project manager who gets results*, and Gayle is making it increasingly clear what results she'd like from Project Leo Brady.

'Yes!' Harris considers the plates of toppings Leo has laid out. 'And some of those crispy bacon bits.'

'Gotcha.' Leo tears off a piece of mozzarella and puts it in his mouth.

'What else?' Harris peruses the table.

'I don't think there's room for anything else, mate.' Leo slides Harris's creation on to a baking sheet. As he's putting it in the fridge ready for this evening, his phone rings again. It isn't Gayle this time, so he hits accept, pressing a finger to his ear to block out the music as he answers. 'DS Leo Brady.' He mimes to Harris to turn down the music, only for the boy to turn it up, laughing hysterically at his mischief.

'Hey. It's me.'

Leo can barely hear himself think, let alone someone else talk. He grabs the remote and turns off the music, rolling his eyes at Harris in mock admonishment. 'Sorry, which me? I don't have this number saved.'

There's a silence so long, then, that Leo thinks the call's dropped out. He's about to hang up when the woman speaks again, and Leo would know that voice anywhere.

'This is DC Ffion Morgan,' she says, and her voice is clipped and crisp. 'North Wales Police.'

'Ffion! Sorry about that, I was—'

'This is just a courtesy call. There's a high-risk MisPer coming your way from the TV show *Exposure*.' Ffion's voice is business-like.

A *courtesy call?* Her tone reminds him of Allie, who conducted divorce proceedings as though Leo had leprosy.

'How are you?' Leo keeps his voice casual, but his heart is pounding. *Ffion.* He'd spent far too long hoping she'd call, and far too many evenings hovering over her name in his phone, contemplating sending her another message. He deleted her number in the end, for his own sanity.

'Helicopter's up, and search-and-rescue are mobilising now.'

'It's good to hear—'

'Our duty DI will talk to yours to agree jurisdiction.'

'—from you,' Leo finishes. But Ffion has gone. Leo leans against the living room door and lets out a breath. His phone buzzes and he snatches at the hope that it's Ffion, following up her abruptness with an explanation. Maybe her boss was listening? Although when did Ffion ever care about what anyone else thought?

Hey gorgeous! Are you free on Saturday? We could take Harris to Chester Zoo! Xxx

Gayle.

Gayle has not met Harris yet. On their last date – on their *third* date, Leo reminds himself – she asked to go with Leo when he picked Harris up from school, and she has taken to FaceTiming rather than calling Leo, on days when she knows Harris is at home with him.

'Children *adore* me,' she keeps telling him.

Leo texts back.

Should be free. Work depending. Bit soon to be making introductions though – hope you understand.

He watches as the message sends and is marked as read. Dancing dots show that Gayle is typing, typing, typing . . .

And then nothing. Leo winces.

'Dad?'

'Sorry, mate, I'm all yours.' Leo smiles. 'Find your reading book and let's see what Biff and Chip are up to, shall we?'

'And Kipper.'

'Of course.'

As Harris runs for his book bag, Leo stares at his phone. He could call her back. Ffion, not Gayle. Or should he WhatsApp her?

But if Ffion had wanted to talk she'd have stayed on the line, wouldn't she? She'd have answered his questions, told him what she was up to, how things were going. Instead, she couldn't get off the phone fast enough.

Leo switches his phone to silent.

Later, after Biff and Chip have found yet another magic kingdom, and Leo and Harris have eaten their pizza (undercooked in the middle, but otherwise excellent), Leo puts Harris to bed, grabs a beer and brings up the search engine on his phone. You'd have to be living under a rock not to have heard about last night's explosive episode of *Exposure*. While Leo was driving to work this morning there had been a phone-in on the radio about reality TV exploitation, and someone in the office had opened a book on which of the *Exposure* contestants would be evicted first.

And now a contestant has gone missing.

The first few search results are news outlets, including a tabloid kiss-and-tell from a woman who once dated Ceri Jones, whom Leo remembers well from the Rhys Lloyd case a year and a half ago; and a line-by-line analysis of the report from the latest inspection of Pam Butler's school. There are several articles devoted to the Reverend Lucas Taylor, who Leo is surprised to learn had spent time in prison, when he was a young man. *Your secret's out!* reads the headline. Leo skim-reads the articles. Further down, the search results include links to viral tweets and Facebook groups dedicated to discussing every move the *Exposure* contestants make. Leo clicks on a YouTube link on the second page. After the obligatory twenty-second advert, a young woman in purple dungarees starts talking at a hundred miles an hour.

'Welcome to *Hart Breaks*! I'm your host, Zee Hart, back with another episode of *Extra Exposure* and I'm telling you, you're gonna want to stick around till the end, 'cause this one is kerr-ay-*zee*! Don't forget to like and subscribe!'

Leo presses his fingers to his temples. Watching Zee Hart feels like being waterboarded.

'So, I'm minding my own business this morning, editing some footage for you lovely lot – and yes, the promised clip of Jason chopping wood is coming, guys! – when I had a visit from . . . the police.'

Leo sits up. Zee Hart's talking head has shrunk. It's bobbing about in the corner of the screen, which is now filled with video footage to which Zee is adding her commentary. 'This is DC Morgan and DC Kent,' she says, as the two detectives walk away from the camera.

Leo presses *pause*. Ffion is turned to one side, talking to her colleague, and Leo recognises the tilt of her chin, the sprinkle of freckles across her face. He feels a jolt of sadness as he presses *play* again, and she walks away.

'As a result of our conversation,' Zee is saying, 'I can exclusively reveal that a contestant has disappeared from the *Exposure* camp. That's right – *disappeared*! Now, I was given the contestant's name in strict confidence, and I'm sorry, you guys, but I'm a woman of my word. All I can do is lay out the facts and let you draw your own conclusions . . .'

As Zee starts to run through the physical descriptions of the four male contestants, Leo stops the video. He notices that the views have increased by several thousand in the few minutes he's been watching, and when he refreshes his search engine Zee's video appears on the first page. The news is going viral.

There's one more piece of research Leo wants to do, before he checks in with his DI. He reaches for the remote and turns on the TV, and there's a crash of chords as the opening titles play. Episode two of *Exposure* begins.

SIX

TUESDAY | DARIO KIMBER | EPISODE TWO

After a decade chasing shoplifters, Dario Kimber had worked on the door at a Manchester nightclub, where he was a little heavy-handed when it came to ejecting patrons. An accusation of assault was eventually dropped, but Dario had found himself unemployed for the first time since he was sixteen.

Exposure felt like an opportunity for a new start. Dario was fit and strong, and survival challenges in the Welsh mountains would be a walk in the park. He was so convinced he was the perfect fit for the show that it came as a surprise to receive a single-line email saying that *Young Productions is sorry to say you have not been selected for the show.*

He was even more surprised, a month ago, to receive a call from Young Productions, asking where Dario was based. Dario was worried he'd been rumbled for the abusive email he had anonymously sent to Miles Young after his rejection, but it turned out to be a location manager checking Dario's availability for a security job.

'I'll be honest with you,' the guy said, 'I've cocked up. I totally forgot to book security, and I need to find someone this week or the shit's going to hit the fan.'

Faced with a ticking clock, a shrinking budget and a contact list full of already booked-up firms, the location manager had thought laterally. *Exposure*'s wannabe contestants had all confirmed they could make themselves available for the show at short notice, and, out of the forty-five thousand people who applied, there had to be at least one security guard, surely?

There was, and, since Dario was currently sofa-surfing and jobless, he'd accepted right away. The location manager, whose responsibilities were growing daily, had ticked 'security' off his list.

And now Dario's here, lying on a musty foldout bed in the old caravan provided as his 'on-site accommodation', watching *Exposure* on a portable television, and wondering for the hundredth time why Miles rejected his application. He knows from the casual chats he has since had with the *Exposure* team that Miles shortlisted the applicants himself, then hired a researcher to dig up the dirt. Dario can't have made the shortlist, otherwise they'd have found out about that assault, or the time he shagged his boss's wife. They might even have discovered that he once accidentally-on-purpose vacuumed up his brother's hamster, to see what would happen. Dario has all manner of juicy anecdotes that would have made perfect telly, and he doesn't give a shit who knows about them. It's not the act itself that makes something secret, but the power it holds over you, and Dario has no shame.

As the opening titles finish, a woman's voice cuts across the theme tune. 'For personal reasons, Ryan has left *Exposure*. He has expressed his thanks to viewers for watching and sends his best wishes to the remaining contestants. There will be no expo-sure or eviction tonight.'

The announcement was Miles's idea, of course.

'Have you seen what that bloody girl's done now?' This

afternoon, Miles had handed Dario his phone, on which Zee Hart was sharing conspiracy theories on the disappearance of Ryan Francis. *I'm not saying any of the contestants are government agents, I'm just saying they know how to disappear without a trace. Makes you think, doesn't it?*

'I've set up an alert for mentions of *Exposure*,' Miles said. He frowned. 'It's not entirely accurate – to be perfectly frank, there are things in my inbox I'd rather I hadn't seen – but it's just thrown up this. So much for keeping it within the team.' He glared at Dario as though he held the security guard responsible for this breach of confidentiality.

'What do you want me to do, smash her tent up? Take her phone?' Dario was joking – the presence of two detectives was already giving him a rash – but Miles had taken a moment to consider the option.

'Better not. But keep her away from the camp, for God's sake. She clearly can't be trusted. I'll have to put out an announcement – we've had press enquiries already. I'll simply say Ryan's gone home for personal reasons. Which he probably has, without giving a thought to the mess that leaves me in.' He glared at Dario. 'Has that hole Ryan dug been filled in?'

'Yes, I did it as soon as you asked me to.'

'Properly?'

'Yes, boss,' lied Dario, who had simply kicked the dirt back against the fence.

Now, Dario reaches for another chocolate chip cookie. On screen, there's no talk of Ryan at all – it's as though he's been written out of the show entirely. The six contestants are sitting in a circle in the chill-out tent, having taken delivery of a box containing that day's task.

'It's a game!' Aliyah says.

Dario wishes his knackered TV had a *pause* button. Aliyah Brown is *perfect*. There's no other word for her. She has a waist Dario reckons he could circle with two hands, a proper arse, and two magnificent tits. Totally natural – Dario can always tell. They jiggle enthusiastically as she leans forward to pick up the instructions.

'Exposure *contestants*,' she reads, '*you will be playing a game of "truth or lie". The objective of the game is to learn more about your fellow contestants' body language when they tell a lie, thereby bringing you closer to uncovering their dark secrets – and protecting your own.*' Aliyah gives a nervous giggle.

God, she's fit. Dario was on the gate when the seven contestants walked into camp, and Aliyah had given him one of those smiles that's basically a massive come-on. He's got no idea what her 'dark secret' is, but he totally forgives her for it.

Earlier today, on the pretext of looking for Ryan, Dario had walked around and around the perimeter fence. Now and then he'd got a glimpse of orange fleece as the contestants roamed among the trees, and heard them shout to each other.

Oi, Henners, have you got that wood yet?

Hey, Pam, what's for tea?

Who finished the loo roll?

Dario was patient. He walked and watched, and walked and listened, and finally he caught sight of a long black plait.

'Aliyah!' His voice sounded too loud – Dario imagined it echoing down the mountain – but she didn't hear him. He tried again – 'Aliyah!' – and this time she came over.

'Alright?' She wasn't in the slightest bit curious about what he was doing there. It made him wonder what else he could get away with, just by wearing a security badge.

'I've got something for you.'

'What's that, then?' Aliyah looked up through long eyelashes. She was definitely flirting with him.

'Come closer, and I'll stick it through the fence.'

Her mouth dropped open (God, that tongue!) and Dario thought for one horrifying second she was going to scream, but then she saw what he was holding, and her gorgeous face split into a smile. 'Chocolate! For me?'

'For you.'

She tore open the bar and took a bite, closing her eyes and giving Dario several seconds of footage for his mental wank bank. 'I've missed this so much.'

Dario laughed. 'You've only been in two days.'

'It feels like an eternity.' The smile disappeared. 'I don't know how much more I can take. I reckon Ryan had the right idea, doing a bunk.'

'I'll help you.' She was so perfect, and so . . . so *helpless*, trapped behind the wire like that.

'Will you? I'm so scared of the confession pod, I just know they'll fill it with spiders, and I hate spiders so much, I'm bound to give in, and then my mum will never speak to me again.' She started to cry.

Dario felt panicked. His offer of help had been reckless; he'd just thought perhaps he could slip Aliyah some extra rations, or—

'Could you find out what the others' secrets are?' Aliyah put a hand through the wire and pressed it against his chest; stepped close enough he could feel her breath on his neck. 'If I expose them, I'll win immunity. Maybe even win the money.' She wasn't crying now. She raised herself up on her tiptoes and whispered in his ear. 'I'll make it worth your while.'

Now, Dario watches Aliyah hand each contestant their

personalised card, each bearing a truth or a lie. The secrets are in the box on the plinth by the fire pit, but how can he get to it, without being seen on camera?

'Um . . .' On screen, the Reverend Lucas blinks rapidly as he reads his card aloud. '*I'm a qualified yoga instructor.*' There's a burst of laughter, and Lucas tries to look affronted. 'It's true!'

'Show us your downward dog, then,' Henry says.

'Downward dog collar, more like,' Pam says wryly. 'Definitely a lie.' Dario can picture the head teacher in her office, ticking off some poor kid for telling fibs.

'You lot are too good.' Lucas spins his card around to show the word LIE, printed in fat black letters.

Dario feels another spike of resentment towards Miles. He would have been brilliant at this game. His poker face regularly wins him card games, gets the police off his back and convinces women he's serious about them. He despairs at this shower on telly, who couldn't lie straight in bed. Henry does the classic 'rubbing the nose' when he tells them he's never ridden a bicycle, and Jason can't keep a straight face for more than a second after announcing his ambition of going into politics.

Aliyah reads from her card. '*I can hold my breath for four minutes.*' Her eyes flick to the right, and postwoman Ceri points and says 'Ha! Gotcha!' but Dario isn't fooled. Not by the eyes, not by the way Aliyah's shifting position and wrapping her arms around herself. She's bluffing.

'Lie!' Ceri says. She looks around the tent for agreement.

'Are you sure?' Aliyah says.

'Hundred per cent.'

Aliyah grins and flips the card. TRUTH. Dario gives a satisfied sigh. It takes a liar to catch a liar.

With no eviction tonight, thanks to Ryan going AWOL, Dario

doesn't bother to watch the rest. He pulls on his boots and steps out of the caravan, trying to figure out how to get into that box of secrets. As Dario takes a slow walk around the camp perimeter, all he can think about are Aliyah's words.

I'll make it worth your while.

SEVEN

WEDNESDAY | FFION

'What the hell did you think you were doing?' Ffion stands in the courtyard at Carreg Plas and stares incredulously at Miles. 'We've got every spare resource searching Pen y Ddraig for Ryan Francis, and you tell the world he's perfectly fine, just chilling at home "for personal reasons".' Her air quotes could dislocate a knuckle.

'I had to! That bloody YouTube woman was sabotaging everything. Issuing an announcement meant it became a non-story. Even the media have backed off.'

'But it isn't true – we've got no idea where Ryan is!'

Miles's gaze keeps flicking back to the monitor on his desk, reluctant to miss a second of precious footage. Above them, the search-and-rescue helicopter takes a slow turn over the trees surrounding Carreg Plas, the sound a pulse in Ffion's ears.

'It's obstruction,' Ffion says.

'It's a potentially award-winning television series, officer, and I'm not alone in thinking it.' Miles picks up an iPad from his desk and thrusts a headline at her. *Indecent Exposure . . . or just damn good telly?* 'Or how about this one?' He swipes at the screen, then reads from an article in *Entertainment Weekly*. '*Miles Young is hot property after his pioneering reality TV series gets everyone talking.*' On Miles's desk, a frozen clip of the Reverend Lucas in prayer waits for whatever Miles plans to splice it to. He brings up another headline, but Ffion's gaze remains firmly on Miles.

Slowly, he puts down the iPad on the desk. When he looks up, he's more subdued, his brow furrowed as he pleads with Ffion. 'Just a few more hours. Please.'

'This is a missing person investigation.'

'Let me at least get tonight's episode in the can. This is the biggest moment of my career. Roxy's too,' Miles adds quickly, when he sees Ffion's incredulous face. 'All I'm asking for is a bit more time before you issue a statement.'

'Let's see what Ryan's wife thinks about that, shall we?' Ffion turns away.

'I'm sorry?'

'I doubt that.' She raises her voice as she walks back towards the farmhouse. 'Jessica Francis just turned up to see her husband. I'll tell her you're on your way.'

Ryan's wife is a petite blonde in black Nike leggings and an oversized grey sweatshirt. When Ffion had seen her by the entrance to Carreg Plas, frowning into her phone as though looking at directions, she'd taken her for a teenager. A fan of the show, hoping for autographs, perhaps; or something to do with Zee Hart. But then the woman had looked up, and Ffion had realised she was in her late thirties, her face creased with concern. 'Is this where they're filming *Exposure*?' she'd said. 'Only I'm looking for my husband.'

Jessica listens in silence as Miles admits that no one has seen Ryan since yesterday morning, and that the activity Jessica noticed on the way up to Pen y Ddraig – the helicopter, the parked cars, the slow-moving clusters of red search-and-rescue jackets – is all because of Ryan.

'But you said he'd left the show "for personal reasons". How do you know what his reasons were, if you haven't spoken to him?'

Ffion glares at Miles, who is avoiding eye contact. 'We tried calling you,' he says, avoiding Jessica's question.

'I switched off my phone.' Jessica looks up. 'All my friends were calling, wanting to know if Ryan had known what *Exposure* was really about, asking if he'd be okay with it.' She exhales sharply. 'Of course, what they really wanted to know was his *secret*.' She spits the final word.

'Officers from Staffordshire police went to your house yesterday,' Georgina says, 'but no one was home.'

'I went to my mum's. I'd already had reporters knocking on the door, offering "sensitive" exclusives, and I knew that the more I told them to get lost, the more it would look like we had something to hide. And we don't. We don't have anything to hide,' she repeats firmly.

'Have you heard from Ryan since he left the show?' Miles says. He never says the word 'missing', Ffion realises. He's reframed Ryan's disappearance – edited it – to make it a voluntary act. If Miles is concerned about Ryan, it's only in terms of his own reputation.

'No.' Jessica's voice breaks. 'When I watched the show last night, and realised he'd left, I called his mobile, but it was turned off. I remembered he said he'd have interviews to do, but it was driving me crazy not knowing how he was. As soon as I woke up, I got in the car and came here.'

'Mrs Francis,' Georgina says, 'I'm sorry to ask, but what is Ryan's secret?' There's a softness to Georgina's voice Ffion hasn't heard before.

Jessica's entire body tenses. She speaks in a low voice, laced with venom. 'He doesn't have a *secret*.' When she speaks again, her words are deliberately airy. 'My husband wears women's clothes. That's it. That's the *big secret*. And yes, Ryan was ashamed of it, but only because people like Miles Young *made* him ashamed.'

'All I'm doing is encouraging people to be their true selves,' Miles says.

'Bullshit. You're outing people for entertainment. You're taking away their freedom to choose when to tell their story and who to tell it to. You're taking something private – something that shouldn't even *be* a secret – and you're making it dirty.'

Ffion imagines Ryan out on the mountain, sick to his stomach with the shame someone else put there. He's been missing for thirty-six hours and the more time that passes, the less chance there is of finding him alive. They're approaching summer, but the nights are still cold and the temperature on the mountain is several degrees colder than in the valleys. All Ryan has with him are the clothes he was wearing when he left camp; no shelter, no food or water.

Miles is still talking. He's still defending his concept. 'Our contestants are having to dig deep into their emotions.'

Jessica gives a humourless laugh. 'You're playing God.'

'We're helping them confront their true selves.'

'And those poor kids watching . . . the ones who are gay or trans, or who are into dressing up, or playing with Lego or whatever else you've decreed is a fucking *secret*—'

'We're supporting journeys of self-discovery.'

'—you're teaching them to feel ashamed of who they are!'

'The contestants will go home transformed.'

'Assuming they make it home at all,' Jessica says coldly. She holds Miles's gaze. 'How did you find out?'

'That's a researcher's job, I don't really get involved—'

Ffion glares at him again, and Miles swallows. 'Something he bought online, as I understand it. A receipt, was it? A pair of shoes . . .' He waves a hand in lieu of a complete explanation.

'Is that legal?' Jessica spins to look first at Ffion, then Georgina. 'That can't be legal.'

'I can give you the contracts. All the permissions are there. *I authorise Young Productions to carry out background research as necessary for the purposes of the production . . .*' The hand again, waving away his responsibilities.

'Jessica,' Georgina says, 'why do you imagine Ryan hasn't been in contact with you?'

'He probably thinks I've found out.' Jessica swallows. 'Maybe he's worried I'll be upset, or disgusted, or—'

Ffion frowns. 'He doesn't know you know he wears women's clothes?'

'I only discovered it a couple of years ago. I wanted to give him space to tell me in his own time. I left a magazine open at an article on cross-dressing couples, kept mentioning LGBTQ people I'd met through work. Trying to show him it wouldn't matter, you know? And at the same time, I figured if he didn't want to tell me, that was cool too. I mean, we're married, but we're entitled to our own lives too, you know?'

'If he'd been open from the start,' Miles says, a pious note in his voice, 'none of this would have—'

'There's only one person to blame for this, and that's you,' Jessica says sharply. Her brow furrows with a sudden realisation. 'I saw a cameraman when I arrived – you're not still filming, are you?' Miles's silence is enough of an answer, and Jessica turns to Ffion and Georgina in fury. 'And you're letting him?'

'It's not a question of *letting* him,' Georgina says. 'He isn't breaking the law.'

'Unfortunately,' Ffion adds, earning herself a reproving look from Georgina.

'Then the law is wrong.' Jessica sinks into a chair, as though her batteries have suddenly run out.

'Mrs Francis,' Georgina says gently. 'When Ryan applied for the show, he disclosed having previously lived with depression. Is that something you're aware of?'

'Aware of?' Jessica gives a humourless laugh. 'It's hard not to be aware of your husband being sectioned.'

'Sorry, what?' Ffion, who is messaging DI Malik with a brief update, snaps her focus back to the conversation. 'Ryan was sectioned?'

'They said he'd had a psychotic episode, that it was for his own good.' Jessica bites her lip. 'And it was – it really was. Even Ryan could see that, once he'd got a bit better. He became a voluntary patient then. We both found that easier, I think. More control, you know?'

'That sounds pretty serious.' Ffion tries to keep her voice calm. 'He really should have disclosed that in the medical section of his application, so the production team had the full—'

'But he did.' Jessica looks confused. 'I made him. I said if he insisted on applying, he at least had to be a hundred per cent up-front about his history. I mean, don't get me wrong, Ryan's been well for years, but—' She breaks off and picks at her finger-nails. 'I guess I hoped he'd be knocked back. But he wasn't.'

Ffion stands and glares at Miles. 'Why didn't you tell us about this?'

'It . . .' Miles swallows. 'It must have slipped my mind.'

'Don't bullshit me. You let a man with a history of severe mental illness on to a reality TV show specifically designed to destroy its participants—'

'You think I should have rejected Ryan's application purely because he'd been in hospital?' Miles takes a step towards Ffion. 'That sounds very much like discrimination to me. Are you suggesting someone with mental ill health can't participate in normal activities?'

'*Exposure* isn't nor—'

'Absolutely not,' Georgina says smoothly, cutting across Ffion's furious response. 'In fact, I think it's admirable of you to look beyond the stereotypes and see the person behind the labels.'

'Well, I—' Miles blinks. 'Yes, exactly.' He shoots a look of pure arrogance at Ffion, who no longer trusts herself to speak. Miles twisted her words the same way he twists what people see on *Exposure*.

'I wonder . . .' Georgina smiles, 'would it be possible to see the enhanced risk assessment you carried out for Ryan?'

'I . . .' Miles's mouth continues moving, but nothing comes out.

'And details of the additional psychological support available, of course. Oh, and I'm assuming you have someone watching the livestream who's been briefed on the contestants' individual psychological history and specific needs, so perhaps we could talk to them, too.'

There's a noise in the courtyard and Miles looks out of the window, visibly grateful for the distraction. His eyes widen. 'What the—?'

The door to the editing studio is wide open.

'I locked it.' Miles turns to the others, as though they might back him up. 'I always lock it when I'm not there.' He crosses to the back door and flings it open with a bang. 'Hey! What are you doing?'

There's a moment's silence, before Dario emerges from number eight. 'There you are!' he calls.

'What the hell are you doing?' Miles shouts back. 'Your keys are for emergencies, not to barrel into my studio whenever you feel like it.'

'I was looking for you.'

Dario's answer is unconvincing, and, if Ffion didn't have a vulnerable missing person to find, she might be tempted to ask the security guard a few questions. But Jessica is on the brink of tears, so Ffion leaves it to Miles to stride across the courtyard and give Dario a piece of his mind. She shuts the back door.

'I'll make a *paned*. Tea or coffee?' she asks Jessica.

'I need to find my husband.'

'And to do that, we need as much information as possible,' Ffion says firmly. 'So, I'll make the tea, and you'll tell us about Ryan.'

Her phone vibrates, and she glances at the message from Mam, who reluctantly agreed to have Dave this morning.

'I'll pick him up at lunchtime,' Ffion had told her, knowing full well it would be six at the earliest.

'If he eats my sofa again—'

'He won't!'

Ffion reads the message Mam's sent her. **Dave 'di bwyta'r blydi soffa eto!**

Ah, well. It's about time she replaced that sofa anyway.

'I should have stopped him,' Jessica says. 'He saw the advert and said *I might apply*, and I should have said *That's a bloody stupid idea, Ry*, but I didn't think anything of it, and next thing I knew, he was filling in the forms. I tried to put him off, but he was determined to do it.'

'And at that stage, presumably he thought it was a survival show?' Georgina says.

'I think he had some stupid idea about proving he was a real man.' Jessica dissolves into tears. 'As if I care about that sort of shit!'

Ffion takes the tea to the table, the bags still bobbing in each mug. 'Has Ryan ever attempted suicide?'

Jessica takes a sharp breath. 'Not as far as I know. Not even when he was ill. He didn't hurt himself, he just lashed out sometimes.' She cuts herself off.

'He was violent?' Georgina says quietly.

'Not with me,' Jessica says fiercely. 'Never with me.'

They wait.

'He smashed up the kitchen just before he was sectioned,' Jessica says eventually, reluctantly. 'Another time, he punched a hole right through a wall. But he wouldn't hurt anyone – you have to believe that. He just . . .' She stares miserably at the table. 'He doesn't love himself like I love him.'

The door opens and Huw barrels in, heading straight for the kettle.

'Jesus, Huw, have you never heard of knocking?' Ffion says. She briefs him in Welsh, figuring it's the fastest way to bring him up to date without upsetting Jessica further.

'*Mae pobl yn siarad,* Ffi,' he replies. 'They're asking is it Ryan we're looking for?'

Ffion's phone pings with another text. **Ffi! Mae Dave wedi neidio dros y ffens a dianc!**

'What's up?' Huw says.

'It's Dave. He's jumped Mam's fence and made off. Keep an eye out for him on the mountain, would you?' Ffion screws up her face. 'Bloody dog.'

'Maybe it would be better if you took him back to the rescue centre.'

He might sound concerned, but Ffion isn't fooled. 'Fuck off,

Huw. You're not getting that twenty quid.' She makes him a coffee, automatically stirring in the precise half-sugar she knows he takes, while Huw introduces himself to Jessica.

'We're doing everything we can,' he says in English.

'Please find him.' Jessica's voice cracks. 'I need him to know I love him not in spite of who he is, but because of it.'

Ffion thinks about Miles's plea for a few hours' grace before they issue a statement. She thinks about his advertising deal with Bet247, and his reluctance to allow the contestants to be 'distracted' by Ryan's disappearance. Giving the volunteer search team Ryan's name could undermine Miles's relationships with his sponsors or impact on the show's viewing figures – no wonder he wants to keep things confidential.

She looks at Huw. 'Round up as many volunteers from the village as you can. Tell them whatever they need to know.'

EIGHT

WEDNESDAY | LEO

The last time Leo drove to Wales, it was with Ffion. They were tying up loose ends following Rhys Lloyd's murder: additional statements, another house search, a final look at the lake from which Lloyd's body had been pulled a few weeks earlier.

Now Leo watches the landscape change as he draws closer to Cwm Coed. He waits for that first glimpse of Mirror Lake. It took his breath away the first time he saw it, and it does the same today – a slash of sapphire, shimmering in the valley. It was winter when Rhys Lloyd died, and there were few boats on Mirror Lake, but today there are dozens. Tiny triangular sails skate across the water, their movements seemingly choreographed, so that each vessel slips past another with what looks like mere inches to spare.

Leo could have sent a DC to liaise with North Wales Police. Probably should have. But his caseload is quiet for once, and Leo feels the pull of the mountains. And Ffion.

As the road drops down towards the village, the lake vanishes behind the belt of green that encircles it. Cwm Coed had felt provincial to Leo, that first time. Too big for a village, yet too small to be a town. Nothing to do except swim, fish or sail; nothing to see but the lake and the mountain. Cwm Coed, Leo had thought then, was a place you drove through on your way somewhere better. Today, he has the oddest sensation as he nears the village. He feels a loosening of the tension in his shoulders, as though he's shrugging off a tight jacket. He feels his body settle back into his seat, the way it does when he sinks into the sofa after a long day at work.

Cwm Coed's been the same for hundreds of years, Ffion once said to him, and she'd meant it as a blessing and a curse. Leo had felt envious of her roots, her history here. He liked that she couldn't walk from one end of the high street to another without a dozen conversations about the weather, or the building work up by the church; without people asking after Ffion's mum, Elen Morgan, or seeing if Ffion knew who'd nicked Osian Edwards' ride-on mower. You don't get that in a city.

Leo's SatNav takes him north of the village, towards Pen y Ddraig mountain. As the road begins to climb, his pulse surges, and he makes himself take several deep breaths. He's a detective sergeant meeting a constable from another force for a briefing, not a sixth-former queuing for the school disco.

Ffion, though.

He messaged her this morning, letting her know he was coming. A single line, mirroring the abrupt tone of last night's call.

Her reply was instant. Noted.

So that's how it's going to be. Leo feels something akin to grief, and he opens the window to let the rush of air blast away his folly. The road narrows. The SatNav says the farmhouse is three minutes away, but Leo's running out of road and there's not a house in sight.

He stops the car and zooms in on the satellite map on his phone.

He's the wrong side of a field.

As Leo reverses cautiously all the way back down the single-track road, he catches sight of himself in the mirror. When did he last get a haircut? He straightens his tie. He's wearing a grey checked suit, but he switched out his office brogues for robust boots more suited to the terrain. Does he look okay? Is the suit jacket too much? He could leave it in the car and wear the cagoule he keeps in the boot in case of rain . . . *For God's sake, man, pull yourself together*. It's only Ffion. And Ffion's made it quite clear she's not interested, so it hardly matters if his hair's a mess, or—

His phone rings as he hits the main road ('main' being a relative term; he'll have to squeeze into the hedge if something comes the other way) and, even though he doesn't really want to speak to Gayle, the distraction is welcome, so he presses *accept*.

'Hello, gorgeous.' Her voice, deep and flirtatious, fills the car. 'I'm in Chester today – I wondered if you fancied meeting up. We could check out that new place by the river; I hear they do an amazing afternoon tea.'

'Sorry, I'm across the border on a job.' Leo has tried several times to explain that he can't take long, boozy breaks. Police meals are eaten in parked cars or at your desk; abandoned the second a job comes in, or Custody calls to say your suspect is ready for interview. As for afternoon tea . . . Leo can just imagine running that one by the DI. *Just popping out for a cucumber sandwich, boss*.

'Everyone has to eat,' Gayle had said once, when he declined her offer to meet at the pub for *a quick bite and a cheeky Pinot*.

'Tell that to Cheshire's criminal fraternity.'

'But Morse and Lewis are always in the pub.'

Leo had laughed, but it turned out Gayle was being serious.

'How are you?' he says now. He ignores the SatNav telling him to make a U-turn and pulls through an open gate on to a wide gravel driveway in front of the farmhouse. A sign on the gate says *Carreg Plas*.

'Horny,' Gayle says, drawing out the word in a sultry stage whisper.

Leo snatches up his phone and turns off the in-car speakers. What is he supposed to say? *That's nice? Oh, dear?* He settles for, 'I'm at work,' then adds, 'unfortunately,' even though he doesn't mean it.

'I'm sure you've got five minutes to help a girl out, haven't you?' She gives a throaty chuckle.

Leo can't do this. Partly because, as time goes on, he likes Gayle less, not more; partly because dirty talk has always made him feel self-conscious. But mostly because Ffion is standing in the drive. Wisps of hair have escaped the clip in the nape of her neck, the wind tangling them about her face. She gives a brief nod as their eyes meet.

'I have to go,' he tells Gayle. 'I'm so sorry.' Ffion walks towards Leo's car, until he can no longer see her face, only a leather belt and a pair of grey trousers, liberally adorned with what looks like dog hair.

'Do you know what I've got on under my dress?' Gayle says.

Ffion opens his car door. 'Are you planning on sitting there all day?'

'Absolutely nothing,' Gayle purrs. 'If you meet me later, you can slip a hand up and see where it takes you . . .'

'Because we're about to talk to Miles.' Ffion's leaning into the car, and Leo can smell her perfume, sharp and citrussy. She's wearing a short-sleeved top with no jacket, and her forearms are goose-bumped from the mountain breeze.

'I'll come in a second.' Leo feels somewhat frantic. He clamps the phone tightly to his ear, but Gayle's voice is so *loud*.

77

'I hope not.' Gayle gives another throaty laugh. 'I need you to go all night.' She draws out the *all* for several seconds.

'I really do have to get on.' Leo is uncomfortably hot, prickles of sweat around his hairline and across his top lip. Ffion is looking at him curiously. 'Work,' he mouths, adding an eyeroll and making a hand gesture to show he's trying to wrap it up. 'I'll call for an update later and see how you've got on.'

'Right now,' Gayle says. 'I'm going to—'

Leo hangs up. He gets out of the car, turning his back on Ffion as he retrieves his briefcase from the rear seat, letting out a long breath in the hope that his heart rate will return to normal. 'Hi,' he says, when he finally turns around. 'It's good to—'

'Shall we?' She starts walking towards the rear of the farmhouse.

Leo catches up with her in a few long strides. There's a label sticking out of the back of her top, and there was a time when Leo would have reached out to tuck it inside and neither of them would have missed a beat, but he keeps his hands in his pockets. 'You've got a—' he starts, but Ffion turns to look at him, and he's reminded how much things have changed. 'How have you been?' he says instead.

'Busy.'

Too busy to reply to his suggestion they have dinner. 'Me too.'

'How's CID? Good team?'

'Yeah, they're a good bunch.' They're talking like colleagues at a business convention, when last time they were together they had shared some of the most intense moments Leo has ever experienced. Even if Ffion didn't want a relationship with him, they could have kept that closeness, couldn't they? They could have been friends.

'Must be demanding, being a DS.' There's an odd note to Ffion's voice as she leads the way around the back of the farmhouse.

'I guess.' Leo glances at her.

Ffion opens a door, the corners of her mouth twitching. 'Especially with a boss who makes you go *all* night.'

Fortunately for Leo, the intense heat that races to flood his face is interrupted by a desolate cry coming from the road. Instinctively, Leo reaches for his radio. An accident? The MisPer himself? Leo wonders what the ambulance response times are around here and hopes they've got a better navigation system than his own.

'Oh, shit,' Ffion says. 'Dave.'

Leo doesn't quite have time to wonder who Dave is, and what is causing him distress, because something the size of a Shetland pony, only hairier and not nearly so endearing, is barrelling into the driveway. Its mournful cries morph into barks of what appear to be joy as it launches itself at Ffion, two giant paws on her shoulders, and starts licking her face.

'Do you . . .' Leo takes a step back. It's not that he's not a dog person. He quite likes dogs, when they're walking meekly on leads, or curled up in baskets by the fire. 'Do you *know* this dog?'

'Off!' Ffion gives a mighty shove and frees herself. 'Leo, meet Dave, a rescue dog with separation anxiety and boundary issues.' She takes off her belt and loops it through the dog's collar. 'Dave, meet Leo, a Cheshire DS with good taste in suits.'

'Pleased to meet you.' Leo stretches out a tentative hand to stroke Dave and is rewarded with a handful of slobber Leo really doesn't want to wipe on his suit. Especially after what appeared to be a bona fide compliment from Ffion Morgan. 'I take it you hadn't planned for him to join us?'

'He escaped from Mam's to look for me.'

'Bright dog.'

'He ate her sofa first.'

Leo doesn't quite know what to say to this. They enter a courtyard at the rear of the house, where the kitchen door is open and a woman with close-cropped dark hair is waiting.

'You must be DS Brady.' She extends a hand. 'DC Georgina Kent, sarge. I work with Ffion.'

'Call me Leo.' Leo shakes her hand. 'Unless there's a member of the public around.' He grins. 'And should I call you Georgina? Or do you have another preferred name?'

There's a surprised pause. 'Well, George, actually.'

Ffion stares at her. 'You never said.'

George holds her gaze. 'You never asked.'

Twenty minutes later, Leo is starting to find his feet. Presenter Roxy Wilde looks younger than she does on television, her manner gentler and less bouncy. It's not the first time Leo has met someone he's seen on TV – you can't cover Cheshire for eight years without bumping into the occasional footballer, or a wannabe celeb from the *Real Housewives of Cheshire* – and he always finds the disconnect unsettling. He supposes the Roxy he's seeing now is the 'real' Roxy and the on-screen persona the fake one, but who knows?

Cameraman Owen hasn't taken his eyes off his phone since Leo arrived. He's already muttered, 'Are we done?' to no one in particular, answering Leo's questions in a laconic, uninterested manner.

Leo has met Caleb Northcote, the production assistant, before, but he's taken aback by how much the lad has changed. An awkward sixteen-year-old in the aftermath of the Rhys Lloyd murder investigation, Caleb has filled out in the last seventeen months, his muscles flexing against the fabric of his black T-shirt. He didn't offer a hand, and, when Leo extended his own, Caleb wouldn't meet his eyes. Still not keen on police, then, although

80

Leo noted Caleb was more relaxed with Ffion, whom he presumably saw around Cwm Coed.

The MisPer's wife, Jessica Francis, has been given her husband's room, a converted stable in the courtyard behind the farmhouse, where Leo learns he will also find Miles Young in his editing suite.

'I told him you were coming,' Caleb says. 'But time's really tight. It's just him on site, you see – everyone else works remotely.'

'Understood.' Leo stands. 'Roxy, Owen, Caleb, thank you for your time.'

It's a moment before the three crew members realise they've been dismissed, but, when they do, Caleb and Owen practically fall over themselves to escape. Roxy holds back, looking as though she wants to say something, but Owen shouts something at her and she follows dutifully.

'Thanks for bringing me up to speed, you two.' Leo nods at George, then at Ffion. He feels self-conscious in a way he never does when he's briefing his CID team. Is she in any way pleased to see him again? If so, the sentiment hasn't reached her face. 'I want to run through a few lines of enquiry – make sure we're doing all we can to bring Ryan home safely.'

'Check the locals haven't cocked it up, you mean?' Ffion emphasises her Welsh accent.

Leo doesn't rise to it. 'I know PolSA's liaising with the search-and-rescue team, and they've got the area immediately surrounding the *Exposure* camp well covered. What about further afield?' He looks at Ffion, but it's George who answers.

'Uniform have searched barns and outbuildings within a five-mile radius.'

'Have any of the property owners noticed anything missing? Clothes from a washing line, milk or bread from the doorstep?'

'I don't think that's specifically been asked, Sarge—' George corrects herself. 'Leo.'

'Then I'd like you and Ffion to do that today, please. Hospitals?'

'No trace.'

'Police custody?'

'Same.'

'Any access to a car?'

George shakes her head. 'All the contestants were picked up from their home addresses and chauffeured here on Sunday.'

'Given the time that's elapsed since Ryan went missing, it's not inconceivable he's got himself to a main road and stuck his thumb out. Get obs circulated among lorry drivers and at service stations, please.' He pauses. 'Ffion?'

She doesn't say anything.

'Okay to do that?'

'Shouldn't your team be doing these enquiries?' Ffion says. 'I mean, Ryan's missing from the Cheshire side of the border, and you're here, so presumably you're claiming the job, so . . .' she points a finger at herself, spins it in a circle then points it at the door, 'we can hand over to you and head off, right?'

'It's been classified as a joint investigation,' Leo says. 'Our MisPer, your local knowledge.'

'I see.'

'Is that a problem?' Leo holds Ffion's gaze.

She tilts her chin up a fraction but doesn't look away. 'No.'

'Good. Where are we with financials and phone?'

'We haven't done them,' George says. 'Ryan's wallet and phone are still here.'

'Do we know if all the bank cards are accounted for?'

George reddens slightly. 'No.'

'Then we check, please. Ryan could have taken a card into

camp with him.' Leo scans the list he made while watching last night's episode of *Exposure*. 'Known associates?'

'Jessica's contacting all friends and family,' George says. 'We're in touch with Ryan's boss, who's checking in with his colleagues.'

'Good job.' Leo snaps his book shut. 'I want to speak to Miles Young, but call me if there are any developments. I've asked the press office to issue an appeal for anyone who's been hiking around the area in the past day or two to check the background of any photos and videos they've taken, so we might have some lines of enquiry to follow up on this afternoon.'

Leo makes his way across the courtyard. He can't hear the helicopter now – it's gone back to base to refuel, perhaps, or been pulled away to another, more urgent job. The mountain summit is stark against the sky, and Leo takes a second to centre himself. His performance in the kitchen just now had been exactly that: a performance. Leo had felt the same soon after he'd been promoted to detective sergeant. He remembered the first briefing he led, and how his heart had thumped furiously from beneath his crisp white shirt and pinstripe jacket; how anxious he was about what the team thought.

'Great job,' his new DI had said afterwards, and Leo had found it extraordinary that his nerves hadn't shown.

Over the course of his first year in post, Leo had grown in confidence. He no longer takes a deep breath before briefings, or practises in the car on his way to work. It isn't that he no longer cares what the team thinks of him; he's simply sure of his ability to do a good job.

But today Leo feels like a rookie again. His head is all over the place – one minute running through MisPer protocol, the next thinking how the curve of Ffion's mouth is at once familiar and brand new. He feels under scrutiny. Is that because he's come back as a sergeant? Or because Ffion is here? It's because she snubbed him, because he wants to show her it doesn't matter, that he's too professional to care that the woman he once thought he was falling in love with has all but forgotten he exists.

A sharp trill cuts through Leo's thoughts and he looks up to see a kestrel hovering above him, wings outstretched and black-tipped tail feathers fanned against the wind. Leo watches for a second, thinking how Harris would love this. They should get out into the countryside more. Six months ago, Allie bought Harris a pair of Le Chameau wellies, then told Leo, *They cost eighty quid, so for God's sake don't let him get them dirty*. But he could get another pair from Asda, and he and Harris could go off for a walk with a picnic and a book on birds. He laughs inwardly. Who'd have thought, a couple of years ago, that city-boy Brady would be dreaming of walking in the hills? That was Ffion's influence, whether she knew it or not. *I can't breathe in cities*, she'd said to him once, and Leo had laughed. But he feels it now, just as he felt it last time he was here. The expanse of sky, the endless stretches of mountainside, even the sun, already high overhead. Everything is so much bigger, so much more open.

The kestrel soars higher up the mountain and Leo focuses. He needs to speak to Miles Young. As the producer of *Exposure*, and the owner of Young Productions, Miles is responsible for the welfare of the seven contestants. If a lack of care results in Ryan's death, Miles could be looking at a charge of corporate manslaughter.

'Excuse me!'

Leo turns. Roxy Wilde is walking towards him. She's fully made-up now and he sees a tiny microphone clipped to her jacket, the wire tucked out of view.

'We're heading up to camp for today's challenge,' Roxy says.

'They're doing an abseiling trust exercise – paired up, you know? Should be fun,' she adds, but her expression disagrees.

'Did you want to say something?' Leo prompts, when it seems as though Roxy isn't going to talk.

'I—' She glances towards number eight. 'Ryan took the announcement really badly. I mean, all the contestants were shocked, but Ryan . . . I've never seen anyone behave like that. He went deathly pale, like a corpse, and he was totally still, like he was frozen with fear.'

'I didn't watch the first episode – was it—'

Roxy gives a humourless laugh. 'You wouldn't have seen Ryan's reaction, even if you had. Miles used footage from earlier in the day, when the contestants were excited about the survival show they thought they were on. He edited that so it looked like it followed on from the announcement. That's why it's all close shots, and why they wear a camp uniform – so you can't tell it's from a different conversation. Everyone whooping and cheering, when the reality was the complete opposite.'

'Is that . . .' Leo doesn't think he's naïve, and he knows there must be an element of airbrushing about reality TV shows, but to manipulate the footage like that. 'Is that normal?'

'Welcome to reality TV.' Roxy closes her eyes for a second and exhales. 'The show's ratings are through the roof, but I've had to come off Twitter – I can't take the abuse any more.'

'Abuse? From who?'

'The #BeKind movement, mostly. Ironic, huh?' Roxy hugs her arms around herself. 'Thing is, I agree with everything they're saying. Bar the death threats, obviously. The show *is* cruel. It's bullying on steroids. If Miles hadn't made my contract so water-tight, I'd walk.'

'Did Ryan say anything to you after the announcement?'

'He could hardly speak, to be honest. The others looked after him, but I know he was in a bad way. He told me he . . . he said he'd rather be dead. I thought it was just a turn of phrase, but—' Roxy's eyes fill with tears.

Leo nods grimly.

'Look, I've got to get on. I just needed you to know not to trust what you see on TV.' Roxy puts a hand on Leo's arm, her eyes large and unblinking. 'The show's all about exposing the contestants' lies. But you should know: Miles is the biggest liar of them all.'

NINE

WEDNESDAY | KAT SHENTON | EPISODE THREE

Kat Shenton watches her husband Jason salivate over a woman young enough to be his daughter. The subtitles are on instead of the sound, and Kat's finger is poised over the remote's off button, because she has told Belle and Aimee-Leigh that Daddy isn't doing *Exposure* any more.

'Apparently he'd rather be doing Aliyah,' she says bitterly to herself, before draining her glass of wine and going to the kitchen for a refill. She slides a ready meal into the microwave and jabs angrily at the controls. Earlier this evening, she'd watched Jason tell Aliyah *I won't drop you, darlin'*, then blatantly stare down Aliyah's vest top as the woman bounced (and boy, did she bounce – those things must be made of rubber) down the side of a rocky outcrop.

Kat has never seen her husband flirt. If she had, she might have found the first three episodes of *Exposure* easier to take. She and Jason have a good marriage, and Kat keeps herself in shape. If Jason flirted with her mates when they were out for drinks, it wouldn't bother her. She's secure in their relationship.

But she has never seen this side of Jason. The sideways glances when Aliyah takes off her fleece; the appreciative nod when her

T-shirt rides up to reveal taut, toned flesh. The mere fact that wherever Aliyah is, Jason will always, always be there too. It's like watching a stranger, and if he's capable of flirting like this, what else is he capable of? What else is he hiding?

Kat, Belle and Aimee-Leigh had watched the first episode together, tucked up on the sofa with hot chocolate and a bowl of popcorn. Kat had had T-shirts printed – *Jase's Girls* – and they'd taken selfies for Instagram. *You can do it, Daddy!* she wrote in the caption, and her phone had flooded with hearts. Kat didn't have a huge reach, but she used the #ExposureTVShow hashtag and her follower count exploded.

She was putting a fistful of popcorn in her mouth when Roxy Wilde made the big announcement on the first episode of *Exposure*. Kat had frozen, too stunned to chew. You fucking *what*?

'That lady's so pretty,' six-year-old Belle said.

'It's wrong to have secrets.' Aimee-Leigh, eight years old and bright as a button, had turned to Kat. 'Why does Dad have a secret?'

It's a bloody good question. Kat and Jason have been married for ten years, together for twelve. They're not supposed to have secrets. Kat has spent the past two days tearing the house apart, looking for something – anything – that will shed some light on what her husband has been up to.

Although, looking at him perving over Aliyah now, Kat's got a bloody good idea.

The pair of them have always known each other's passwords, so Kat has been through all Jason's bank statements and his phone records but found nothing untoward. Should she speak to the other firefighters to see what they know?

'You must be so worried,' Kat's mum had said when she called – the second the credits rolled on episode one.

'Not a bit,' Kat had lied. 'Jason and I don't keep secrets from each other.'

Last night, Kat had seethed at the telly as Jason relaxed in the hot tub with the accountant, Henry. Aliyah had just left and Jason was talking about her.

'She's so fit.' He'd closed his eyes and rested his head back, a smile on his face. 'Perfect tits, gorgeous arse. The full package.'

Kat had felt she should be chucking the remote at the telly or running upstairs to slash Jason's favourite shirts. But she couldn't move. She'd sat numbly in the centre of the leather sofa, tears rolling slowly down her cheeks. All through today, her phone has pinged with notification after notification: friends checking if she's okay, frenemies revelling in her public humiliation.

'The sex,' Jason told Henry last night, 'is phenomenal.' The camera had cut away to Aliyah stepping out of the shower, a towel wrapped around her perfect figure. Kat's heart had splintered. *He's slept with her.*

She knows she shouldn't have turned on the telly again tonight – that watching it is the worst form of self-harm – but she can't tear herself away from the car crash that is her marriage. Jason and Henry are back in the hot tub today – mercifully without Aliyah – and Kat turns up the volume, keeping one eye on the lounge door.

'I'm thinking of 'fessing up. Ripping the plaster off, you know?' As Jason talks, the image on screen is replaced by an earlier shot of Aliyah and Jason laughing in camp. No prizes for guessing what Jason's thinking of 'fessing up to, Kat thinks bitterly. She wonders how he'll do it. Whether he'll call her when he leaves camp or wait till he gets home.

'What would you use the prize money for?' Henry's saying to Jason.

'Whatever makes her happy.' Jason smiles, and Kat squeezes her eyes shut as the camera follows his gaze to where Aliyah's sitting in camp, her hands cupped around a coffee. 'I'd definitely book a holiday somewhere,' he says. 'Sun, sea and . . .' He finishes his sentence with a wink, and Kat's eyes fill with hot tears. She and Jason have never been abroad together and their honeymoon was two nights in her mum's caravan. He's known this girl all of five minutes and he's ready to hand over his prize money to her.

By the time the men leave the hot tub – all back slaps and winks, and that stupid gun thing men do with their fingers to say *I got you, bro* – Kat's had enough. She's about to switch off, vowing she won't put herself through this tomorrow, when the footage cuts to later in the day. Henry's now dressed and on his way to the confession pod. Despite Kat's angst, she's gripped. Is he going to confess his secret? The microwave beeps insistently from the kitchen, but Kat doesn't move.

In the confession pod, Henry is looking into the camera. 'I've agonised over whether to say what I'm about to say.' He rubs his head, messing up his still-damp hair. 'I'm not good with words – I'm a numbers guy – and if I'm honest, I'm not good with relationships.'

Kat leans forward. Has Henry been cheating too? Has everyone? Maybe the producer has brought these contestants together to expose their infidelity. There is some small comfort, Kat thinks, in not being the only partner going through this.

But Henry is talking about Jason. 'He's a cool guy, and I feel bad doing this, but that's the game, right? Survival of the fittest. So here goes . . . I expose Jason.'

Immediately, the show cuts to an ad break. Kat lets out a cry of frustration. She drops to the carpet and drags herself to the telly; stays crouched before it while the adverts play and her phone pings with messages she daren't look at.

When *Exposure* starts again, the contestants are gathered in camp for the live segment that rounds off every episode. The meat of Henry's accusation has been dangled out of reach, and now Roxy is striding into camp with her perfect hair and glossy lips, and Kat wants to die. *Just tell me*, she thinks. *Rip off the plaster.* 'What have you done?' She directs the question at her on-screen husband, who – by the relaxed look on his face – has no idea he's up for exposure. Or perhaps he doesn't care. Maybe he put Henry up to it; maybe this is Jason's way of ripping off that bloody plaster. *Hey, Kat, hey, kids – I'm leaving you for a woman I just met!*

Roxy addresses the camera. 'Earlier today, Henry made a bid to expose Jason. Let's see if he was right.' There's a flash of images: Jason's betrayed expression; Henry's discomfort; the shock on the others' faces. 'Remember,' Roxy says, 'if Henry's wrong, he'll face the confession pod himself.' She turns to Henry. 'Tell everyone what your phobia is.'

Henry blinks rapidly. 'Um . . . water.'

The screen cuts to an empty confession pod, water rushing in through a pipe in the wall, filling the narrow, windowless booth. Up and up the level rises, till Kat feels her chest tighten in vicarious panic.

Roxy hands Henry a key and gestures to the box of secrets, padlocked to a wooden pillar by the fire pit. 'The moment of truth. Open the box and give me Jason's secret.'

Kat can't look away. She can't breathe. She watches Henry unlock the box and flick through the seven envelopes inside, looking for the one marked *Jason*.

'Mum?' The lounge door opens and Aimee-Leigh comes in, rubbing her eyes.

Everything happens at once.

A close-up on the envelope as Roxy opens it. A cut away to Henry's earlier accusation. *I expose Jason.* Contestants' faces. Aimee-Leigh's excitement. 'Dad! You said he'd left! Is he back in?'

I expose Jason as a bigamist.

The open envelope. Henry's relieved yet guilty expression. Jason's despair.

'Mum, what's a bigamist?'

The room spins.

On screen, Roxy is talking to viewers. Jason is saying a muted farewell to every one of his fellow contestants except Henry, at whom he shoots a murderous look.

At home, Kat's tears have dried up. She switches off the telly and pulls her daughter in for a cuddle. Her phone is going mad, but it couldn't be as mad as Kat herself.

Her husband has another wife.

Kat's going to bloody kill him.

TEN

THURSDAY | FFION

'Inside. Quick.' Ffion glances both ways up the narrow street. Her tiny rented house is in a terraced street on the opposite side of Cwm Coed from Mam's house. The houses are red brick with slate roofs, and would once have been identical, before new owners replaced windows and painted doors and had little porches built for their coats and boots. There are no yards and no rear entrances, making it a challenge to come and go without an audience.

Ffion pulls the front door shut. 'Did anyone see you?'

'No.'

'Are you sure?'

'I'm not stupid. Now cough up.'

Ffion hands over a tenner. 'That's all the cash I've got.'

'I take PayPal.' Seren smiles sweetly. 'Unless you'd like me to tell Mam I'm spending the day here instead of in the library . . .'

But Ffion's already on her phone, transferring another twenty quid to Seren's account. 'Who taught you how to blackmail?' she mutters.

'My mam.'

The two women lock eyes for a second. Ffion shakes her head and lets out a laugh.

Seren was sixteen when she found out that Ffion wasn't her

93

sister but her mother. Only sixteen herself when she'd given birth, Ffion had gone along with Mam's idea – even made herself think it was for the best. As Seren grew up, the family secret had become so long-buried, it felt like the truth.

It had shattered Seren's world when she'd found out. She hadn't spoken to Ffion for days, and when she did, the hurt in her eyes had almost broken Ffion's heart. 'I don't know how to *be*,' Seren had said. 'You were my sister, and I knew how to be around you. But now . . .'

It had been months before they'd settled into a new normal. Everything had changed, and yet, in many ways, nothing had. Ffion had a go at Seren, the way she always had. Seren backchatted her, the way she always had. They both called Mam *Mam*, the way they always had.

What had changed was deeper than that. It was in the unfiltered way Ffion felt when Seren was watching telly in her PJs, her hair still damp from the shower. It was in the way she felt when Seren came home an hour later than agreed. Revealing the truth had been like peeling off a layer, and everything Ffion felt was more raw, more vivid.

Seren flops on to the sofa and picks up the remote.

'You're here to revise, not watch TV.' Ffion didn't dare ask Mam to have Dave again, not after his remake of *The Great Escape*. She figures Dave will be more settled in his own house, and Seren can study as easily at Ffion's house as in the library. Mam does not share this view, hence the subterfuge.

'I thought I was here to watch Dave?' Seren gets up and wanders into the kitchen.

'You are. But you've got studying to do – that's why they call it study leave.'

'Riiight. And exactly how much studying did you do when you

were doing your A-levels?' She drops two slices of bread into the toaster.

'That's not the point,' Ffion says archly, remembering little of her final year at school besides the Friday night challenge to procure that weekend's vodka. 'You're predicted an A star and two As, which is a long way from my solitary C in Welsh lit.' She hesitates, glancing at Dave, who already looks mournful at the prospect of being left. 'Promise me you'll at least look at your notes.'

'My next exam isn't for ages, and it's only chemistry – I can do that standing on my—'

'Promise!'

'Okay!'

'It's important, Seren. Good grades open doors. Bangor's a great uni to have on our doorstep and—'

'Yeah, about that—'

Ffion holds up a palm like a traffic cop. 'You're going to university. End of. If Caleb's worth his salt, he'll wait.'

'But—'

'No buts.' Ffion downs the dregs of her coffee, then grimaces when she realises it's stone cold. 'How's he getting on with Miles, anyway?'

'He's not. Miles still hasn't added production assistant to the credits, and he won't let Caleb anywhere near the editing suite even though he already knows all the software – not even for experience. Caleb's basically just making coffee and loading the quad bike with emergency bog roll. He's raging.'

'Gotta start somewhere, I guess.'

Ffion crouches and holds Dave's huge head between two hands. Unable to move, he swivels his eyeballs towards the kitchen counter, where Seren is scraping margarine on to her toast.

'Now listen, mate,' she says. 'I've got to work, but you'll have fun with Aunty Seren. I love you, but if you let me down, you're off to the knacker's yard.'

'Touching,' Seren says, opening the Marmite. 'It's a mystery to me why you're single.'

'Me too.' While Dave is distracted by the possibility of toast crusts, Ffion makes a dash for the door. 'Don't take your eyes off him for a second.'

Ryan Francis has been missing for more than forty-eight hours. The search-and-rescue team – bolstered by volunteers from Cwm Coed – has been out since dawn, but the updates are thin on the ground. Dim newyddion, reads Huw's latest message to Ffion. No news. Yesterday, Ffion and George visited every property on Pen y Ddraig. None of the farmers or tenants reported any unusual activity. 'What next?' George said, as they left the final house, but Ffion was at a loss. When someone goes missing in a city, the investigation moves fast. CCTV alone prompts dozens of actions: dashcam footage, petrol stations, smart doorbells, town centre cameras . . . there might be multiple streets in the search area, officers speaking to residents in every house. Mobile phone tracing, financials, computer search history . . .

It's different out here. Harder. A person can be lost for days, even if they want to be found.

Ffion's phone beeps with a message from Leo. She hates that her stomach still gives a flip, as though his communications might be anything other than professional. Sure enough, the message is brief and perfunctory.

Three of the *Exposure* cameras were trashed last night. Am on my way up to camp with George to take a look.

She looks at the screen, annoyed at the flicker of misplaced jealousy she feels. Not that she imagines the robotic George is likely to turn Leo's head, but . . . Ffion closes her car door with unnecessary force. She misses him, that's all.

It's still too early in the year for the sun to burn off the morning mist that rises from the lake. It ribbons through the trees around the lakeshore, and, as the Triumph climbs towards Carreg Plas, the lake dips out of sight completely, hidden beneath a haze of white.

When Ffion arrives at the back door of the farmhouse, she finds the kitchen teeming with people. Jason Shenton sits ashen-faced at the table, talking to a woman with a tight ponytail and a recording device. A second woman, with a camera slung across her body, is helping herself to a pastry. Next to her, on the kitchen counter, a laptop plays a breakfast chat show on mute. At the other end of the table, Zee Hart is holding an animated conversation with a short, balding man. Neither Leo nor George is here.

Caleb is skulking in the pantry.

'Who's Jason talking to?' Ffion says.

'Some women's magazine. The bald bloke is from the *Sun*. He's found Jason's other wife in Australia – it's been kicking off big time.'

'I'm amazed he agreed to talk to them.'

'He loses his fee if he doesn't.'

Ffion looks at Zee, who is taking a card from the *Sun* reporter. 'What's she doing here?'

'She's got some kind of press ID.' Caleb shrugs. 'You know what Miles is like. No proper briefing – just shoved me in here and told me to babysit. Too tight to pay a press officer,' he scoffs, a far cry from the sycophantic Caleb Ffion saw at Mam's house three days ago.

97

'Turn it up,' someone says.

An Australian voice cuts through the kitchen. 'We were so young. I mean, like, eighteen? It was a mad summer.' The speaker laughs. Curious, Ffion moves so she can see the screen. The Australian woman is tanned and lithe, with caramel hair and deep chocolate eyes. 'I loved Jason, though. I haven't seen him for twenty years, but maybe this is God's way of telling us to give it another shot.' She flashes perfect white teeth at the camera. 'Hey, Jason, if you're watching – what do you reckon?'

Jason puts his head in his hands and lets out a long moan.

'How do you feel about that?' The magazine journalist pushes her recording device closer to Jason. 'Do you still love Addison?'

'No! Christ!' Jason rubs his face, then looks up as though he'd hoped to discover he'd been dreaming. 'I didn't even know what love was back then. I'd known her for three weeks and we were off our heads the whole time. After we got hitched, we sobered up and realised it was never going to work. We went our separate ways and . . .' He tails off miserably.

'You never thought about getting divorced?'

'Not till later, when I met Kat. Only by then I didn't know how to get in touch with Addison. I convinced myself it wasn't a proper marriage, it didn't count . . .' He looks around the room. 'I'm not a bigamist!'

'I mean, technically, you literally are,' Zee says.

'Kat wants a divorce.' Jason is bitter. 'She won't even take my calls. Says if I turn up at the house she'll call the police.'

The female journalist pats his arm. 'I'm sure she'll come around.'

'I hate to say it,' Zee says, 'but you did bring this on yourself.'

Jason stands with such force that his chair crashes to the floor. Ffion hears a series of clicks as the photographer captures the moment. 'My entire world has fallen apart, and it's all down to

Miles Young. The second he comes near me, I'm going to fucking kill him.'

There's little chance of that happening, Ffion reasons, because Miles has locked himself in the editing suite. He answers only after she has hammered at the door for a full minute.

'What is it?' Miles is in his running clothes, the vibrant yellow jacket adding an unhealthy tinge to his already pale skin. 'Ah – do you have my crime number? I need it for the insurers. Your superior officer said someone would—'

'Sorry, my what?'

'Detective Sergeant Brady, is it? He said—'

'No, I don't have your crime number.'

'But I need it.' Miles glares at her.

'And I need somewhere to live, a pay rise that matches inflation and a dog who doesn't eat his way out of a room in order to find me. I guess we're both out of luck.'

'I've had to request new cameras right away, but the insurance company won't pay up till it confirms the old ones have been damaged, and that won't happen till I have a crime number, so I'm out of pocket to the tune of several thousand pounds.'

'Ryan Francis has been missing for two days,' Ffion says. 'I think that's more important than a criminal damage report, don't you?'

The door slammed in Ffion's face suggests Miles disagrees.

Your superior officer. What does that make her – inferior? 'Inferior, my arse,' she mutters.

From within the editing suite comes a strident North Wales accent Ffion instantly recognises. *Enough with the praying! Every time I come back to camp, you're on your bloody knees.* Ffion can't help but smile. Ceri's a laugh on a night out, but you wouldn't

99

want to get on the wrong side of her. Ffion saw that first-hand last year.

'Rhywbeth ti isio'i ddweud wrthon, Ffion?' Efan Howells had called, from the other side of the pub. *Something you want to tell us?*

It was a few days after they'd put the Rhys Lloyd case to bed. Efan was wearing blue overalls, the arms tied around his waist, and his expression was sly and knowing.

'Been hearing a few things about the Morgan family. About that *sister* of yours, in particular.'

'If I wanted to hear from an asshole, Efan Howells, I'd fart.' Ffion had carried two pints across to the table Ceri had nabbed. She hadn't cared that people were still talking about whether the rumours were true – whether Seren really was Ffion's daughter. Let them talk. Ffion would neither confirm nor deny it.

'You took that well,' Ceri said, nodding at Efan and his mates, who were roaring with laughter.

'He's not worth getting wound up over.' Ffion picked up her drink, only to put it down when she realised she was shaking.

'He needs putting in his place, he does,' Ceri said darkly.

It was Mam who told Ffion, a few days later, that Efan Howells had come a cropper with next door's prize black bull. 'Someone let him into the top field and he charged at Efan,' she said. 'He only just got out in time.'

Ceri claimed to know nothing. 'It's karma, is all,' she said, but Ffion saw a glint in the postwoman's eyes.

Enough with the praying! Ffion hears now, as Miles replays the clip.

'He always has it that loud.' Caleb appears at her side. 'Says

100

he needs to *immerse* himself in it.' He opens his mouth, then closes it, before repeating the movement.

'What's with the guppy impression?'

'I just . . .'

'Spit it out, mate.'

'Well . . . isn't it against the law to promise someone something, then not do it?' His expression morphs between hurt and anger. 'Because Miles promised I'd have a production assistant credit, and then he gave me some bollocks about the graphics going wrong, but it wasn't there last night either and—'

'Caleb.' Ffion touches his arm. 'I totally get why this is frustrating, but I'm a detective, not an agony aunt.'

'But it can't be legal!'

'You need a union or something, not the police.'

'He promised,' Caleb says, in a growl that is almost a threat.

'Give it up, mate.' Ffion walks away. Caleb's on a hiding to nothing. Miles Young doesn't strike her as a man who keeps his promises.

ELEVEN

THURSDAY | LEO

In the centre of the camp, flames lick at the fresh logs Lucas just added to the fire. The air is crisp on the mountain, and the smoky haze above the flames puts Leo in mind of November nights, bonfires and sparklers. Only the canopy of green around them reminds him it's almost summer.

Leo and George are examining the damaged cameras when Lucas appears. Owen immediately rounds on the vicar. 'You were told to stay in the tent.'

'We will, we will.' Lucas's calm manner invites confidences, and Leo wonders whether he's the sort of priest who takes confession. 'If we let the fire go out, though, it won't be hot enough to cook on later.'

Reluctantly, Owen lets him continue. He stands guard by the fire as Lucas works, supposedly to prevent Leo or George imparting information 'from the outside world' that might influence the show. The cameraman is Miles's henchman, Leo realises – self-appointed or otherwise – and, judging by his smirk as he frog-marches Lucas back to the other contestants, he enjoys it a little too much. In contrast, Dario hangs back, seemingly uneasy with the situation – or perhaps with the police presence.

Beside the fire is the pillar that holds the small metal box containing the contestants' secrets. Created from a section of tree trunk with the bark removed, it's buried so deep in the ground it may as well be set in concrete. Galvanised staples and a heavy-duty padlock secure the box, which Leo now sees is more like a small safe, to the top of the plinth.

'Look at these marks.' George points to a series of gouges around the staples. Similar-sized scratches appear around the lock of the safe. 'Someone tried to force the box open, and, when that didn't work, they tried to lever it off the base.'

Leo looks around. 'How many cameras have been smashed?'

'Three,' Owen says. 'All the ones pointing at the fire.' He indicates the first lot of damage, showing George the circle of broken glass beneath the unit. 'Whoever did it knew exactly where they were – they stayed completely out of shot. All you can see is something hurtling towards the screen, then it goes black.'

'What time did it happen?'

'The first one went at eleven minutes past two this morning.'

'How easy would it have been for someone to come into camp from the outside?' George looks at Dario, who flushes.

'I can't be everywhere at once! A walk around the perimeter on the hour, that's what Miles said, and even that's against my human rights – how am I expected to function properly on half an hour's kip here and there?'

'Have you checked the fence for signs of entry?'

Dario's silence speaks volumes.

Owen sighs loudly. 'If you want a job done properly, do it yourself, I suppose. This way, DC Kent.' As the two of them walk off towards the edge of the enclosure, Dario stares after them with a look of pure thunder.

There's a movement in the trees behind Leo. He turns to see Ffion walking towards him. She's dressed for the mountain, in lightweight trousers and walking boots. Her ID, hanging from a lanyard around her neck, is the only thing marking her out as a police officer. Leo feels overdressed in his suit.

Ffion takes in the smashed cameras and the marks around the box of secrets. 'What do you reckon – was it Ryan?'

'If he tried to take the box to protect his secret, it means he was on the mountain last night. It'll give us a fresh trail for a tracker dog.'

'Did the contestants see anything?'

'They're refusing to talk to us – Miles has muzzled them.'

'He's done what?' Ffion immediately starts walking towards the tents.

'He told them their contracts prohibit them from talking to anyone except the prearranged media outlets.' Leo follows her inside the central bell tent, where the contestants are sitting on bean bags.

'And then there were five . . .' Ffion says cheerfully. 'How are you all doing?'

The contestants look at the floor.

'This is a serious investigation,' Leo says. 'Someone has caused thousands of pounds' worth of damage to the production company's cameras – if you know anything about it, we need to know now.'

Nobody speaks.

'If it transpires that one of you is involved,' Leo says, 'or that you have information pertinent to the case, you could be in serious trouble for withholding it. No contract can stop you giving information to the police, whatever Miles has told you.'

Aliyah hugs her knees tighter.

'Ryan didn't go home,' Ffion says.

Henry takes in the others. Slowly, they're looking up, checking in with each other, seeing if anyone is going to crack.

'He didn't leave "for personal reasons",' Ffion says. 'He's missing.'

'What?' Pam says. Henry nudges her and she glares at him. 'Since when?'

'Since he left camp,' Ffion says. 'Miles lied to you.'

'The bastard!' Henry gets to his feet, and it's as though it's unlocked something in the others, who jump up too and all start talking at once.

'I knew there was something going on.'

'I saw the helicopter and I thought it was press.'

'He threatened to withhold our participation fee if we spoke to anyone.'

'Is it popular?' Aliyah suddenly asks. 'The TV show – are people watching it?'

Leo could tell her it seems as though *everyone* is watching it; that radio shows are inviting listeners to confess their secrets; that #ExposureTVShow has been trending on social media since Monday night. He could tell her the show has the highest viewing figures of any UK reality TV show – a fact which astounds him.

He doesn't tell her that. Not because of Miles's warning about influencing the outcome (like Ffion, Leo couldn't care less about Miles's sponsorship deals), but because Aliyah's question isn't motivated by a desire for fame. It's motivated by fear. She wants to know how big the audience will be for her public flogging. She stares at Leo, dark circles ringing anxious eyes, and Leo finds it hard to reconcile the broken girl he sees now with the smiling young woman on his TV set last night. He supposes Miles has twenty-four hours of footage from which to find the smiles. Leo remembers Roxy's warning: *Miles is the biggest liar of them all.*

'You know, you could all just leave.' Ffion looks around the group. 'You're not prisoners.'

'We may as well be,' Pam says grimly. 'This is TV's version of Death Row, and we're all waiting for our turn in the chair.'

'So leave,' Ffion says.

'The secrets, though . . .' Ceri shuts her eyes for a second. 'Once mine's out, I'll be sacked. If I don't stay in long enough to win the hundred grand, I need that participation fee.'

'Sweetheart, don't go sharing that sort of information.' Pam nods towards the others. 'Now they know your secret is something that'll lose you your job.'

'"They"?' Aliyah says. 'Like you wouldn't expose Ceri if you had the chance!'

'I wouldn't,' Pam says firmly. '*Exposure* might be trying to destroy my life, but I'll be damned if it's going to destroy my morals.'

Henry snorts. 'Laudable, I'm sure. Let's see how strong that moral fibre is when you're facing the confession pod. What is it in store for you? Rats, isn't it?'

Pam flinches.

'Expose one of us and you escape the confession pod,' Henry says. 'It's survival of the fittest here, and you know it.'

Just then, Owen sweeps into the tent in a fury. 'What are you doing in here?' He glares at Leo. 'Miles just radioed me – I told you the tents were strictly off limits.'

'Mate,' Ffion says, in a tone that's far from matey, 'you do know we're the police, don't you?'

'I don't give a f—' Owen cuts himself off, presumably remembering that he does, in fact, give a fuck about being arrested for obstruction, public disorder or any of the other offences for which Leo and Ffion would be glad to arrest him if he carries on. 'Um . . . your colleague wants you,' he finishes meekly.

George has seized a number of palm-sized stones, several of which glint with fragments of glass. 'I found this, too, trodden into the dirt by the edge of the camp.' It's a pocket knife, identical to those issued to each of the contestants at the start of the show. Engraved in the handle are the letters RF.

'That's Ryan's,' Owen says.

'Cheers, Poirot,' Ffion says, then turns pointedly to Leo. 'If forensics find prints on these stones – which I think we can safely assume were used to smash the cameras – they can get comparisons from the items in Ryan's overnight bag.'

'I'll see if there's a dog free,' Leo says. As they leave camp, he looks over his shoulder at the bell tent, from which Pam, Henry, Lucas, Ceri and Aliyah are emerging. Miles maintains the contestants will be relieved once their secrets are out, but Leo doubts it. All five look desperate.

When they arrive back at Carreg Plas, Huw is waiting for them in the courtyard.

He pre-empts Leo's question. 'Nothing, sorry. The drone picked up someone wild camping, but it was just a birdwatcher. One of your lot debriefed him.' Huw looks between Leo and Ffion with something more than professional curiosity, and Leo wonders how much Ffion shares with her ex-husband. He can't help but compare himself to Huw, who has the weathered complexion of a man who works outside, with fine lines around his eyes from blinking against the sun. Leo hits the weights as often as he can, but there's a difference between biceps built in the gym and arms made strong from lugging bricks up ladders. He glances at Ffion. Does she still have feelings for Huw?

'Sarge?'

Leo's glad of the interruption to his thoughts. He looks around to see a uniformed officer walking towards them, accompanied by a woman in walking trousers. An Ordnance Survey map in a plastic wallet hangs around her neck and a metal water bottle clinks against the fastenings of her rucksack.

'This lady's seen our MisPer,' the officer says.

The woman is taken aback at suddenly finding herself the centre of attention, as all eyes turn to her. She rallies well. 'I walked up Pen y Ddraig this morning – I wanted to be at the summit for sunrise – and I left my car by the lake. When I got back – it must have been around eleven o'clock, I suppose – there was a man in the lake.'

'*In* the lake?' George says.

'Up to his knees. I thought he was fishing at first. Then I realised he didn't have a rod, and he was crying. He started walking deeper into the water, and I shouted at him to stop. I said *Are you alright?* which was so stupid, because of course he wasn't alright.'

'What did he do?'

'Well . . .' The woman falters. 'He started shouting back. It wasn't particularly coherent, but it was rather aggressive, and I'm afraid I was frightened, so I went back to my car. I wasn't sure whether to phone the police, then this nice chap drove past, so I flagged him down and he brought me up here.'

'The description matches Ryan Francis,' the officer says.

Leo hears a strangled cry. He turns to find Jessica Francis standing in the courtyard, and he curses himself for not taking the witness somewhere more private.

'Ryan can't swim,' Jessica says. 'If he was in the lake, he . . .' She doesn't finish.

She doesn't need to.

'Update the PolSA,' Leo tells George. 'We need to refocus the search area.'

He only hopes they're not too late.

TWELVE

THURSDAY | ZEE HART | EPISODE FOUR

Zee Hart was born to be famous. Unfortunately for Zee, it's taken a while for anyone else to recognise this. Despite her slogging away at her YouTube channel for years, her viewers have always been in the hundreds rather than the thousands, and the Twitter account she set up to spill behind-the-scenes tea on *Exposure* didn't gain the traction she'd hoped for.

But all that changed when Ryan went missing.

Zee checks her stats and grins fit to burst. It's happening. It's really happening. The numbers are spiralling, not just on her YouTube channel but on Twitter too. Her video breaking the missing contestant story has gone viral and now everything she posts is shared within seconds.

Wait till she posts her interview with Jason Shenton. People are going to go INSANE.

Zee is still buzzing from actually scoring an interview with a contestant. When she snuck down to Carreg Plas this morning, she'd hoped to get a photo, or – at best – a soundbite answer in response to a yelled question. But the courtyard had been deserted, and a hastily written sign on the back door to the farmhouse read MEDIA CENTRE.

Zee was media, wasn't she?

She looked around for Miles, who had made it clear he hated her, but the only member of the production staff around was the runner, who gave a suspicious glance at the ID Zee flashed. 'That's a business card.'

'Right,' Zee said. 'For *Hart Breaks*. My media company.'

'You're a YouTuber; that's not—'

'And where do you get your breaking news, Caleb? The ten o'clock news, is it, when you're tucked up with your cocoa? Or is it on your socials, like a normal person?' Zee flicked her business card. 'Social media *is* media.' She was quite pleased with that – she thought she might put it on her website.

'Ten minutes. Only once the other journos have finished.'

The *other* journos! She was a journalist! Well, as good as. Zee had tried to look nonchalant as she sat next to a guy from the *Sun* newspaper. She made the most of her ten minutes by flirting with him in exchange for some of the dirt he'd dug up on the other contestants, then filming multiple clips of Jason being interviewed, to roll out on her socials over the next few days.

Now back in her tent, Zee checks Twitter and, once she's sure #ExposureTVShow is trending, she presses *post* on her own interview with Jason. It's only a few minutes long, thanks to Miles throwing her out, but she figures the abrupt ending is on brand for an investigative reporter. She takes a long pull on her joint, closing her mouth over the bittersweet smoke before letting it out through her nose. She brings up her tweet and plays the interview again, watching it through the eyes of the public. The footage ends abruptly just after Zee's yell of *Get your hands off me!*

'I'm nowhere near you,' Miles had said at the time, somewhat confused. By then Zee's phone was back in her pocket, complete with the dramatic ending to her interview, which was sure to get everyone talking. Fortunately for Zee, Miles had been somewhat

110

distracted by Jason, who had launched himself at the producer with the full force of his fury. Zee had taken the opportunity to slide away, going back to her tent to have a spliff and edit her footage.

She refreshes Twitter and is thrilled to see dozens of people have already shared the link.

Anyone know who the bloke is at the end? Hope @ZeeHart is pressing charges.

Sounds like Miles Young. Voice is the same as in this interview.

The tweeter drops a link as evidence.

Zee's conscience pricks at her, but, if what Jason said is true, Miles has done his fair share of editing the truth. Maybe it's time he got a taste of his own medicine.

No bruises, she tweets, which is entirely true. It was worth it to hear from Jason himself, she adds, which isn't. In fact, the brief interview is pretty boring. *I love my wife, I never meant to hurt her, yada yada yada*. It seems Twitter agrees, as Jason is hardly mentioned in Zee's replies and quote-tweets.

Total abuse of power from the producer. Share and shame!

Has the #MeToo movement passed him by completely? What an arsehole!

Looks like Miles Young is the one being #Exposed here . . .

Zee's follower count ticks steadily upwards. She turns on her iPad and uses more precious phone data to stream tonight's episode of *Exposure*, so she can tweet while she watches. Every few minutes her phone loses signal, and she has to walk around to find it again.

In tonight's episode, the contestants have been given a lie detector.

'Each of you must introduce yourself with the three true facts we've provided you with,' Roxy says. 'These will act as a control, giving a baseline for the polygraph. After that, your fellow contestants may ask ten questions in an attempt to find out more about the secret you're keeping.'

Aliyah goes first, slipping her fingers into a wired glove, before Roxy attaches a monitor around her chest. '*Um, my name's Aliyah*,' she reads from her card. '*I have black hair and brown eyes*.' She simpers and the camera swings round to the object of her attention: Henry.

Zee frowns. Zee has a bit of a thing for Henry, the best-looking bloke in the line-up (Lucas isn't bad, but you're not allowed to fancy vicars, are you?). Now that Jason has gone, Aliyah has clearly decided to turn her attention to Henry.

The contestants are scrutinising Aliyah's polygraph reading.

'Have you ever broken the law?' Ceri says.

Aliyah hesitates. 'Yes.' All eyes snap to the reading.

'No change,' Lucas says. 'She's telling the truth.'

'Have you been unfaithful to a partner?' Pam says, after prompting from Roxy.

'No.'

Henry asks the next question. 'Lied on a CV?'

'No.'

'Liar!' Ceri says triumphantly, as the polygraph reading shoots off the scale. Keyed up by their success, the contestants fling questions thick and fast at Aliyah, until she is reeling. She rips off the heart monitor and Zee wonders if she's going to freak out, but the footage cuts to Henry, already strapped to the machine. Aliyah has been forgotten – the dogs have been thrown fresh bait.

Earlier, Henry announced he would take over Jason's morning firewood chore, which Zee knows means he's likely to come close to the perimeter fence in search of logs. If she spends the morning walking around the camp, she's bound to spot him through the trees, and maybe he'll come close enough for a decent picture. She might even deploy her flirting skills again and see if she can score an interview. Imagine – the first ever interview actually from *within* the camp! It'll go viral for sure. Zee has tried to get Ceri to talk – the postal worker walks a loop around lunchtime each day – but hasn't got anywhere. She'll have more luck with a man, she's sure.

'*My name's Henry, I have brown hair and blue eyes.*' As Henry gives his 'control' truths, the others scrutinise the reading.

'It's ever so high already,' Pam says, concern in her voice. 'I hope you don't have an underlying heart condition – a lie will send it sky-high.'

'I don't plan on lying,' Henry says simply. 'I don't know what *Exposure* think they've got on me, but I have nothing to hide.'

'Ever broken the law?'

'No.'

'Cheated in a test?'

'No.'

'Crashed a car?'

Henry answers every question in the same calm manner, the polygraph reading following the same steady line as his control questions. Zee's crush intensifies. Hot *and* honest. There aren't many blokes like that around, in Zee's experience. If she doesn't manage to interview Henry tomorrow, she's definitely going to track him down once he leaves. He's an accountant, so he should be easy to find on Google, and, since Zee is expecting a flood of advertising offers now her profile's on the rise, it would be perfectly normal to make an appointment with an accountant . . .

Back on *Exposure*, it's time for the live segment. This is Zee's favourite bit. She gets such a thrill from knowing she's only a short distance from something she's watching on television *right now*. She pinches off the end from her joint, then pushes her feet into her trainers in case there's an eviction and she might be able to bag her second contestant interview.

'It'll kill me,' Aliyah is saying, as the group waits for Roxy to start. 'All those spiders, in that tiny space.' Her bottom lip wobbles.

Pam puts a comforting arm around her. 'I'm sure it won't come to that, sweetheart.'

Alone in her tent, a slow smile spreads across Zee's face. She'd pay good money to see Aliyah in a room full of spiders, and she's suddenly worked out how she can put her there.

'We've had no accusations from contestants today,' Roxy says, and there's audible relief from the huddled group hanging on her words. She flashes a wicked smile to the camera. 'But the public have spoken!'

'Oh!' Aliyah clasps a hand to her mouth. Lucas pales, and even Henry – who says he doesn't have a secret – looks rattled. Ceri's eyes are tightly shut, and Pam's are fixed on Roxy.

'The contestant who has received the least support from the public,' Roxy says, 'who will now face the confession pod, is . . .'

The pause is unbearable.

'Pam!'

Zee scrambles her kit together. She takes the iPad with her as she hastens to the camp entrance, because if Pam gets evicted – as she surely will – Zee wants to livestream her exit. She walks with one eye on the path and the other on the TV screen, where Pam is stepping down into the confession pod. Her eyes take a moment to adjust to the dim lighting, flicking into the dark corners of the tiny space. She lowers herself gingerly into the throne-like chair and looks squarely at the camera.

'Come on, then,' she says. Zee has a flashback to being chivvied on to the hockey pitch on a freezing Monday morning. 'Let's see what you've got for me.'

Zee slows to a walk, transfixed by what she's watching, holding her breath as Pam holds hers. Pam's gripping the arms of the chair, knuckles white, chin raised, eyes wide in fear and determination. 'Rats,' she says to the camera. 'You're putting rats in, aren't you?'

There's a sudden noise – a mechanical whir – and Pam's brow furrows as she listens. 'I take it back,' she says. 'That doesn't sound like a rat. So what is it, then, some kind of machine? A rack, to stretch me, maybe – I've always wanted to be a few inches taller, you know.' Pam carries on talking, covering her nerves with nonsense, and Zee stares at the screen in horror, because she can see what Pam hasn't yet realised.

The mechanical whir was a metal disk on the wall, spinning away from the hole it covered. Zee sees a flicker of movement, a hesitation of whiskers and then a *hop!* as a rat enters the confession pod. It sits up and looks around, and as though she can feel its presence Pam turns around. Her breathing quickens and she draws her feet closer to the chair.

'One,' she says. 'I can handle one.'

Zee can hardly bear to watch, because it's so obviously not going to be one rat, and even as she's forming the thought there's another twitch from the hole in the wall and then another and another, and now they pour from the pipe in a torrent of tails and feet and whiskers.

Pam's scream echoes across the mountain a split second before it comes through Zee's screen. Zee presses on. Any moment now, Pam's going to crack, and Zee doesn't want to miss a second of that walk of shame.

'Two minutes and thirty seconds to go!' Roxy's clear voice cuts across the footage. 'If you want this to stop, Pam, all you have to do is confess your secret.'

Pam's crying now, her hands no longer gripping the chair but clawing at her body, pushing off the rats as they swarm up her legs. A huge brown one leaps from the wall on to Pam's head and she screams again, and now Zee can't watch because she's clawing at her own head, certain she feels sharp feet in her hair.

'I confess, I confess!' Pam leaps out of the chair and steps towards the camera, her tear-stained face filling the screen. 'I've been taking money from parents who want to get their kids into my school. Now let me out, please!'

Zee shoves her iPad in her bag and runs, adrenaline coursing through her veins. The rats are forgotten – a corrupt head teacher is social media *gold*. And Pam looks so respectable!

'Not so fast, young lady.'

Zee just manages to avoid colliding with fifteen stone of security guard.

'Where do you think you're going?' Dario says.

'To interview Pam Butler.'

'Not without press accreditation you're not.'

Zee flashes the same card she showed Caleb. Dario plucks it from her fingers. Slowly, keeping his dark eyes fixed on Zee, he pushes the card into his mouth. He works his jaws and Zee hears the saliva smacking against his lips.

'You're not right in the head,' she says, uncomfortable under Dario's stare.

His eyes still fixed on hers, he shoots the wet ball of card at her feet. 'I'm giving you ten seconds to get back to your tent before I call Miles.'

Zee hesitates for a moment, before huffing her discontent and turning back towards the tent. She's *fairly* certain she can't be arrested just for standing here, but she wouldn't put anything past Miles, and who knows what Dario's capable of? Okay, so Zee would prefer to be closer to the action, but being moved on by the cops would ruin everything. She's styled herself as an *Exposure* expert with exclusive access.

Zee stops dead.

An *Exposure* expert . . .

Excitement fizzes inside her. Miles and Dario aren't going to let her anywhere near the farmhouse, which means the chances of another 'official' interview are slim. But what if she tried a different tack? She feels in her pocket for the business card the *Sun* reporter gave her this morning.

Miles is trying to expose the contestants.

Maybe it's time someone exposed Miles.

THIRTEEN

FRIDAY | FFION

Down by the lake, Ffion and Dave are sheltered from the wind that whips around the farmhouse, further up the mountain. The morning is warm and hazy, the sun casting sparkles across the surface of the water. Boats tack lazily from one shore to the other. In the shallows drifts a flat-bottomed boat, fishing rods resting on stands while the fisherman reclines, only his hat visible above the boat's hull.

The scene would be idyllic, were it not for the police divers.

The lake can be as stubborn as the sea for keeping hold of its treasures. It lodges them under rocks, or within the wrecked carcasses of abandoned rowing boats. It spins them over and over, breaks them into pieces. It washes them up into inlets and crevices, on to coves too small and uninviting for boats or walkers. Lost shoes, dropped oars, shopping trolleys nicked on a whim and shoved in the lake. Bodies.

Today's police activity is at the opposite end of lake from where Cwm Coed's last body was found, drifting through the mist towards the New Year's Day swimmers. Rhys Lloyd had been in the water for a matter of hours before he was spat out. Even the lake wanted rid of him, Ffion thinks. She glances at Leo, heat rising within her as she thinks about where she was – where they were – when Rhys's body was being hauled out of the water.

'Penny for them?' Leo says, catching her eye.

'I was just thinking about Rhys.'

'Do you think about him a lot?'

'I try not to.'

Leo nods, then he smiles suddenly, as though it's caught him off guard. 'Your face, when you saw me in the mortuary.'

'*Your* face!' It had been mere hours since they'd parted company – work the last thing on either of their minds.

'Well, I hadn't expected to see—'

'I thought I was imagining—'

They both talk at once, then stop to allow the other to finish, and the silence is abrupt and unwelcome.

Ffion bends to pick up a stone from the shore. 'Seems like a lifetime ago.'

'Longer,' Leo says quietly. He waits, perhaps for her to say more, but Ffion rolls the smooth pebble between her fingers and looks out over the water. A minute passes, then she hears the stones shift under his feet as he walks away.

They had hoped to find Ryan yesterday. After he'd been seen in the lake, the helicopter was immediately scrambled. It flew low above Llyn Drych, streaming the resulting footage back to Control Room. *Eastern shore clear*, came the commentary, above the *whomp whomp whomp* of the rotor blades. Below them, two search-and-rescue operators in a tangerine boat responded to the helicopter crew's requests, checking out an upturned kayak, a burst inflatable, carrier bags. *Negative*, came the response every time.

And so this morning, at first light, the police underwater search team arrived. Frogmen in black dry suits and scuba gear, ropes guiding them from the shore. They'd check the area where Ryan had been standing, the skipper said. Look for his clothing, his shoes. His body.

A chill runs down Ffion's spine. She pictures Ryan walking deeper and deeper into the lake, desperate for it to be over. She imagines his fear – not only of what faced him in the depths of Llyn Drych, but of what brought him there. She knows exactly where the lake bed drops away, and she imagines Ryan's feet stepping into nothing, his head ducking beneath the surface. *Ryan can't swim*, Jessica told them. Did instinct make him draw breath before he went under? Or did he force himself to sink with empty lungs, determined to end the nightmare?

Dave pulls at the lead, unsure why everyone is suddenly getting in the water but convinced he should be part of it. Last night, when a weary Ffion had returned home after a long and frustrating day, she found Dave and Seren bundled up under Ffion's duvet, revision cards scattered around the room like confetti.

'He's been crying for you all day,' Seren said. 'I've hardly done anything.'

No matter how desperate Ffion is for a dog-sitter, Seren's A-levels – and the degree course she'll start in Bangor in September – are more important. Seren is back in the library today and Dave has come to work with Ffion, under strict orders not to disgrace her.

Ffion walks over to where the Major Incident wagon is parked up. Unsurprisingly, Huw has already sniffed out the free coffee. Through the vehicle's open door, she glimpses the Family Liaison Officer sitting with Jessica Francis, whose face is streaked with tears.

A few metres away, Leo and George are talking to Jim Morris, a North Wales dog-handler Ffion has known since she joined the job. Well-built and tasty in a pub fight, Jim has grown a beard since Ffion saw him last, which adds to his already imposing presence. Many a North Wales burglar has thrown in the towel at the sight of Jim and his German shepherd bearing down on them. Right now, the dog is sitting patiently while his master talks to Leo. A long, coiled line hangs on Jim's belt.

'*Ti'n iawn,* Jim?' Ffion bends to stroke Foster. 'Aren't you a gorgeous boy?'

'Thanks,' Jim says. 'You're not so bad yourself.'

Foster is doing his best to ignoring Dave's enthusiastic buttsniffing.

'Sorry.' Ffion yanks him away. 'He didn't learn that from me.'

'Rescue dog?'

'How did you guess?' Dave leans so hard against Ffion's legs she almost falls over. 'He's a bit . . . clingy. Eats the house if I go out, and howls if he can't see me.'

'Get him working. Most behavioural issues can be solved by keeping a dog busy. Got any game shoots in your area?'

Ffion pictures Dave running amok through a flock of pheasants. 'Not sure that's quite his bag.' She eyes Foster enviously. 'Could he be a trail dog?'

'He'd be perfect for that.' Huw appears beside them, hands cupped around his coffee. 'As long as Ffion's the one missing.' He holds an open palm out to Ffion. 'I'll take my twenty quid now, if you like.'

'I'm not sending Dave back.'

'You will.' Huw grins again.

'I could come over some time if you like,' Jim says. 'Do some training with you? Be good to catch up outside work.'

'Thanks – I might take you up on that.'

Leo clears his throat. 'I hate to break up your social plans, but Ryan was sighted over twenty hours ago—'

'Yeah, sorry about that, mate – I was at an armed robbery in Caernarfon.'

'—so if we could leave the chit-chat and get on? Ryan could have been spooked by the witness and left the water. Let's not waste any more time.'

Ffion stares at Leo. What's with the snippy attitude? Being promoted has clearly gone to his head – she's never heard him speak to anyone like that.

'Will there still be a trail?' she asks Jim.

'Only one way to find out.'

'Actually, Ffion,' Leo says tersely, 'George and I have got this covered, so can you go back to the house?'

He's *sending her away*? 'I—'

'Thanks.' And, with that, Leo turns to watch Jim, who has moved Foster a few metres from the group. The dog's big ears are pricked, his eyes locked on his master's. Jim clips the long line on to Foster's collar and stands on it, then takes off the short lead, looping it over his head and one arm. Foster strains at the line now, his nose twitching.

Jim opens the bag containing Ryan's jumper and holds it by Foster's nose for several seconds. He leans towards the dog. 'Away find!'

Instantly, Foster's off, sniffing at the ground, at the air. He breaks into a run, Jim feeding out the long line expertly, keeping pace with him but letting the dog lead, zigzagging through the trees and away. Ffion gets out her baccy tin and rolls a cigarette.

'How are things between you and lover boy?' Huw says, in a low voice at her ear. 'He seemed a bit tense just now.'

Ffion whips her head around, glaring at Huw. 'The fuck are you talking about?' They're only a few metres from Leo.

'No need to be coy about it. Everyone knows you slept together.' Huw pulls a face at Ffion's cigarette. 'Are you still doing that? You know no one smokes any more?'

'That's why I do it.' Ffion checks her pockets for a lighter. 'When you say everyone . . .'

'Your mam, Seren, Steffan at the boathouse, the girls in the café—'

'Alright!' Ffion widens her eyes, her palm raised to ward off the rest. 'Just drop it, will you? It was one time, there's unlikely to be a repeat performance and anyway, talking to my ex-husband about my sex life is very wrong.'

'If you're worried about me, you needn't be.' Huw finishes his coffee and crumples his paper cup in his fist. 'What is it they say? *I give you my blessing.*'

'You give me . . .' Ffion's too outraged to finish.

'My blessing.'

Ffion narrows her eyes. There's only one explanation for this sudden benevolence from Huw, who a few months ago was begging her to come back. 'You're shagging someone, aren't you?'

'Are you jealous?' Huw's tone is jokey, but there's a vulnerability in his eyes which makes Ffion feel at once guilty and homesick.

'Not in the slightest. I hope she's The One,' Ffion says. 'Now, if you'll excuse me, I'd like to smoke this in peace.'

Still smarting from Leo's dismissal, Ffion reaches Carreg Plas to find Miles in a full-blown argument with Caleb.

'Then you should have got a proper press officer!' Caleb says, sounding close to tears.

'Oh, *should I*? Who do you think you are, telling me what I *should* have done? In case you've forgotten, young man, I am the producer and you are merely a runner.'

'Am I?' Caleb says bitterly. 'I guess I'd forgotten my job title, seeing as you haven't put it on the credits yet.'

'Are you still banging on about that? It's still a line on your CV, isn't it?'

'But you know I won't get a listing on IMDb unless I have an on-screen credit, and you promised!'

Ffion steps into the room before Caleb bursts into tears and makes even more of a tit of himself than he's currently making. 'The trail dog's just started,' she says. 'Divers haven't found anything yet, so there's still a chance—'

'Have you seen this?' Miles waves a newspaper at her.

'I've been busy. Looking for your missing contestant,' Ffion adds, although the barb is lost on Miles. He reads out the article.

'*Miles Young, producer of controversial reality television series* Exposure, *is facing increased criticism as the contestants and even his own team turn on him.*' The grainy photo – clearly taken on a phone – shows Owen restraining a furious Jason, who is trying to take a swing at Miles.

Ffion takes the paper and continues reading aloud. '*A source close to the* Exposure *team reported that Roxy Wilde, the show's frontwoman, was "tricked" into taking the presenter job. "She's furious with Miles for putting her in this situation," the source said.*'

'I'm not the source,' Caleb says quickly.

'It was that bloody vlogger, or Twitterer, or whatever she is,' Miles says. 'Zee bloody Hart.'

Beneath the exposé from the 'source', an emotional interview from Jessica details her husband's battle with his mental health.

He was honest with *Exposure* from the start, she's quoted as saying. He thought he was there for a survival competition, and he would have given that his best shot, but it was all a set-up. The researchers knew the truth about the show, and they knew Ryan was vulnerable. If he's hurt himself, it's all on them. It's all on Miles Young.

'There's more,' Miles spits.

Over the page, a photo of Pam appears alongside a heartfelt apology.

It's true that I took money from parents hoping to secure a place for their child in the school. What those parents didn't know is that the places were there anyway – there was no need for them to bribe me. I took the money they tried to bribe me with and used it to pay for food and uniform for students from less privileged backgrounds.

Robin Hood Head, reads the headline.

Ffion hands back the paper without a word. It seems the tables have well and truly turned on Miles.

'The network's getting twitchy,' Miles says. 'Several papers have run similar front pages, and a bunch of mental health charities have issued statements "condemning" the concept of the show.' Miles waggles his fingers around the word to show his own contempt. 'No doubt it was a *campaigner* who tried to sabotage us by damaging the cameras – it's cost me well over the odds to get replacements in at such short notice.' He turns on Caleb. 'And it's all your fault!'

Ffion's phone rings, and she steps out of the room to take George's call.

'You let Zee Hart into the media centre!' Miles is yelling at full volume. 'If I get my hands on the bitch—'

'The dog's followed the trail to a house in the woods,' George says. 'It's right by the lake, in a clearing, apparently.'

'I know it.'

'You're fired!' Miles shouts.

'Fired from what?' Caleb gives a bark of laughter. 'From unpaid work experience with no credit, no proof I even did it?'

'Did what?' Miles retorts. 'Delivered loo roll? Forget the TV industry, kid. You're not cut out for it.'

'Do you want to meet us there?' George is saying.

Ffion hesitates. 'Leo made it quite clear I wasn't—'

'I assumed you'd ignore him.'

Ffion is momentarily speechless. Where does George get off, making assumptions about what Ffion would or wouldn't do?

She takes another look at Miles and Caleb, still yelling at each other, then finds her voice. 'You assumed right.'

FOURTEEN

FRIDAY | LEO

Leo runs through the trees. He hadn't planned to follow Jim and Foster (partly because no specialist wants a DS cramping their style, but mostly because he didn't stand a hope in hell of keeping up with them) so he and George had instead turned their attention to the activities in the lake. The underwater search team had finished searching the reeds, and were in deeper water, the long line showing where they were submerged.

'He seemed friendly,' George said.

It was innocuous enough, but Leo shot her a look. He knew he'd been short with the dog-handler. It had surprised him, the rush of jealousy he'd felt when Jim had suggested meeting up with Ffion. He would have to work on that. Ffion was free to meet whoever she wanted.

In the lake, a diver had surfaced, signalling something to his colleague on shore, before releasing the air from his buoyancy jacket and sinking slowly back beneath the surface. Leo had felt a prickle at his neck as he'd pictured the dark depths of the lake-bed and imagined the weeds catching at the diver's legs.

'Do you want a coffee?' George had nodded towards the major incident wagon.

Leo did, but not the instant stuff he'd tried this morning. Miles's expensive coffee machine – and its accompanying tray of pastries – was calling. There was nothing Leo and George could do until – and unless – the search team found something, so the two of them had begun walking back to the car.

'Talk-through with DS Brady?' Jim's voice crackled through the radio in Leo's pocket. 'Apologies, Control, I don't have his shoulder number.' His voice came in bursts, his breathing keeping time with his running feet.

Leo grabbed his radio. 'DS Brady. Go ahead.'

'Sarge, we're on. Cottage in a clearing close to the lake – around a mile from where you briefed me. No access by road, as far as I can tell. Looks like whoever lives here keeps animals.'

Leo and George exchanged glances, then they ran.

As they sprint through the trees, Leo vows to get back in the gym, a habit he has lost since working more flexibly to spend time with Harris. The ground is uneven and every few metres his foot catches on a tree root or in a rabbit hole. George hangs back to make a call, but she catches him up quickly and runs lightly by his side, making easy work of it.

'You look like you know where you're going,' she says.

'I think so. There's only one cottage that close to the water and I went there with Ffion during the Rhys Lloyd job. It should be just around this corner . . .'

Angharad Evans's cottage is clad in wood. At first glance, Leo thinks Angharad has installed a living roof, but as they draw nearer he sees that the tiles have been overrun with emerald moss, as though the forest is slowly claiming back the house. Around the building is a sprawl of outbuildings and cages with mesh doors.

'Angharad takes in rescue animals,' Leo says. He sees a glimpse of what might be a badger. They slow to a walk and Leo pulls his T-shirt away from his neck for a breath of fresh air. He put on walking trousers this morning rather than his suit, knowing they'd be outside most of the day with the search teams, but he hadn't anticipated a cross-country run. 'Anything?' he says, when he reaches Jim. Leo's breath is heavy and ragged, while the dog-handler hasn't broken a sweat.

'Nothing in the outbuildings. We told the occupant to stay inside with the door locked till we searched the outside.'

'We?' Leo wonders if Jim means Foster, then he sees the quad bike parked at the end of the track that leads down from the mountain, and the rider leaning against it.

'It was quicker than walking,' Ffion says.

Leo feels acutely aware of his laboured breathing, and the line of sweat he knows will be around his hairline.

'The MisPer was definitely here,' Jim says. 'I've never seen Foster so certain. He's a bit distracted now, mind.' He nods towards the animal pens.

Leo walks towards the cottage.

Angharad is tall, with long hair the colour of steel. Her weather-beaten face is a maze of tiny lines, but her forearms are strong and sinewy. She could be anything from forty to seventy, but Leo knows she is closer to the latter.

The tiny kitchen has stone walls and dark beams, and Leo ducks to avoid bashing his head. The room smells musty, like the mothballs Leo's mum used in her jumper drawer.

Ffion leans against the oiled pine worktop. '*Sut mae pethau, Angharad?*'

Jim must have called Ffion, Leo supposes, to let her know where the search had ended up. The thought makes him disproportionately glum. A bit of him (the petty part) would like to send Ffion on an errand, but he knows enough about Angharad to know she prefers to deal with someone Welsh.

'*Prysur, fel arfer,*' Angharad says. She looks at Leo. 'Busy,' she translates, 'as usual.'

'We're looking for a man in his thirties.' Leo starts describing Ryan and the clothes they believe he is wearing, but Angharad cuts him off.

'I haven't seen anyone for a week or more. I'm working on a new project – I'm a translator for a Welsh publishing house – and I've been at my desk.' She smiles. 'I'm not one for company, as you've probably gathered.'

'Has anything been disturbed?' Ffion asks – the English for Leo's benefit, presumably.

Angharad thinks. 'I had a blanket go missing off the line.'

Leo gets out his notebook. 'When was this?'

'Just yesterday. I thought I'd not pegged it properly – the wind was fierce.' She opens her mouth as though to continue, but stays silent.

Ffion notices too. '*Be?*'

'It's nothing. Just . . .' Angharad sighs. 'I never lock the back door at night – don't give me that look, Ffion Morgan; tell me one person round here who does – and this morning I noticed there was some food missing.'

Leo and Ffion exchange glances.

'Not much. The end of a loaf of bread, a piece of cheese. A packet of biscuits.'

'Listen to me,' Ffion says. 'You need to lock your door. Not just if you go out, but when you're home. Especially at night.'

'But if he needs food—'

'He's not well,' Leo says. He hesitates. They don't know for

130

certain that Ryan Francis is having a breakdown, but they do know his wife considers his mental health to be fragile. They know that his frustration has resulted in acts of violence on at least one occasion, and they know that *Exposure* has pushed Ryan to his limits. 'He may not be acting rationally.'

'It sounds as though he needs help.'

'He does,' Ffion says.

'Then—'

'From a doctor.' Ffion moves to stand by Angharad, touching her arm. 'I know you think you're tough as old boots—'

'Less of the old, *diolch yn fawr* . . .'

'—but if Ryan comes to the house, you call on the nines, *iawn*?'

Angharad sighs. '*Iawn*.'

'Would you like us to check the house?' Leo says.

'*Diolch*, but I'm fine.' Angharad smiles. 'The advantage of living in a house as small as this one is that you know exactly who's in it.'

'Lock the door,' Ffion says, as they leave.

'I will.'

'Promise me.'

'I promise.'

They wait until they hear the clunk of the lock.

Leo scans the surrounding woodland. Is Ryan out there, watching them? Hiding out in the trees until darkness falls, and he can return to Angharad's cottage in search of food? For Angharad's sake, Leo hopes he's moved on. The longer Ryan goes without food and shelter – without seeing Jessica and his daughter – the greater the stress he'll be under. He'll be frightened, and fear makes people unpredictable.

Leo's worried about Ryan.

But he's just as worried about where Ryan might go next.

FIFTEEN

FRIDAY | ANGHARAD EVANS | EPISODE FIVE

Angharad Evans doesn't own a television. Her work as a literary translator – work she has no intention of stopping, despite having reached retirement age some time ago – requires long hours at her desk, and the last thing Angharad feels like doing in the evening is staring at another screen. She prefers to listen to the radio, or to linguistics podcasts, or she simply revels in the sounds of the forest, and tends to the animals she treats like her children.

This evening, though, Angharad is watching *Exposure*.

Her laptop is on a kitchen chair in front of the sofa on which Angharad is eating her supper. This in itself is unusual – Angharad prefers to eat at the table, where she can prop up her book against the vase in the centre – but then it's been a rather unusual day. She feels unsettled by the police's visit. She remembers DS Brady from last year and likes him no more now than she did then. She knows Ffion of old, and still cannot reconcile the wild child she knew – Ffion *Wyllt*, as everyone called her – with the job she does now. And then there was the dog – that beautiful, strong German shepherd – made to do the police's dirty work. Angharad's animals had confused him, she was pleased to see. He'd changed direction, running between the badger and the deer, sniffing out

132

the rabbits. Losing the scent he'd been tasked with following.

There is a vicar on *Exposure*. Angharad knows this because, whenever the Reverend Lucas Taylor is speaking, a banner appears on the screen, informing her of this fact. Do people nowadays have so little concentration they must be spoon-fed? Angharad has only seen fifteen minutes of this vacuous yet profoundly damaging television programme, but she has the measure of all four contestants. The young woman, Aliyah Brown, works in a children's nursery. Angharad isn't a parent, but she imagines Aliyah gets on well with infants, largely because she is still rather childish herself.

It astounds Angharad that Ceri Jones, the postwoman Angharad has always found eminently sensible, has put herself in this appalling situation. Angharad suspects Ceri is thinking the same, as the programme started a quarter of an hour ago and Ceri has yet to smile.

Angharad doesn't like Henry Moore. She might be alone in this view, as even Angharad can see that he makes himself useful in camp, and doesn't talk behind the others' backs. But his eyes are too close together, and in Angharad's experience men with close-set eyes are not to be trusted.

That only leaves Lucas, to whom Angharad might have lent her support, were it not for his obsession with all things celebrity. Angharad's faith might not be conventional – she hasn't set foot in a church since she was a child – but it is strong, and she feels let down by this self-proclaimed 'modern vicar'.

'There's quite a few celebrity vicars, aren't there?' Henry is saying.

'There *are* quite a few,' Angharad says from the sofa. 'Plural, Henry. Being an accountant is no excuse for poor grammar.'

'Yes, it's quite the trend.' Lucas is searching his bunk for something.

'Is that what you're after, then? A programme on Radio 4? A chat show?'

'That would be nice.' Lucas tuts. 'Have you seen my socks? They're hot pink and they have a small hole on one heel.'

There's some nonsense on screen about voting by text message, accompanied by several bars of the ghastly *Exposure* theme tune, then the graphics swirl away and the screen returns to Lucas hunting for his socks.

'Magazine interviews, TV adverts, a book deal for a cosy crime series.' Lucas runs through his ambitions, which Angharad notes are entirely self-serving. 'And a podcast, of course.' He finishes his wish list, distracted. 'Someone's taken my bloody socks!'

Angharad frowns. If Lucas is a 'modern vicar', she'll stick with the old-fashioned ones. 'And these are the ones in the lead,' she exclaims. 'I shudder to think what the others were like.'

'They were alright,' says a voice next to her.

Angharad's expression softens as she turns to her guest. *Exposure* is on at his insistence. She refused at first, citing her lack of television as an excuse, but Ryan became increasingly demanding and Angharad wondered if it might, in some way, prove cathartic.

'Pam was kind. She looked after me when I—' He breaks off. Angharad doesn't push him. He'll talk about it when – and if – he's ready.

Yesterday, Angharad had been feeding the animals when she'd heard a commotion coming from the lake. A man was shouting, but he'd sounded distressed rather than angry, and Angharad had walked down to see what was occurring. She found the man – Ryan – standing waist-deep in the water with tears streaming down his face.

Many moons ago, Angharad was a teacher in a particularly

134

challenging school. When the students were disruptive (as they often were), the other teachers would raise their voices above the throng and call for quiet. The students would talk louder, the teacher would shout more forcefully, and so it would go on. But when Angharad's class grew rowdy, she became still and quiet. She would make eye contact with every pupil, her expression open and curious. Slowly, like spilt water seeping across a table, the room would fall silent.

When Angharad saw Ryan in the lake, she took off her shoes and walked into the water with him. She stood quietly, feeling the delicious cool of the lake enveloping her feet. She waited.

'You can't stop me,' Ryan said. Angharad acknowledged the truth with a nod. 'I've got nothing left to live for.'

'I'm sorry to hear that.'

She let him guide their conversation, never speaking until he spoke. She learned about the television programme, and what could only be described as a gross betrayal of trust. She learned how Ryan tried a dress on for the first time on his thirty-third birthday, and that the moment he did, he felt indescribable joy as he wriggled the fabric down over his hips.

'I don't want to be a woman, though,' he said. 'I don't even want to dress as one all the time. That doesn't make any sense, does it?'

'If it feels right, then it makes sense.' Angharad had wiggled her toes. 'My feet have gone numb. Shall I put the kettle on?'

'He's going to destroy all their lives, too.' Ryan gestures to the screen, where the four contestants are grouped in a circle. 'He doesn't care who he hurts, as long as he gets the ratings, the kudos. Why are they still there? Why don't they leave?' His voice gains volume until he's yelling at the laptop, and Angharad sits very still and very quiet. She knows what the police would do if they saw him now, shouting and waving his arms about. They'd restrain him and bundle him into a van, then they'd write their statements and say it was necessary *for his own protection* – and just how would that protect Ryan's fragile state of mind?

In the middle of the contestants is a tray of objects, covered by a rich purple cloth.

'Each of the seven objects on this tray relates to an *Exposure* contestant, past or present,' says the presenter. 'But will they bring you a step closer to exposing your campmates?' Roxy is game-show-host breezy, but above the mischievous smile her eyes are flat.

'Past or present,' Ryan says. '*Past or present!*'

Angharad stays calm. 'We can switch it off.'

'No, no, no, no, no!'

It's not clear if he's responding to her suggestion, or to the prospect of what's under the purple cloth. Angharad weighs up her choices. If Ryan keeps watching, he is likely to become even more distressed. But if she turns it off without his agreement . . . She cannot win.

'Ready?' Aliyah says. Her fellow contestants nod, and Aliyah whips off the cloth. The items are eclectic. A pregnancy test, a single red rose, a condom, a birthday card, a wedding ring, a twenty-pound note and a pair of stockings. Despite herself, Angharad, who does Sudoku every morning to keep her brain sharp, finds herself leaning forward to see what can be gleaned from these mundane yet supposedly significant items.

Ryan's forehead glistens, one knee bouncing up and down so fast it becomes a vibration. Angharad can feel it through the sofa, and for the first time since she took Ryan in she feels a kernel of unease. There is not a malicious bone in Ryan's body, Angharad is quite sure of that. But Ryan is not himself right now.

Ceri's eyes flit to the other end of the tray. The money? The birthday card? It irritates Angharad that she's been sucked in, that she's positing theories about which object belongs to whom. The pregnancy test will be Aliyah's, she thinks. Perhaps the girl terminated a pregnancy, or gave a child up for adoption, although neither act should be shamed. Angharad is beginning to understand Ryan's vitriol towards Miles.

'How about this rose, then?' Henry brandishes it like a sword, then tickles Lucas's nose with it. 'Been buying flowers for a lover, have you, Reverend?' It gets a laugh from Ceri and Aliyah, but their mirth is cut off by the look on Lucas's face. He catches himself and laughs too, but the damage is done.

'You've got a lover,' Ceri says, her eyes wide.

'You've got the wrong end of the stick,' Lucas says.

'You have!'

'Back off!'

There's a stunned silence.

'He's making them turn on each other,' Ryan says. His knee is still going – up down, up down, up down – and now he's pinching his fingers, left on right, then right on left. Over and over. Angharad steals glances at him, her mind whirring. She won't call the police – a custody cell is no place for a man in the throes of a mental health crisis – but could she summon a doctor? Angharad has little faith in modern medicine, but even she is beginning to realise Ryan needs more than the camomile tea growing cold by his side.

On screen, Henry picks up the stocking.

'That's supposed to be mine, isn't it?' Ryan says. 'The stocking. I'm not even there, and Miles is still twisting the knife. He's determined to expose me, even though I walked. *Because* I walked!'

'Maybe this relates to Jason's bigamy?' Henry is suggesting.

Ceri shakes her head. 'The wedding ring would be his, surely?'

'Why do you keep looking at the birthday card?' Aliyah is staring at Ceri.

'I don't.'

'You do! You lied about your age, or something?'

'Don't be stupid,' Henry says. 'That's not a proper secret. Not like Jason being a bigamist, or Pam taking bribes.'

'What was Ryan's secret, do you reckon?' Aliyah says.

In Angharad's tiny living room, Ryan emits the sound of an animal in pain. Angharad reaches for her mobile phone; makes a show of checking the time. 'Only ten minutes left. I can turn it off—'

'Must have been bad, him running off like that.' Ceri leans into the conversation, visibly relieved to no longer be at the epicentre of it.

Angharad starts typing a message to Elen Morgan.

Don't panic, I'm fine, but can you ask Dr Alwen to come? I'll explain everything later. It's urgent.

Henry runs the stocking over his fingers seductively, then looks up with a laugh. 'Maybe this is Ryan's.' He gives a pantomime pout. The roar of laughter it prompts is fuelled by self-preservation and fear, but the sound is pure cruelty.

Ryan's moans intensify. 'Jessica will leave me.'

'She loves you.' Angharad doesn't know this for sure, but there are times when you have to say what needs to be heard.

'She'll be disgusted.'

'There's nothing disgusting about it.'

'*I'm* disgusted!' Ryan shouts it, and Angharad checks her phone. Has Elen read the message? Is she calling Dr Alwen? On the screen, the *Exposure* candidates are grouped around the fire pit in camp; Roxy Wilde is talking to camera.

'Tonight, the public have decided that a contestant will face the confession pod! And that contestant will be . . .' She leaves a pause. 'Lucas!'

Ryan is no longer watching the programme. He's on his feet, pacing, pacing. On the screen, the Reverend Lucas is in a narrow, poorly lit chamber. He sits on a high-backed chair, his hands clasped loosely in his lap. His eyes are closed.

'Are you ready?' The presenter's disembodied voice comes through a speaker in the tiny room, and Lucas nods. 'Then your three minutes begin . . . now!'

'It's over, it's all over,' Ryan cries.

'Shh,' Angharad soothes. 'Let's turn it off and—'

'Don't touch it!'

Angharad stays very still. Her hands, she realises, are mirroring Lucas's. She does not understand – perhaps because she did not watch the first few episodes of this awful show – why Lucas is sitting in this narrow space. The 'confession pod', they called it, and it does have the look of a church confessional. Angharad scans the walls of the chamber, looking for a grille or a window, wondering if there is someone sitting on the other side, waiting to hear Lucas's confession.

There is still no reply from Elen Morgan.

Ryan looks sharply at Angharad's hand. 'What have you got?'

'Just my phone.'

A metal circle on the wall behind Lucas opens and there's a movement like water, falling to the ground. Only it isn't water but snakes.

'Oh, this is too much!' Angharad can hardly watch. 'How dare they?'

'It's torture,' Ryan says, although he isn't watching the programme. He's looking at her hand, closed around her phone. 'Are you messaging someone?'

'Those poor innocent creatures.' Tears prick Angharad's eyes. 'Snakes are highly sensitive – they shouldn't be subjected to this abuse.' An anaconda coils lazily around Lucas's neck, flickers a sharp black tongue in his ear.

Ryan stares at Angharad. 'You're telling everyone my secret, aren't you?'

'No, of course not!'

'One minute to go!' Roxy says. Lucas's lips move in silent prayer as a serpent makes its way up his trouser leg.

'You said I could trust you!'

'You can.' Angharad stands, and the sudden movement is too much for Ryan. He rushes for the door, but the room is small and he knocks over the kitchen chair, smashing the laptop to the floor.

'Wait!' Angharad reaches for him but he knocks her away and he doesn't mean it – she knows he doesn't mean it – but she falls, smashing her head against the stone-slabbed floor.

The laptop lies upended beside her.

Angharad sees another flicker of tongue, a slither, a coil.

Then it goes black.

SIXTEEN

SATURDAY | FFION

Ffion's ringtone crashes into a dream in which Dave is competing in an agility class at Crufts. He's just run through an extendable tunnel and now he's soaring over jumps, taking them in his stride before reaching the finish line and ringing the bell.

Riiiiing. Riiiing.

Ffion answers the phone, her voice thick with sleep. 'Mam, it's four o'clock in the morning. *Ti'n okay?* What's happened?'

'It's not me, *cariad*. It's Angharad.'

Ffion puts her phone on speaker, pulls on yesterday's clothes and scrapes her hair into something approximating a ponytail. Anticipating a walk, Dave leaps off the bed with a thud.

'She doesn't want the police involved,' comes Mam's tinny voice through the phone.

'I hate to break it to you, but remember that funny black and white hat I used to wear . . . ?' Ffion takes the stairs two at a time.

'You don't count.'

'Thanks.'

'You know what I mean.' Elen exhales sharply. 'I'm kicking myself for not looking at my phone last night. Thank heavens for a menopausal bladder, otherwise I might not have checked it at all. You'd think the HRT would have—'

141

'Mam. Focus.' Ffion's downstairs now, looking for her car keys and casting a longing glance in the direction of her coffee machine. 'Is Angharad conscious? Breathing?'

'Yes and yes. Poor thing was lying at the foot of the stairs when I got here.'

'Have you called an ambulance?'

'I'm not an idiot, Ffion Morgan.'

'I'll get uniform there.'

'She's adamant, Ffi. No police.'

'Mam, she's been assaulted.'

'She says she had a dizzy spell and fell down the stairs.'

'Then why is she insistent the police aren't called?'

Mam doesn't answer.

'I'm letting Control Room know now.' Ffion hangs up and picks up her radio.

Many years ago, a fallen tree made the road leading to Angharad's cottage impassable, and, since Angharad doesn't drive and is selective about visitors, she left it that way. Now, Ffion leaves the Triumph next to the ambulance, ducks under the trunk and jogs the half-mile to Angharad's cottage. The dawn light is breaking through the trees, throwing dancing tree shadows across the dirt track. Ffion keeps Dave on the lead, despite his pleas to chase rabbits.

'Most people would be thrilled by the prospect of staying at home,' she admonishes him. 'What's the big deal? The entire bed to yourself, Radio 4 on all day, and Sian popping across the road to fuss you at lunchtime . . . what more do you want?'

Dave doesn't answer. Ffion's plan to sneak out by scattering a distraction of gravy bones across the kitchen floor had been an abject failure: Dave had hoovered up the bones in four seconds, then hurled himself at Ffion as she made a dash for the door.

Up ahead, Ffion sees flashes of fluorescent through the gloaming. When she reaches the cottage, two paramedics are strapping Angharad on to a wheeled stretcher.

'I'm perfectly fine,' she snaps.

'Standard practice for a head injury,' replies the male paramedic firmly. 'Two secs,' he adds, *sotto voce*, to his colleague, before pulling Ffion to one side. 'She claims she felt a bit rough last night,' he continues, his voice low. 'She texted a friend to ask the GP to visit, then went to bed, but she fainted when she got up in the night and came to at the bottom of the stairs.'

'Are her injuries consistent with that?' Ffion loops Dave's lead around a sturdy branch, hoping he hasn't noticed the baby deer recovering in the nearest pen. Angharad is still arguing with the female paramedic, and Elen Morgan has stepped in to mediate.

The male paramedic jiggles his head from side to side, hedging his bets. 'She's got a cut on her head which is already healing, and a contusion to the side of her face I'd say was a good few hours old. No bruises anywhere else, which is odd after a tumble down the stairs, but they might still come out, of course.'

They walk back to Angharad, who has finally fallen silent. Elen looks at Ffion. 'I'll go with her to the hospital.'

'Angharad,' Ffion says. '*Pwy oedd yma neithiwr?*'

The answer comes fast and firm. 'No one was here.'

'Was it Ryan?'

'Who?' Angharad turns her head away.

Ffion looks around the empty cottage, careful not to touch anything. Outside, two local officers have arrived and their conversation drifts through the open door.

'Creepy, isn't it? I couldn't live here, not on my own.'

'Not exactly on her own, not with all these animals.'

'That's what makes it creepy! What even *is* that?'

'I think it might be a polecat.'

'And that is one ugly dog.'

Ffion lets out an indignant huff on Dave's behalf. It's no wonder the lad has issues.

Don't panic, I'm fine, reads the text from Angharad. Elen had forwarded it to Ffion's phone after she'd called her. But can you ask Dr Alwen to come? I'll explain everything later. It's urgent.

Angharad eschews modern medicine. Her kitchen shelves are lined with herbs she swears will cure all ills, and Ffion knows full well what she thinks of the town's medical practice. The only reason she'd call for a doctor is if she were desperate (which she surely wasn't if she told Elen she was *fine*) and if that were the case why hadn't she called Dr Alwen herself?

Ffion checks the stairs and hall for marks, or smears of blood from the cut on Angharad's head. There's nothing there. But the moment Ffion enters the tiny living room, her nerve-endings jangle. There are two empty mugs, one on either side of the sofa. A kitchen chair lies on its side in the centre of the room, a laptop beside it.

Ffion picks up the laptop. The machine has gone to sleep, but, when Ffion presses a button with a sleeve-covered finger, the screen springs into life. The frozen logo of *Young Productions* appears – the final frame of last night's episode of *Exposure*.

There's no doubt in Ffion's mind that Ryan Francis was here with Angharad last night.

The question is: where is he now?

SEVENTEEN

SATURDAY | LEO

When Leo arrives at Angharad's cottage, CSI are packing up.

'We've swabbed and lifted prints from two coffee cups.' A woman in tortoiseshell glasses pulls off her paper suit and balls it into a bag. 'Your colleague found blood on the corner of the table in the living room, so we've swabbed that, too, and taken photos.'

'How soon can you have a comparison with the MisPer's forensics?'

'I'll see what I can do.'

Ffion looks up from Angharad's kitchen table when Leo comes in. 'I haven't sat down in almost seven hours,' she says defensively.

'Good morning to you, too.' Leo pulls out the chair opposite her and sits down. Just as he puts his phone on the table, it rings, Gayle's number flashing on the screen. He switches it to silent and ignores Ffion's curious glance.

'Why are you here?' she says. 'Angharad's assault is a North Wales job.'

'Committed by a suspect currently missing from *our* side of the border,' Leo says mildly.

'I suppose you think we don't know how to manage a crime scene. Because of course round our way it's all sheep and—'

'Ffion?'

She glares at him.

'What's going on?'

'A GBH, if I can swing it, although most likely an ABH, almost certainly downgraded to a common assault once it gets to—'

'With us,' Leo says quietly. 'What's going on with us?'

The ensuing silence is broken by the whine of an animal in one of Angharad's pens. Leo wonders who will feed them, in Angharad's absence. When Ffion finally looks up from the table, she's biting the inside of her cheek. Dark circles ring her eyes. Leo decides now is probably not the time to mention that her jumper is inside out.

'This isn't how things were the last time we worked together,' he says.

'So?'

'So if I've done something wrong . . .'

'You haven't done anything wrong,' Ffion snaps. Two lines furrow between her brows.

'Then . . .'

Ffion opens her mouth then closes it again. She looks at him. 'Then why am I being such a cow?' she offers, and the edge to her voice has tempered a little.

Leo makes a show of contemplating the accusation. 'Look, *I* wouldn't have used that word, but . . .'

The ghost of a smile crosses Ffion's lips. 'I'm sorry.' Immediately, she holds up a flattened palm, blocking Leo's face from hers. 'Don't.'

'What?'

'Don't do that face. Your *wonders will never cease* face because I apologised. It's fucking annoying.'

'That makes two of us, then.' Leo stands, hiding his own grin.

'Would Angharad mind if we made coffee?' He unscrews the lid of the tin closest to the kettle and sniffs at the ochre-coloured contents.

'It's chicory – I've already checked. Who's Gayle?'

'A woman.' Leo puts back the tin. 'Where's George?'

'At the hospital. Says Angharad's adamant she fell down the stairs. A colleague?'

'A . . .' Leo hesitates a fraction too long '. . . friend. How is Angharad?'

'Well enough to discharge herself against the doctors' advice. George is bringing her back now.' There's a pause. 'Would that be the same *friend* who wants you to "go all night"?'

It's suddenly incredibly hot in Angharad's kitchen. Leo wonders if it's possible to spontaneously combust. 'She didn't . . . I mean, I wouldn't . . .' He swallows. 'I don't want to talk about it.'

'Chill!' Ffion laughs. 'I'm winding you up. I'm happy for you.'

'It's complicated.'

'Isn't it always?' They lock eyes for a beat before Ffion breaks away. 'She can't be any worse than your ex, anyway.'

'I guess not,' Leo says, but then he thinks about how, the last time he took Gayle out for dinner, he spent five minutes psyching himself up in the mirror.

'Are you getting on better with her nowadays?' Ffion looks up. 'The ex – is she letting you see Harris?'

Leo doesn't know if it's hearing Harris's name that makes him want to smile, or the fact that Ffion remembered it. He leans against the counter. 'Yeah, it's all good. She's moved on, I think. Dominic's dad died and left him some money and they've moved to a street with three footballers on it, so Allie's in her element.'

'I can't imagine you with someone like that,' Ffion says.

'Nor can I.'

Something unspoken passes between them. This time, Ffion

doesn't look away. 'You know . . . it'll be another half-hour before George gets here with Angharad.'

'Do you have something in mind?' Leo lets his gaze travel over her face, taking in the tiny scar on her chin, the freckles across her cheeks.

'I do.'

'I'm all ears.'

'I reckon there's time to run to the garage for coffee,' she says, dropping the tease.

Leo shakes his head, laughing at himself as much as at her. 'You're impossible.'

'I don't know what you mean.' Ffion grins.

'Go on, then. I'll have a flat white.'

'You can't send me for coffee just because I'm a woman, you know.'

'How about I send you for coffee because you've been deeply unpleasant to me for reasons even you can't seem to explain, and because, deep down, you know you probably owe me more than a simple sorry?'

Ffion considers this for a moment, then pushes back her chair. 'I'll get a muffin too, shall I?'

The hair around Angharad's stitches is matted with blood. She cups her hands around a herbal tea. 'Stop looking at me like I'm going to keel over. I had a bump on the head, that's all.'

'You've got concussion.' George taps the leaflet in front of Angharad, which says *All about head injuries* at the top. 'You have to take it seriously.'

'I'll stay with her tonight.' Elen's busying herself at the sink, wiping down the counter and washing fingerprint powder from the crockery found in the living room.

'Two mugs.' Ffion looks meaningfully at Angharad. 'Two plates. Two sets of cutlery.'

The older woman's expression doesn't change. 'I'm lazy about washing up.'

'You were watching *Exposure*.'

'I like to keep up with popular culture.'

Ffion arches a brow. 'We won't find Ryan Francis's prints anywhere in your house, then?'

'Like I said when you came before: I've had food go missing. He could have touched—'

'Oh, Angharad!' Elen turns around, tea towel in hand. 'Give it up, *blodyn*.'

There's a pause, then Angharad sighs. 'He's not well.'

'He hurt you,' George says.

'He didn't mean to.'

'We'll make sure he gets help.' Leo holds Angharad's gaze. 'Will you make a statement?'

'No.'

'We'll need your testimony to—'

'I'm not pressing charges,' Angharad says. 'Ryan's been treated appallingly by that television show – is it any wonder he's had a breakdown? The only crime committed here is that *Exposure* was ever commissioned. You want a manhunt? Go after Miles Young. He's the one with blood on his hands.'

George takes out her pocketbook. 'What was Ryan wearing when he left here?'

'I didn't see him leave, but I gave him a pair of walking trousers and a warm jumper when he got here.' Angharad nods towards the stairs – presumably where the clothes had been stored.

'Colour?'

'Mmm? Oh, the jumper was dark green.'

Angharad's distracted. Leo follows her gaze to the door. 'What is it?' he says.

She hesitates. 'My backpack,' she says, reluctantly. 'I keep it hanging behind the door.' The hook is empty.

'Ryan's taken it?' Ffion asks.

'I suppose you'll be wanting to add that to his rap sheet too.' Angharad sniffs. 'Well, I won't be pressing charges for that, either.'

'What was in the bag?' George says. 'Bank cards?'

'No, I keep my wallet upstairs. There wasn't much in there. A few pounds in cash, a first aid kit, a—' She stops herself. 'Hardly anything,' she finishes, but Leo and Ffion exchange glances.

'A what?' Leo says.

There's a pause. 'A fishing knife.'

George leaves the room, one hand reaching for her radio. She stands in the small clearing in front of Angharad's cottage, and Leo hears her calm voice in his earpiece, appraising Control Room of the increased concern for Ryan's welfare. A bird cries out – either from the forest or from one of Angharad's pens – and the trees behind George rustle in the breeze.

The second George finishes, the operator circulates observations across the main channel. 'All units, be aware the suspect has warnings for violence and may be in possession of a knife.'

Leo feels a growing sense of apprehension. Maybe Angharad's right, maybe Ryan didn't assault her intentionally, but nevertheless his actions caused her harm. And now he's armed. It's only a matter of time before he goes too far.

'If only I saw your message when you sent it,' Elen says. 'I'd have come right away and—'

'Your mobile,' Ffion says suddenly. 'I didn't see it when we searched the house – did you take it with you to hospital?'

'I didn't take anything. I wanted to go upstairs and choose a book – those doctors can keep you waiting for hours – but they said—'

'Where is it?' Ffion says.

Angharad thinks. 'I had it in my hand when Ryan – when I fell. It should be in the living room.' She tries to stand, but George puts a firm hand on her shoulder.

'You've been told to rest.'

'It's definitely not there,' Ffion says, looking at Leo.

'What's the number?' he says.

'Here.' Elen's already finding it in her contacts, showing Leo the screen.

Now they have something to trace. If Ryan turns on that phone, they can find him.

EIGHTEEN

SATURDAY | HUW ELLIS | EPISODE SIX

Huw Ellis has heard so much about *Exposure* over the last week, he could happily go his entire life without seeing a single second of footage, yet here he is, watching episode six. Bronwen, Huw's girlfriend of six months, suggested they stay in and watch telly tonight, instead of going for a curry. Imagining a Netflix-and-chill scenario, Huw was quick to accept, but Bronwen is glued to the screen, and has so far resisted his attempts at seduction. Huw takes a surreptitious sniff at his left armpit, just in case, but all he can smell is washing powder. He had a feeling it wasn't going to be that sort of night when Bronwen answered the door wearing Winnie-the-Pooh pyjama bottoms.

There's still another half-hour to go. Why do women like this shit? Admittedly Huw hasn't been concentrating, but the four contestants (Bronwen keeps telling him their names, and he has already forgotten the three who aren't Ceri) seem to do nothing but sit around all day bitching about each other. Even the vicar took a swipe just now at the young girl, for not doing her fair share of washing-up.

'He's terrified of snakes,' Bronwen says, pointing at the vicar, 'but he didn't crack in the confession pod. That's how desperate he is to keep his secret.' Her hair is twisted into a plastic clip on her head, exposing the tiny silver hoop in the top of her ear.

'Mmm,' Huw says, wondering if he might take the bike out for a spin after work tomorrow.

Bronwen is obsessed with the contestants' secrets. She keeps going on about how awful Miles is to 'out' them, and how everyone's entitled to privacy, which is ironic, given how Bronwen's been on at Huw for weeks to tell people they're seeing each other. 'Are you embarrassed by me? Is that why you won't tell anyone?'

'You're reading too much into it,' Huw always says. Bronwen's great. Really great. She's the first woman he's met since Ffion left with whom he can imagine being for a long time. Maybe even marrying, although he hasn't said that to Bronwen yet.

But it's complicated.

Huw would no more live with Ffion Morgan again than he would take up pole-dancing, but nevertheless he still loves her, and telling her he's seeing Bronwen puts a full stop to something Huw once thought was forever. Also, telling someone – telling *anyone* – in Cwm Coed is tantamount to taking out an advert in every newspaper in the country. There's no going back from it. Everyone will know.

'They've not found him yet.' Bronwen checks the news on her phone during the adverts. *Exposure*'s missing contestant is now a national news story, with many of the papers running critical stories about Miles's role in Ryan's disappearance.

'Hmm.' Huw and his search-and-rescue team have been stood down, the police taking over the search. They cited *increased risk factors*, and, even though they won't say what they are, the rumours are that Ryan knocked Angharad unconscious, then robbed her.

'Poor man,' Bronwen says.

'Hmm,' Huw says again, thinking of Angharad.

'Elen Morgan says he's having a breakdown.'

'That's what they all say nowadays, when they don't want to face up to what they've done.'

Bronwen stares at him.

'Although,' Huw adds, 'obviously he might genuinely be ill.'

Satisfied, Bronwen turns back to the TV.

Huw's relieved the search-and-rescue team are finally off the mountain. They might look like another emergency service, with their marked-up off-roaders and high-vis kit, but everyone's a volunteer. For the last six days, they've abandoned their jobs and families to look for Ryan Francis.

Bronwen clutches his arm. 'Oh, my God!'

Huw, who hasn't been watching, and who has no idea what is happening, has run out of interested noises to make. On the telly, the young pretty one – Ali something? – is stepping down into what Huw only knows is the 'confession pod' because Bronwen won't stop banging on about it.

'What if she exposes Ceri?'

'That would be . . . bad.' Huw feels on fairly safe ground with this, but Bronwen turns to him in horror.

'Bad? It would be disastrous!'

'Absolutely disastrous.' Huw should get some sort of an award for this. Boyfriend of the Year, or something. He bets Bronwen won't sit and watch the motocross with him next weekend.

'Oh, God, I can't stand it!' Bronwen sounds close to tears.

She's going a bit over the top, isn't she? Huw likes Ceri – they'll chat over a pint if they happen to be in the pub at the same time – and he gets that Bronwen is Ceri's boss at Royal Mail, so she's kind of invested, but . . . does it really matter?

'It's the birthday card. That's what's done it,' Bronwen says. 'Aliyah saw Ceri looking at the card, and she guessed her secret.'

154

On the telly, the young girl in the confession pod takes a deep breath. 'I expose Ceri.'

'No!' Bronwen digs her nails into Huw's arm as the adverts cut in.

'Ow!'

'This can't happen. We have to do something!'

Huw peels her off him and goes to the loo. 'Chill out, Bron,' he calls from the kitchen, where he opens another beer. He returns to the sofa and tries to *cwtch* up a bit, but Bronwen is rigid with tension. 'Ceri's a tough cookie. Whatever her secret is, it's not going to bother her if people find out.'

'Shh!' The music is playing, and the contestants are back on screen. Huw slumps back into the sofa. He'll get no sense out of Bronwen till this is over.

'Good evening from Dragon Mountain,' Roxy says to the camera.

'Pen y Ddraig,' Huw mutters automatically.

'God, Huw, it doesn't matter! Ceri's about to be exposed!' Bronwen is almost hysterical.

They'll have to get a second telly, Huw decides, if they move in together.

'Aliyah,' Roxy says. 'Earlier today, you attempted to expose Ceri. Let's find out if you were right.' She holds up a small key. 'Open the box and find Ceri's envelope, please.'

Aliyah's hands are shaking so much she fumbles the key, but eventually she gets it open and flicks through the envelopes, handing one to Roxy. Huw catches a glimpse of Ceri in the background, silent and white-faced.

'I can't bear it.' Bronwen slaps splayed fingers over her eyes.

The screen cuts to the confession pod, and to Aliyah's recorded accusation.

'I expose Ceri,' Aliyah says. 'Ceri set fire to her own car to make a false insurance claim.'

By the campfire, all eyes snap to Ceri, whose mouth drops open.

'She got it wrong,' Bronwen says through sobs. 'Thank God.'

'Aliyah, do you stand by your accusation?' Roxy has opened the envelope and is holding a slip of paper.

'I do,' Aliyah says.

'I'm afraid, Aliyah . . .' Roxy pauses, 'you're wrong.'

Aliyah gasps. 'That's not possible.'

'You know what that means, don't you?' Roxy says.

'You bitch!' Aliyah looks wildly around as she hurls the insult. Huw isn't sure if she means Ceri or Roxy, although she isn't looking at either of them, but out beyond the camp, on to the mountain.

'Back to the confession pod, Aliyah.' Roxy turns a dazzling smile to the camera. 'Maybe we'll have an exposure tonight after all!'

'Oh, my God,' Bronwen says again. She collapses in the sofa, tears streaming down her face.

'Bron.' Huw picks up the remote and presses mute. He turns Bronwen gently to face him. 'What on earth is going on?'

She blinks at him miserably.

On screen, Aliyah screams silently. Spiders pour into the confession pod, swarming up her legs and over her contorted face.

'I know Ceri's secret,' Bronwen says miserably.

Aliyah has climbed on the seat, but the spiders are nimbler than her and, as fast as she brushes them off, they come back. Her eyes widen in horror and she scratches at her back, then tears at her shirt, the buttons shooting towards the camera.

'Is it bad?' Huw says. He doesn't know how long Aliyah's been in the confession pod – thirty seconds, forty? – but it's clear she's had enough. She's jumped off the chair and is hammering at the door, and Huw doesn't need the volume up to understand the words she's screaming.

I confess, I confess!

'She'll lose her job.' Bronwen bursts into fresh tears.

'Ceri?' Huw pulls his attention away from Aliyah, annoyed to realise he's been sucked into watching the show. 'You've got other postal workers though, right? And if you're short staffed, you can recruit—'

'I'll lose mine, too,' Bronwen says. 'We might even go to prison.'

'Prison?' Huw tries to make sense of what's going on.

'Please help me.'

'Of course, but Bronwen—'

'People mustn't find out what's in that envelope – promise you'll help?'

'I promise.' Huw puts his arms around Bronwen, hushing her as sobs rack her body. His head is reeling. Ceri has done something illegal, which somehow implicates Bronwen, and Huw has to stop anyone finding out.

How on earth is he going to do that?

NINETEEN

SUNDAY | FFION

'Former sex worker' hadn't been on Ffion's *Exposure* bingo card. Along with twelve million other viewers, she had watched open-mouthed as Aliyah hammered on the door of the confession pod last night and screamed her secret to the world.

'I wasn't expecting that, were you?' Ffion had said. Dave, midway through the critical business of licking his balls, did not acknowledge her. On the telly, Aliyah walked out of the *Exposure* camp and down the mountain, tears streaking her beautiful face. Ffion had switched off. She didn't want to watch any more, didn't want to contribute to the viewing figures inflating Miles's ego, when she knew the whole thing to be a sham. Seven days behind the scenes of *Exposure* had shown her there was nothing real about reality TV.

'There has to be a way to make them stop filming,' she says now. She's walked away from the farmhouse to call DI Malik without being overheard by the production team. 'Miles Young is morally bankrupt.'

'Half the government's morally bankrupt,' Malik says. 'But unless they commit a criminal offence, we're stuck with them.'

Ffion stops, out of breath from marching up the hill, and looks down at Carreg Plas. It looks idyllic. Criss-crossed above the courtyard, unlit string lights wait for the next wedding party, and Ffion imagines the cobbles covered with trestle tables and trailing ivy. She and Huw had got married at the chapel in Cwm Coed; had the reception in a marquee at the back of Y Llew Coch. White dress, veil, the whole lot.

'What a waste of money,' Mam said with a sigh, when Ffion moved back home, eighteen months later.

'I'll pay for the next one myself,' Ffion told her.

DI Malik is still talking. 'There's nothing we can do to make Young Productions stop filming. All we can do is advise them of the risks.'

'Miles doesn't listen to anything unless it's viewing figures,' Ffion says. Public opinion has swung wildly in Ryan's favour over the last two days, with several high-profile experts condemning the show, but the ratings continue to soar. It seems everyone loves a train crash. 'He doesn't even care that the crew have received death threats, or that someone posted the location of the farmhouse on Twitter. It's only a matter of time before protestors start showing up.'

'I'll speak to the duty superintendent – put uniform on standby.'

'I've got a bad feeling about this, boss.' Ffion starts walking back down the mountain. '#FindRyan has been trending since yesterday, and everyone's blaming *Exposure*.'

As well they might, she thinks. Angharad's phone hasn't connected to the phone network since Friday evening, when Angharad had messaged Elen, and Ryan himself has disappeared without trace. Either someone else took him in last night, or Ryan spent another night sleeping on the hills. Ffion doesn't want to think of the alternative. The one where Ryan uses Angharad's knife to end it all.

'It's a sensitive situation,' Malik says. 'The media have polarised the situation – woke lefties crying for everyone to *be kind* versus right-wing columnists praising Miles and mocking the contestants for being *snowflakes*. The chief's wary of being seen to take sides.'

Ffion explodes. 'What's woke about trying to stop a mentally unwell man doing himself or someone else harm, for fuck's sake?'

'Ffion, did we, or did we not, set an action plan around professional language in the workplace?'

Ffion sighs. 'We did.'

'It would be nice if you at least pretended to be working on it. Forget about trying to stop *Exposure* filming,' Malik adds. 'Just find Ryan Francis.'

If only it were that simple, Ffion thinks, as she makes her way back down to the farmhouse. If Ryan wanted to disappear, he would have left the mountain immediately after breaking out of camp. If forensics confirm Ryan's prints on the stones thrown at the cameras, it will make sense of his decision to stick around until then, but what about after that? Is he hoping for another opportunity to try to break open the box of secrets? Or does he have something else planned?

Ffion glances through the window of Ryan's stable room as she walks through the courtyard. Jessica's on the phone, pacing the tiny room, a hand tangled in her hair. None of Ryan's friends or relatives has heard from him since he left *Exposure*. They all agree how out-of-character his disappearance is.

It's around ten when Ffion reaches the house. She's almost at the back door when she hears a door being locked, and she turns to see Miles in his bright yellow running jacket and beanie. He bends to slip the key to his studio under the doormat.

'Miles!' Ffion calls. If the well being of the contestants isn't enough for him to pull *Exposure*, maybe the safety of his staff will be. Among the barrage of online abuse are several graphic threats against Roxy, who, as the public face of Miles's toxic creation, is taking the worst of the hate.

But Miles doesn't even glance in Ffion's direction. He sprints up the mountain for the daily exercise he insists on, clearly unable to forgo it even with all this shit going on. Talk about fiddling while Rome burns, Ffion thinks. It would serve him right if Ryan did catch up with him with that knife . . .

Just outside the entrance to Carreg Plas, a television crew are speaking to Aliyah. Now that the media are no longer dancing to his tune, Miles has declared the kitchen off-limits, and is refusing all interviews. That hasn't stopped some of the contestants doing them on their own terms, and Ffion hovers by the corner of the house, watching Aliyah talk to a journalist in a long camel coat.

'The argument isn't whether women should be doing sex work,' Aliyah is saying. 'It's how we ensure their safety while they're doing it.'

'Smashing it, isn't she?'

Ffion turns to see Pam watching proudly from the side.

'I gave her a pep talk last night. We have to own the narrative, I said. Can't let that bastard Miles win.'

Ffion takes in the nodding journalist, and Aliyah's confident stance. 'Impressive.'

'ITV is doing a feature about how the cost-of-living crisis pushes students into sex work, and the BBC want to interview her about "men who shame women".' Pam checks a note on her phone. 'After that, Aliyah and I are speaking to Sky News about the exploitation of reality television. Oh, and I'll be on *Woman's Hour* tomorrow.'

'What's happening with your job?'

'I've got a phone call with the chair of the Board of Governors this morning.'

161

'Good luck.'

'I'll need it.' Pam gives a rueful smile, before turning back to Aliyah with something akin to maternal pride. Ffion can see why parents want a place for their daughters in Pam's school.

Roxy's in the kitchen. Her face is pale and blotchy, as though she's been crying. 'I was just about to go for a walk,' she says, when Ffion comes in. Ffion wants to say that's a bad idea, given the venom directed at her online, and the doxxing of the farmhouse location, but she thinks of Pam, empowering Aliyah to *own the narrative*. Isn't it bad enough that Miles wanted his contestants cowering in fear, without the crew feeling the same?

'Be careful,' Ffion settles for. 'Don't go too far.'

'I tried to quit.' Tears brim over Roxy's dark lashes. 'But Miles said he'll sue me for breach of contract. Said he'll make sure I never work in television again.'

'He can't do that, surely?'

'I hate him,' Roxy says bitterly. She lets the door slam behind her.

'Join the club,' Ffion says to the empty room. 'There's quite the membership list.' She checks in the drawing room for Caleb, before remembering that Miles fired him. There are two voicemails from Seren on Ffion's phone, which will no doubt be pleas for Ffion to argue Caleb's case with Miles. Ffion hasn't played them. Miles isn't going to listen to Ffion.

She's rolling a cigarette when Jessica bursts into the kitchen.

'Ryan just called me!' His wife fumbles with her phone, showing Ffion the number on her screen. 'He didn't say anything, but I know it was him. He was—' She breaks off. 'He was crying.' Jessica's face crumbles and she grabs at the table as though it's the only thing that will hold her up.

Ffion checks the digits against the ones written in her notebook, making sure it's Angharad's number. She brings up Leo's number on her phone and dials.

'Ryan's clever,' Jessica says. 'He's a good boss – runs a team of people at work. He's funny, sociable . . .' She looks through the window, towards Miles's studio. 'That bastard's broken him.'

Leo answers. 'What's up?'

'Ryan's used Angharad's phone.'

'What Miles has done is criminal,' Jessica is saying. 'But it's not just him.'

Leo doesn't hesitate. 'I'll get authorisation for a trace.'

'All those people,' Jessica says. 'Glued to reality TV shows, desperate for the gossip.'

'Sit down,' Ffion says. 'I'll get you some water—'

'Have you watched it?'

'I beg your pardon?'

'Have you watched *Exposure*?' Jessica demands.

Ffion hesitates. 'Yes, but—'

'Then you're just as guilty!' Jessica points an accusatory finger at Ffion. 'You and everyone else watching. Gossiping about people you don't know, waiting for the next victim to be torn apart.'

'I only watched . . .' *For work*, Ffion was going to say, but that isn't true, is it? She thinks about the first episode of *Exposure*, cosy on Mam's sofa with Dave and a plate of pie. She recalls how they dissected the contestants, how they treated them like exhibits in a zoo, not real-life people. She thinks about last night, how she switched off the telly only after she'd seen Aliyah's confession.

'If people like you didn't watch reality TV, then people like *him* – ' Jessica turns her finger towards Miles's studio ' – wouldn't make it. You're all part of it. You've all got blood on your hands!' She storms out of the kitchen, slamming the door behind her.

Ffion sinks into a chair, horrified to discover she's shaking.

TWENTY

SUNDAY | LEO

Leo is well aware of the limitations surrounding cell site analysis – particularly in an area like Cwm Coed, where there are fewer mobile phone masts than in cities – but nevertheless he's disappointed by the limited information the analyst can provide about Ryan's likely movements.

'West of the nearest mast,' Leo tells Ffion and George.

'Is that it?' Ffion blows out her cheeks.

George shrugs. 'At least we know he hasn't left the area.'

'Angharad said there was money in her purse,' Leo says. 'Ryan could have got on a bus, even called for a taxi, but instead he's stayed near Dragon Mount—' He catches Ffion's eye. 'Near Pen y Ddraig,' he says self-consciously. 'Why would he do that?'

'Because his wife's here,' George says.

'No.' Ffion looks out of the open kitchen door across the courtyard. 'Because Miles is here.'

It's sixty metres or so from the kitchen to the studio, but they can hear the muted sounds that indicate Miles is back from his run and is editing. Leo can't make out the words on the clip being played, just the rise and fall of male and female voices, played at Miles's customary loud volume.

'We should warn him,' Leo says.

'I tried, earlier, when he was going for a run,' Ffion says. 'He totally blanked me.'

Leo considers their options. The intelligence isn't specific enough to issue Miles with an Osman warning – an identified and imminent threat to an individual's life – but it's clear from what Angharad has told them that Ryan harbours deep resentment towards everyone involved in *Exposure*. Especially Miles.

On Leo's phone is a screenshot of the type of knife Angharad kept in her bag.

'I don't carry it around as a matter of course,' she'd explained when she'd seen Leo's reaction. 'I'd been fishing, and it was still in my bag.'

The filleting knife has a long, tapered blade like a stiletto heel. *Ideal for slicing*, reads the website description, and a chill runs down Leo's back as he thinks of it. The knife in the photo has a wooden handle, but Angharad's is bone – *it belonged to my father* – and Leo imagines it gripped in Ryan's anxious hand.

Miles is playing the *Exposure* footage louder, and now Leo can make out the words. A man shouts, 'What are you doing?'

'He's going to damage his hearing, editing at that volume,' George says.

'Are you threatening me?' comes the voice, loud but indistinct, muffled by distance and doors. 'Get off me!' The only men left in the *Exposure* camp are Lucas and Henry, but, even as Leo is wondering which man was shouting, he realises it's neither, because the shouts are followed by a bloodcurdling scream and an anguished cry. 'Help, help!'

Then nothing.

Leo, Ffion and George stare at each other.

Ffion moves first, but George runs faster, reaching Miles's stable and hammering on the door. The curtains are closed, and she bangs on the glass then rattles the door handle. 'Open the door!'

'What's going on?' Jason appears behind them. 'Did you hear that scream? Was that Miles?'

'Stand back!' Leo takes a step back then aims a kick at the lock. There's a splintering sound, but the door holds, and he goes in with his shoulder, slamming his full weight against the wood. The door crashes open, and Leo just manages to stop himself from falling into what he immediately sees is a crime scene.

Miles is slumped at his desk. Above his head, the *Exposure* contestants are talking and laughing; a grotesque juxtaposition that turns Leo's stomach. He feels for a pulse, but they're too late.

Miles Young is dead.

STATEMENT

In light of today's tragic events, this evening's episode of Exposure *will not be broadcast. All filming has now ceased, and the remaining contestants and crew are being supported. The matter is in the hands of the police, and we will be making no further comment at this time.*

Young Productions

PART TWO

TWENTY-ONE

SUNDAY | FFION

George is already calling in the job, passing the details of Miles's murder in the same detached voice she uses to order a sandwich. *Uniformed support and dog section, please, Control. CSI, FME, SIO . . .*

While George reels off initials, Leo moves the crowd back. Everyone is in the courtyard now, summoned either by Miles's shouts or the chaos that followed. Roxy's hands are clamped to her mouth; behind her, Owen stares in disbelief. Ffion sees Pam, Jason, Aliyah. Caleb has turned up too, she notices.

Only Jessica is missing.

'Everyone in your own rooms.' Leo's tone brooks no argument.

'Is he . . .' Jason looks past Leo to Miles's studio. 'Is he dead?'

'Now,' Leo says firmly. The two men lock eyes for several seconds before Jason turns reluctantly away. The others follow, peeling off as they reach their respective rooms.

Ffion's chest is tight. The voices in the courtyard echo as though they're coming through a tunnel.

Miles Young is dead.

Ffion has seen countless dead bodies. She's been first on scene to dozens of assaults and traffic collisions, and more incidents of self-harm than she wants to remember.

She has never *heard* a murder take place.

Ffion replays the sounds in her head; thinks about how they all ignored Miles's shout of *What are you doing?* and *Are you threatening me?* How they'd imagined Miles was listening to a recording – how they had discussed the impact the volume would have on his hearing, for heaven's sake – and all the time . . .

Ffion thinks about the guttural scream that followed and imagines how desperate Miles must have felt, hoping someone would hear him calling out.

Help, help!

Did it feel like an eternity?

It was over in less than a minute.

Less than a minute, Ffion repeats to herself, and even in her head she can hear the defensiveness. They couldn't have done anything. They couldn't have stopped this.

Less than a minute.

It takes less than a minute to cross the courtyard, says the voice in her head. She's glad when her phone rings, and she answers with a crisp, 'DC Ffion Morgan.'

'Detective Chief Inspector Christine Boccacci,' comes the voice. 'You're with the murder victim, I understand?'

'Yes, ma'am.' Ffion snaps back to focus, glad of the distraction. 'Scene's contained, and witnesses are—'

'Who's the senior officer on scene?'

The DCI's interruption leaves Ffion momentarily without words. 'There isn't—' She remembers Leo. 'Well, we've got DS Brady from Cheshire CID here.'

'Ah, excellent.' Boccacci sounds relieved. 'Get him on the line, please – I'd like a detailed update.'

Ffion opens her mouth to protest – a detailed update was precisely what she'd been about to give – but she knows it's

172

pointless. She's never chased promotion. She wants to solve crime, not unpack personnel issues, and the most interesting work is on the front line, not in an office. But as she passes her phone to Leo, with a curt, 'SIO wants to speak to you,' she feels a stab of resentment.

Lying on the carpet of Miles's room is his door key, attached to a slim leather fob embossed with the number eight. It will have dropped to the floor when Leo booted open the door, Ffion realises. She leaves it where it is.

Miles's body is slumped over a large desk brought in by the production company – Ffion has seen the other stable rooms, which each have a small sofa in place of this expansive workstation. There are two computer screens, both connected to a laptop and external hard drive. One screen is blank. Ffion recalls Caleb complaining that Miles could easily have shared the workload, had the producer not been such a control freak.

'He's got two editing stations,' Caleb had said. 'But the great Miles Young won't let anyone sit next to him, oh no.'

The second screen shows the live feed from camp, where Ceri and Lucas are sitting by the fire pit.

'—saw her talking to the woman with the camera,' Lucas is saying.

The sound is uncomfortably loud. How could Miles bear it? At the top of the screen, red labels invite the user to click on different camera views: CAMP 1, CAMP 2, CAMP 3, BOYS TENT, GIRLS TENT, CONFESSION POD. The temptation to play around with it is huge – Henry isn't with Ceri and Lucas by the fire, and Ffion would like to know where he is – but she settles for pressing the mute button with the tip of her pen. The silence that descends makes her instantly calmer.

The converted stables have the feel of upmarket university study rooms, each with compact wardrobes and small double beds. At the rear of Miles's room, the casement window is wide open. It's easily big enough for someone to climb through, and the stables on this side look on to the woods, meaning it would have been easy for the murderer to make off without being seen. Ffion puts her hands in her pockets as she walks around. It's a habit she knows looks shockingly casual to an observer (she's been reprimanded more than once by DI Malik) but it's a foolproof way of guarding against thoughtless touching.

With the toe of her shoe, Ffion pushes open the shower room door. As she does so, it occurs to her that the open window could be a bluff, to make them think the killer ran off into the woods. Or opened the window but didn't have time to climb out, and instead hid in the only place possible . . .

She's both relieved and disappointed to find the tiny bathroom empty. The glass shower cubicle is bone-dry, and Ffion wonders if Miles showered after his morning run, or pulled on clothes and got straight back to work. She grimaces at the thought. Now that she thinks about it, there's a tang of sweat in the air, like a locker room after rugby.

She moves to stand next to the body.

Miles's arms hang by his side, his chest on the desk and his head to one side. He could be stealing forty winks, except that his eyes are open. They bulge disconcertingly in Ffion's direction. He's wearing a loose-fitting T-shirt which reveals angry red marks around his neck.

'Strangled,' Leo says from the door.

'Looks that way.' Ffion gestures to the computer screen, where the now silent Lucas and Ceri have been joined by Henry. 'We'd better bring them down.'

Leo shakes his head. 'Everyone stays where they are till the dog gets here.'

'But—'

'DCI Boccacci's asked me to take temporary command.'

The subtext is clear – *I'm the boss around here* – and Ffion thinks it's just as well she fucked up the relationship side of things, because how could you hope to have an equal partnership when one half outranks the other?

'George has taken an initial account from everyone staying in the stables, and they all say they were in their rooms at the time of the murder,' Leo says. 'That's Jason, Pam and Aliyah.'

'No Jessica,' Ffion says.

Leo makes a note. 'Can you speak to the three in the farmhouse? Roxy, Owen and Caleb. There shouldn't be anyone else in the house – uniform have got an outer cordon on at the gate.'

Leo is much more at ease giving orders than Ffion is taking them, which confirms to Ffion that what happened – or almost happened – between them is firmly in the past. Leo sees Ffion as a colleague, nothing more.

'Sure thing,' she says, with a lightness she doesn't feel. 'Sarge.'

It seems surreal that less than an hour ago Ffion was leaning against the kitchen counter, wondering whether to have a cigarette or another coffee, or both. She was frustrated by the inevitably slow pace of a missing person enquiry; now they've hurtled into a murder case with enough speed to cause whiplash.

She finds Owen in the drawing room, looking out of the bay window at the blue and white tape fluttering across the entrance to the drive.

'I've let the office know,' he says.

'You were specifically told not to make any calls.'

'Someone needs to pick up the editing, otherwise—'

'Editing?'

'Of the show.' He speaks to her as though she's a few cards short of a deck.

Ffion stares at him. 'Miles has been murdered.'

'Exactly. So someone else needs to step up.' He flexes his knuckles. 'I've asked the office to send a freelance cameraman to replace me. I'll take over from Miles.'

Ffion almost feels sorry for him.

'Don't worry – I know what I'm doing. I started on low-budget shorts, where you're producer, director, camera . . . the works. I'll pick up as editor and producer now; the viewers won't even see a difference.'

'Mate, it's game over.'

'What do you mean?'

'*Finito*. No more *Exposure*. This is a murder investigation.'

'No!' It's almost a cry. 'You can't just cancel the show.'

'I can and I have,' Ffion says. 'From now on, the only cameras around the place will belong to CSI.'

'Thank God for that.' Roxy flushes. 'How awful, I'm sorry. I don't mean I'm glad Miles is dead, of course not, but I don't think I could have done another week of *Exposure*.'

'It wouldn't have lasted a week, would it? There were only three contestants left.'

Ffion's perched on the windowsill of Roxy's room, which is next to Miles's at the back of the house, overlooking the courtyard. Roxy is sitting on the cream throw which drapes the end of her bed. Sage-green panelling runs around the lower half of the room. There are four bedrooms in the farmhouse, all as large as this one, into which Ffion could probably fit the entire ground floor of her rented cottage. On a clothes rail by the door hang several identical sets of Roxy's presenting uniform.

'Miles had it all planned out.' Roxy takes in Ffion's curious look. 'You didn't think the evictions were random, did you?'

'Are you saying the public vote is irrelevant?'

'Miles uses—' She stops. 'Used it as a guide to see who people liked, but the final say was his. Jason was always going to be first out, for example.'

'Why Jason?'

'Bigamy.' Roxy shrugs, as though it's self-evident. 'Juicy enough to keep people watching, get the media hyped up. If one of the contestants hadn't exposed him, Miles would have put Jason in the pod. He had all sorts of tricks up his sleeve. It wouldn't surprise me if he was passing stuff to the contestants through the security guard. Manipulating them, you know?'

Poor Jason, Ffion thinks, remembering his desperate attempts to get his wife to take his calls. No wonder he took a swing at Miles in the kitchen.

'Did you hear Miles shout for help?' she asks Roxy, but the presenter shakes her head.

'I was here, getting changed. I had music playing.'

'What were you listening to?'

Roxy pauses. 'ABBA, I think.' She gives an awkward laugh. 'Tragic, I know, but it helps me get in the zone.'

Caleb doesn't officially have a room at Carreg Plas. He lives at The Shore, the resort on the edge of the lake, and cycles up each day – Ffion's seen him pushing his bike up the steep bits. But she also knows, from Seren, that Caleb has appropriated the empty bedroom next to Owen's, across the landing from Roxy's. She knocks on the door.

Eighteen-year-olds possess an uncanny ability to look a variety of ages, Ffion has found. Seren barely looks twelve when she's dripping cereal milk on her pyjamas and watching morning cartoons, yet transforms into a woman in her twenties with a lick of mascara and fifty quid's worth of Shein.

Today, Caleb looks like a kid. A scared kid. His window looks down on to the valley, where the midday light casts a silvery sheen across Llyn Drych. On the far side of the lake lies The Shore, and the lakeside lodge owned by Caleb's mum, where Ffion imagines Caleb would like to be right now.

'What's happening?' he asks. He's been crying, although Ffion knows he'd deny it.

'A murder investigation,' she says.

Caleb chews on his bottom lip.

'How long have you been in your room?'

'Since the other detective told me to come here.'

'Where were you before that?'

'On my way up to camp with the day's rations.'

'I thought you'd been fired.'

'I was, till he realised there was no one to give the shit jobs to.' Caleb exhales in a sharp *huh*. 'No apology of course, just *get up to camp*, like he's leader of the fucking universe.' He stops, his expression suddenly wary, as though he's realised bad-mouthing a recently murdered boss is perhaps not the smartest idea.

'Did anyone see you heading up to camp this morning?'

'Is this an interview?'

There's a long pause. 'No,' Ffion says eventually. Caleb's an adult, but only just. And he's not a suspect, surely? Because that would really put the kibosh on Seren's A-level prep.

*   *   *

178

She takes the long way back to the courtyard, leaving the farmhouse by the front door and skirting around the house and behind the stables. She won't get too close to the scene – with any luck, Jim and Foster will pick up a scent from the open window – but it might give her an idea which way the murderer is likely to have gone.

She hadn't bargained on coming face to face with her ex-husband.

'What are you doing here?'

'I could ask you the same question,' Huw blusters.

'You could, but I'm a police officer and you're skulking about a murder scene.'

'A what?' His mouth drops open.

'You heard. What are you doing?' There's no footpath on this narrow strip between the back of the stables and the mountain forest, no reason for Huw to be here.

'Looking for Ryan.'

'No, you're not. The civilian search was called off when we received intelligence Ryan was in possession of a weapon.' It's cold in the shadow of the trees, and Ffion feels the hairs on her forearms rise.

'I dropped a radio clip around here. I was looking for it.'

'Don't you want to know who's been murdered?'

'What?'

'You didn't ask.' Ffion stares at him. 'It's the first thing I'd ask.'

'I suppose I just assumed it was Miles.' Huw blinks rapidly. 'Is it?'

Ffion doesn't answer. She's thinking about something far more useful than what her ex-husband is doing creeping about the woods; the only thing Huw murders is 'Sweet Caroline' when Y Llew Coch runs a karaoke night. 'That software you use to pinpoint people's locations,' she says. 'How does it work?'

'What?' Huw's thrown by the change of subject.

'Can you use it for Ryan?' When Ffion lived with Huw, she would watch in amazement as Huw sat at an open laptop, guiding members of his team to trace an injured hiker or a lost walker. How much easier it was, she thought, to find someone who wanted to be found.

'It wouldn't work,' Huw says.

'Why not?'

'Because the text we send says, *This is mountain rescue, please click on this link so we can see your location.* If he's on the run, he's not likely to—'

'Does it have to say that?' Somewhere in the forest, a dog barks, the sound echoing across the mountainside.

Huw hesitates. 'I guess we could change it . . .'

Ffion feels a fizz of energy. 'So it could say something like . . . *Hey, it's Jessica, I've been so worried, I love you so much blah blah. I'll meet you . . . here.*'

'That won't work.'

'It could.'

'It's a serious breach of protocol, changing the message – isn't it some kind of deception?' Huw looks uncertain. 'Seriously, Ffi, this could get me into trouble.'

'Tell me again what you're doing wandering around a murder scene?'

There's a long pause. 'Okay. I'll do it.'

'Great. Now get the fuck out of here before someone sees you.'

Ffion thinks about Huw's words. *I just assumed it was Miles.*

Of course it was going to be Miles who was murdered. Who else would it be? Who else has thrown a grenade into seven ordinary lives? Who else has manipulated viewers into believing they had a role to play, when all the time the script was half written?

Ffion has watched six episodes of *Exposure*, but she might as well have watched none for all she's learned. Six days of twenty-four-hour footage, slashed and manipulated and shrunk into six fifty-minute episodes, presenting the story Miles chose to tell. Nothing in those episodes tells Ffion what the contestants think of Miles, or of the situation he's put them in. The truth is somewhere on the cutting room floor.

Three of the contestants are still locked in camp, but four are out, and all four have reasons to hate Miles for what he's done to their lives.

Miles was a puppeteer.

Was it one of his puppets who snapped the string?

TWENTY-TWO

RYAN | DAY ONE OF *EXPOSURE*

In the weeks leading up to his appearance on *Exposure*, Ryan has been feeling increasingly nauseous. Yesterday, when he arrived at Carreg Plas and was issued with his rucksack of branded clothing ahead of the first day of filming, he'd felt almost faint with fear. He desperately regretted his application to the show, which had been a reckless attempt to reinforce his manliness to Jessica. She had taken to leaving magazines featuring effeminate men about the house, so Ryan knew she was becoming suspicious. Taunting him.

Are you tough enough to survive two weeks in the mountains of Snowdonia? The advert had popped up between *Gogglebox* and *Jimmy Carr*, a bright orange banner flashed across the screen. *Can you handle the Exposure?*

'I could do that,' Ryan had said wildly.

Jessica had chuckled. 'I'd love to see you try.' She'd squeezed his thigh affectionately, but it was too late. Now Ryan had to prove it. He could handle the 'Exposure', couldn't he? He could do wild camping, rock-climbing, abseiling. He could light fires and catch fish; tie barrels together to make a raft. He could be the real man Jessica wanted him to be.

When the email arrived – *Congratulations! Get ready for*

Exposure! – Ryan had vomited. He'd contemplated ignoring the email, but just that morning Jessica had said, *Did you see, they've got a same-sex couple on* Strictly *again?* Ryan had always thought Jess was pretty liberal, but lately she'd started pointing out every transgender or gay man she saw, as though their very presence was an offence. He had replied to the email from Young Productions with an enthusiastic *Yes!* and spent the next eight weeks sick with anxiety.

As Ryan and his fellow contestants have breakfast on the first day of *Exposure*, Ryan's nerves begin to dissipate. The others aren't all beefcakes with shaved heads and biceps the size of France. They aren't brimming with confidence, boasting skills in fire-starting and water filtration systems. He looks around the breakfast table in the farmhouse kitchen and decides his competition all looks pretty normal. Maybe he can do this after all. He spears another sausage and dips it in ketchup.

Maybe he even stands a chance of winning a hundred grand.

As the other contestants get to know each other, Ryan loses himself in a daydream in which he's standing at the summit of Pen y Ddraig mountain with an enormous cheque, Jessica looking on with newfound respect.

Later, when the seven contestants are making their way up the mountain to camp, Ryan smiles at Ceri, the postwoman who is walking next to him. 'Stunning, isn't it?' Above them, the mountain peak is lost in a haze of morning sun, and when Ryan looks down he sees the whole valley stretching out before them. He was too preoccupied to notice the lake when he arrived last night, but now it takes his breath away.

'It's alright.' Ceri sees his expression and laughs. 'This is my back yard.'

'How d'you mean?'

'I grew up here, didn't I?' She winks. 'Unfair advantage, right?'

Ryan catches his foot in a rabbit hole. He lurches forward, landing on his knees, and feeling a fool.

Ceri hauls him upright. 'They're a bloody nightmare, them rabbits. I came up here the other day and went arse over tit.' She shows him, exaggerating her stupidity then bursting into laughter. 'Proper clumsy, I am.'

Ryan's eyes shine. He's never been part of a gang before. He's never even tried, because he won't fit in, so what's the point? But all seven *Exposure* contestants have something in common: they applied to be on the show. Ryan slips his arm through the elbow Ceri proffers.

Sometimes, Ryan fantasises about telling Jessica he likes wearing women's clothes. He isn't gay, or transgender, and he's very happy being married, so it wouldn't change anything . . . not in his fantasy, anyway. Just that, in the evening, Ryan might put on a skirt, or cigarette pants with a three-inch heel. Maybe they'd go out together on a Friday night, in silk dresses that swish about their shins.

That's the dream.

The reality, of course, is that it would change everything.

A few years ago, Ryan had left the gym without his sports bag, in the bottom of which was a pair of lace knickers. If the gym rang, he'd say they were Jess's, he decided, except then Jess had texted to say she was at Pilates, and sent a picture of his bag. Is this yours?

Ryan has no clear recollection of what happened in the next ninety minutes, but by the time Jessica got home – having not even unzipped the bag – he had punched a hole in the kitchen wall and smashed an entire set of plates. The strain of not being

184

able to explain to her why he'd had some kind of breakdown had exacerbated the breakdown itself, and Ryan had found himself spiralling. Jessica had stood by him until he got better but, although she never mentions it, he knows she thinks about it all the time.

'Are you sure you want to do this?' she'd said, when Ryan was filling out the application form for *Exposure*. 'Are you sure you're . . .' She'd paused, choosing her words carefully. 'Are you okay to do it, I mean?'

'I'm fine,' Ryan had said. And he was. It had been a long time since the world had spun away from him.

When the contestants reach the *Exposure* camp, they meet Roxy Wilde. They actually met her at breakfast, but they've been instructed to pretend this is the first time they've seen her, and Ryan feels self-conscious as he shakes her hand and says, 'Hi, I'm Ryan.' The others are better at acting. Ryan would swear blind Henry and Pam had never seen Roxy before, and even Lucas, the vicar, clasps her hand with believable sincerity.

'Are you guys excited?' Roxy leads them in a cheer.

'Bring it on!' cries Jason.

'I am *so* up for this!' Aliyah says.

Ryan adds his *whoop!* to the others' cheers.

'Ladies and gentlemen,' Roxy says. 'You think you're here for a survival show, don't you?'

'We are!' Henry shouts.

Ryan's anxiety jangles. There's something in Roxy's eyes, beneath the twinkles and the wink.

'You're wrong.'

When Roxy Wilde tells them the true objective of *Exposure*, Ryan floats out of his body. He hovers above the camp, watching himself shrink, taking in the horrified faces of his fellow contestants.

Jason runs at Roxy, and there's a moment where it looks like there'll be a full-blown fight, until Henry pulls him back and says, 'There must be some mistake – let's hear them out.' Only there isn't a mistake, is there? They're really planning to expose everyone's darkest secrets.

Ryan thinks about his job in a software engineering firm, and what it will be like if his colleagues find out. He thinks about his parents, who should be allowed to go to their graves without trying to understand something Ryan hardly understands himself. He thinks about his daughter, and what the kids at school will say to her.

Pam is marching up to Roxy and Owen. 'Turn off that camera right this second.'

'You can't do this,' Aliyah sobs. 'We didn't agree to it.'

'Actually,' Owen says, 'you'll find it's all covered in the small print. *Young Productions reserves the right to alter, amend, rework, etcetera etcetera.*'

Ryan is spiralling. His chest is tight and he feels the same spacey, out-of-body experience he felt as he waited for Jessica to come home from Pilates. He wants to leave, but he can't move, and if he leaves, he'll have to explain himself.

It's over. His life is over.

And it's all Miles Young's fault.

TWENTY-THREE

SUNDAY | FFION

By the time Ffion has sent Huw on his way, and circled back to the entrance of Carreg Plas, there's a crime scene vehicle parked by the gate, next to Jim's dog van. A volley of barks coming from the courtyard suggests Foster has already been put to work, and Ffion's relieved not to have the complicating factor of Dave, who would no doubt want to play.

At six o'clock this morning, Ffion had coaxed a reluctant Dave around the side of Mam's house and posted him through the back door. 'Shh!' she said, as he began whining. 'You'll wake—'

'Ffion Morgan!' Mam had appeared in the kitchen in her dressing gown. 'You're lucky I haven't got a shotgun.'

'I used my key, Mam. Burglars don't use—'

Mam eyed Dave with distaste. 'It's not the burglars I want it for.'

'Please, Mam. This missing person case is dragging on and I haven't a minute to sort out a permanent solution. Just today. Please. *Caru ti* . . . Love you.' Ffion scarpered, half expecting to be rugby tackled on the path by Dave on an early escape bid.

Much as it pains her to admit it, Huw's right about Dave. Ffion needs to call the shelter and ask them to take him back. She's used every dog walker in the area, and all have refused to have

Dave again. Such is his reputation, a walker in a village ten miles away refused without meeting him. As soon as this job is squared away, Ffion will go on bended knee to the shelter and admit defeat.

There's no sign of Jim and Foster when Ffion reaches the courtyard. A CSI tent has been erected in front of Miles's studio at the entrance to the crime scene and a uniformed officer stands guard. It's started to drizzle. Glistening droplets cling to the fabric of the tent, and the officer turns up his collar.

Ffion hears a series of excitable barks. Seconds later, Foster emerges from behind the block of stable rooms, Jim feeding out the long lead. The dog's picked up a scent. They head off up the mountain trail and Ffion watches until they disappear into the trees. They're heading straight for the *Exposure* camp.

'FME's pronounced life extinct, and CSI have filmed the body in situ,' Leo says. 'DCI Boccacci's authorised a transferral to the morgue.'

They wait in the tent as Miles is moved from chair to bag. It's a laborious process, filmed every step of the way by a Crime Scene Investigator. Miles's hands have been wrapped in bags to preserve evidence that might be trapped beneath his fingernails, and on a large sheet of paper next to the body bag the CSI has laid out the contents of Miles's pockets: a wallet, a watch and an iPhone. Ffion bags each one separately and begins filling out exhibit tags.

'He has to have known his attacker,' Leo says. 'There's no sign of a struggle, so Miles must have opened the door then sat down to carry on editing. He was obsessed with preventing leaks – there's no way he'd have let someone watch him work, unless he knew them.'

'The killer waited till Miles was sitting down again, then attacked him from behind when he was less able to defend himself,'

Ffion says, and, in spite of her assurances to DI Malik that she'd rather work alone, she feels a buzz inside. This is her favourite part of an investigation – better, even, than slapping the cuffs on someone. Turning over the clues, piecing together the events leading up to the crime. The back-and-forth as they toss ideas around. Ffion realises she's smiling, and is glad Leo's gaze is still on the spot where Miles was sitting when he was killed.

'Yes. Although it might not have been that calculated.' Leo has one hand raised towards the chair, as though he's trying to conjure up a suspect. 'Miles could have said something that made his visitor snap.'

'Or maybe he was editing something that triggered the killer?'

The volume on the TV screen is still muted, and Ffion sees Ceri, Henry and Lucas talk silently around the *Exposure* fire pit. For them, nothing has changed. She wonders if Owen – in his grand plan to take over from Miles – would have told the three remaining contestants about the murder right away, or only as they emerged from camp. Anything could happen in the real world, and those three would only know about it if someone chose to tell them. Was that what Miles had liked about his job? The chance to play God?

'We can't wait for the tech analysis,' Ffion says. 'We need to know what Miles was working on when he died.'

Leo nods. 'Agreed. Owen knows how to operate the editing equipment, right?'

Ffion thinks of the cameraman's keenness to take over as producer. 'I'm not sure I trust him.' She gets out her phone. 'I'll tell George to give Caleb a shout.' *He already knows all the software,* Seren had said.

'DCI Boccacci's on her way,' Leo says. 'By the time she gets here, we need a full breakdown of where everyone was when Miles was killed – including the three contestants in camp. They're unlikely to be suspects, since they're locked in the compound, but Ryan's already proved that you can get out if you're determined enough.'

'Does that mean you don't think Ryan did it?' Ffion is tapping out a message to George.

'I'm keeping an open mind. On that note, although all the indications are that the murderer was known to Miles, we shouldn't close down lines of enquiry. Miles said that the application process for *Exposure* was fierce, and that he received abuse from some of the rejected applicants.'

Ffion knows where he's going with this. 'I'll get a list of everyone who applied.'

Through the open flap of the CSI tent, she sees the farmhouse door open. Caleb and George appear, hesitating at the worsening rain, before making a dash for it.

'We can see if any of them have a criminal record or markers for violence,' Ffion continues. 'Perhaps start with applicants who live within a fifty-mile radius?'

'Ideal. And I want full PNC checks on all the contestants and crew,' Leo says. 'Lucas's conviction – when was it and what was it for? Has he been in trouble since? Vicar or not, he gets looked into in as much detail as the others. Understood?'

'On it.'

'Boccacci's got the analysts looking at social media to see if any of the threats levelled at Miles online are credible,' Leo says, just as Caleb appears. He has a little more colour in his face than when Ffion saw him earlier. 'Don't touch anything,' Leo warns him. 'I just need you to talk Ffion through the computer system. I need to know exactly what time Miles's last edit was, as well as what was being streamed from camp at that exact time.'

Ffion is pulling protective covers over her shoes. When she

enters the crime scene, she doesn't touch Miles's chair, but leans awkwardly over it, using the tip of a pen to follow the instructions Caleb issues from the doorway.

'Now press the up arrow twice,' Caleb is saying. 'If he hadn't been so insistent on no one helping him, he wouldn't have been on his own when the murderer came. I told him I knew the software, I said I'd do all the basic stuff, to free up his time, but he wouldn't let me.' He wraps long, lean arms around himself. 'If I'd been at that second deck, he might not be dead.'

'Or we might be zipping you into a second body bag,' Ffion says. 'So there's that.' She calls to the others. 'The last edit was made just before ten.' She looks at Caleb. 'What time would Miles usually get back from his run?'

'Between 10.30 and 10.45. He pretty much always did the same route.'

'So let's say it's eleven by the time he's changed and at his desk,' Leo says.

Ffion nods. 'That fits. It was maybe quarter past when I heard audio clips – I remember thinking that he was back from his run. He must have been replaying what he'd done before he went.'

'And he shouted just before 11.45,' George says. 'I noted the time when Leo was kicking the door in.'

'I want to establish everyone's whereabouts between 11.15 and 11.45,' Leo says.

'What was the edit he made before his run?' George says.

Ffion turns around. 'Caleb? This is the computer he worked on, right?'

'Yeah, he only used the other one for streaming. A waste, when I could have been—'

'How do I find it?' Ffion says, before Caleb can go off on one again.

191

The teenager's fingers press the air, like a pianist relying on muscle memory. 'Right-click,' he says. 'Then control seven – no, eight. There. That's every edit made, with the time it was made.'

Ffion selects the top listing – made at 9.52 – and the screen fills with a close-up of a fire.

'He had loads of those,' Caleb says. 'Owen told me. The fire, the hot tub bubbling, an axe chopping wood . . . They were all done before the contestants arrived, to speed up the compilation process. He used them as cutaways from the main action.'

Ffion frowns. 'I'm finding it hard to believe Miles would have let Ryan in when we'd identified him as a potential risk. There are no indications a struggle took place, so what . . . the two of them watched the feed for a bit then Ryan strangled Miles? It doesn't make sense.'

Just then, Ffion hears her name. George pulls open the entrance to the CSI tent, and Ffion sees Huw striding towards them. He's brandishing a tablet encased in tough rubber, and it's clear from his expression that he has news.

'It worked,' he says, as he reaches the tent.

'What worked?' Leo says.

Swiftly, Ffion fills in Leo and George on the GPS software used by search-and-rescue teams, and her long-shot plan to lure Ryan in. The rain drums insistently on the tent, and she has to raise her voice to be heard.

'What did you replace the message with?' Leo asks.

'*Hi, this is Jessica.*' Huw reads from the tablet. '*I'm using a pay as you go so they can't trace our messages. I love you. Are you okay? Meet me here as quickly as you can. I promise everything will be okay.* Then the link.'

'And he clicked on it?' George says. 'What will he have seen?'

'A standard search-and-rescue message telling him to stay where he is, we now have his location.' Huw gives a rueful shrug. 'Sorry, I couldn't change that bit.'

'Great,' Leo says tersely. 'So now it's obvious to Ryan we know he has Angharad's phone.'

'Don't have a go at him.' Ffion looks at Leo and then Huw, their disgruntled expressions remarkably similar. 'It was my idea.'

'*Diolch*, Ffi,' Huw mutters. 'Thanks a bunch.'

'This is arrest strategy stuff,' Leo says. 'You should have run it by the SIO, or at least spoken to me as the senior officer present.'

'The plan worked, didn't it?' Ffion holds her hand out for Huw's tablet. 'Where is he?'

Huw points. 'That red dot is where the phone was when he clicked the link a few minutes ago.'

The screen shows a satellite view of Pen y Ddraig. Ffion sees the farmhouse with its distinctive courtyard of parallel stables, and the clearing further up the mountain, where the *Exposure* camp is.

In the centre, equidistant between Carreg Plas and the camp, is a bright red dot.

TWENTY-FOUR

SUNDAY | LEO

'George, you're coming with me.' The surge of adrenaline Leo now feels overshadows the resentment sparked in him by that conspiratorial look between Ffion and Huw. Ffion's right, the plan worked – that's all that matters. 'Tell Control we need two uniformed officers with taser capability. There should be some already looking for Ryan.'

Ffion moves a hand to her waist to check for cuffs, an instinctive gesture Leo knows is redundant. Ffion hates wearing a stab vest, and always leaves her kit and radio in the boot of her car.

'You're staying here,' he says, before she gets any ideas.

'I'm bloody not. The GPS tracker was my idea.'

'You've been in the scene. Stay put and carry on going through the tapes, see if anything happened that might be connected.'

Ffion falls silent. It doesn't need further explanation. Even a watertight case can fall apart if the defence find a chink in the evidential chain, and cross-contamination is an all-too-easy win. When they swab Ryan's hands for traces of Miles's DNA, there must be no possibility that it was transferred by an officer.

Within minutes, two uniformed officers are crossing the court-yard, bright yellow tasers in holsters at their sides. Leo has taken a photo of the map on Huw's tablet, and five of them – Leo,

194

George, Huw and the uniformed crew – start walking. Leo pulls up the collar on his jacket and wishes he'd brought a raincoat. Twenty minutes has elapsed since Ryan's location was confirmed, and Leo prays he hasn't gone far.

He hasn't moved a muscle.

Precisely where the red dot was flashing on Huw's tablet, they find Ryan cowering in the undergrowth. His hair is dirty and matted, his face gaunt and stressed. He looks up as the four police officers approach, but his eyes are unfocused. He appears not to notice the rain, which lashes against his face. Clasped in two trembling hands is Angharad's fishing knife.

'Drop the knife,' Leo says. Behind him, he hears George notify Control.

Ryan grips the knife tighter.

'*Drop the knife,*' Leo repeats, louder this time.

Ryan makes a sudden movement, scrambling to his feet and lunging towards Leo, slicing the blade through the air. 'Get away from me!'

The uniformed officers move, one in Ryan's line of sight, one off to the side. It disorientates Ryan, who spins between the two, still pointing the knife in Leo's direction, still shouting, 'Get away, get away!'

'Drop the knife or I'll taser you,' shouts one of the officers.

'No,' George says suddenly. She steps forward. 'Don't.'

Leo opens his mouth – he's surprised to hear her undermine other officers – but something in George's expression makes him close it again.

'Let me try,' she says.

Leo hesitates, then nods.

George walks forward until she's six feet or so from Ryan, then stops.

'Ryan, my name's George Kent. I'm a detective constable with North Wales Police.'

To a casual observer her stance might seem relaxed, but Leo notes that her knees are flexed, one foot placed slightly ahead of the other. She holds her hands loosely at her belt. She's ready to move in any direction; ready to raise her arms, or reach for her baton.

'Ryan, are you hurt?' Unlike Leo, George has a raincoat, but she pushed back the hood when she started talking, and her dark hair flattens itself around her ears.

Ryan's breathing is jagged and guttural. The two uniformed officers have their hands on their tasers.

'I've been speaking with Jessica,' George says.

Ryan's eyes snap on to her and Leo thinks she's misjudged it, but he simply lets out a low moan.

'She's very worried about you. She loves you a lot. She wants to see you.'

'She won't.' Ryan gives a harsh laugh. 'Not when she knows.' He rotates the knife handle in the palm of his hand and the blade glints in the sunlight.

'She does know.'

Ryan inhales sharply. Leo hopes George knows what she's doing.

'It doesn't make any difference to her. She's totally behind you, Ryan. Everyone is. But we need you to drop the knife.'

'I'm so sorry. I didn't mean to do it.'

Immediately, Leo glances at the bodycams clipped to the uniformed officers' vests, checking for the red blinking light.

'We can talk about that later,' George says. 'Right now, I just want you to focus on me. On what I'm saying, okay?'

Ryan doesn't move.

'You look like you could use something to eat, maybe a hot

drink, am I right? And that's a nasty cut to your head; we should get that looked at.'

'You won't take me to a hospital, will you?'

George sidesteps his question. 'It looks like it just needs a bit of a clean-up.'

'I'm so tired.'

'Drop the knife, Ryan. Let's get you sorted out.'

'I can't.'

'You can.'

'I've lost everything.' Silently, Ryan starts to cry.

'You've got everything that matters, Ryan, I promise. Jessica loves you.'

Several seconds pass.

Slowly, a degree at a time, Ryan lowers his hand to his side. Leo keeps his eyes trained on the knife, hardly taking a breath as Ryan's fingers begin to open.

'You're doing great, Ryan,' George says.

The knife falls to the ground.

'Great job. Now I want you to take six steps forward – can you do that? One, two, three . . .' As Ryan moves forward, George moves back, the distance between them never changing. 'That's brilliant, well done. Now can you kneel? That's it, great. Now put your hands on your head, fingers together like mine – can you see? Perfect.'

George holds up a hand to stop the uniformed officers, who are twitching like greyhounds in a trap, from rushing in.

'Ryan, in a moment, a police officer is going to put handcuffs on you, okay? That's for your safety as much as ours. He's going to put one of his hands on top of your hands, then he's going to use his other hand to apply the cuffs, and I want you to stay very still and just keep looking at me, alright?' She's crouching now, her eyes level with Ryan's, a supportive smile on her face. 'Ready? Okay.' She drops her hand. 'Now.'

'You were really good with him,' Leo says, as they walk down the mountain. It's slow progress. Overcome with exhaustion and stress, Ryan stumbles every few steps, held upright by a uniformed officer on each side.

'I didn't want him tasered,' George says. 'It's bad enough we've arrested him.' She's put her hood back up, but the rain's driving into them and the gesture is futile. Leo's grey trousers are black with rain, and his muscles are tight from the unexpected cold.

'Ryan is our primary suspect for Miles's murder,' Leo says. 'He put Angharad in hospital. We had to arrest him.'

'Still. It's not exactly going to help him get better, is it?'

They walk on in silence, Leo casting the occasional glance at George. She's rattled by what's just happened, her forehead creased in concern. Her thoughts seem somewhere else, and when Leo asks how she is finding being paired with Ffion she has to ask him to repeat the question.

'It's . . . an experience,' she says. 'You worked with her on the Rhys Lloyd murder, didn't you? I heard that was quite the job.'

'It had its moments.'

'The two of you must have got to know each other pretty well.'

Leo glances sharply at her, but George is looking straight ahead, her expression neutral. He doesn't answer. He isn't sure he can. Does anyone really know Ffion Morgan?

Ryan is taken in the back of a marked car to Bryndare custody, where they will request a doctor to establish whether he's fit for interview. Jessica drives behind them, despite Leo's warning that she's unlikely to be allowed to see her husband.

When Leo and George go into the kitchen at the farmhouse, they find Ffion with an older woman wearing a burgundy trouser suit.

'DCI Christine Boccacci.' The woman shakes Leo's hand. 'Have your ears been burning? Ffion's been telling me all about you.'

'It's all lies, ma'am,' Leo says seriously, before cracking a smile. 'Unless it's good.'

'Good enough for me to ask you to stay and oversee things here, if that's alright with you? I'll clear it with your DI when I get back to the incident room.'

'No problem.'

'Ready to brief me?'

Leo would have liked a little more time to gather his thoughts, but the DCI's question was rhetorical.

'Miles Young was killed at approximately 11.40 this morning, in stable number eight, which he was using as *Exposure*'s production suite.'

'That much I know. And I'm aware you've arrested Ryan Francis, after an extensive missing person investigation failed to locate him prior to this incident.' The implication, Leo knows, is that if they'd done their job properly, and found the MisPer, there wouldn't be a murder to investigate. 'Is he our man?'

'We're keeping an open mind,' Leo says. 'Francis is a strong suspect, but several others have motives, including the crew, and the evicted contestants who have had their secrets exposed.'

'Do they have alibis?'

'Roxy Wilde and Owen Havard were here in the house,' Ffion says. 'The production assistant, Caleb Northcote, was running an errand to camp, and security guard Dario Kimber was by the perimeter fence. Jason Shenton, Pam Butler and Aliyah Brown claim they were in their rooms.'

'Can we rule out the three contestants still in play?' Boccacci asks. 'I understand one of them has a previous conviction for violence.'

'Lucas Taylor,' Ffion says. 'We've requested full details. But he was on live camera at the time of the murder, as was Henry Moore. Lucas was by the fire, and Henry was in the confession pod.' Ffion hesitates. 'Out of the three contestants still in the *Exposure* camp, only Ceri Jones was off camera when Miles was killed.'

'The MisPer's wife, Jessica Francis, says she was out looking for her husband,' Leo says. 'We've yet to verify that. Miles also received a number of death threats on Twitter, which I understand your team is looking into.'

'What about Automatic Number Plate Recognition?' Boccacci suggests. 'Cars not registered to the local area?'

'I've considered that, ma'am, but the nearest route with ANPR feeds a large area, and as North Wales is such a popular tourist destination we're talking a fair amount of traffic, with no way to narrow it down to vehicles coming all the way to Cwm Coed. It's resource-intensive – I think we should park it until we've eliminated the more likely lines of enquiry. The evidence so far suggests prior knowledge of the victim's routine, which points towards one of the individuals already identified.'

Boccacci looks impressed. 'Agreed. Anything else?'

'Scene parameters identified and secured, no CCTV, no house-to-house,' Leo lists. 'There's a key missing which is believed to have been in the victim's pocket, so CSI have been asked to look out for that.'

'What's the significance of the key?'

'It opens the box containing the contestants' secrets.' Leo explains. 'It's the only key, and we're told Miles was very protective of it. The secrets of three of the contestants are still unknown. The murderer may have gone to see Miles specifically to get the key, in order to stop one of those secrets being exposed.'

'Interesting.' Boccacci thinks for a moment. 'Was the dog unit deployed?'

'Within fifteen minutes, ma'am, but unfortunately he lost the trail.' Jim's update had come in as they were bringing Ryan down the mountain, the dog-handler's frustration at the worsening weather evident even over the radio. The negative result has re-inforced Leo's decision to keep an open mind in relation to suspects. With Ryan hiding in plain sight just a short distance from the crime scene, Leo would have expected Foster to find him quickly. So perhaps the scent from Miles's open window wasn't Ryan's.

'Sounds like you've got everything under control,' Boccacci says, with a small smile. 'Anything you'd like to know from me?'

'I'm aware Miles's parents have been informed . . . I assume an FLO's been appointed? And is there a press strategy?'

'DC Jules Monroe, and we'll be issuing a statement in the next hour.' Boccacci doesn't miss a beat.

'We're likely to have press turn up. We can easily prevent access at the front of the house, but the property's exposed at the rear – can we have additional uniformed resources?'

'I'll see what I can do.'

'I'd like urgent data analysis on the victim's phone and smart-watch – are you happy to authorise that?'

'Yes. Anything else?'

'Not right now, ma'am.' The briefing has helped to get things straight in Leo's own mind too, and now he's keen to get going, starting by breaking the news to the three contestants still in the *Exposure* camp, now that Jim and Foster have been stood down.

'Remember our priorities,' Boccacci says, including Ffion and

George in her briefing. 'Trace, interview, eliminate. Get those alibis checked out as a matter of urgency, and I want confirmation that the live cameras don't have a time lag, before we definitively rule out Lucas Taylor and Henry Moore.'

'Yes, ma'am,' George says.

'I'd like a DC with me in Bryndare to brief the wider team.' Boccacci looks first at Ffion, then George. 'Decide between you – I'm going to take a look at the crime scene.' She pauses at the door, giving Leo an appraising look. 'That was an excellent briefing, by the way.'

As soon as the DCI is out of earshot, Leo exhales noisily. 'That felt like a job interview.'

'It was.' George produces a coin from her pocket. 'Heads or tails?' she asks Ffion. 'Loser gets to be the DCI's bag-carrier.'

'Heads.'

'What do you mean, it *was* a job interview?' Leo says.

George tosses the coin. 'There's a DI vacancy on Major Crime. They've been running light for months but Boccacci's a hard taskmaster and she hasn't found anyone she likes.' She lifts her hand to check the coin. 'Heads it is. Bugger. Wish me luck.' She heads into the courtyard to find the DCI, leaving Ffion and Leo in the kitchen.

'You and me, then,' Ffion says.

'Looks like it.' Leo turns away to make a coffee, feeling suddenly adrift. He saw that coin land, and he could have sworn it was tails.

TWENTY-FIVE

ALIYAH | DAY TWO OF *EXPOSURE*

'Knock, knock.'

The flap to the girls' bell tent is pulled open and Aliyah sees Jason. The sun is behind him, and his face is in shadow, his features blurred.

Aliyah shields her eyes from the harsh stream of light. 'What time is it?' Her head aches from crying and her face feels puffy and swollen. She remembers the cameras and groans, pulling the covers over her head.

'No idea. Is Ryan in here?'

'This isn't *Love Island*.' Ceri's pillow muffles her voice. 'Anyway, he's not exactly my type.'

'Maybe he's gone for a shower.' There's a creak from Pam's bunk. Aliyah peeks out of her covers and sees the head teacher pulling her orange *Exposure* fleece over her pyjamas. She looks wide awake.

'I've looked everywhere.'

'Could it be part of the game?' Aliyah says. 'Like a test, or something?'

'His stuff's still scattered around his bunk, but he's vanished.' There's real concern in Jason's voice.

Game or not, Aliyah throws off her covers, pushing aside the thought of being on telly without having even brushed her hair. Her appearance is the least of her concerns, given last night's bombshell. Their worst secrets, exposed to the whole world. Aliyah has a sudden thought that maybe she dreamed it, but despite Pam's alertness there are dark circles under the older woman's eyes, and Ceri is staring into space with a look of despair on her face. Aliyah's heart sinks. This is really happening.

'I'll help you look.' Aliyah copies Pam and pulls on her clothes over her pyjamas.

Roxy and the cameraman had made a sharp exit after last night's live segment finished. This was hardly surprising given the carnage that had erupted following Roxy's announcement. Jason took a swing at Owen, almost smashing his camera, and Ceri screamed obscenities at Roxy. Afterwards, Ceri told Aliyah she'd done it deliberately. 'It goes out before nine p.m.,' she said. 'So, the more you swear, the less footage they can use.' Aliyah said how clever she was, but she was wary of Ceri after that. The postwoman had seemed totally out of control, spittle flying from her mouth as she raged at the crew.

Aliyah had been too stunned to get angry. She knew exactly which secret the *Exposure* researchers had dug up. She liked to believe she'd covered her tracks – her escort work had all been done under a different name – but she supposed there would still be photos online. A digital trail. Last night, she'd looked at Ryan, the only other contestant still sitting down while the others ranted at Roxy and Owen. 'This is going to kill my dad,' she told him. Tears ran down her face.

Ryan hadn't answered. His eyes were wide, staring at a spot on the floor in front of him, and his hands were clasped tight. Aliyah could feel movement through the log between them as he rocked back and forth.

'Are you okay?' Aliyah asked. Ryan's lips moved, but he wasn't answering her. He was talking to himself – or to someone in his head – and he didn't stop, even when Aliyah moved closer and said, 'It's going to be okay,' which was a blatant lie of course, because everything was an absolute shitshow.

After Roxy and Owen left, Henry had gone too. He'd stuffed his clothes in his rucksack and said *I'm not putting up with this crap*, and left without saying goodbye to anyone. It would have been a waste of time anyway, because he was back in ten minutes.

'The security guard wouldn't open the gate!' Henry was apoplectic. 'That jumped-up jobsworth Dario said only Miles could authorise it. They're keeping us locked up like animals!'

'They can't do that,' Pam said firmly. 'It clearly said in our contracts that we can leave the show at any time.'

'If we're prepared to forfeit the appearance fee,' Lucas reminded the group.

'And have our secrets exposed anyway.' Jason tuts. 'The only way out of this is to keep immunity and win the show.'

There was silence as this sank in. Keeping immunity meant exposing someone else's secret. Getting close enough that they let down their guard – let something slip.

Yesterday, when they'd arrived in camp, *Exposure* had felt like a friendly competition, but today the game was on. The stakes were higher now.

The six contestants have been searching for Ryan for what feels like hours when a recorded announcement rings out across camp.

'Contestants, Ryan has left *Exposure* for personal reasons. He is safe and well and will not be returning to camp. For this reason, there will be no public vote this evening.'

'Oh, thank goodness!' Pam throws her arms around Henry, the

nearest contestant to her. He stiffens a little and claps her back awkwardly.

'So glad he's okay,' Lucas says, and Aliyah thinks that maybe the Reverend Lucas Taylor's relief seems genuine, whereas everyone else – including her – is simply giddy with relief that no one will be exposed during the live section of tonight's episode. Whether he meant to or not, Ryan has given them all twenty-four hours of immunity.

Jason and Henry decide they should celebrate by christening the hot tub. It's big enough for six, but Pam demurs (*no one wants to see me in a swimsuit, dear*) and Ceri takes a raincheck (*you know hot tubs are basically skin cell soup?*), so it's just Jason, Lucas, Henry and Aliyah. Aliyah bought a new bikini especially for *Exposure*. It's blinding white, with strategic boob coverage and complicated straps that cross her taut stomach and tie at the back. Aliyah knows it's shallow, but an approving look or three from the boys will make her feel a bit better about her life crashing about her feet.

But none of them gives her a second glance. Oh, they're polite enough – she's included in the conversation, and Lucas smiles and asks if she's okay, and does she have enough room – but you know when a bloke's checking you out, don't you? And these ones aren't.

'He's twisted,' Henry is saying. They're talking about Miles, who has been the subject of ninety per cent of conversations in camp since last night's revelation. It's small comfort, but Aliyah thinks that at least the people watching at home will know exactly how she and the others feel about the show's producer – they haven't exactly held back.

'He'll get his come-uppance,' Lucas says grimly. 'There's a special place in hell for people like Miles Young.'

Aliyah's eyes widen. She'd thought the vicar was fairly mild-mannered, but there was a definite flash of hellfire and damnation about him just then. He gets out shortly afterwards, and Jason and Henry start talking football, and then wives, and Aliyah thinks she may as well get out too. She's obviously losing her touch. Or maybe it's obvious she's tainted, which is the charming word her ex-boyfriend used when she told him about the escort work she'd done as a student. Aliyah hoped he'd be supportive – maybe even help her come to terms with how ashamed she felt – but he made it a million times worse. Aliyah wishes she could be one of those women who feel empowered by sex work, but she doesn't. Her dream is to be a children's TV presenter. That's why she applied for *Exposure* in the first place – loads of reality TV contestants end up with TV jobs – but it's backfired badly. How many former prostitutes have you seen on *Blue Peter*?

As Aliyah towels herself dry, Jason's talking about his wife, Kat, who he met at work and 'fell madly in love with'. Aliyah feels even sadder. Will anyone ever talk that way about her? The guys she meets from now on will be split into two camps: the ones who think she's a sure thing, and the ones who wouldn't touch her with a bargepole. Aliyah doesn't want either type.

'She's so fit.' Jason is lying back against his seat, smiling as he thinks about his wife. 'Perfect tits, gorgeous arse. The full package. And the sex is phenomenal.'

'Too much information, mate!' Henry laughs.

'I love her to bits.' Jason looks around, spotting a camera and shouting at it. 'Do you hear that, KitKat? You and the girls are my world.'

All the *Exposure* guys are cool, Aliyah thinks, but Jason's definitely the nicest.

'Have you been with your wife for a long time?' she asks, once Jason and Henry are back in camp.

'About twelve years?' He says it as though he's doubting himself.

'She's a lucky woman.'

'Remind her of that when this is all over, will you?' Jason says darkly.

Aliyah frowns. 'Is your secret something to do with your marriage?'

Instantly, the shutters come down. Jason stands. 'I'd better see if Pam needs help with tea.'

Aliyah files the information away. She wishes she had paper and pens, or a big whiteboard she could make notes on. Is Jason being unfaithful? He clearly adores Kat, so maybe his secret is some other kind of betrayal. An older child Kat doesn't know about? A second family?

Aliyah is still mulling over possibilities by the afternoon, when she takes a walk through the trees surrounding the central camp. It's a relief to be away from the cameras and she wonders how long she can spin out her walk before someone is despatched to send her back to the central camp. The perimeter fence is only a few hundred metres from the tents, but the woodland is dense, away from the clearing, and it feels good to be alone. She's lost all sense of time. This is only the second day, but it feels as though they've been trapped here forever. Aliyah follows the fence, trailing a hand along the wire mesh. Henry's right, they are like caged animals. As she starts walking back to camp, she hears someone calling her name. She stops and turns around.

'Aliyah!' Standing by the fence is a man in a fluorescent jacket – the security guard who let them into camp yesterday. Dario, Aliyah remembers.

'Alright?' she says.

'I've got something for you.'

'What's that, then?'

'Come closer, and I'll stick it through the fence.' He winks.

Aliyah's mouth drops open. God, men are *so* disgusting. Even after she sees the chocolate bar, and realises Dario's remark had been innuendo, she's still annoyed. But chocolate is chocolate, and so Aliyah flashes him a fake smile. 'Chocolate! For me?'

'For you.'

Aliyah takes a bite, thinking fast. 'I've missed this so much,' she says, and she knows she has him – he's practically salivating. 'I don't know how much more I can take.'

'I'll help you,' Dario says, just as she knew he would. Men are so predictable.

Aliyah lays it on thick: the confession pod, the spiders she knows she'll be faced with (to be fair, she doesn't have to lie about that, she's absolutely terrified of the things), before delivering her request. 'Could you find out what the others' secrets are?' She reaches through the wire and touches his chest, feeling faintly nauseous at the whiff of aftershave and body odour she receives in exchange. 'I'll make it worth your while,' she promises.

'I'll do everything I can,' Dario says, nodding feverishly. He reaches for her, but she steps back before he follows up on that thought of sticking something through the fence. There's an ominous lump in his trousers and he's breathing heavily.

'What's public opinion like?' Aliyah says, all business now.

'What?' Dario looks dazed.

'What do they think of us?'

'Um . . . they like the vicar. They think Pam's bossy.'

'But Pam's lovely! What about me?'

'They think you're a . . .' Dario hesitates. 'A bit flirty.'

'A bit *what*?' Aliyah's outraged.

Dario swallows. 'They're hoping you might get it on with Jason.'

However unpalatable this is, Aliyah recognises it could work in her favour. The public won't vote to expose and evict someone they're hoping to see shagging on screen. 'How about Ceri?'

'Miserable.'

'Jason?'

'Jack-the-lad.'

'Henry?'

'Boring.'

'Fair,' Aliyah concedes. She eyes Dario. 'Same time tomorrow?'

'I'll be here.'

Armed with the remainder of her chocolate bar, and the reassurance of an ally on the outside, Aliyah heads back to camp with renewed determination. The only way to avoid exposure is to get the other contestants out, and that's exactly what she plans to do.

TWENTY-SIX

SUNDAY | FFION

'Miles is dead?' Dario stares at them. 'But I saw him running this morning.'

'When was that?' Ffion asks. They're standing by the entrance to camp, Ffion and Leo slightly out of breath from the brisk walk up from Carreg Plas.

'Maybe quarter past ten? Same time as always.'

'Did he speak to you?'

Dario snorts. 'The only time Miles speaks to me is if I do something wrong.'

'And have you done anything wrong?' Ffion says, because something crossed Dario's face just now. Something secretive. She hears a noise in the undergrowth beside them and turns to look, but there's nothing there.

'No. Why, what have you heard?'

Leo ignores the question. 'Have you seen anyone hanging around?'

'Hang on a minute . . .' Dario's eyes narrow. 'You're not trying to put this on me, are you? I'm hired to keep the site safe, but I can't be everywhere at once. If Miles has been murdered, that's not my fault.'

Ffion frowns. 'We didn't say he was murdered. I told you he was dead, that's all.'

'You wouldn't be poking around asking questions if he'd died of natural causes, now would you?' Dario folds his arms across his chest. 'But I'm telling you: I've been nowhere near Miles Young. He must have been forty metres or so from me this morning – didn't even wave, let alone say hello. I haven't moved from this spot since.'

'Miles told us you did hourly checks of the perimeter,' Leo says.

Dario coughs. 'I mean, apart from my checks, I haven't moved from here.'

'Would you have seen if any of the contestants had come in or out of camp?' Leo asks.

Ffion hears the strange sound again. A tinny clink, like metal on metal. She walks towards the undergrowth.

'The gate's been locked all morning.'

'What if they got under the fence, like Ryan did?'

'I guess.' Dario shrugs, but there's a defensiveness to his expression. 'I can't be everywhere.'

Ffion has her eyes trained on the undergrowth. There's definitely something in there. She catches a glimpse of blonde hair. Not *something*, she thinks – *someone*. She reaches into the bushes and grabs a handful of dungarees.

'Ow, you're hurting me!' Zee's bracelets jangle as she clutches her phone to her chest.

'How long have you been there?' Ffion demands.

'Has someone really killed Miles? Do you know who it is?' She lifts her phone. 'Can I get an interview for my—'

'No.' Ffion claps a hand over the lens. 'Put that away or I'll find a reason to seize it.' Ffion looks at Leo and sees that, like her, he's assessing whether to include the YouTuber in their list of potential suspects. Like many of the others, she had opportunity, but did she have a motive?

'Was it Roxy Wilde?' Zee says. 'She was absolutely raging over

212

Miles the other day – I heard her slagging him off to the camera-man. Said he'd trashed her reputation.' Zee's eyes widen as a thought seizes her. 'Or is it a contestant?' She drops her voice and glances through the wire fence. 'I was going to save this for Twitter, but now that there's a police investigation I guess it's my duty to tell you.' She takes a loud and overly dramatic breath. 'I saw Ceri talking to someone in the woods earlier today.'

'Outside the *Exposure* camp?' Ffion clarifies.

'No, through the fence. I couldn't see who she was talking to, but it was definitely a man.' She places a hand on her heart. 'Do you think it was Miles? Maybe they were having an affair!'

'What time was this?' Ffion says.

Zee screws up her nose. 'Like . . . lunchtime? Some time between twelve and one?'

Not Miles, then, Ffion thinks. 'What did he look like?'

'It was an IC1 male.' Zee stops, suddenly uncertain. 'That's white, isn't it?'

'You can just describe him normally.'

'Oh, okay. Um, he was white. Quite old . . . like, thirties?'

'Anything else?'

'Sorry. I didn't get a clear view of him.' Zee switches her gaze towards Dario, who is walking into camp alongside Leo, to bring out the *Exposure* contestants. 'I wouldn't trust that Dario bloke,' she says. 'I've been timing his walks around the perimeter and some of them take way longer than others.' She brightens. 'Hey, would you like me on your incident room? I could do your social media updates.'

'I'll get back to you on that one,' Ffion says.

The remaining three contestants are as incredulous as Dario was.

'This is a joke, right?' Lucas looks around for cameras. 'Some kind of test, to see how we'll react?'

213

'Are you even real detectives?' Henry says.

'They're real, alright.' Ceri looks at Ffion. 'Are you serious, mate?'

'Deadly serious. Miles was killed at quarter to twelve this morning.'

'Shit,' Henry says.

Lucas's face is ashen. He leans against the fence to steady himself.

'So what happens now?' Zee says.

'We find the murderer and lock him – or her – up,' Leo says.

'I meant with this. *Exposure*. Who wins?'

The others stare at her.

'It's just that . . .' Zee looks around the group. 'My stats are really picking up, and now *Exposure*'s going to get even more attention, and I thought . . .' She trails off.

'Show's over,' Leo says. He turns to Henry, Lucas and Ceri. 'Everyone will be accommodated in the stable rooms until you've given statements and the preliminary investigation has been concluded.'

'Our stuff's still in camp,' Henry says. 'Do you mind if I just nip back and—'

'No.' Ffion is firm. 'You're coming with me.' Leo is staying in camp so they can test the cameras, and she leads the others down the mountain. Ceri, Lucas and Henry follow, and Dario brings up the rear.

'Me too?' Zee calls after them hopefully.

Ffion shakes her head. 'But don't go far – I want a statement from you.'

'How was he murdered?' Ceri asks, as they pick their way down the path.

'Was he shot?' Lucas says. 'Because I heard a shotgun this morning – or was it yesterday morning?'

'That'll have been someone shooting rabbits,' Ceri says. 'You hear it all the time.'

214

'No talking!' Ffion stops so suddenly the others almost plough into her.

'Steady on!' Henry says crossly. 'You're treating us as though you suspect one of us of—' He stops, his determination waning under Ffion's stare.

'And?' she says coolly.

They continue to the courtyard in silence.

The CSI tent outside Miles's studio hides the work of the crime scene investigators Ffion knows are inside. Henry and Ceri stare, transfixed, as they pass. Lucas looks away, and Ffion sees his lips move in silent prayer. One by one, Ffion delivers them to their allocated rooms, wondering as she does so whether she is walking with a murderer.

'What's your secret, then?' Ffion asks Lucas, as she hands him his key.

He blinks. 'Is this an interview?'

'Should it be?'

The vicar holds her gaze. There's a look of despondency in his eyes, and his shoulders sag like ancient cushions. 'Only God can judge us,' is all he says.

Next door, Henry wipes clammy hands on his trousers when Ffion asks him the same question. 'Ah, you see I . . .' He coughs. 'You won't tell anyone, will you? I know it's an outrageous thing to say, but Miles dying like this has done us all a favour. I really would rather no one knew.'

'If it's illegal,' Ffion says, 'I'm duty-bound to—'

'Gosh, it's nothing like that!' Henry looks horrified. He flushes. 'I'm an alcoholic. I'm on a final warning at work – I came in drunk a few times – and I promised them I'd quit, but . . .'

Ffion follows Henry's gaze to the bed, where he's been unpacking the bag that has been waiting for him since he and the others set off for the *Exposure* camp. Ffion sees an ironed shirt and a pair of cream trousers, and she imagines him at home, picking out an outfit for the media interviews, not knowing what horrors would later unfold for him and his fellow contestants. Next to the small pile of clothes is a bottle of whisky. Ffion glances back at Henry. 'You don't look the type.'

'Big red nose and drinking Stella on a park bench?' Henry gives an empty laugh. 'I'm what they call a functioning alcoholic, which is the technical term for a middle-class alkie who drinks Merlot instead of own-brand vodka and who's still holding down a job.'

The definition hits a little close to home, and as Ffion walks away from Henry's stable, she thinks maybe she'll do Dry January next year. Just to prove she can.

She walks back across the courtyard, ducking inside the CSI tent. 'Okay to check something on the cameras?'

'Go ahead,' the CSI says. 'Everything around the desk has been dusted and swabbed.'

Ffion pulls on a paper suit and a pair of latex gloves. The monitor is still on, the camera still trained on the campsite view Miles was watching when he was killed. Ffion watches Leo walk slowly around the fire.

She calls his radio. 'Put your hand on your head.'

Leo does as he's told.

'You lose – I didn't say *Simon says*.'

'I take it we're live.'

'Seems so.' They test the connection with numbers, Ffion calling 'one, two, three, four, five', while Leo holds up the requisite fingers in time with the beat.

'There's no time delay,' Ffion says. 'Lucas was definitely on live camera at the time of the murder. He can't have killed Miles.'

216

They repeat the exercise from the confession pod, Leo sitting on the throne-like chair. 'Still no delay?' he asks through the camera.

Ffion radios her answer. 'None.' Henry's alibi was as solid as Lucas's.

That leaves Ceri, who claims to have been collecting kindling at the time of the murder. And, since her two campmates were otherwise engaged, there is no one to vouch for her movements.

'You don't seriously think I killed him?' Ceri leans in the doorway of her stable room.

'You can see our predicament, though.' Ffion scuffs her boots on the gravel in front of the door, then looks at Ceri. 'What secret was Miles holding over you?'

Ceri shrugs. '*Dim syniad.*'

'You must have some idea.'

'I don't. Maybe he found out I was a lesbian.'

'This is the twenty-first century, Ceri – that's hardly breaking news.' Ffion can't make Ceri meet her eyes. 'What are you keeping from me?'

'Nothing.' Ceri puts a hand on the door. 'Now, are we done?'

Ffion looks at the woman she goes drinking with; the woman who laughed like a drain when her trousers split that day they went to Chester races, and who always puts the kettle on when Ffion needs a *paned* and a moan about work. She suddenly feels she doesn't know her at all.

'We're done,' she says. 'For now.'

Ryan Francis has been seen by the doctor and declared unfit for interview. He's been taken to a psychiatric ward, to be reviewed in the morning. When he's well enough, detectives in DCI Boccacci's team will put the murder to him, along with allegations of assault and criminal damage.

But Ryan didn't kill Miles.

The more Ffion thinks it, the more she believes it. Miles's murder was planned. It was methodical and tidy, carried out in a high-risk environment with extraordinary levels of control. The murder scene is a stark contrast to Angharad's cottage, where the chaos Ryan left behind seems to more accurately reflect his state of mind.

He could be putting it on, of course – he wouldn't be the first suspect to try to wriggle out of a charge by pleading insanity – but Ffion doesn't think so. From what she's seen and heard of Ryan, he's a man genuinely pushed to the brink.

If Ryan didn't kill Miles, the killer is still out there.

Ffion looks at the dense woodland surrounding Carreg Plas, and the formidable mountain rising towards the sky. She thinks of the keyboard warriors who made death threats towards the *Exposure* team, and wonders if any of them were bold enough to take it further. The CSI tent flaps noisily in the wind and Ffion pulls her attention back to the courtyard, to the seven closed stable doors, and the shuttered rooms of the imposing farmhouse.

Is the killer out there?

Or in here?

Ffion is suddenly cold. She retreats to the warmth of the kitchen, but she feels on edge. She drinks a cup of coffee standing by the sink, looking on to the courtyard, and it's only when she sees Leo coming through the gate from the mountainside that she realises she was waiting for him.

She opens the kitchen door, but before Leo reaches the house Ffion hears the crunch of a second set of footsteps on gravel. A woman wearing a blue denim apron appears around the corner.

'*Ti'n iawn*, Ffi? Thought I might see you here.'

'Alright, Ceinwen?' Ffion frowns. 'How did you get here? There's supposed to be a cordon on the front.'

'There is, but it's Rhodri's lad, isn't it? I told him I needed to just pop in for two minutes and he said to go on through but not to let Sergeant – Brody, is it? – see me.'

'Brady,' Leo says, behind her.

Ceinwen keeps looking at Ffion. She pulls an *oops* face.

'*Be ti'n da yma*, anyway?' Ffion asks her.

'I'm doing the catering. I'll just pick up my cash and I'll be out of your hair.'

Ffion goes to the foot of the stairs to shout for Roxy, who appears on the landing in an old pair of joggers and a voluminous sweatshirt. Ffion passes the message. When she returns to Ceinwen, the caterer is quizzing Leo on the best condiment for a beef sandwich.

'French or English?'

Leo looks as though he thinks this might be a trick question. 'French,' he opts for.

'Not horseradish, then?'

'DC Morgan?' Roxy calls out.

Ffion finds her hovering at the foot of the stairs. 'What is it?'

'I can't pay the caterer.'

'Are you asking me for a loan? Because I don't want to be rude, but if the production company has a cashflow issue that's not really my—'

'The petty cash was in a tin in Miles's bedroom.' Roxy indicates up the stairs. 'There was around a hundred quid, last time I looked.' She looks back at Ffion. 'It's all gone.'

TWENTY-SEVEN

SUNDAY | LEO

The tin is small, with a hinged lid and a label left over from the days when it contained Earl Grey teabags. Leo has placed it in an exhibit bag, along with the handful of receipts it contained – most of which were issued by Ceinwen's Catering.

'Who used the petty cash?' Leo says.

'All of us.' Roxy shrugs. 'Owen and I got a pizza the other night after we wrapped. Miles sometimes took a tenner out of it for petrol for the quad bike.' She looks at Owen, who nods his agreement.

'And you'd stick the receipt in the tin and fill out this sheet?' Leo unfolds the expenses form with gloved hands.

'That's right. I popped to the garage for some throat sweets before the live segment on Saturday. That's the last time I touched the tin.'

The black pen Roxy used to sign the form has bled through the page. Leo puts it back in the exhibit bag. 'Which means the money went missing some time in the past twenty-four hours.' He looks between Roxy and Owen. 'I have to ask this: did either of you take the money?'

Owen shakes his head. 'No.'

'Absolutely not,' Roxy says.

'Apart from the four of you,' Ffion says, 'did anyone know the tin was there?'

'No.' Roxy stops. 'Oh . . . Caleb ran out for milk when the contestants were having breakfast here the day we started filming.'

'Was the tin mentioned then?'

'I don't know. Maybe.'

Leo picks up the exhibit bag. 'Don't go anywhere,' he says. Roxy and Owen nod mutely. Leo gestures to Ffion, who follows him outside.

'Do you think it was Roxy?' Ffion says, as they cross the courtyard. 'She thought she'd get away with it, but when Ceinwen turns up wanting to be paid, she panics and decides to "discover" the theft?'

'I don't get that vibe from her, do you?' Leo hands the bagged and tagged tin to a white-suited CSI, who is standing outside the forensics tent. 'Can you book this in for prints?'

'Same job?' The CSI has pulled his paper suit down to the waist and the sleeves trail on the ground. A North Wales Police lanyard around his neck identifies him as Alistair Langham.

'Possibly.'

'I'll need a new budget code if it's not for the murder job.'

'In that case it's definitely for the murder job.' Leo looks through the open door of the tent. 'Speaking of which, did you find any evidence of forced entry?'

'None whatsoever.'

'Then Miles definitely knew his attacker,' Leo says. 'They came to the door, Miles let them in and sat back at his desk, then something happened to—'

'Not quite.' Alistair stops him. 'We can be fairly certain the suspect left via the window, right? You guys were on scene in a matter of minutes and if someone had made off through the courtyard you'd have seen them.'

'Right,' Ffion says.

'Well, you'll be pleased to know the forensics support that. We

221

found a mark on the outside of the window frame, exactly where you'd grip it to pull yourself through.'

'Prints?' Leo says hopefully.

Alistair shakes his head. 'The mark shows a fabric weave – most likely woollen or a wool mix. Often this will tell us the suspect was wearing gloves, but in this case there are no individual finger marks. I've yet to hear of a burglar wearing mittens, so my best guess is a pair of socks.'

So far, so logical. When Leo worked in Liverpool, half the kids he nicked wore socks on their hands when they broke into cars. Easier to get hold of than gloves, and the cannier lads used the ones from their feet, instead of carrying an extra pair they'd have to explain in a stop-and-search.

'But here's the thing,' Alistair says. 'We found a similar mark on the *inside* of the frame.'

'But no forced entry.' Leo follows the CSI's train of thought. 'Which means Miles let his attacker in through the window, presumably so they wouldn't be seen.' He looks at Ffion. 'Could he have been having an affair?'

'I think it's more likely to have been work-related,' she says. 'We saw how secretive he was – he didn't tell Roxy or Owen the true purpose of *Exposure* until the first day of filming. Maybe he was planning another plot twist.'

'He could have been arranging to put one of the evicted contestants back in.'

Leo is beginning to share Ffion's misgivings about Ryan Francis. Why would Miles open the window for a missing man known to be carrying not only a grudge against Miles but a stolen knife? They need to establish who else has an alibi – and who doesn't.

* * *

222

Aliyah blinks rapidly when Leo asks where she was in the run-up to Miles's murder. 'I was in h-here,' she stammers. 'B-but I can't prove that.'

'What were you doing?' Ffion asks her.

'Nothing.' Aliyah sits on her bed. 'You told us to stay in our rooms while you were looking for Ryan, so that's what I was doing. I think maybe I was on my phone – I can't remember. I came out when I heard everyone shouting.'

'I saw you being interviewed this morning,' Ffion says. 'How did that go?'

Aliyah gives a weak smile. 'It was good. I was terrified, but they were really lovely. The journalist said I had nothing to be ashamed of. She even offered to talk to my boss if I needed moral support.'

'You work in a . . .' Leo checks his notes, 'children's nursery?'

She nods. 'They've actually been great. My boss was like, that's all in the past, but you have to promise not to do sex work while you're working for us.' Aliyah gives a short laugh. 'Like I'd want to.'

'How about your parents?' Ffion says.

Fresh tears roll down Aliyah's cheeks. 'We've talked a lot. I thought they'd be ashamed, but they were more sad that I hadn't told them how much everything was costing me; that I didn't ask them for help.' She lets out a shuddering breath. 'And Dad made me swear nothing bad had happened to me.' Aliyah's eyes darken, and Leo wonders how much she's kept from her parents. 'But they haven't disowned me.'

'So . . . you're okay?'

'Don't get me wrong, the past week's been pretty horrific, but now that it's out there it's kind of a relief. It's always been there, you know, lurking in the background. I was always terrified a

223

new dad would drop his kid to nursery and it would be someone I . . .' She swallows. 'That it would be a former client, you know?' Aliyah lets out a long breath. 'But it doesn't matter now. Everyone knows. The worst has happened.'

'When you were in camp,' Leo says, 'you talked with the other contestants, right?'

'There wasn't much else to do.'

'Did you get a sense that any of them were . . .' Leo searches for the right words '. . . harbouring violent thoughts towards Miles?'

'No.' Aliyah shakes her head. 'I know where you're going with this, and okay, Miles wasn't exactly popular, but no one would have actually—' She breaks off, shaking her head again.

'You trusted them all, then?' Ffion says pointedly.

Aliyah flushes. 'Well, I mean obviously it was difficult to trust people when they were literally there to betray you, so—'

'Did you trust Jason?' Leo takes over.

'Hundred per cent.'

'Pam?'

'I love that woman so much.'

'Lucas?'

'Of course,' Aliyah says, with less conviction.

'What is it?' Ffion notices it too.

'Nothing. It's just that . . .' Aliyah sighs, 'I overheard Roxy say something about a #MeToo contestant and it kind of triggered me, I guess. The idea of being locked in that camp with a sexual predator.' She closes her arms around herself and shudders.

'What made you think Roxy was talking about Lucas?' Leo says.

'Process of elimination. Jason's a genuine guy, and I only got good vibes from Henry. Ryan was – well, bless him, there was nothing predatory about him. That only leaves Lucas.' She glances out into the courtyard and lowers her voice. 'You know he has a criminal record?'

'Is that right?' says Leo, who is now fully up to speed on the Reverend Lucas Taylor's prison sentence – and his exemplary behaviour ever since.

'He told me himself.'

'That was very honest of him,' Ffion says.

'I suppose it was.' Aliyah sighs. 'It's hard to know who you can trust, isn't it?'

'She's not wrong,' Ffion says, once Aliyah has closed the door. 'I wouldn't trust this lot as far as I could throw them. Lucas's conviction didn't have a sexual element, did it?'

'No, and half of me wonders if she's trying to distract us with this #MeToo stuff.'

'Stop us looking at her for the murder, you mean? She's tiny. There's no way she could have strangled Miles unless he just sat there and took it.'

'I'm inclined to agree,' Leo says. 'But I'd feel happier if she had an alibi.' His phone rings, but when he sees it's Gayle again, he drops it back into his pocket.

'Your girlfriend calls a lot,' Ffion says, as they make their way to Pam's stable.

'She's not my girlfriend.'

Leo has tried several times now to end things with Gayle, who seemingly has the skin of a rhino, interpreting his *I don't have time to see anyone right now* as *please call me several times a day to suggest different ways we could hang out.*

'Friend with benefits?' Ffion's voice is teasing. 'Booty call? Stalker?'

225

'You're not far off,' Leo says morosely.

'Really?'

'Not really. She's just . . .' Leo pauses. 'Persistent.'

'So tell her where to go.' They reach Pam's door and Ffion gives Leo a sidelong glance. 'Grow a spine.'

The throwaway insult smarts, and Leo opens his mouth to say something back, but it's too late: Ffion's knocking on Pam's door.

When Ffion asks Pam who she saw in the courtyard when Miles's body was discovered, the head teacher closes her eyes to think. 'I saw you two,' she says slowly. 'And your colleague. Georgina, is it? And the runner, Caleb.' She places invisible figures around the room with her hand, her eyes still closed. 'Jason was *there*, then Roxy and Owen came out of the house and stood *there*, and then Aliyah was *here*.'

'Aliyah?' Ffion looks at Leo.

Pam opens her eyes. 'I asked her how the interview went.'

'You're sure?' Leo says.

'DS Brady, there are a hundred and seventy-four girls in my sixth form and if any of them skip assembly I could give you their name in a matter of seconds. I think I can remember who was standing in the courtyard a few hours ago.'

Leo doesn't doubt it. Pam Butler is a formidable woman. 'What were you doing immediately before the murder?'

'Being suspended,' Pam says quietly. Her eyes glisten. 'The chair of the Board of Governors called me. Apparently the decision was unanimous.'

'We'll need to speak to someone who can verify that,' Ffion says.

Pam reaches for a spiral-bound notebook and flips through the pages. 'This is his number.' Beneath the digits, Pam's neat writing

226

gives a summary of her call. *Full pay*, Leo reads. *Appeal?* He takes a photo of the page.

'This must be very difficult for you,' Ffion says.

'It's my girls I'm worried about.' Pam sighs. 'I hate to think what they've been told. The deputy head's covering but, well . . . you worry when you're not there, don't you?'

Leo does indeed. He was gratified when DCI Boccacci asked him to take command of the scene, but, now that the initial rush has dissipated, he's desperate to know what's going on in the incident room.

'We'll move things along as quickly as we can,' he tells Pam. 'In the meantime, please stay in your room and don't speak to the other contestants.'

'Of course. I must say, you're awfully nice for police officers. Very reassuring.' She gives Ffion an appraising look. 'Have you ever thought of teaching?'

Ffion waits until she and Leo are out of earshot. 'Can you think of anything worse than being a teacher?'

Leo certainly can't think of anything worse than *Ffion* being a teacher, but he decides to keep that to himself. 'Jason next?' he says instead.

'I fucking hated Miles.' The firefighter sits with his arms folded tight across his chest. 'But I didn't kill him.'

'We need to establish where everyone was at the time of the murder,' Leo says.

'I was on a video call to my solicitor.'

Leo flips open his notebook, which is rapidly filling up with actions. 'I'd like their details, please.'

'Are you calling me a liar?'

'This is a murder investigation,' Ffion says. 'And, as it stands, you don't have an alibi. So if I were you, I'd give us your solicitor's details, before you find yourself wearing a fetching pair of bracelets.'

As they cross the courtyard on their way back to the kitchen, Leo's phone rings.

'Sarge? It's George.'

'How's the incident room?'

'Busy.'

'When's the post-mortem happening?'

'Tomorrow.' George's voice is muffled, as though her phone is clamped between shoulder and ear. 'Izzy Weaver's doing it.' Leo recognises the name – it's the same pathologist who did the autopsy on Rhys Lloyd. 'We've had forensics back on the stones used to smash the cameras, by the way. There's DNA on the stones.'

'And?'

'It's not Ryan's.'

Leo lets this sit awhile. Ryan didn't smash the cameras. In some ways, this isn't surprising – Leo is increasingly feeling that Ryan has been in no fit state to carry out meticulously thought-out plans – but it raises more questions than it answers. If Ryan didn't smash the cameras, who did? The same person who murdered Miles?

'Has it been run through PNC?' he asks.

'Yes, no match.'

Which means whoever smashed the cameras doesn't have a criminal record. Leo is reminded of the list he requested from Miles's production office, of people who applied to be on *Exposure*. Might one of them be responsible?

'The DCI says everyone but scene watch can stand down,'

228

George says. 'On again at zero eight hundred hours tomorrow, when I'll be back with you and Ffion.'

Leo finishes the call. 'George can speak to Caleb Northcote and Jessica Francis first thing tomorrow,' he tells Ffion. 'I'll interview Roxy Wilde and Owen Havard.'

'What do you want me to do?' Ffion says.

They lock eyes for a second and Leo feels a surge of heat. He fights the impulse to answer her question in an extremely unprofessional way. 'See if Pam Butler's and Jason Shenton's alibis check out,' he says instead. 'And get that box of secrets open – find out who had the most to lose.'

Out of the seven people with uncorroborated alibis, Ceri Jones is the only one who still has a secret in that box.

Is it big enough to kill for?

TWENTY-EIGHT

JASON | DAY THREE OF *EXPOSURE*

You have to be fit to be a firefighter, and Jason Shenton's the fittest on his watch. He's at the station gym every day, switching between legs, arms and cardio. When the advert for *Exposure* came out, so many of Jason's mates sent him the link he ended up posting on Facebook to say *Yes, I've applied!* He wasn't even surprised when he got picked – it felt as though it was meant to be. Jason was fit and strong, and he was going to boss this survival show.

So when Roxy made that announcement on the first night, Jason's first reaction was one of disappointment. He was gutted, to be honest. All the extra training he'd done, all the egg-white omelettes and protein shakes. That bloody fake tan Kat put on him, so he'd look buff for the cameras.

'Are you saying I'm not buff already?'

'Even more buff.' Kat had grinned, rubbing on lotion. They'd got distracted then, and Kat had ended up with a fair amount of fake tan on her, too . . .

A second after Roxy's announcement, it hit him.

'You fucking *what*?' he said. Even then, Jason didn't realise the implications. He only knew that they'd all been lied to, and there's nothing Jason hates more than a liar. The cameraman was grinning like an ape, and Jason ran at him, not thinking about anything except wiping that smile off Owen's stupid face.

The passing days have served only to fuel his rage. Jason knows which secret of his they want to expose, of course. It took him a while to figure it out, which might sound ridiculous, except that marrying Addison feels like something someone else did. It was such a long time ago, when he was a different person. *Kat* is his wife. Not his second wife, not a bigamous wife, just his wife. And he adores her with a fierceness that surprises even him.

A bigamist. Fucking hell. It makes him sound like a total bastard – a complete player. The stupid thing is, Jason's literally only had three girlfriends in his life. And he married two of them. If his secret's exposed, he could go to prison. Worse than that, he'll lose Kat and maybe even the girls. He can't let that happen.

By the third day of *Exposure*, Jason comes up with a plan. The contestants have been pitted against each other, tasked with uncovering each other's secrets. The questions are ramping up, every conversation a potential trap.

'I reckon Lucas's secret is to do with a woman,' Aliyah whispered to Jason over breakfast. 'He gets well flustered if you ask him about relationships.'

As a result, everyone's pulling up the drawbridge, scared of giving something away. It doesn't seem to have occurred to anyone – except Jason – that there's another way to play the lying game . . .

'I gotta say, man, the stress is really getting to me,' Jason tells Henry, during what has quickly become a regular heart-to-heart in the hot tub. 'I'm thinking of 'fessing up and getting it over. Ripping the plaster off, you know?'

Henry considers this. 'I guess it depends on what you're likely to face as a result.'

Jason leaves a long pause. When he speaks again, it's intentionally casual, as though he's just thought of something. 'Do they send people to prison for old crimes, do you know?'

'You what?'

'Like . . .' Jason makes like he's plucking a crime from thin air. 'Burglary, for example. Would they bother? Like, if it was years ago? If the person was a teenager at the time, and the house belonged to their grandad or something, so—'

'What are you saying, Jase?' Henry looks suddenly serious. He glances towards the cameras.

'Nothing. Forget it.' Jason holds his nose and sinks under the water, hiding his grin. Hook, line, sinker.

'What would you use the prize money for?' Henry says, when Jason surfaces.

Jason doesn't hesitate. 'I'd give it to Kat. She can buy whatever she wants. Whatever makes her happy. I'd definitely book a holiday somewhere hot. Ten years we've been married, and we've still not saved enough for a proper honeymoon. Yeah, that's what I'd do first.'

Afterwards, he sees Henry whispering with Aliyah, who casts furtive glances in Jason's direction. It doesn't bother Jason to be the subject of gossip, not when it's Jason himself who put it there, and he gives the pair a cheery wave. Aliyah looks quickly back to Henry.

When Roxy and Owen assemble the contestants in camp for the evening's live segment, there's a palpable tension in the air. Roxy is pacing by the edge of the trees, practising her lines, while Owen fulfils barked requests from Miles. *Move Pam ten centimetres to the left. Have Lucas standing. No, try him leaning against the table.*

'*Exposure* contestants!' Roxy leaves a long pause. 'Henry has attempted to expose one of you. Do you have an idea who it might be?' Jason matches the blank expressions of his campmates, taking care not to meet Henry's eyes. Double-crossing bastard.

Roxy looks at each contestant in turn. Pam, Henry, Aliyah, Lucas, Ceri . . . Her gaze comes to a stop. 'Earlier today, Henry made a bid to expose Jason. Let's see if he was right.'

The camera will be zoomed in on him now. Jason adopts a betrayed expression, then mouths *I love you, Kat*, hoping she'll see it.

'Remember,' Roxy says, 'if Henry's wrong, he'll face the confession pod himself.'

Roxy is handing a key to Henry. 'The moment of truth. Open the box and give me Jason's secret.'

Henry takes ages to find Jason's envelope among the others, but eventually he hands it to Roxy and shoots an apologetic glance in Jason's direction, which Jason ignores.

Roxy turns to the camera, the envelope held aloft. 'Let's remind ourselves of the accusation Henry made earlier in the confession pod.' She holds her smile for a second, then her shoulders slump and she cricks her neck.

'Are you okay?' Aliyah asks Jason.

'I'm fine,' he says curtly, remembering the whispered conversation he'd seen between her and Henry earlier. It could just as easily have been Aliyah running to the confession pod, accusing Jason of robbing his grandad.

'Twenty seconds,' Owen says, pressing a finger against his earpiece. Jason knows that, right now, the viewers at home are watching Henry's exposure attempt. *I accuse Jason of burgling his grandfather's house.* Jason tries not to laugh. Kat's going to be so confused – both Jason's grandads were dead before Jason hit double figures.

'Ten seconds,' Owen says. 'Five, four.' He finishes the countdown on silent fingers, as Roxy re-assumes her smile for the camera.

'Let's find out if you're right, Henry.' She opens the envelope, and despite everything, Jason's heart races. His real secret's in there – what if Roxy reads it out by mistake, or drops it, or—

'Congratulations, Henry.' Roxy turns the card so all the contestants can read the writing. 'Your accusation was correct – Jason is indeed a bigamist.'

The camp spins. This isn't possible.

'Say your goodbyes, Jason.' Roxy's exaggerated sad face flips quickly to one of glee. 'You've been . . . exposed!'

This can't be happening. What was Henry whispering to Aliyah about, if it wasn't the information Jason fed to Henry in the hot tub? Jason hasn't said a single word that would enable Henry – or anyone else – to guess his secret . . . Unless . . . he thinks about the way Aliyah pumped him for information yesterday. *Is your secret something to do with your marriage?* Maybe it wasn't Henry sharing information with Aliyah, but the other way around.

'Oh, my God.' Aliyah reaches for Jason as he says goodbye to the group, but he brushes her off. He's thinking about Kat, who he knows will be watching. He's thinking about how devastated she'll be, how she's probably even now packing his bags, slinging them out into the street. White-hot rage builds within him as Roxy leads him out of the *Exposure* camp. None of this would have happened if it weren't for Miles Young creating this hell of a show. Miles hasn't been near the *Exposure* camp since filming started, but he can't hide now.

He's going to get what's coming to him.

TWENTY-NINE

MONDAY | FFION

As Ffion drives towards Carreg Plas, she sees that several vehicles are parked in the narrow road, including a large van with a satellite dish on top. She leaves the Triumph a hundred metres away and walks towards the gate, where a uniformed officer has clearly been on all night.

'What time's handover?' she says.

'Another half-hour.'

'Media?' As Ffion nods at the row of vehicles, she sees the side door of the satellite van slide open.

'They've been arriving for the past few hours. I told them DCI Boccacci would be holding a press conference at Bryndare, but they want to speak to someone at the—' He breaks off to speak to a woman wearing a beige raincoat belted at the waist. 'Can I ask you to wait in your vehicle please, madam?'

'Are you a detective?' The woman addresses Ffion. 'Can I get a few words from you?'

'You wouldn't like them,' Ffion says.

'I understand the television producer Miles Young has been murdered. Do you have a comment about the investigation?'

'Where did you hear that?' Ffion opens the five-bar gate across the driveway and slips through it.

'It's all over social media. I think the original story came from a YouTuber called . . .' the woman tails off, trying to remember.

'Zee bloody Hart,' mutters Ffion, as she marches around the side of the farmhouse and into the courtyard. There are no signs of life from the stable rooms, and no lights on in the main house. Behind the courtyard, the mountain is clinging on to the pinky hues of this morning's sunrise. As she and Dave head up the path away from Carreg Plas, Dave takes an enthusiastic leap over a stream and lands on his nose in the boggy ground surrounding it.

'Part dog, part elephant,' Ffion mutters. She looks at her watch. Still another twenty minutes till she's due to meet Huw at the *Exposure* camp.

'I need the bolt cutters,' she'd said, when she rang him last night.

'You what?'

'You got custody of them in the divorce.' Ffion was at home, stabbing the plastic on a microwave curry.

'I did,' Huw said. 'Because they're mine.'

Ffion stabbed a few more times, for good measure. 'Can I borrow them, then?'

'What do you want them for?'

'I need to open the box of secrets in the *Exposure* camp. I tried today with a screwdriver, but I snapped the bloody handle off.'

'I'll do it for you.'

'It's fine, just leave them by the back door, and I'll swing by and—'

'I don't mind. First thing in the morning? Meet you up there?'

Ffion paused midway through putting her curry in the microwave. 'Why are you being so nice?'

'Because last time you borrowed tools from me, you lost my favourite spanner.'

'Only you could have a favourite spanner.' Ffion selected *high* and pressed *start*. 'See you in camp.'

Ffion sees the perimeter fence up ahead, and the flash of fluorescent she knows will be Dario Kimber. She remembers Zee Hart's insinuation that the security guard was up to no good – *I've been timing his walks around the perimeter and some of them take way longer than others* – and decides she'll put her extra twenty minutes to good use. She calls Dave, who is nosing something that looks horribly like a rotting animal, and follows the fence to where Zee's dark blue tent is pitched.

The flap of the tent is half open and a gentle snoring sound comes from inside. Ffion is just contemplating how to announce her arrival when Dave does the job for her, barrelling his boggy paws and stinking snout into the tent.

It's difficult to scream when you're winded, but Zee manages admirably. The noise propels a terrified Dave back outside, where he attempts to climb up Ffion's legs.

Zee, still in her sleeping bag, has shuffled outside. 'What just happened?'

'Consider it an alarm call.'

'What do you want?' Zee reaches for her phone.

'Don't even think about filming me,' Ffion says. 'You've done enough damage – half the country's news agencies are camped outside Carreg Plas.'

'Really?' Zee's eyes light up.

Ffion takes a step forward. She rests her hands on her knees so her face is inches from Zee's. 'This is your final warning. If you Tweet, Facebook, Snapchat, blog or YouTube one iota of this murder investigation, I'll arrest you for interfering with the course of justice.'

'How about TikTok?' Zee takes in Ffion's furious face. 'Okay, no TikTok. Or any of the others. Got it.'

'Yesterday, you suggested the security guard took too long doing his perimeter checks. What did you mean by it?'

'Just that. He walks round three times a day, but the second time takes longer than the first. I reckon he's been talking to one of the contestants.'

'Any idea which one?'

'Sorry. He went into camp one night, too. I couldn't sleep, so I went for a walk. It was like, two in the morning? I walked past Dario's caravan. The light was on, so I peeked through the window, but the van was empty. I thought *what's he up to, then?* so I went looking.'

'And?'

'I saw him unlock the gate to camp and go inside. I waited, but he was ages and I was freezing, so I went back to bed.'

'What night was this?'

Zee's head bobs about as she thinks. 'The night Jason was exposed. Oh, my God, I was so shocked – imagine marrying someone, then discovering they were—'

'Wednesday,' Ffion says, thinking back. Which means Dario snuck into camp in the early hours of Thursday morning. Two o'clock on Thursday morning, to be precise; just when the camp cameras were smashed.

'Is it significant?' Zee's eyes light up. 'If you issue a statement, will you mention my YouTube channel?'

'No.'

'How about if I said I'd remembered something about the man I saw Ceri talking to yesterday?' Zee gives a sly grin.

'How about you just tell me, and I don't nick you for withholding evidence?'

Zee stares at her for a second, then clearly decides Ffion's not joking. 'He was wearing a dark green beanie.'

'Dark green? Are you sure?'

Zee nods.

'Anything else?'

'No. I just remembered the hat.'

Ffion whistles for Dave.

'Do you need to know anything else?' Zee says. 'Because I've got a theory about Pam Butler. I reckon she's stronger than she—'

'Thanks.' Ffion's already walking away, her head buzzing. Loads of people must have green beanies, she thinks. It doesn't mean anything.

Huw is waiting for her by the fire pit, an array of tools laid out beside his backpack. 'I thought you'd want me to wait.' He indicates the metal box, padlocked to the tree trunk by the fire. He's wearing his search-and-rescue jacket, and on his head is a dark green beanie.

'Thanks.' Ffion lets her gaze move over him, knowing it makes Huw uncomfortable. 'You been to the camp before?'

'Just for the search,' Huw says easily.

'You haven't been lurking around the fence, then, trying to speak to the contestants?'

'You what?' Huw laughs.

'Ceri, for example.' Ffion lets the silence stretch between them.

'Who told you?' Huw says eventually.

'A witness.'

'A witness? You mean, this is part of your murder investigation?'

'What are you playing at, Huw?'

'We were just talking.'

'Sure.'

'It's got nothing to do with what happened to Miles, Ffi, I promise.'

'You don't get to make that call. I do.' They stare at each other.

Huw looks away. 'I went to ask her not to drag Bronwen into it.'

'Bronwen *Post*? Ceri's boss? What's she got to do with it?'

'Ceri's secret. It could get Bronwen into trouble too.'

'Okay, but what's that got to do with you?' Ffion stares at Huw, at the flush creeping from his collar, and she feels a sudden rush of something she can't explain. 'Oh . . .' she says quietly. 'Bronwen's the woman you're seeing.'

'I was going to tell you.'

'It's none of my business.' Ffion's talking too fast. Too loud. It really isn't her business – they're divorced, and heaven knows, Ffion doesn't want to revisit that particular chapter of her life – and yet . . .

'I saw you moving on,' Huw says, 'and—'

'Moving on?'

'That English detective.'

'Oh, God, that's—' Ffion laughs, but her protestations sound false, even to her. She almost had moved on, she thinks. Would have done, if she were less of an idiot.

'And it made me realise I had to do the same.' Huw kicks at the dirt.

'That's good,' Ffion says, and she means it.

'I don't want her to get into trouble, Ffi.'

'What's Ceri's secret?'

He doesn't answer.

Ffion exhales, frustrated. 'What did she do, Huw?'

'I can't – I shouldn't even have got involved.'

'No, you bloody well shouldn't.' Ffion is fast losing patience, but it occurs to her that Huw's idiotic interference might just provide Ceri with an alibi. 'What time did you talk to her?' Zee told her it was after midday, but if it had been earlier – say around ten to – there was no way Ceri could have killed Miles at 11.45, then got back—

'About twenty past twelve,' Huw says. 'I went back down the mountain after I spoke to Ceri – that's when I saw you by the stables.'

'Right.' It still could have been Ceri, then. *Or Huw*, says the voice in Ffion's head, before she can stop it. But that's absurd. Huw has his faults, but he's one hundred per cent honest.

Isn't he?

Ffion picks up the bolt cutters and holds them out. 'Will you do the honours, or shall I?'

There are seven secrets in the box, including those already exposed. If Ceri's secret implicates her boss, it must be something Ceri's done at work, and it's clear the stakes are high, otherwise Huw wouldn't have gone to such lengths to keep Bronwen out of it.

But are they high enough for murder?

Ffion pictures Ceri in her postal uniform. Shorts, whatever the weather, and brown boots that give way to sandals in summer. Ceri knows everyone in Cwm Coed, and everyone knows her. At least, they think they do.

'Promise me you won't drag Bronwen into this?' Huw hesitates as he puts the bolt cutters to the padlock.

'You know I can't—'

'I really like her, Ffi,' Huw says quietly.

Ffion thinks about her ex-husband with his new woman, and the sadness she feels is mixed with relief. No more guilt for ruining Huw's life. He's moved on. She thinks about Ceri, who is as much a part of Cwm Coed as the lake and the mountain. She thinks about Miles, gasping for breath, as hands closed around his throat.

Ffion snaps her focus back to the box of secrets. 'Just open it.'

THIRTY

MONDAY | LEO

'It's a playlist I put together.' Roxy is sitting on her bed while Leo stands. 'I always listen to it when I'm getting ready for filming.' She shows Leo the list of songs and he sees 'Don't Stop Me Now', 'Eye of the Tiger', 'Ain't No Mountain High Enough', 'Dancing Queen'. . .

'Very motivational.'

Roxy flushes. '"Dancing Queen" had just started when Owen's door banged. I heard him running down the stairs, so I came out to see what was happening.'

'You didn't hear the commotion yourself?'

'I had the music up loud, and I was doing my make-up. Over there.' She points to a dressing table across the room from the window, which is strewn with cosmetics. 'If you look at the "recently played" tab, it'll give you the time.'

Roxy hands Leo her phone, seemingly untroubled that he could tap on any of her messaging apps. A sign she has nothing to hide, perhaps? He scrolls backwards until he finds 'Dancing Queen'. The time stamp reads 11.44. So far, so corroborated.

'Of course, this only tells us what your phone was playing,' Leo says. 'Not where you were at the time.'

'I was here, in my room.' Roxy's tone isn't defensive. It doesn't

242

need to be, Leo thinks – he's playing devil's advocate. Owen has already confirmed that Roxy followed him down the stairs, and that they ran out of the kitchen door seconds apart. With no love lost between the two of them, it's unlikely either would cover for the other, which means neither of them could have killed Miles.

Leo is about to leave, when he remembers Aliyah's concerns about there being a sexual predator among the contestants. 'Do you remember saying something in camp about there being a "#MeToo" contestant on the show?'

Roxy frowns, then her expression clears. 'Yes. It was after we'd finished filming on the first night. I turned to Owen and said something like, *I wonder which one is the #MeToo bloke*. Miles had given me a heads-up before we'd gone up to camp.'

'I thought he was the only one who knew the contestants' secrets?'

'Oh, I don't think that was one of the secrets – he was just making sure I kept my wits about me, you know? Didn't find myself alone with some creep. He did the same with Lucas's prison sentence. Like a kind of risk assessment, I suppose.'

'That was very considerate of him.'

Roxy snorts. 'Nothing considerate about it. Nowadays, you can sue the ass off a production company if they don't protect staff from harassment. Miles was thinking about his bottom line, the way he always did.'

'Roxy's and Owen's alibis are solid,' Leo says. They've concluded their respective interviews and have regrouped in the kitchen, coffees in hand.

'As is Jessica Francis's,' George says. 'She used a running app to map her search routes for Ryan, so she didn't cover the same area twice. She was well over a mile from the scene at the time of the murder.'

Leo makes a note next to Jessica's name.

'And that's not all.' George takes a sip of coffee. 'Jessica spoke to Caleb Northcote, who was also out on the mountain. She didn't know his name, or even that he was the production assistant, but she recognised him and they exchanged a few words.'

'What time was this?'

'She reckons ten minutes or so before the murder. He wouldn't have had time to get down the mountain.'

Leo nods slowly, mentally placing everyone at the scene like chess pieces on a board. Roxy Wilde and Owen Havard were in the farmhouse; Caleb Northcote and Jessica Francis were up the mountain. Henry Moore was in the confession pod and Lucas Taylor was tending the fire – both recorded on the live camera feed. 'That still leaves Pam Butler, Jason Shenton, Aliyah Brown, Ryan Francis, Ceri Jones, Dario Kimber and Zee Hart without confirmed alibis,' he says.

'We can rule out Pam,' George says. 'The chair of the Board of Governors called back first thing this morning. He rang Pam from his mobile and he's sent me a screenshot of the log – the call ran from 11.25 till 11.47.'

Leo looks at his list and draws a thick black line through Pam's name. 'How about Jason?'

'His solicitor's being a jobsworth.' George rolls her eyes. 'He's demanding a data protection waiver before he even speaks to us, and banging on about legal privilege.'

'Can't Jason just give him permission to speak to us?' Leo says.

'He can, but he says the solicitor charges him a hundred quid every time he answers a call or an email, and he wants us to pay for it.'

'Is he on another planet?' Leo laughs. 'I had a stationery order

244

knocked back last week because I'd requested one pen more than the number of people in the office. Keep working on him.'

'Is he broke?' George says suddenly.

Leo shrugs. 'He's getting a ten-grand participation fee, so—'

'But the contestants haven't received that yet, right? So he's broke, he's got an expensive solicitor to pay for, and he knew there was a tin of money sitting around in the farmhouse . . .' She leaves the suggestion hanging.

Leo thinks out loud. 'He could have slipped in here when everyone's attention was on Miles's studio.'

She shakes her head. 'I remember seeing him. I'd have noticed if he'd disappeared.'

Leo taps the lid of his pen against his teeth. The petty cash tin has been submitted for forensics, but CSI are – quite rightly – prioritising the samples they obtained from the murder scene. It could be another couple of days before they get a comparison with the elimination prints. He moves on, turning to the next item on his mental list. 'What have the analysts turned up from the death threats made online?'

'A lot of hot air, plus a couple of more worrying tweets that DCI Boccacci's team are looking into,' George says. 'She's particularly keen to establish if they came from people who applied for the TV show but didn't get picked.'

'I get that they might have been pissed off at the time, but not once they realised what *Exposure* was all about, surely?' In Leo's inbox is a spreadsheet containing all applicants' details, filtered by the analysts to highlight those with criminal records or warnings for violence. 'I imagine the rejected applicants are overwhelmingly relieved not to have been chosen,' he says. 'I know I would be.'

The back door opens and Ffion heads straight for the coffee

machine. There haven't been any deliveries of pastries or trays of sandwiches since Miles died, and Leo supposes someone in the Cheshire office cancelled them. Detectives from Leo's own team have interviewed the handful of staff who work there. They reported that Miles was generally liked, but that staff felt his projects had progressed from edgy to unpalatable. Everyone agreed *Exposure* crossed a line, but no one had walked out. No one had challenged Miles. No one wanted to lose their job in a recession.

'No dog today?' Leo keeps one eye on the door, half expecting a cannonball of wet fur to fly through it.

'Huw's looking after him.' Ffion's voice sounds strange and Leo wonders if that means they're back together. He immediately reminds himself he doesn't care.

'That's good of him.'

'He owes me a favour,' she says shortly. She turns around, coffee in hand and all business. 'Dario Kimber's looking good for the smashed cameras.' She fills Leo and George in on intelligence she gleaned from Zee Hart earlier.

'Should we arrest him for murder, too?' George says. 'If he smashed the cameras, he must have been after the box of secrets. When he couldn't get it open, getting the key from Miles would be the logical next step. Maybe he thought Miles wouldn't be there, they had a confrontation and things got out of hand.'

'We saw him,' Ffion says suddenly. She looks at George. 'When was it? Wednesday? The day Jessica Francis showed up. Miles was in the kitchen with us, and Dario let himself into Miles's studio. Miles was raging.'

'You think he was looking for the key?' Leo says.

'And yesterday, when we were by the entrance to the camp.' Ffion looks at Leo. 'Dario said Miles had gone for his run at the *same time as always.* As though he'd been watching Miles and knew his movements.'

'Okay.' Leo nods. 'Let me run it by the DCI. Did you get the box open?'

Ffion dumps her rucksack on the kitchen table and takes out a plastic exhibit bag holding the metal box from camp. The hinges have been forced open.

'Have you looked inside?' Leo says.

'I thought you'd want to do that.' Ffion tips the rest of her coffee into the sink and runs the tap.

George pulls on latex gloves and removes the box from the bag, laying it carefully on a sheet of paper before taking off the broken lid. She lifts out the pile of envelopes inside, each marked with a contestant's name. Four of them are open. The envelopes each contain a printed card.

> Jason is a bigamist.

> Pam takes bribes from prospective parents.

> Ryan wears women's clothes.

> Aliyah is a former sex-worker.

'We know all those,' Leo says, impatient for the others. Henry has confessed to his alcoholism, but Lucas maintains the only person he needs to confess to is God. Since the vicar's alibi means he isn't the frame for Miles's death, his potential motive is academic, but a murder investigation requires the full picture.

> Lucas is having an affair with a married woman in his congregation.

George looks up from the card, eyes round. 'The dirty old goat!'

'Maybe Aliyah was right about him,' Leo says. He leans forward to take the next card. 'Is that one Henry's?'

> Henry has refused to pay child support for three years.

It seems Henry has more than one secret.

'What an arsehole,' Ffion says.

'There might be more to it than that.' Leo is trying to be fair, although privately he's inclined to agree. 'None of the others' stories were straightforward, after all, and, given what he told you about his addiction problems, he's clearly not been in a good place.'

George rifles through the envelopes, frowning.

'What is it?'

'There's one missing. There's no secret for Ceri.'

Leo looks at Ffion. 'Could it have dropped out? Where did you bag and tag it?'

'In camp, then I came straight here.' Ffion shrugs. 'Weird.'

'Not weird,' Leo says slowly. 'Suspicious.'

'I'm sure it's—' Ffion starts.

'There's no reason why Miles would let Dario climb in through the window,' Leo says. 'It only makes sense if Miles's visitor was someone who shouldn't have been there – someone Miles didn't want anyone to see in the courtyard.' Leo looks at the others. 'Such as a contestant who should have been in camp.'

George puts the envelopes back on the table. 'Ceri killed Miles and stole the key so she could remove her envelope from the box and protect her secret.'

Leo pushes back his chair.

'What are you doing?' Ffion says.

'What do you think I'm doing?' He takes out his phone and pulls up DCI Boccacci's number. 'I'm getting the go-ahead to bring her in.'

THIRTY-ONE

PAM | DAY FOUR OF *EXPOSURE*

It was Pam's 'can do' attitude that secured her the post of head teacher at Heath Hill School for Girls.

'It's clear you're not easily intimidated,' said Mr Wolfson, chair of the governing board, when he rang to offer her the job. 'We're confident you can handle anything Heath Hill can throw at you.'

Pam likes to tell her girls there's little that can't be fixed with a cheery smile and a positive approach, but it's the fourth day of *Exposure* filming and if you told Pam to be positive now, the response would be worthy of detention. Pam's 'can do' attitude has abandoned her, her cheery smile a distant memory.

Henry's clearing the remnants of lunch. He dumps the metal plates in the sink with a clattering noise that goes right through Pam.

'For God's sake, Henry!'

Heath Hill is a state school, but it offers boarding to girls who live too far away to travel in each day. Pam often chats with those who are struggling to settle into dorm life.

'It's Camilla,' they'll say (or India, or Verity, or Lily). 'She does the most annoying thing.' They'll go on to describe how poor Camilla (or India, or Verity, or Lily) breathes the wrong way, or gets into bed in an irritating fashion, and Pam will explain how they all need to live peaceably together. Pam didn't go to a boarding school herself, and, although she lives in the confines of Heath Hill School, she does not of course sleep in a dormitory. She retires to a lovely three-bedroomed house with a private garden, disturbed only by her emails and phone, and occasionally by the jangle of the iron bell above the door.

Living with the other *Exposure* contestants has given Pam a newfound respect for her boarders. Aliyah sobs gently at night, pressing her tears against the pillow. On the first night, this was understandable. When it happened the second night, Pam dutifully trotted over to the younger woman's bed to stroke her hair and tell her it would all be alright, even though Pam had just that second been about to drop off. Last night, Pam rolled over when she heard the muffled sobs and pulled her pillow over her ears. If Aliyah bawls tonight, Pam is contemplating smothering her. Crying isn't going to help anyone, and the rest of them would quite like to get some sleep, thank you very much.

The more time Pam spends with her fellow contestants, the less she likes them, despite – or perhaps because of – their attempts to ingratiate themselves. Earlier, Aliyah slipped Pam half a chocolate bar, one finger to her lips to keep the secret.

'Where did you get that from?' Pam whispered. No one has told them how many cameras and microphones there are, and paranoia is rife. Chocolate, though! The contestants weren't allowed to bring snacks in with them and although their tasks have won them treats, there hasn't been any chocolate.

'Don't worry about that.' Aliyah winked. 'Just enjoy it.'

This was contraband, Pam realised. Aliyah was cheating, and Pam absolutely did not approve. She did, however, eat the evidence. Waste not, want not.

Henry is still clattering the dishes against the metal sink.

'Could you do that any louder?' Pam snaps. 'I don't think they can hear you in Outer Mongolia.'

'Would you prefer me to leave it for you?' Henry says archly.

'Now, now!' Lucas moves to sit next to Pam. 'You seem very tense today, Pam. Is there something on your mind?'

Only the impending collapse of my career, and the tarnished reputation of the school I love, Pam thinks. She doesn't say it, because she knows it would give the others ammunition for an exposure attempt. It's terrifying how easily things slip out, and how much you can glean from various asides. Aliyah's secret, for example, is about sex, something Pam established very quickly from Aliyah's wails about *shame, the only choice I had*, and *I've already lost a boyfriend over it*. Pam worries Aliyah is giving too much away – she's seen the sharp looks from some of the others, each time Aliyah lets slip another slice of her secret.

'I'm not tense,' Pam tells Lucas, somewhat tensely.

'Would you like me to pray with you?' Lucas has a kind, open face, rather soft around the edges. Pam feels a sudden urge to slap it.

'No, I bloody well would not.' She stands. 'And, since you brought it up, is it really necessary to pray before every sodding meal?' Pam sailed through the menopause without a single symptom (there's no space for middle age mood swings in a school full of adolescent girls) yet now she is teetering on a knife-edge, flying into a rage if someone even looks at her the wrong way.

'It's a quick Grace, just to give thanks to—'

'Give thanks?' Pam snorts. 'For subjecting us to this hideous social experiment?'

'I think you're confusing God with Miles,' Ceri says. She considers this. 'Which, to be fair, he seems to be doing himself, so as you were.'

'Prayer has brought me great comfort since we found ourselves in this horrendous situation.' Lucas stands. 'If anyone would like to join me in asking the Almighty for forgiveness, I'll be in the chill-out tent.'

Aliyah goes with him. Pam does not. Even if Pam were a believer, she wouldn't be asking for forgiveness. She hasn't done anything wrong. The uber-rich parents who throw money at her to secure their daughters' places in the school won't miss the cash, and the working-class girls Pam helps as a result are appreciative and relieved. Miles won't be thinking about them, of course. He won't even have considered that, by exposing Pam's secret, he'll be stopping bright, ambitious girls from achieving their potential. It's ironic, really, given that Miles is clearly exceptionally bright and ambitious himself – he has to be, to have conceived *Exposure*. A show designed to ruin lives. Someone needs to ruin Miles's, just to show him.

Pam finds the thought soothing. She pictures a broken Miles, standing amid the wreckage of his career. She's a little hazy on the finer details of modern television production, and so her fantasy-Miles is surrounded by thousands of metres of unspooled cine film.

Ceri has wandered off – she's either seeking God's forgiveness with Lucas and Aliyah or she's gone to the loo. Henry is washing up with a slowness that can only be deliberate, and Pam can't bear the clattering any more. She crosses to the sink and picks up a tea-towel. Anything to make it finish more quickly.

Henry turns on her. 'What are you doing?' he shouts. 'Put that down!'

'I'm helping,' Pam says indignantly.

Henry's angry face crumples. 'Sorry. God, I don't know what's happening to me. I feel like all my nerve-endings are exposed.'

'That's what he wants.' Pam narrows her eyes at the cameras, high up in the trees. 'It's like when they play white noise at hostages, or stop them sleeping. He wants us weak.'

'Well, it's working.' Henry leans on the sink.

'Come on, now.' Pam has a burst of head-teacherly stoicism. 'Don't let him win.' It is easier, she finds, to bolster someone else's morale than it is to boost your own.

Henry turns to her as though she's said something profound. 'You're right. We need to beat him at his own game.' Something sparks in his eyes. 'What if we teamed up?'

'I don't—'

'Expose the others, secure immunity, both win the money!'

Pam hesitates. 'How would we . . . hypothetically . . . if we were to do that . . . how would it work?' The money isn't important to her, but keeping her job is.

'We need to combine our knowledge,' Henry says. 'You say what you know about Aliyah, or Ceri, or Lucas. I tell you what I've found out. We build a picture and then BAM!' Henry slams his hand on to the edge of the sink. 'Are you in?'

Pam considers this. If she could avoid being exposed, she wouldn't need the money. But the two go together, and, in any case, she knows the Heath Hill governors will already be nervous. They're probably already digging for the truth. They'll speak to the teachers, to parents, and people's tongues are loose. Pam's secret will come out and, when it does, she'll lose her job, perhaps even be barred from teaching. A hundred grand is enough to keep her afloat till she retrains, maybe even with enough left over to do some good. Charitable support, a bursary . . .

'Take Ceri.' Henry leans closer, whispering so he won't be heard. 'Her secret's something she's been doing at work. What has she said to you about it?'

'She— No. This is wrong.' Pam had promised herself she'd play fair, that she'd be able to hold her head up high whenever she was evicted. She walks away.

'Wrong?' Henry follows her. 'This is a game, Pam. We have to play it.'

'Not like this. Not in an underhand way.' They're standing among the trees now, away from the cameras.

'But don't you see? Everything about this is underhand. Even Miles – no, especially Miles.' Henry grips Pam's shoulder. 'Remember when he joined us for breakfast, before filming started? We all thought it was great how he took time to speak to each of us personally.'

'I remember.' Pam swallows. She considers herself a good judge of character, but Miles had had them all fooled. He was all smiles and excitement, telling them he was going to make them all stars.

'He said something about you,' Henry says.

Pam's mouth falls open. 'What?' she breathes.

'He said, *greasy hands*.' Henry's cheeks flush. 'I didn't know what he was talking about, because obviously they hadn't told us what the show was really about, then. It was only afterwards I realised he must have been trying to give me a clue – manipulate me into exposing you.'

Pam realises she's shaking.

'You're alright.' Henry gives a sheepish laugh. 'I still haven't got it. I'm like, *greasy*?' He holds up his own palms and shakes his head. 'But maybe Miles said something to some of the others, too. Planted seeds to get us to form alliances and pool our knowledge.'

'He didn't say anything to me,' Pam says, but it's clear from Henry's watchful expression that he doesn't believe her.

'Just think about it, okay? And if you want to team up – I'm in.'

Pam nods, and, as Henry walks off towards the tents, she leans against a tree, her legs suddenly incapable of supporting her. She can't think about Henry's offer, because she's thinking about Miles throwing her under a bus before the cameras had even started rolling. Pam thought she wasn't capable of hating Miles Young any more than she already did. Looks as though she was wrong.

THIRTY-TWO

MONDAY | FFION

'Ceri isn't a murderer.' The kitchen is suddenly too hot, too small, too full of people. Ffion picks up her upturned coffee cup from the drainer and rinses it again. Fills it with cold water and drinks half of it in one go. She thinks about how, despite living in the same village, she's only really got to know Ceri recently. Ceri's a private person – guarded, almost – and that's always suited Ffion, but is there a dark side to her?

'How well do you know her?' George says.

'She's the postwoman in the village.'

'What does that mean? You know her well, or you don't know her at all?' There's a touch of irritation in George's voice.

'It's a small community. Everyone knows everyone.' Ffion's voice sounds high and strained. 'We should wait till Ryan's been interviewed. He might cough straight away.'

'It could be days before he's declared fit,' Leo says. 'Besides, you said yourself, he doesn't fit the MO.'

'And there's Dario Kimber. He doesn't have an alibi, and we have a witness putting him in camp the night the cameras were smashed.' Ffion talks quickly, trying to drown out the buzzing in her head. 'Also, I don't trust Zee Hart. What if she killed Miles to inject some drama into her behind-the-scenes reporting?

257

Then there's Jessica Francis – she had just as much motive as Ceri—'

'She's been alibied,' George says. 'She bumped into Caleb more than a mile from here, ten minutes before Miles was killed. He was walking up to camp with fresh supplies. Her running app shows she was nowhere near the scene, and Caleb couldn't have got back in time.'

At the back of her mind, Ffion remembers the quad bike she borrowed from Caleb to zip down to Angharad's cottage, which would cover the distance easily. Caleb might have been on foot when he saw Jessica, but was the bike parked nearby? She pushes the thought aside. The buzzing in her head is loud enough already.

'Ceri must have gone straight back to camp after killing Miles,' George says. 'And you brought all the contestants out of camp four hours later, so she has to have removed the envelope in that time.'

Leo turns to Ffion. 'Can you have a look at the footage? I guess she thought that, with Miles dead, no one would be watching the livestream, and she could open the box without being seen.'

Ffion nods mutely, glad to be dismissed. By the time she reaches the back door, Leo's already on the phone to the DCI. *A team effort, boss*, she hears. *That's very kind of you . . . let's see how it pans out . . .*

In the courtyard, Ffion takes a lungful of cool air.

'Are you having an asthma attack?'

She opens her eyes to find Seren leaning against the farmhouse wall. 'What are you doing?'

'Waiting for you. Did Ceri really kill Miles?'

'You shouldn't have been listening.'

'It's not my fault. Tell your boyfriend to keep his voice down.'

'Don't call him that.'

'Don't you fancy him any more? Does he give you the ick?'

'No, but—'

'Oh, do you give *him* the ick?' Seren juts out her bottom lip in sympathy.

Ffion exhales slowly. 'Why are you here, Ser?'

'I want to talk to you about uni.' Seren scuffs the toe of her shoe on the ground. 'I might have changed my plans a bit.'

Fucking hell, she can't deal with this right now . . . Ffion exhales sharply. 'No. I know you think I'll be softer on you than Mam, but no. You're going to university and that's final.'

'Yes, but Caleb—'

'—will have to wait.' Ffion glares at her. 'Bangor's two hours away, Ser, and some days you won't even have lectures. You'll have plenty of time with him.'

'You never *listen* to me!' Seren almost screams it, and Ffion walks away from the house, striding across the courtyard so the younger girl has to follow. 'I'm trying to explain what—'

'Look.' Ffion stops dead, turning to Seren. 'I know it feels like Caleb is the be-all and end-all right now – and maybe he always will be – but getting a degree is . . .' She stops, thinking of Jessica running into Caleb on the mountain. Wondering again how long it would have taken for him to reach Miles's studio if he'd been on the quad bike. She can see it now, parked by the gate at the back of the courtyard, and she tries to remember if it was there yesterday morning. 'How is Caleb, anyway?'

Seren narrows her eyes. 'He's fine. Why?'

'He was pretty pissed off with Miles.'

'The guy promised him a TV credit. A credit's a big deal, apparently.' Seren shrugs. 'I don't get it, to be honest, but he's gone mental over it.'

259

Ffion glances up at the bedrooms above them. 'I wouldn't let him hear you saying that.'

'His room's at the front of the house – he'd have to be a bat to hear me.'

'When you say "mental",' Ffion says, 'have you heard him, say, make any threats against Miles?'

'Oh, my God.' Seren takes a step back, shaking her head. 'I don't believe you.'

'What?'

'You think he killed Miles.'

'I don't. I'm just covering all bases.'

'By treating my boyfriend like a suspect!'

'I'm just doing my job, Seren.'

'You're shitting on your own doorstep.'

Seren turns and runs, and Ffion doesn't go after her. She presses her fingers to her temples. Thinks about Caleb, about Ceri.

Seren's right. The police service says it values officers with 'local knowledge', but that knowledge comes at a cost. Once again, Ffion's dealing with suspects as familiar to her as family, and the stress of it is a thunderstorm in her head. She's too close to this job, but how can she walk away?

The Crime Scene Investigators have finished in Miles's studio and Ffion sits down gingerly. It feels bizarre to be in the chair where he died, looking at the same monitors he was looking at when his attacker arrived.

Was it Ceri?

Or Ryan?

Or someone else?

Ffion goes through the motions of checking the footage, already knowing what she'll find. The contents of the hard drive have

260

been downloaded and recorded as an exhibit, but nevertheless Ffion is tentative with the controls, wary of accidentally deleting something. The system is surprisingly straightforward, with a clickable tracker enabling the viewer to jump directly to a specific time. Ffion plays with the tracker, jumping between days, watching a few minutes then diving into another day, another conversation. It feels even more voyeuristic than watching the TV show.

Ffion moves the tracker to start a few minutes before the murder. She watches Lucas lost in thought by the fire, then moves back in time and clicks on the label marked CONFESSION POD. Henry is already in full flow, although – like a lot of men Ffion knows – he's using a lot of words to say nothing of great importance.

'I've been racking my brains,' he says to the camera. 'And I honestly don't know what "secret" *Exposure* plans to reveal, so I just wanted to jump on here quickly to say sorry.' His eyes flick to the left.

Quickly? Ffion snorts. Henry's self-indulgent apology – *Sorry to anyone I might have unwittingly hurt. Sorry to my parents, sorry to my friends, to my colleagues* – is almost forty-five minutes long, and not once does he mention the mother of the kid he's allegedly abandoned, or the alcoholism he reluctantly disclosed to Ffion. Instead, he rambles on about making *better life choices*. Henry was hoping to get away with his secret, Ffion realises. He was hoping to win.

She clicks back in time and sees Henry enter the pod; rewinds a second time and there's Henry again, making another visit to the pod only a few minutes before his great Shakespearian confession. The man takes navel-gazing to a whole new level.

Ffion switches to the camera giving the best view of the box of secrets and plays it quadruple speed from the time of Miles's

261

murder until she sees Dario, acting on Leo's and Ffion's orders – appearing in order to extract the contestants.

No one goes near the box.

Ffion walks up the mountain towards the *Exposure* camp. She's heading nowhere in particular, she's walking to delay the moment at which she goes back to Carreg Plas and does what she should have done the moment she opened the box of secrets. She sees a dirty white outline through the trees and realises she's walked around the edge of the camp, to where Dario's caravan is pitched.

Could he have murdered Miles? Ffion would like to believe it – for Ceri's sake – but Leo's point about the window was valid. Dario going into Miles's studio via the door wouldn't give anyone cause for suspicion, so why would Miles let him in through the window?

Ffion looks through the window of the caravan. It's empty. The seats have been folded out into a bed, and two pillows are bunched on one side. There's no sheet, just a duvet in a striped cover. In the kitchenette, a mug stands on the counter next to a saucepan and an open tin of beans.

She walks around the caravan and tries the door, but it's locked. Ffion's almost glad – she can imagine what the inside smells like. There's a pair of wellington boots under the caravan, but otherwise there's nothing outside except for an oil drum a few metres away, its outside blackened and cracked. Ffion wanders over to it, knowing she has to get back, that Leo will be wondering where she is.

The drum is empty apart from a few charred scraps of paper. Ffion considers them. There's no stack of logs, no sign that Dario has been keeping a fire going to stay warm. Has he been burning something? Ffion leans into the drum and fishes out the burnt paper. It's nothing but scraps, but what's left of the printed letters shows the same word again and again.

Exposure.

'Did you find anything?' Leo says, when Ffion returns.

Ffion doesn't answer. She's looking at DC Alun Whitaker, who should be in the CID office at Bryndare and is instead installed at the kitchen table. 'What's he doing here?'

'The DI asked me to drop by. See how you were.'

'Check up on me, more like.' Ffion scowls at Alun.

'I met your sister,' Alun says. 'She was just leaving when I got here.'

'I'll book her in for therapy.'

'She had some choice words to say about you.'

Ffion doesn't bite.

'Boccacci's authorised Ceri's arrest,' Leo says. 'Do you want to interview her with me? George and Alun are going to nick Dario for the criminal damage.'

'You'll be wanting these, then.' Ffion drops a handful of charred paper on to the table. Just as she does, she remembers something Seren said, and she looks up at the ceiling, trying to place everyone.

'What are they?' Alun picks up a piece of paper between finger and thumb.

'I found them by Dario's caravan. They're contracts, or disclaimers, or something – look, this one has Pam's signature, and this one has the word *indemnify* on it.' She looks at George. 'Owen's bedroom is at the front of the house, isn't it? Next to the one Caleb's been using?'

'Um . . . yes.' George is distracted, peering at the scraps of paper. 'Dario must have taken paperwork from Miles's studio that day we saw him. Nice one, Ffi.'

263

'So if Owen's room looks out towards the lake, how did he know what was going on in the courtyard when Miles was murdered?' Ffion says.

There's a beat while everyone thinks this through.

Leo stands. 'I'll go and get him, and let's find out, shall we?'

'Before you do . . .' Ffion looks at him, and her stomach lurches. 'Can I have a word?'

'Sure.'

'Not here.'

They walk up the mountain, away from Carreg Plas and in the opposite direction to the *Exposure* camp. Something's nagging at Ffion – something about the footage she watched earlier – but her head's too full to understand what it is, and whether it matters. All she knows is that she needs to come clean.

'What's going on?' Leo says, as Ffion's march slows and she stands still, her hands deep in her coat pockets. Below them, Llyn Drych is a slash of blue. Ffion can see Mam's house, on the edge of Cwm Coed, and Steffan's boatyard. Over on the English side of the lake, The Shore's log cabins stretch from the water's edge back into the forest.

Ffion takes Ceri's envelope out of her pocket and hands it to Leo.

He looks at it, puzzled. 'You found it?'

Ffion says nothing. She tries to hold his gaze, but she's too ashamed and she has to break away, although not before she's seen his face switch from confusion to understanding to disbelief. She looks back at the lake before it progresses to disgust. 'It's complicated,' she says quietly.

Ffion hears the snap of latex gloves – only Leo would have a

264

pair in his pocket, just in case – and the whisper of card sliding out of paper.

Leo reads it aloud.

Ceri stole thousands of pounds from her postal
delivery round.

A crow hops from one stone to another, its head jerking from side to side. Ffion watches it peck at something on the ground.

'She got caught,' Ffion says, when it's clear Leo isn't going to say anything. 'She promised to stop, and pleaded with her boss, Bronwen, not to tell the police. Eventually Bronwen took pity on her, but, when *Exposure* started, Bronwen realised she risked being dragged into Ceri's lies.'

'But . . .' Leo is struggling to speak. 'Why?'

'Bronwen's going out with Huw.'

'So?'

'He begged me.' Ffion plucks a leaf off the tree next to them and shreds it into pieces. The sudden movement spooks the crow, which flies off down towards the lake. 'I think he really likes her. I think she's mending him, after I . . .' She lets the sentence trail away.

'Plenty of people leave their marriages, Ffion, and a whole bunch of them feel guilty about it.' There's an edge to Leo's voice. She can feel his eyes on her as he speaks again. 'Concealing evidence isn't making amends, though, it's crazy.'

'I'm crazy, am I?' Ffion snaps, finally looking at him.

'Yes! Do you still love him, is that it?'

'What? No! God.'

'Have you any idea how stupid this is going to make me look?' Leo says. 'DCI Boccacci said she was impressed with me, that Cheshire was lucky to have me. She even asked if I'd consider transferring.'

For one tiny moment, Ffion tortures herself with the idea of seeing Leo every day at work; catching up over a canteen coffee at lunchtime.

'She said she trusted my judgement on arresting Ceri Jones,' Leo says bitterly. 'A judgement I based on the compelling evidence that Ceri's envelope was the only one to have been taken.'

'I—'

'Because you took it!'

'I messed up, alright!' Ffion knows she sounds broken, that her throat is thick with the threat of tears.

'But you're *always* messing up. You don't think things through, and then everything crashes around you, whether it's work or . . . or . . .' Leo blinks, and there's a flash of pain in his eyes before they harden again.

'Or what?' Ffion says urgently. If he means their relationship, she'll just do it. She'll tell him how she really feels, and—

'Fuck up your career if you want.' Leo starts walking towards the house. 'But don't drag mine down with it. I'm done.'

'Done with what? You can't just walk out on a murder investigation.'

'No, Ffion,' Leo says, without looking over his shoulder. 'I'm done with you.'

THIRTY-THREE

TUESDAY | LEO

Bryndare mortuary is an uninviting single-storey building at the rear of the hospital. Leo presses the buzzer and a second later, the door clicks open.

'Have you been here before?' George asks, as they follow the mortuary technician through a door and down a long corridor. The smell of disinfectant doesn't quite mask the underlying stench of death, which grows steadily stronger as they draw nearer to the windowless morgue.

'Once.' Leo still remembers the look on Ffion's face when she realised who she'd be working with on the Rhys Lloyd murder. His own expression must have been pretty similar, he supposes, and, despite everything, a smile tugs at the corners of his mouth. It's not every day you encounter last night's one-night stand in a morgue.

Miles Young is already on the slab, his naked body covered with a green sheet. Izzy Weaver, the forensic pathologist, whips it off like a stage magician. 'The ultimate exposure,' she says, in lieu of hello. She nods a greeting to George as Leo casts an eye over the body. Miles is lean, rather than toned, with visible hip bones and a bony chest. His hands are encased in paper bags.

'What are your first impressions?' Leo asks.

'I'd say he's dead,' Izzy says drily, 'wouldn't you?' She picks up a recording device and holds her finger over the record button. 'Well-nourished Caucasian male, no visible scalp trauma. There's a reality TV show for everything nowadays, isn't there?'

There's a pause, before Leo realises Izzy is talking to him.

'Cooking, dancing, ice-skating. Everyone's an expert after six episodes.'

'I guess so.'

'External auditory canals patent and free of blood. They should do one about pathologists.'

'I'm sorry?'

'A reality TV show. Six amateur sleuths, a fridge full of bodies . . .'

George grimaces. 'Bit macabre.'

'Aren't they all?' Izzy presses record. 'Did you ever see *Who's Your Daddy?* Win a hundred thousand dollars if you can guess which of these twenty-five men is your biological father. Left lower eyelid on the inner conjunctival surface: a one-millimetre petechial haemorrhage.'

'That's horrific,' George says.

'Very normal for strangulation.' Izzy examines Miles's face. 'No, reality TV shows are the scourge of modern society.' She presses record again. 'Similarly sized petechial haemorrhages can be seen on the skin of the upper eyelids.'

'You didn't watch *Exposure*, then?' George asks.

'I'd rather gouge my eyeballs out with a Durham retractor.' Izzy resumes her examination, lingering on the angry marks around Miles's neck. 'Ligature mark, width approximately three millimetres. Horizontal with upward deviation.' She stops. 'Was he sitting down?'

'Yes,' George says.

'Thought so.' Izzy looks pleased with herself. 'Ligature furrow crosses the anterior midline below the laryngeal prominence, level with the cricoid cartilage.'

Leo tunes out, as he might if he were sitting in a café abroad, surrounded by people speaking a foreign language. He didn't see Ffion again yesterday after he'd left her on the hillside. He'd heard the Triumph backfire, and the angry spray of gravel as she spun out of the drive, and he'd responded to George's quizzical look with what he hoped was an equally curious shrug. 'I'm going to Bryndare,' he'd told her. 'I need to have a conversation with the DCI.'

'I thought you wanted to talk to Owen?'

'Put him on ice,' Leo had said tightly. 'New information has come to light.'

Two hours later, Izzy snaps off her gloves. 'In the least unsurprising update of all time, I can confirm your man was strangled.'

'With?' George says.

'A flat close-fibre cord. My best guess would be a shoelace, or something resembling a shoelace. No fibres, but we should be able to pattern-match it if you come up with the cord.' She picks up a ring from a dish next to the sink and slips it on to the fourth finger of her left hand, briefly admiring the square-cut diamond.

'Might he have injured his attacker in any way?' Leo says. Miles's nails have been scraped and carefully clipped into labelled bags.

'There was tissue under two of the nails on his right hand,' Izzy concedes. 'But if you look here . . .' She indicates two crescent-shaped wounds above the ligature mark, then brings her own hands up to her neck, tugging at an invisible cord. 'I think we'll find that's his own skin. I suspect it happened so fast he didn't have time to react.'

She gives them an overview of her findings from the internal examination, pointing out the disrupted blood vessels in the brain cortex consistent with strangulation. 'No indicators for drug use, although we'll send samples for toxicology, of course.' Izzy looks at Miles, whose organs – carefully weighed and photographed – are now on a trolley beside him. 'Do you have a suspect?'

'Two,' Leo says. 'One's under the care of a mental health team at the moment – we've not been able to question him yet. The other's in the traps as we speak.'

Boccacci had asked Alun Whitaker to interview Dario. 'Best to keep this one in-house,' she said to Leo, disguising the slight behind a smooth smile. 'Let me know how the post-mortem goes tomorrow.' The subtext was clear: Leo was benched.

'Are the suspects left- or right-handed?' Izzy says.

'Not a clue,' Leo says. He'll have to ring Boccacci again, he thinks, feeling a little sick at the prospect. Whitaker will be interviewing Dario now, first about the damage to the cameras, then about the murder. The security guard might even roll over. By the time Leo and George are done here, Whitaker could be charging him and taking all the glory.

'Dario's left-handed,' George says. 'He smudged the signature on his witness statement. I only noticed because I do the same.' She waves her hand in the air. 'Leftie.'

'Then he's not your murderer,' Izzy says. 'The abrasions from the ligature are deeper on the right side, the angle more intense.' She mimes a strangling action, her victim's neck level just above her waist. Leo pictures Miles at his editing desk. He'd been comfortable with his visitor. Relaxed enough to carry on working, perhaps with his guest looking over his shoulder. 'Your dominant hand naturally pulls harder.' Izzy tugs again.

Leo pictures the sudden panic on Miles's face as he felt a tightening against his windpipe; the shoelace whipped around his neck too fast to get his fingers beneath it, clawing as it dug into his skin, fighting for breath . . .

Izzy has finished her mime, but, rather than let her imaginary shoelace drop, she rolls it up and places it on the stainless-steel gurney beside her. Leo and George exchange glances. Forensic pathologists, thinks Leo – not for the first time – are not entirely normal.

In the car on the way back to Carreg Plas, George calls Jessica. Leo listens as she asks after Ryan, fighting the urge to turn to her and mouth *Get to the point!* Eventually, she does.

'Bit of an odd question, I know, but is Ryan right- or left-handed?' There's a pause. 'Thanks. No, it's not important. Okay, take care of yourself, alright? Bye.'

'He's left-handed, isn't he?' Leo says, once George has ended the call.

'Yes. He can't have strangled Miles.' She glances at him. 'I'm glad, aren't you?'

'That it wasn't Ryan?' Leo thinks. 'I guess. But who the hell was it? It can't have been Ryan or Dario because they're left-handed. Lucas and Henry were on the live cameras at the time of the murder. Pam and Jason have been alibied, as have Caleb and Jessica, and Aliyah just wouldn't have been strong enough . . .' Leo rattles off the names, feeling increasing despair as each possibility evaporates. 'Where do we go from here?'

'We speak to Owen,' George says. 'Roxy said she realised something was going on when she heard Owen's bedroom door bang, but maybe she was mistaken. He could have murdered Miles, climbed out of the window then run around to the front of the farmhouse. Maybe it wasn't a bedroom door Roxy heard, but the *front* door.'

'But the front door doesn't open,' Roxy says, when they put the theory to her. 'That's why we all come in through the kitchen.' The three of them are upstairs at Carreg Plas, clustered on the landing by the door to Roxy's room.

'Could it have been the kitchen door?' Leo tries, but it feels like a stretch.

Roxy shakes her head. 'It was definitely up here – that's why I heard it over the music. And when I opened my door I saw Owen haring down the stairs like something was on fire. I was literally seconds behind him.'

'Thanks.' Leo turns. 'Sorry to disturb you.' As he walks away, he hears Roxy drop her voice, whispering to George.

'Does he think Owen killed Miles?'

'We're just trying to build a picture of exactly what happened that day, that's all.'

'He was desperate to take over as producer, you know,' Roxy is saying.

Leo has tuned out. He's looking further down the landing, through the open door into the room Miles slept in. 'Owen wasn't in his bedroom,' Leo says. He walks towards the open door. George follows him.

'I'm telling you,' Roxy said, a note of frustration in her voice. 'I saw him at the top of the stairs.'

In Miles's bedroom, Leo takes in the window overlooking the courtyard, and the chest of drawers where the petty cash tin was kept.

'Oh, of course!' George says. 'He was in here.'

THIRTY-FOUR

LUCAS | DAY FIVE OF *EXPOSURE*

The Reverend Lucas Taylor has been talking to God a lot. This isn't unusual – it does rather come with the job – but if praying had league tables, the last few days would have put Lucas in the premiership.

Is he technically having an affair? This is what Lucas has been asking himself (not God – you can't ask the Almighty questions like that). Lucas is a single man, and the Church doesn't require him to remain so, so really, Lucas hasn't been having an affair, has he?

But he has been having sex. And Helena Barnsby, the woman to whom Lucas has been making love in the vestry every Wednesday evening, is already married. To Lucas's organist.

'Shall we see who plays the organ best?' Helena said, as she got on her knees and lifted Lucas's surplice. Lucas groans at the memory (and not in the way he did at the time). Of course it's an affair. God doesn't deal in semantics. The question is, what will He do about it? And what will the Bishop say?

Lucas rifles through his rucksack. Someone has taken his socks. Normally, Lucas would send up a prayer for whichever poor unfortunate found themselves in need of socks, but these are not normal times and his five fellow contestants are no less fortunate than he is. Right now, if Lucas were to find the person who stole his socks, he would rip them off their feet and shove them up their—

Lucas breathes out. It's frightening how quickly the old ways have come back to him. Unusually for a vicar, Lucas found God in prison. Or rather, God found him, leaning over a fellow inmate, about to slam a fist into his face. Then Lucas felt it, clear as anything: a hand closing around his, holding it back. When Lucas turned around, there was no one there, but Lucas had an over-whelming sense that he wasn't alone. That Sunday, he went to chapel and prayed for the first time since primary school.

It would be a relief, Lucas thinks now, if his criminal past were the 'secret' Miles Young planned to expose. But Lucas has been upfront from the start. In his audition tape, he'd outlined the rocky start he'd had in life and the events which had resulted in a custodial sentence. He'd made it clear he didn't consider it a secret – in fact, Lucas often speaks of prison in his sermons, he told Miles, to show his parishioners no one is beyond redemption.

The Church holds strong views on sin, and Lucas has been part of it long enough to understand there is a right kind of sin and a wrong kind. The right sort is stealing cars, going to prison then repenting, finding God, doing a theology degree then serving as curate in the parish of Lower Deansford. The wrong sort is bending Mrs Barnsby over the harvest festival display.

'There's quite a few celebrity vicars, aren't there?' Henry is saying.

Lucas hasn't been listening. 'Yes, it's quite the trend,' he says vaguely. Where are his bloody socks?

'Is that what you're after, then? A programme on Radio 4? A chat show?'

'Definitely not.' Lucas has no aspirations to fame. By applying for *Exposure*, he hoped only to show that the clergy were no different from the people in their congregations.

'I saw one on the cover of a magazine, the other day,' Henry says. 'Dog collar and all.'

'Magazine interviews, TV adverts, a book deal for a cosy crime series. And a podcast, of course.' Lucas sighs. 'I find it a little tasteless, to be honest. A vicar's job is to serve God and their parish, not to be a celebrity pin-up.' He clenches his teeth in frustration. 'Someone's taken my bloody socks!'

'You just want a quiet life, then?'

'That would be nice,' Lucas says wistfully. 'Have you seen my socks? They're hot pink and they have a small hole on one heel.'

'Sorry, mate.'

'Are you sure? I left them on my bunk.'

'I'm not sure I like your tone.' Henry stands then, and before Lucas knows what he's doing he's standing too, squaring up to Henry.

'Well, I don't like people who take my socks,' he says with icy calm, 'so you'd better—'

'Are you threatening me?' Henry glares at Lucas, but a second later his eyes crease into laughter. He claps Lucas on the back. 'Chill! I haven't got your socks, mate. Here, I'll help you look for them.'

That evening, Lucas sees a glint in Roxy Wilde's eyes. He knows even before she says it that he's been sentenced to the confession pod. All his life, Lucas has hated snakes, and as he leaves behind the supportive cheers of his campmates (he isn't fooled: their enthusiastic support is entirely down to relief at not being in the firing line themselves) he steels himself. He will not give up his secret.

He will not give up Helena Barnsby.

Lucas loves her, he realises, as something slithers through the dark towards him. And he thinks she loves him. A snake passes over his left foot; another climbs up the back of the chair and coils itself around his neck. Lucas fights the urge to scream. He thinks of Helena, and how – when he finishes this horrendous ordeal – he will ask her to leave her husband (organists are hard to come by, but such is the strength of Lucas's feelings for Helena). And somehow, he will make his peace with God.

While he's asking forgiveness for his part in the Barnsby adultery, Lucas can also ask forgiveness for grievous bodily harm. He hasn't actually committed GBH yet, but he intends to. Because when Lucas leaves the *Exposure* camp, he's going to find Miles and kick the shit out of him.

THIRTY-FIVE

TUESDAY | FFION

Ffion is on her way to Carreg Plas when DI Malik calls. There's no hands-free system in the Triumph, so she puts her phone on to speaker and balances it on the dashboard, from where it immediately slides into the footwell. 'Oh, fuck,' Ffion says.

'Ffion?'

'Sorry, boss. Morning.'

'Are you driving?' Malik's tiny voice comes from somewhere beneath the passenger seat.

'Yes,' Ffion shouts back. 'But I'm hands-free.'

'Pull over.'

Ffion tucks the Triumph close into the hedge and cuts the engine. 'Okay, I'm all yours.'

'You're off the *Exposure* job.'

'What? Why?' Ffion says, although she knows why. Ceri's envelope. How could she have been so stupid? Huw owes her – big time.

'I should have trusted my gut from the start,' Malik says. 'You're too close to this case, Ffion – it's a conflict of interests.'

No prizes for guessing who's been talking to Malik, Ffion thinks. What an absolute shit Leo is. He could at least have given her the heads-up that he planned to drop her in it.

'I suppose I'll be getting a call from Professional Standards?' She says it airily, as though she doesn't care, but she wonders how much trouble she's in. Interfering with an investigation could land her with a criminal charge, never mind the internal disciplinary.

A sheep trotting down the middle of the road stops and stares at Ffion. She glowers at it. Even the bloody sheep looks judgemental.

'I think we can probably keep this one in-house,' Malik says, after a pause. Ffion lets out a breath. 'I've told DCI Boccacci I need you back on CID. I'm letting her keep Alun instead.'

'What's she done to deserve that?' Ffion says automatically, but her heart's not in it. Alun will be unbearable now. She's surprised he's not rung her on some pretext, just so he can rub it in her face, but perhaps he's still bruised from not getting a cough from Dario Kimber last night.

Ffion had listened to the interview recording this morning.

'I thought I'd be able to lever the box off with my knife,' Dario said, after he'd confessed to smashing the camp cameras. 'But it wouldn't budge. Then someone called out from one of the tents and I made myself scarce. I was only trying to help Aliyah,' he added. His embarrassment was clear. The bloke had fallen for a woman half his age; kidded himself she was into him. The question was: did he kill for her, too?

'Absolutely not.' Dario didn't miss a beat when Alun put that very question to him. 'Miles was an arsehole, but I didn't kill him.'

'You stole confidential papers from his office,' Alun said.

Dario didn't deny it. 'I didn't have time to read them, I just grabbed them from the drawer in Miles's desk and shoved them in my pocket. I thought they might have the secrets in them, but they were useless.'

Miles's Cheshire-based production team had confirmed the burnt documents were health and safety forms, signed by each contestant before filming started.

The sheep continues down the road. Ffion presses her forehead against the steering wheel. She can understand why Leo's pissed off with her, and okay, he's a DS now, but reporting her to the DI? How dare he?

Ffion lets the anger inside her build. Encourages it. It's easier to be angry than heartbroken.

'Work from home today,' Malik says. 'Stay out of harm's way. Catch up on paperwork. And while you're doing it . . .' He breaks off, and Ffion hears his hesitation.

'Yes?'

'This is your last chance, Ffion. Work out where your loyalties lie.'

Ffion goes to Mam's house. Elen Morgan is unpacking a food shop, and without saying anything Ffion picks up a bag and starts putting things away. Dave helps by tearing open a multipack of crisps.

'Bloody hell, Dave.' Ffion snatches it away from him. 'I can't take you anywhere.'

'What's wrong?' Mam looks at her daughter with sharp eyes.

'They're spicy beef flavour. He'll be farting like a racehorse.'

'I meant with you.'

'I know what you meant.' Ffion puts a packet of spaghetti in the larder cupboard.

'You don't want to talk about it, then?'

'You've got four types of pasta here, Mam. Are you setting up an Italian restaurant?'

'I'll take that as a no.'

'Can I work here for a bit?'

'What's wrong with your place?'

'Nothing.' For once, Ffion wants company. She wants to be annoyed by Mam's incessant gossip and interrupted by requests to hold a tape measure or go up in the loft. Anything to stop her dwelling on the fact that she's essentially been placed on gardening leave, when they're within a breath of solving the most high-profile murder North Wales Police has ever had.

Ffion's phone rings.

'Is that DC Morgan?' It's an analyst from Bryndare police station.

'Speaking.'

'I've got your name on the exhibits seized from the Miles Young murder. We're still working on retrieving the data from Young's phone, but I've got the results from his watch, if you want them?'

Ffion should say she's not working the case any more – tell the analyst to call Leo or DCI Boccacci – but it'll be all around the station if she does, so she simply says, 'Shoot.' She'll email George with anything useful.

'It's a fairly cheap watch. No texts or emails. It looks as though he mostly used it as a PB tracker. He was obviously a keen runner.'

'He went every day,' Ffion says.

'Except Sunday.'

Ffion frowns. 'I'm sorry?'

'I was just saying, he didn't run on the day he died. The watch logs duration and distance, and his history shows that he ran for approximately the same amount of time every morning, but he didn't go on Sunday. Day of rest, I suppose.' The analyst laughs.

'No, that's not right,' Ffion says. 'He definitely went for a run.'

For a second she doubts herself, and she pulls up the memory for scrutiny. She remembers Miles stooping to put the key under the mat; remembers him deliberately ignoring her shouting across the courtyard and sprinting up the mountain away from her.

'Maybe he just forgot to track it,' she says, but it doesn't fit with what she already knows. Miles was obsessive. A creature of habit.

'Are you going to put that away? Mam says, once Ffion's off the phone, and she realises she's cradling a jar of honey as though it's a baby. She puts it in the cupboard, still distracted by the analyst's call. Miles *did* go for a run on Sunday morning. She *saw* him.

Her eyes widen as something suddenly hits her.

She saw a runner.

But was the runner Miles?

THIRTY-SIX

CERI | DAY SIX OF *EXPOSURE*

A year ago, Ceri Jones's life was perfect. She'd started seeing a woman called Lou, who had been on holiday in North Wales the same week Ceri decided to give Tinder a go. A weekend's dalliance had become a long-distance relationship, and they'd alternated between Ceri's house in Cwm Coed, and Lou's swanky apartment in London's Canary Wharf.

'The great thing about dating at our age,' Lou said, the first time Ceri visited her in London, 'is we're both grown-ups.' Lou had picked a stunning restaurant, with prices that made Ceri choose the cheapest thing on the menu, even though aubergine tastes like sponge. 'We're both working, both homeowners . . . we're equals.' Lou smiled as the bill arrived. 'Shall we go Dutch?'

Ceri got out her bank card and ignored the alarm bells ringing in her ears. Yes, they were both working, but Ceri was a postie and Lou a pension fund manager. Yes, they were both home-owners, but Ceri's mortgage was eighty-five per cent and interest-only, and Lou had casually mentioned having bought her apartment outright.

Over the next few months, the two women visited museums and galleries, and enjoyed theatre trips and spontaneous weekend city breaks, during which Lou sought out the best restaurants and

Ceri suggested picnics in the park. Ceri's credit card was soon maxed out, so she took out a loan.

It was a relief when the relationship ended. Lou sent her a text message (Darling, I've had the best fun, but all good things must come to an end! Lots of love, Lou x) and Ceri took a deep breath and added up her debts.

The money she owed kept her awake at night. Each morning, as she trudged around the back streets of Cwm Coed, she tried to come up with money-making schemes, but the interest alone was more than she could afford.

The ten-pound note was almost an accident.

She found it at the bottom of a post bag when she finished her round. It would have fallen out of a birthday card; it happened occasionally. The protocol was to list it in the book and put it in the safe, where it would wait until someone reported it missing.

Heart pounding, Ceri slipped it into her pocket, then used it to put fuel in her car.

Nobody reported the missing cash, but Ceri felt sick with guilt. It would be someone's birthday money; hard-earned by a doting aunt, sent with love and a *buy yourself something special*.

'There's not a parcel for me is there, Ceri love?' Dee Huxley asked a few days later. Ceri was delivering at The Shore, the holiday resort on the opposite side of the lake.

'Nothing in the van,' Ceri said.

'My new kettle's gone astray.' Dee tutted. 'Never mind. I'll get them to send a replacement.'

Something pinged in Ceri's mind. If she took the right parcel, she could sell the contents online. Big companies could afford to take the hit, the customer would get their replacement, and Ceri could pay off her debts and get her life back.

Over the next six months, Ceri took a parcel from every morning round. Every evening, she listed her spoils for sale. Once a week, she drove to Chester to send her packages from a post office where no one knew her. Slowly, her debt shrank.

People reported the losses, of course. There was even some gossip about a temporary postal worker who'd been shipped in to cover a maternity leave. But no one ever pointed a finger at Ceri. She'd grown up in Cwm Coed. She wouldn't steal from her own community.

Then one day Bronwen came into the break room just as Ceri was transferring a parcel from her locker to her rucksack, and it was all over.

'I'll have to report this,' Bronwen said, after a tearful Ceri had told her everything.

'I won't do it again, I promise. I can't lose this job, Bron, I won't be able to pay my mortgage.'

'How much have you stolen?' Bronwen said.

'I'm not sure. I've got a list.' Ceri had meticulously noted down what each item was worth, and what she sold it for; how much it was chipping away at her debt.

'I want to see it.'

Ceri sent it to Bronwen that evening, along with a long email begging for forgiveness. They settled into an uneasy agreement. Ceri wouldn't steal anything again, and Bronwen would keep Ceri's secret.

But did she?

The moment Roxy Wilde made that awful *Exposure* announcement, Ceri knew which secret of hers would be in that metal box.

It's the sixth day of filming, and Ceri knows her days are numbered. Jason and Pam have been exposed and evicted, and the atmosphere in camp is charged with suspicion. She lies in her bunk and stares numbly at the tent's walls, feeling simultaneously sick with dread and bored out of her mind. Like being a remand prisoner, she thinks, waiting for trial.

Trial by public jury.

Will she be given a chance to explain? Ceri can't excuse her actions, she knows that, but the debt was crushing her. She felt as though she couldn't breathe, as though she'd never be free from it.

Outside, one of the men is making a song and dance about something. At first Ceri ignores it, but there are so few of them now, there's nothing else to do – no one else to talk to. She hauls herself upright and pushes through the flaps of the tent.

Henry is performing what looks like a tribal dance by the campfire, slapping his back and waving his hat around his head. 'Get off me!'

'What's going on?' Ceri says.

Lucas is doubled over with mirth. 'He was sitting under that tree and a spider dropped on his head. I know it's ungodly to make fun, but . . .' He creases into laughter again, pointing at Henry, who is now leaping from one foot to the other.

'Where's Aliyah?' Ceri's not in the mood for a pantomime.

'She said she was going for a walk.'

Ceri has grown suspicious of Aliyah, who frequently disappears on her own. Yesterday, Aliyah had claimed to have been trapped in the loo by a dodgy tummy, which had to be a lie, because Ceri had been in the loo herself.

She walks away from the men – Henry has finally rid himself of the offending spider, thank goodness – and looks for movement between the trees. She follows the line of the fence, her heart thumping, even though she's doing nothing wrong. Why shouldn't she go for a walk? It's only what Aliyah's doing, after all.

Except Aliyah isn't walking, but talking – to someone on the other side of the fence. Who is it? Ceri creeps closer, but her foot finds a branch and the resulting crack cuts through the still air. Aliyah turns her head sharply and Ceri freezes. If she tries to get closer they'll see her, but Aliyah's standing directly in front of whoever it is and all Ceri can see is dark trousers and a glimpse of fair hair, when Aliyah moves. Is it a woman she's talking to?

There's a holler from camp, followed by the clang of a wooden spoon on a metal pan. Lucas or Henry have got a brew on. Ceri looks back and although it's only for a split second, it's too long. When she looks back, the woman – yes, definitely a woman – is walking away and Aliyah is coming towards Ceri.

Shit! Ceri stoops to pick up the stick she trod on. When she stands upright, Aliyah is looking right at her.

'What are you doing here?'

'Collecting kindling.' Ceri brandishes the stick.

'You haven't got much.'

'Only just started. Who was that?'

'Who?' Aliyah starts walking back to camp.

Ceri falls into step with her. 'The woman you were talking to.'

'I dunno. Some walker. She was lost, I think.'

Ceri shoots a sideways look at the younger woman. Aliyah's lying. But why?

As that evening's live segment approaches, there's none of the fevered excitement Ceri remembers from when the contestants first sat around the fire pit. Then, there had been laughter and camaraderie; arms thrown around their new friends.

Now, Ceri sits at one end of the long log that serves as a bench, Aliyah at the other end. Henry is in the middle, several arm lengths from either woman.

Lucas has opted to stand, his hands twitching nervously in his pockets. 'And then there were four,' he says ominously.

'Could be three, after tonight,' Henry says. 'Not that I've accused anyone,' he adds quickly.

'Nor me,' Ceri says.

'Judge not, that ye be not judged,' sighs Lucas. 'It doesn't have to be an accusation – the public vote could put any one of us in the confession pod.' He looks at the others in alarm. 'The show wouldn't make me do it twice, would they?'

'I wouldn't put anything past Miles Young,' Henry says darkly.

Aliyah is quiet. Ceri takes in the younger woman's downcast eyes, the way she's picking at her nails. That's more than nerves, she thinks. That's guilt.

'Did you make an accusation, Aliyah?' Ceri says.

Whatever Aliyah is about to say is interrupted by the arrival of Roxy and Owen, who sweep into camp and immediately start ordering the contestants around.

'Lucas, on the bench with the others, please,' Roxy says. 'Bunch up – that's it. Henry, can you put an arm around Lucas?'

'No, I can't.'

'We haven't got time to play games,' Owen says, more sharply than Roxy. 'Unless you'd like us to go off-script?' He dangles a small key in the air. 'Miles is currently the only keeper of your secrets, but we could always open the box and—'

'No!' There's a collective cry from the four contestants. The odds might be smaller now, but each of them still has a chance. A week tomorrow, those with their secret still intact will leave the *Exposure* camp with a hundred grand.

'Then play your parts,' Owen snaps. 'And look happy about it.'

Ceri forces her mouth into something approximating a smile.

The more sanguine she appears, she reasons, the less interesting viewers will find her, and the less likely they are to try to expose her. It's clear the others are thinking along similar lines, because Henry has draped an arm around Lucas, and Aliyah is clapping like a performing seal.

'Five, four,' Owen says. He counts down with his fingers. *Two, one.*

'Good evening from Dragon Mountain,' Roxy says to the camera. 'Aliyah, earlier today, you attempted to expose Ceri. Let's find out if you're right.'

'You what?' Ceri twists to face Aliyah, who has dropped the seal act and is staring back defiantly.

'You'd do the same.'

Ceri doesn't answer, and only partly because Aliyah's right. Of course she'd expose Aliyah's secret, if she had the first clue what it was. Ceri doesn't answer because she can't. Because every muscle in her body is trembling, because her jaw is rattling and she suddenly feels at once too hot and too cold. She knows that in this brief interlude, when Owen is fiddling with his camera and Roxy is checking her make-up, Aliyah's accusation is playing on TV screens across the country. Right now, everyone is hearing Ceri's secret. All Ceri's customers – all her *friends* – know she stole from them.

'Back on in ten,' Owen says. 'Positions!'

And, like the whipped dogs they are, Henry, Lucas, Ceri and Aliyah shuffle into place. A hot, shameful tear slides down Ceri's cheek.

'Open the box, Aliyah.' Roxy hands her the key. 'And hand me the envelope marked with Ceri's name.'

Aliyah's long hair falls over her face as she fiddles with the lock and opens the box. Ceri hears Lucas swallow a moan at the sight of the envelopes, but she can't summon up any sympathy, can't give his shoulder a squeeze the way Henry is doing. *Their* secrets are still safe; they're not being carried to Roxy, not being held up to the camera for inspection.

'Time to find out if Aliyah's right.' Roxy tears open the envelope. 'Aliyah, do you stand by your accusation? Did Ceri really set fire to her own car and commit insurance fraud?' She slides out the card.

Ceri can't catch her breath. She thinks perhaps she's lost her mind, that she's starting to hear things. Roxy's eyes have widened. She glances at Ceri then turns to the camera, her mouth a circle of surprise, drawing out the moment. Ceri starts crying, not only with the emotion of today's exposure, but the stress of the last week, the guilt of the last few months.

'I'm afraid, Aliyah . . .' Roxy is sliding the card back into its envelope. 'You're wrong.'

There's a stunned silence.

'What?' Aliyah stares at Roxy. 'That's not possible!'

'Your exposure attempt has failed – you made an incorrect accusation. You know what that means, don't you?' Roxy says.

Aliyah looks beyond the trees around the camp, her head snapping left then right as she searches for something. 'You bitch!' she shouts.

'Back to the confession pod, Aliyah.' Roxy beams to the camera. 'Maybe we'll have an exposure tonight after all!'

As Aliyah is led away, Ceri sinks on to the damp ground and leans against the log, still shaking. She isn't sure why or how, but she's safe.

For now.

THIRTY-SEVEN

TUESDAY | LEO

Owen had made an admirable attempt to protest his innocence.

'I don't know what else I can say to convince you,' he had said last night, looking across the kitchen table at Leo and George. 'You can search my room if you like. Search me.' He held out his arms, inviting them to frisk him.

'Once the tin's been examined by forensics,' Leo had said, 'we'll be comparing any fingerprints with the elimination prints you provided following Miles's murder.'

Owen wasn't thrown by this. 'Well, you'll find mine, I expect. It's a petty cash tin. We all used it.'

'When was the last time you went into Miles's room?' George said.

'No idea . . . Saturday? Friday, maybe? A couple of days before he died, definitely.'

'Not the day of the murder, then?' Leo said.

'No.' Owen didn't blink.

'The thing is,' Leo said, 'to my mind, there are only two ways you could have seen or heard something going on in the courtyard. One . . .' he counted them off on his fingers, 'you were in Miles's bedroom. Or two, you were in the courtyard itself. Either way, you've lied to us, which makes me think you had something to do with Miles's death. So I guess what I'm saying is, did you murder Miles, or did you steal a hundred quid from the petty cash.' Leo leant forward. 'Because, in case you haven't worked this out, one of those things is more serious than the other.'

There was a long pause.

'I took the money,' Owen said eventually.

There is some irony, Leo thinks now, as he fills out the paperwork for Owen's charge file, in Owen's cementing his own alibi by confessing to a different crime.

Leo has never known a case where so many potential suspects have so many alibis. He is beginning to feel they will never identify who killed Miles; that he will be stuck in this loop of suspects and alibis forever.

Jason Shenton continued to grumble about the money it would cost for his solicitor to support his alibi, until Leo pointed out that if Jason were to be nicked for obstruction he'd be engaging a criminal lawyer as well as a family one. The recording of Jason's video meeting arrived within the hour.

She can't refuse to let me see them, can she? Jason asks, on the left-hand side of the screen. On the opposite side, a man in a navy suit is making notes.

'There's no time stamp on it,' George says.

'I don't think we need one.' Leo turns up the volume. There's some sort of commotion happening in the background. Jason looks to the side, away from the camera, then frowns. There's a faint but unmistakable *Stand back!* then a crashing sound.

'I'm kicking the door in,' Leo says, half to himself.

Something's going on outside, Jason says on the video. *Can I call you back?*

I'll have my secretary book in a time. I'm afraid I will have to charge you for the full—

291

The screen goes black. Leo looks at George. 'That's that, then. Another one who couldn't have done it. We're going to have to cast the net wider.' He closes the recording and brings up the spreadsheet he's already spent hours poring over. It includes the names of every person who applied to be on *Exposure* – all forty-five thousand of them. The analyst has added categories so Leo can group them geographically, by gender or date of birth, or separate out those who made it through each round of shortlisting. Even with the filters, the list is still overwhelming. Leo would like to know which of these applicants has a criminal record, but the man hours (*person* hours, Leo silently corrects himself) required to check each name against the Police National Computer make it an impossible task. Instead, the analysts have cross-referenced the list against the individuals identified as having made threats against Miles and his crew. There's no match. No disgruntled applicant with an axe to grind.

'Or a shoelace,' Leo says, out loud.

'Hmm?' George looks up. They're in the farmhouse kitchen – now their satellite incident room – which is distinctly less tidy, Leo notes, than when the production team were in charge. At the front of Carreg Plas, additional resources have been brought in to deal with the constant flow of 'murder tourists' who drive up the narrow road – made tighter still by the row of media vans still camped by the gate – to gawp at what they imagine lies behind the fluttering blue and white tape. Earlier, Leo had had to intercept Zee Hart giving what she'd introduced as an 'official statement' to a reporter from the *Evening Standard*.

'But I've got breaking news,' she'd declared, as Leo marched her off the grounds. 'I can rule out Ceri Jones as a murder suspect.'

Leo had stared at her. 'That's not breaking news, that's evidence, and evidence goes to the police, not the media.'

'I *am* the media,' Zee said petulantly.

'Whatever you know, you need to share it with me,' Leo said. 'Now.'

Zee had waited a moment, before reluctantly producing a memory card from her pocket. 'At the time of the murder,' she said, 'Ceri was still in camp.' She'd opened the photo storage on her phone, scrolled to a video and pressed *play*. The picture was grainy – clearly zoomed in from a distance – but Leo could make out Ceri, sitting on a fallen log inside the *Exposure* enclosure, around twenty metres from the fence.

'She was crying,' Zee said. 'Mind you, that wasn't unusual. A few of them came out to the edge of the enclosure to have a good bawl.'

'Did you talk to them?' Leo said.

'Sometimes. That's not a crime, is it?'

'Not as far as I'm aware. What did you talk about?'

'What it was like in there, mostly. You know, for my content. And . . .' Zee gave a sly grin '. . . I played a few games.'

'Like what?' Leo was checking the date and time on the video. Everything checked out.

'I told Aliyah I knew what Ceri's secret was. And she totally fell for it.'

'Why?'

'Because I'm a really good actress. My drama teacher said—'

'No, I mean why did you lie to Aliyah?'

'For the views!' Zee gave a patronising sigh. 'If I knew when someone was going to be chucked out, I could be in the right place at the right time. Anyway, it served her right,' she muttered, 'putting it about like that.' She saw the look on Leo's face. 'What? I was just playing the game, like the rest of them were.'

293

'A game that ended with someone getting murdered,' Leo said. 'Why didn't you show us this video sooner?'

'I've got a lot of footage. Like *a lot*. I basically just film everything, 'cause you never know what you're going to need later. Anyway, Caleb reckons his girlfriend overheard you lot saying Ceri was the murderer, so I figured I'd need some background shots for when she's arrested – like, behind-the-scenes stuff, you know? – and I remembered this. So that alibis her, right?' Zee grinned.

'And you filmed this yourself?' Leo said.

'Obvs.'

'So it alibis you, too.'

'Yeah, but . . .' Zee's mouth had fallen open. 'I wasn't . . . Oh, my God, was I on your suspect list?'

'Everyone's on my suspect list,' Leo said. 'Right, you're coming with me. I want every second of video footage you've got from the day of the murder.'

Over the next hour Leo had gone through the downloaded contents of Zee's photo album, satisfying himself that she'd recorded nothing else of interest, before updating DCI Boccacci that they could eliminate both Ceri Jones and Zee Hart from their enquiries.

'Who does that leave?' the DCI had said. The question was rhetorical.

It left no one. Not a single suspect with the means, motive and opportunity to kill Miles Young.

The final column of Leo's spreadsheet gives the decision made by Young Productions in relation to each applicant. A series of red 'No's blurs before Leo's eyes, as he scrolls mindlessly down the alphabetical list. He almost misses the first green 'Yes', but scrolls

294

back. Aliyah Brown. Leo clicks on the verdict column and sets the filter to find all the successful applicants. Six lines appear on the screen.

Leo counts them. 'George, how many *Exposure* contestants are there?' he asks, even though he knows the answer.

'Seven.'

Leo reads the names to himself. 'That's odd.'

'What is?'

'It's probably nothing,' he says, but his nerve-endings are tingling. Experience tells him that if something looks like a duck and quacks like a duck, it's almost certainly a duck.

'What?' George is out of her seat, reading the names over Leo's shoulder. 'Oh,' she says. 'There's one missing.'

'Miles put seven contestants into the *Exposure* camp.' Leo looks at George. 'But only six of them applied.'

THIRTY-EIGHT

TUESDAY | FFION

Ffion knocks on the door of number four, The Shore. There are thirty wood-clad cabins in the now-sprawling resort, but few with the enviable views of numbers one to five. These flagship cabins, which stood alone for the best part of a year, have decks that stretch over the water, so that standing on the balcony of the master bedroom is like being on the prow of a ship.

Nowadays The Shore boasts a restaurant – the Shore Shack – and a luxury spa called *Shh!* which sends blissed-out berobed clients out to the covered hot tub on its raised platform. The new rows of cabins have been built on a terrace, each row higher than the one in front, so that every bedroom has a view of the lake. Ffion feels the weight of them above her, watching.

Caleb's mother, Clemmie Northcote, opens the door. She's a short, curvy woman with short hair accented with streaks of blue and pink. She smiles broadly at Ffion. '*Bore da, Ffion, sut wyt ti?*'

'*Da iawn, diolch.* Is Caleb in?' Ffion doesn't have time to indulge Clemmie's faltering Welsh beyond the obligatory *how are you*s. 'I need to speak to him urgently.'

'I'll give him a shout. Do you want to come in?'

'Better not.' Ffion looks down at Dave, from whose jaw dangles a thin but impressively long strand of drool.

Caleb is in boxer shorts and a T-shirt, a pillow crease bisecting one cheek. He yawns, treating Ffion to his molars. 'Zee was looking for you.'

'What did she want?'

'She's trying to find a good accountant, I think. I wasn't really listening.'

'What does she think I am, Google?' Ffion shakes her head. 'Look, I haven't got time for this. Where did Miles keep his running kit?'

Caleb screws his eyes tight, opens them wide then blinks rapidly. He yawns again.

Ffion wants to shake him. 'His running kit, Caleb. That yellow jacket he wore. His beanie.'

'Um, in the studio.'

'Are you sure?'

'Yeah. He slept in the house, but he was at the editing desk at, like, six each morning? And he literally didn't come back in till after the show aired.' Caleb's expression hardens. 'He just texted me when he wanted coffee, sandwiches, his arse wiping—'

'What time did he run?'

'Ten.'

'Every morning?' Ffion knows this from Miles's smartwatch, but the pieces of the puzzle aren't fitting together, and she can't work out why.

'Yeah. He'd shower when he got back. Sometimes he'd want a smoothie.'

Ten was when Ffion had seen Miles leave the studio and push the key under the mat. So . . . had the real Miles gone somewhere else, instead of for a run? Or had he still been in the studio and it was someone else she'd seen leaving? Was it some sort of a conspiracy gone wrong? None of it makes sense.

'I need you to watch Dave,' she says.

'I'm allergic.'

'Bullshit.' Ffion presses the lead into his hand.

'Seren wants to talk to you.'

'I know. As soon as this case is over.'

'It's important. It's about uni.'

Ffion locks eyes with Caleb. 'She's going to uni, mate. And if I find out you've persuaded her not to—'

'I'd never do that!'

'I've got to go.' Ffion goes back to her car, ignoring Dave's whimpering.

She leaves her car a hundred metres up the lane from Carreg Plas, and slopes around the outside of the building. She needs to see Miles's studio, but Leo's car is parked on the drive. If he and George are in the kitchen, Ffion can't risk crossing the courtyard. Not when she's been taken off the case.

Her plan was to come at the courtyard from the mountain side, but, as she runs lightly along the trees behind the stables, she sees that the window of number eight – Miles's studio – is slightly ajar. If she climbs through the window, there's even less chance of her being seen. She can lock the door and work undisturbed.

There's movement inside stable number six – the room allocated to Ceri – and Ffion sprints past, then presses herself against the back of Miles's studio until she's certain she hasn't been seen. She slips a hand through the window and pops the latch, opening it wide, then pulls herself on to the ledge and swings her legs inside.

Miles's running shoes are still by the bed, but Ffion can't see the distinctive yellow jacket worn by whoever it was she saw leaving the studio on Sunday morning, or the beanie and sunglasses Miles always ran in. She locks the door, then takes out the key and crouches down, checking part of her theory. The gap under the door is wide enough for the key to pass through easily. When Leo kicked the door in and Ffion saw the key on the floor, she assumed it had been knocked out of the lock, but that wasn't the case. The door had been locked from the *outside*. Whoever Ffion had seen presenting as Miles on Sunday morning hadn't been putting the key under the mat for safekeeping, but pushing it under the door.

Ffion sits at the editing desk and turns on the computer. The files have been copied, but the original footage is still here. Something has been nagging her ever since she watched some of the raw film from the sixth day of *Exposure*. She'd dismissed it as irrelevant, but now everything has changed. If the person presenting as Miles was the murderer, was it possible Miles was already dead? The pathologist could only pinpoint the time of death to within a time frame of a couple of hours, and, since the murder was heard by police officers, that didn't present a problem.

But what if Miles was already dead when the murderer put on the yellow jacket and fled the scene? If Ffion's theory is correct, the alibi range they've been working with – of between 11.15 and 11.45 – is wrong. They'll need to re-interview everyone who was in the courtyard or in the farmhouse. Jason, Pam, Aliyah, Roxy, Owen, Caleb. They'll have to check where Ceri, Lucas and Henry were almost two hours earlier.

Ffion drags her cursor along the screen, trying to trigger the same feeling she'd had the last time she was here – what was it about the footage that hadn't seemed right? She rubs her fingertips across her forehead. It feels like coming to the end of a jigsaw puzzle, only for someone to throw it in the air and then add another hundred pieces for good measure. If Miles was already dead when Ffion saw the impostor, how can Ffion, Leo and George have heard the murder happen, just before 11.45? It doesn't make sense . . .

On the screen, Ceri is talking to Lucas. He's only half listening, a wry smile on his face at something just off screen. Ffion clicks to another camera. The something is Henry, who flailing his arms around, and Ffion finally realises why this didn't feel right the first time she saw it.

A spider dropped on Henry's head.

Ffion thinks back to the first episode of *Exposure*. She thinks about sitting in Mam's cramped lounge with Mam and Seren and Caleb, watching Aliyah run out of the bell tent, shrieking. She remembers her throwaway comment as the contestants were introduced. *Imagine being stuck in camp with an accountant.*

Why would Henry, who chivalrously checked Aliyah's bed for spiders on the first day of *Exposure*, react in such an extreme way to one a few days later?

Ffion turns up the sound.

'Get off me!' Henry shouts.

Ffion catches her breath.

That's why.

He set it up in order to say something he wanted to capture on camera for later.

Get off me.

Ffion fast-forwards, only stopping to listen to the sound when she sees Henry's lips moving. Nothing stands out, so she clicks on the previous day. Fast-forwards again. While she works, she pulls out her pocket notebook and finds the page on which she noted everyone's contact details in the aftermath of the murder. She dials Zee Hart's number.

'Hello?'

'This is DC Morgan. Caleb said you wanted to ask me about an accountant?'

'Not ask you – tell you!' Zee's voice thrums with excitement. 'I wanted to interview all the contestants now they're out of the show, and every time I come near the house I get grief from one of you lot, so—'

'Get to the point, Zee.' Ffion's still scrolling through episodes at warp speed, pausing every time Henry's in the frame. Henry in the shower, singing to himself. Henry chatting with Ceri over breakfast.

'I thought, I'll try another way. So, like, for Jason, I left a message at the fire station, and I knew Henry was an accountant, and they have to be, like, registered, don't they? So I googled him but—'

'You didn't find an accountant called Henry Moore.' Ffion presses play on another clip of Henry, who is watching Lucas search for something in the men's tent.

'Oh, I found one. He's got a LinkedIn account. But his photo looks nothing like the guy from *Exposure*.'

'Thanks, Zee. That's really helpful.'

'Oh, you're welcome! I think it's great when the media and the police work together, so if you want any—'

Ffion ends the call.

'You just want a quiet life, then?' Henry is saying on screen.

'That would be nice,' Lucas says. 'Have you seen my socks? They're hot pink and they have a small hole on one heel.'

'Sorry, mate.'

Ffion's about to fast-forward again when Henry's tone changes.

301

He becomes defensive, even though Lucas has barely raised his voice.

'Are you threatening me?' Henry says, then he drops the angry man pretence and bursts into laughter. 'Chill! I haven't got your socks, mate.'

Are you threatening me? Get off me!

Ffion feels the heady sense of euphoria that comes with a breakthrough. She could stop now – she has enough; almost enough – but she wants Henry to know he isn't as clever as he thinks he is. She wants the missing piece of the script.

She finds it on the fourth day of filming, when Pam picks up a tea-towel to help Henry with the washing-up, only for him to round on her. 'What are you doing? Put that down!'

What are you doing? Are you threatening me? Get off me!

Ffion plays the third clip again, turning the volume up high. As Henry flails at his imaginary spider, his shouts are deafening in the small space. 'Get off me!'

Ffion feels exhausted and exhilarated all at once, as though she's run a marathon. They weren't hearing Miles being murdered at all. They were hearing a reconstruction. Miles was already dead, his attacker long gone, off to put the finishing touches to his alibi.

She navigates to footage she's already watched, of Henry in the confession pod, at what they'd all thought was the time of the murder. No wonder he'd stayed there so long, she thinks, revolted by the self-deprecating look on his face. Every few seconds, his eyes flick to one side. Because he's lying? She pauses the footage. She remembers seeing him make an earlier visit to the confession pod, and she clicks back to eleven a.m. and then forward, minute by minute, until she sees the door to the pod open. The first time she'd seen this, she assumed Henry was about to launch into another introspective monologue, but now she sees that he doesn't sit down at all. He steps in for just a moment, and his eyes flick back to that spot on the wall.

Ffion has a feeling she knows exactly what he's looking at, and, once she's confirmed it, she can present the others with the final piece in the puzzle they were beginning to think was unsolveable. She sets off up Pen y Ddraig, leaving the studio door wide open.

THIRTY-NINE

HENRY | DAY SEVEN OF *EXPOSURE*

The secret to being undercover, Henry has found, is to be as boring as possible. No shade on accountants, but you don't seek them out at parties, do you? Not unless you want advice on your tax return. Over his fifteen years working as an investigative journalist, Henry (whose name is actually Clive) has used his accountant cover story more often than any of his others. He has travelled across the world in pursuit of the truth, sometimes for anonymous tell-alls in the Sunday papers; sometimes at the behest of some big corporation, acting on whistleblower intelligence.

The funny thing about secrets is that one invariably leads to another. Sent to investigate allegations of modern slavery in a cigarette factory, Henry stumbled upon a drugs ring. A few months later, as he was writing an exposé on counterfeit watches, he discovered that the CEO had a predilection for dogging. It had no bearing on the article, but it fuelled Henry's lucrative sideline in opportunistic blackmail. It no longer surprises Henry when he comes across these dirty little second lives. Everyone has a secret. Everyone is playing their own game.

He met Miles at an award ceremony, where a documentary to which Henry had contributed was up for a gong. Henry, who was usually discreet about his involvement, had a few drinks too many and boasted to Miles of his unrivalled research skills. 'I can find out anything about anyone.'

'Is that right?' A slow smile spread across Miles's face. 'How would you feel about collaborating on a concept I've been working on?'

They developed *Exposure* over the next twelve months, before Miles advertised for contestants. He gave Henry a list of shortlisted applicants and charged him with digging up the dirt. 'Hopefully at least six of these have something to hide.'

Henry was blasé about it. 'Everyone has something to hide.'

'I don't.'

'Sure about that?' Henry had done a little research of his own; he knew about Miles's fondness for recreational drugs. He held Miles's gaze until the producer looked away.

There was dirt aplenty among the applicants, as it turned out. Miles rejected any who seemed as though they wouldn't care enough about protecting their privacy. 'It isn't just about how big the secret is,' he reminded Henry. 'It's about how much they want to keep it. It's about the consequences of that secret getting out.'

Slowly, Miles chose his favourites, while trying to maintain the right balance of contestants. 'This one'll have to go,' he said, plucking a photo from the line of images on the table in front of them. 'He's too old.'

'He's the same age as Pam.'

'Yes, but she's there for comedy value – I mean, look at her. This guy's too basic.' Miles flipped over the photo to read the back, reminding himself of the man's dirty little secret. 'Imagine how relieved he'll be when the show airs and he realises he escaped a #MeToo take-down.'

'Bloody feminists,' Henry said, with uncharacteristic bitterness.

'You too, huh?' Miles fist-bumped him. 'Solidarity, mate.

They're all keen enough when you're paying for drinks, right? Then suddenly it's all *but consent isn't consent unless it's signed in triplicate.'*

'Exactly!' Henry shuddered. 'Christ, I've had a few like that over the years.' He picked up the photo of the rejected applicant and dropped it in the bin. 'Consider yourself saved by the brotherhood, mate.'

They were both satisfied with the final line-up of six contestants. Each had a different type of secret, and each seemed likely to react differently to the threat of exposure. Although *Exposure* was reality television and supposedly unscripted, Miles had clear storylines in mind, setting out storyboards well in advance of filming. There would be the Declaration of Friendship and the subsequent Betrayal. The obligatory shot of a hot girl (Aliyah) in a bikini. Every scene was anticipated, the contestants' behaviour steered to suit Miles's narrative.

'So we're agreed on Jason as the first exposure?' Henry said, as they planned the order of events.

Miles nodded. 'Bigamy's huge. As soon as we come off air, I'll get that anonymous tip-off into the papers with the location of the first wife.'

Unable to trust a member of Miles's production team not to leak *Exposure*'s dynamite twist, Miles trained Henry on the editing software. In the weeks leading up to filming, Henry and Miles set up templates and graphics, ensuring Miles would be able to drop in the footage he wanted on the day.

'You're a fast learner,' Miles said approvingly, when he came back from his morning run and saw the framework Henry had created for the first exposure. There would be a close-up of someone crying (someone always cried) then a cutaway to Roxy, then a pre-recorded shot of an axe hitting wood, before cutting back to the contestants. 'I'm almost disappointed you can't stay and help me put it together once we're live.'

'Why can't I?' Henry said.

Miles's face broke into a slow smile. 'Because you're going into camp.' He held up a hand before Henry could say anything. 'Think about it: even if I control the exposures so that only one contestant stays in the show till the end, I've still got to pay out a hundred grand. Meanwhile, you're earning a few thousand.' He grinned. 'But if you go into *Exposure* as a contestant, knowing all their secrets, you can make sure things go the way we want, and I can make sure you win. Even if someone goes into the confession pod and doesn't crack, you can expose them later and they'll be gone. I won't have to pay out the full hundred grand, and you'll take home . . . let's say forty thousand quid.'

Henry was reeling, but forty grand was forty grand. He was used to changing his appearance; he could dye his fair hair brown, wear blue contacts. 'Eighty grand,' he said.

'Fifty.'

'Seventy.'

'Sixty,' Miles said. 'Final offer.'

They shook on it.

Henry should have known not to trust him.

At the end of the third day of filming, after Henry had, as arranged, accused Jason of bigamy, Henry flicked through the envelopes in the box of secrets, drawing out the final few seconds before handing Jason's envelope to Roxy.

And then he saw it.

His own name.

He wanted to believe it was empty, a prop included to avoid suspicion, but through the envelope Henry could see the faint outline of printed letters. He battled to keep his composure, knowing the cameras were on him.

'*Jason is a bigamist*,' Roxy read.

Henry's mind was turning somersaults. What was in that envelope?

On Sunday morning, Henry wriggled through the hole under the fence Ryan had made, which Dario had made a pathetic attempt to fill in. He jogged down towards Carreg Plas. He had laid his trail carefully, burying the key phrases he would need in nonsense about tea-towels, lost socks and spiders. He smiled at the thought of Miles listening to what would become his own murder soundtrack.

He crouched beneath the window to Miles's studio and removed a shoelace from his trainer, before slipping Lucas's stolen socks on to his hands to act as gloves, then knocking on the window. Inside, Miles looked round. Confusion turned quickly to alarm, and he practically leapt across the room to open the window.

'What are you doing? You'll be seen.'

'I was careful.' Henry climbed inside. 'The others will think I'm collecting firewood. How's it all going?'

'Good.' Miles looked a little wary – perhaps expecting Henry to have a go at him about the envelope – but, as Henry enthused about how ground-breaking *Exposure* was, Miles relaxed.

'Come and see what we're going to lead with tonight.' He returned to the desk and pulled up a clip so Henry could look over his shoulder.

Henry wrapped the shoelace around both hands.

He took no pleasure in killing Miles. It was a necessary evil – self-defence, if you will – and then, with no time to lose, he set about building his alibi. He searched for his carefully performed voice clips and edited them together, before raising the pitch a notch, to match Miles's voice, which was reedier than Henry's. Miles had shown him how he liked to do this when women were arguing on screen, presenting them as hysterical and unreasonable. Ahead of the voice clip, Henry added an hour of silence followed by thirty minutes of general clips at a lower sound level – sufficient time so that by the time the 'murder' played, Henry would be installed in the confession pod.

He had worried the key might be hidden – that he would spend precious minutes searching for it. The longer the gap between Miles's real murder and the staged one, the more likely it would be that a pathologist would query the time of death. But the key to the box of secrets was in Miles's pocket, and was swiftly transferred to Henry's.

Henry loaded the video clip on to the secondary system and pressed *play*. He re-laced his trainer, then pulled on Miles's fluorescent running jacket along with his beanie and sunglasses. Lucas's socks were tucked away in his pocket now, and Henry covered his hand with his sleeve to open the door, his heart beating furiously as he turned to lock it behind him.

As he was pushing the key under the door, a woman called Miles's name, and Henry felt a dart of fear. He didn't look to see who it was, but sprinted out of the courtyard and on to the mountain.

The next few minutes were agony. Was the woman suspicious? Did she knock on Miles's door? Henry imagined the alarm being raised, police swarming over the mountain. And where would Henry be? Alone on the hills, wearing Miles's clothes, with no alibi.

But as Henry grew closer to the *Exposure* enclosure, he heard no sirens. He took off Miles's jacket and pushed it deep into a rabbit hole with the glasses, socks and hat. He squeezed back under the fence and patted down the earth to replicate the pathetic repair job Dario had done.

'What have you been up to?' Lucas said, when Henry mooched into camp.

'Having a kip.' Henry glanced at the cameras. 'I can't sleep properly in the tent, can you? Knowing we're on TV, imagining what the voiceover guy's saying about us.'

Lucas gave a hollow laugh. 'I've slept in worse places.'

'I went for a wander and sat back against that big oak – you know the one – and promptly nodded off. Must have been even more knackered than I thought. Do you fancy a coffee?' Henry walked towards the fire, in case his racing pulse was somehow visible. He threw on a handful of kindling, hesitated, then gathered the remaining pile of sticks and added them all to the flames.

'Tea for me, if you're making!' Ceri emerged from the women's sleeping tent.

'You've got the hearing of a bat,' Henry said.

Ceri grinned. 'Only when there's a *paned* in the offing.'

As the kettle boiled, Henry's heart rate returned to normal, and a slow smile spread across his face. Phase one of his plan was complete.

Now, Henry hears Miles's shouts – Henry's *own* shouts – ring out across the courtyard, and he knows with a sinking dread exactly what has happened. His voice clips have been discovered. Someone has worked out how Henry pulled off what he'd thought was the perfect crime.

He looks outside, expecting to see dozens of police, but there is only Detective Constable Morgan, leaving Miles's studio and setting off at a run towards the camp. Is it possible, he thinks, with a desperate spark of hope, that DC Morgan is the only one who knows that Henry killed Miles?

Henry doesn't hesitate.

He follows her.

PART THREE

FORTY

TUESDAY | LEO

'What was that?' Leo looks at George, who is already pushing back her chair.

'It sounded like . . .' Her words tail off, ending in a self-conscious laugh.

'Like Miles being attacked.' Leo shakes his head. 'Which obviously it can't be.' They run out to the courtyard, where the stable doors are opening and people are spilling into the courtyard. Leo sees Ceri, Jason, Pam . . . it's as though they've been plunged into a reconstruction of Miles's murder, and for a single insane moment Leo wonders if they've all imagined it: some kind of collective delirium brought on by long days and lack of sleep.

'Who was that?' Pam says, looking at Leo.

'Is it happening again?' Aliyah has wet hair; one eye made-up and the other bare. 'Has there been another murder?' Her voice rises and her panic spreads through the others like fire. 'Is everyone okay?'

'Miles's studio door is open,' George says. Suddenly, she starts herding everyone to the opposite side of the courtyard. 'Get back! Everyone stay back!' She draws her baton and Leo does the same, and the two of them approach the converted stable from opposite sides, their focus switching between the open door and each other.

'Police!' George shouts, when they're a few strides away, but from the angle Leo is approaching he can see into the studio. There's no one there.

'Could Miles have somehow recorded his own murder?' George says, once they have searched the tiny room – in the shower room, under the bed – and established it is indeed empty. 'And the system had some kind of a glitch and played it?'

'Have you seen Ffion?' comes a voice through the open door.

'You were told to stay—' Leo stops when he sees Caleb standing there. He has Dave with him, straining at the lead. 'What are you doing here?'

'Looking for Ffion, so I can get rid of *this*.' Caleb holds the end of the lead away from his body, as though Dave is radioactive. 'She didn't say how long she'd be, and the dog won't stop whining for her.'

'She's working from home today,' Leo says shortly. DCI Boccacci had emailed this morning to say that Ffion had been replaced by Alun Whitaker, who would join the DCI in the incident room. The tone of her email didn't invite further questions.

'No, she's not.'

'I assure you she—'

'Then why did she need me to watch Dave?'

It's a fair comment. Leo feels a familiar sense of trepidation in the pit of his stomach. Surely Ffion wouldn't go rogue again, so soon after what she did with Ceri's envelope?

Caleb is still talking. '. . . and Ceri said she saw her just now.'

'What?' Caleb has Leo's full attention now.

'Ceri's room is number six.' Caleb points to the stable two down from where they're standing. 'She says Ffion ran past her window not long before the shouting. She was worried something had happened to her, but Pam pointed out it was a man's voice shouting, so—'

Leo and George exchange glances.

'Miles must have somehow hit record when he was attacked,' George says. 'It's the only explanation. Ffion must have found the recording and played it.'

'Then where is she?' Leo says. He pulls out the chair from under Miles's desk and motions for Caleb to take the other. 'Since you're here, you can make yourself useful and show me how to use this.'

For a work experience lad, Caleb certainly knows his way around, Leo thinks.

'This is from Saturday.' Caleb points to the date stamp in the corner. 'And that reference in the bottom left tells us it's raw footage. It's whatever was streamed from camera three on day six of *Exposure*, before any editing was done.'

'Why would Ffion be watching that?' George says. 'It's a blank screen – there's nothing there.'

'Not now,' Caleb says. He toggles swiftly to an activity menu, scanning the times there. 'Someone pressed *play* on this section of footage eleven minutes ago.'

'Can you take the footage back eleven minutes?' Leo says, but Caleb's already on it, and now they're watching Henry windmilling his arms in an attempt to brush off a spider.

'Get off me!' Henry's yell is followed by a series of anguished cries.

'Imagine being that scared of a spider,' Caleb says. 'I'd be mortified if everyone saw me screaming like a girl just because—'

But Leo and George are no longer listening to him. They're

staring at each other in horror, as the implications of what they've just seen sink in. Henry. The only contestant who never applied to be on the show. A plant. A fake.

A murderer.

FORTY-ONE

TUESDAY | FFION

It's no more than a mile from Carreg Plas to camp, but it's all uphill and Ffion's out of breath as she reaches the enclosure. Dammit, maybe she really should give up smoking. Not right away, though, otherwise Huw will think she's taking his advice.

The door to the confession pod closes behind her as she steps down into its depths and slides into the throne-like seat. The space is even smaller than it looks on screen and the chair is narrow despite its high back and arms. It's dark, the only sources of light a sliver of sun coming through the narrow band of glass right at the top, and a red glow coming from one side of the now defunct camera.

A digital clock.

Ffion grins. Being right never gets old. Henry had looked into the pod to check the time, then clearly decided it was too early. He'd come back later for his mammoth session, giving himself the perfect alibi.

Or so he'd thought.

Suddenly cold after her burst of energy, Ffion shivers as she remembers the rats swarming over Pam, the snakes that writhed around Lucas's neck. Cold sweat prickles across the small of her back.

Ffion should call this in. Notify DCI Boccacci or DI Malik, or at least let Leo and George know what she's discovered.

Only, she isn't going to.

Fuck Malik, for taking her off the job. Fuck Leo, for grassing her up to the boss. And fuck George, for . . . Ffion feels for the door handle in the dark, grappling for a reason to hate her erstwhile partner. Fuck George, for . . . *working with Leo when you're not*, finishes the voice in her head.

No, she's not going to tell anyone what she's worked out. She'll run back to the farmhouse – easier on the return journey – and arrest Henry, and once he's safely in handcuffs she'll casually call up and fill in the rest of the team.

Except it seems she can't do that.

Because the confession pod door won't open.

Ffion is locked in.

FORTY-TWO

TUESDAY | LEO

'I don't get it.' Caleb looks to Leo for an explanation. 'How can it be Henry? He was in the confession pod when Miles was murdered.'

But Leo's heading for the courtyard, where pockets of people cluster nervously.

'Is anyone hurt?' Aliyah says.

Pam's eyes are shrewd. 'It's a recording, isn't it?'

'Was Miles's death fake?' Ceri looks at the others. 'Is he still alive?'

Jason gives a humourless laugh. 'He won't stay that way for long, if he is.'

Aliyah gasps. 'Is this all part of the show? Are we still being filmed?' She looks at Owen, but he's not holding a camera.

'Officer.' Lucas steps forward. 'Will someone please tell us what's going on?'

Leo ignores them all. 'Where's Henry?'

Everyone looks around.

'He's in the room next to mine,' Pam offers. 'But I haven't seen him.'

Aliyah cries out again. 'Has Henry been murdered?'

Leo doesn't answer. He reaches Henry's door in six long strides and, for the second time in a week, kicks open a stable door.

It's empty.

Henry's gone.

FORTY-THREE

TUESDAY | FFION

Ffion's chest is tight. She forces herself to slow her breathing. It's claustrophobia, that's all; there's plenty of air. Plenty, she tells herself, over and over, because her body doesn't seem to be getting the message. It's hammering her heart and squeezing her throat shut so she has to drag each shallow breath past the blockage.

She tries the door again. She thinks back to watching the contestants enter the confession pod and she doesn't recall seeing a lock, so the door must have jammed somehow; perhaps a log fell across the door or a clump of earth or . . . On and on Ffion runs with this stream of thoughts, because that way she doesn't have to face up to what she knows is the truth.

Henry has trapped her.

'Hey!' Ffion shouts.

Was that a sound she just heard? A rustle, like an animal in the trees. Like a hunter, watching his prey.

Why has he shut her in here? Perhaps he's just buying himself time to make his escape, in which case she just has to sit tight and wait. And it might be a while, and she'll have to keep telling herself that tightness in her chest is panic, not a heart attack, but eventually, they'll find her.

Or does Henry have other plans for her? Now that he has her trapped, does he plan to silence her?

In which case, Ffion needs to get out. Fast. She takes out her phone and dials 999, ignoring the lack of signal, hoping that somehow the call will get through. Even if the operator can't hear her, if the call connects they can trace the number, they'll know it's Ffion and—

The call fails. She tries again and again, but it's no good.

She looks at the narrow band of glass that runs around the top of the pod. It's too high to reach, but if she climbs on to the back of the chair . . . She looks around for something she can use to break the glass, but there's nothing. Even the camera is just a lens, embedded in the smooth walls. She climbs anyway, taking a second to weigh up the usefulness of her phone, before smashing it against the glass. The phone shatters instantly, but the band of toughened glass doesn't so much as chip.

What was that noise?

A whirring – no, more mechanical, like someone turning a handle. Ffion jumps off the chair and looks around for the source of the noise. She catches something out of the corner of her eye and turns to see a piece of wall moving. The section is circular, about the size of a fist.

The size of a drain, Ffion sees now, as the circle completes its hundred-and eighty-degree turn to reveal a black pipe. That's where they came from, she realises: the spiders, the rats, the snakes. Poured in, tumbling over each other and falling into the dark, coffin-like room. Forcing confessions.

Ffion backs into the corner furthest away from the pipe. Pointless, of course, because whatever Henry is about to inflict on her won't confine itself to the opposite side, but it's giving her space, it's giving her time in which to compose herself.

And Ffion can handle this. She's not frightened of spiders, and granted, she'd prefer not to be covered in rats, but it's all about mental strength, right? She breathes deeply – *in, out, in, out* – and tries to remember the contestants' discussion about their phobias.

I hate spiders, Aliyah had said, and sure enough she'd been faced with them when her turn in the confession pod came. Pam was rats; Lucas was snakes . . .

What were the others?

There's a sound from the pipe. A creak of the plastic, a low rushing as the momentum gathers. And Ffion remembers.

What are you scared of? Aliyah had asked Henry, at the start of the show.

Me? he'd replied. *Water. I almost drowned when I was a kid.* Water.

It rushes into the confession pod like a pipe just burst, hitting the wall on the opposite side, spraying Ffion from head to foot, covering the floor within seconds. In the tiny metal box the sound is magnified, as though she's standing by a waterfall, a roaring in her ears. In the seconds it takes to shake herself into action – although what action can she take? she thinks, as she hammers in vain at the door – it covers her boots.

And still it comes.

FORTY-FOUR

TUESDAY | LEO

There will be questions later, Leo knows, but for now he's grateful for DCI Boccacci's brisk acceptance of this turn of events.

'Helicopter's on its way,' she tells him. 'The dog unit's committed but they'll make their way over as soon as they come free.'

A second after she ends the call, Leo's phone rings again. Caleb has tied Dave up, and the dog is howling worse than ever, the lead pulled so taut it looks as if it might snap. Leo moves away from the noise.

'I've got a team of six going up Pen y Ddraig now,' Huw says. 'We'll hold off if we get a sighting on Henry, given the risk assessment, but it'll give you more eyes on the ground.'

'Thanks, Huw.' There's silence on the other end of the phone and Leo wonders why Huw called him. He should have had all the information he needs from the dispatcher who requested search-and-rescue support. 'If you've got any questions,' Leo says, 'just give me a shout.'

Huw clears his throat. 'Control Room said Ffion's gone after him.'

'It looks that way.' Or it's the other way around, Leo thinks, but doesn't share.

Another pause. 'It's times like this when I'm glad I'm no longer married to her.' Huw laughs, but it sounds forced.

'Ffion's a front-line officer,' Leo says, surprised by his sudden urge to defend her. 'She's committed.' The sound of Ffion's name prompts a torrent of barks from Dave, followed by a mournful howl.

'She bloody should be.' Beneath the poor joke, there's a crack in Huw's voice.

Leo takes a moment. 'We'll find her,' he says. He ends the call and puts his phone in his pocket, his gaze fixed on the ground.

There's a light tap on his shoulder. 'You okay?' George says.

'Fine.' Leo doesn't mean to sound so snappy. He softens it. 'Thanks.'

'The dog's going nuts.'

'So I see.'

'He's desperate to be with Ffion.'

'Look, I don't mean to be heartless, but I don't have the band-width to worry about a distraught dog when one of our officers is missing.'

'No, listen to what I'm saying. He wants to find Ffion.'

'We all want—'

George cuts him off. 'So why don't we let him?'

FORTY-FIVE

TUESDAY | HENRY

As Henry makes his way out of the *Exposure* encampment, the detective's shouts become more frantic. When she first rattled the door – pointless, given the weight of the log Henry had rolled across it – she had sounded more angry than scared, but now he hears a note of hysteria in her voice.

Good. The woman's messed everything up.

When Henry had returned to camp after killing Miles, it had proved impossible to open the box of secrets. He had made coffee and given Ceri her tea, and all the time his mind had been racing. Could he drop his fleece over the box and swiftly turn the lock as he retrieved it? Repeat the manoeuvre a short while later, but, this time, remove his envelope?

No, it was too dangerous. He'd worked hard to make it look as though he was nowhere near the crime scene. He couldn't now risk attracting suspicion by behaving oddly in camp, when the police were bound to look at the footage to establish where everyone was at the time of the murder.

So Henry had proceeded to phase two of his plan.

It was hard to keep track of time in your head; all the contestants had discovered that. Henry had finished his coffee and was

328

forcing himself to concentrate on what Lucas and Ceri were talking about, all the time mentally calculating how many minutes had passed. He had walked casually to the compost toilet, then ducked into the confession pod, where the red blinking digits told him it was precisely 11.18 a.m. Henry had let out a long, steadying breath. It was almost time.

He was reluctant to stay by the campfire. He and the other contestants had watched from their bell tents on Friday as the damaged cameras were replaced, but what if the new ones had a different field of view? What if Henry's meticulously executed alibi came to nothing, simply because a camera had been moved a few millimetres to the right? No, the only safe place was here in the confession pod, where the camera was fixed on the seat in front of it.

But first – Henry looked again at the clock – there was time to cast a little suspicion of his own. He returned to the others, still sitting where he'd left them, and glanced towards the fire. 'Who's on kindling duty?' he said, knowing full well it was Ceri. They'd divided the chores three ways: Lucas cooked, Henry collected the heavier logs and Ceri filled a basket with tinder-dry twigs. No one had cleaned the loo since Pam had left.

'Me. But I collected loads yesterday; it'll last till tomorrow at least.'

'There's none there now,' Henry said.

'Oh, bloody hell, you two.' Ceri continued grumbling as she grabbed the basket and headed into the woods, and Henry made his way back to the confession pod. There, he launched into a long and rambling overview of his life to date, and the way he planned to live it in the future. Every few seconds, he checked the time. At the precise moment Miles was being 'murdered', Henry was feigning a coughing fit in order to suppress a sudden urge to laugh. He'd done it. He'd committed the perfect murder.

Afterwards, Henry's confidence had grown as hours went by without anyone arriving to slap him in cuffs. Even as the detectives took the three remaining contestants down the mountain, it was obvious they had all but been ruled out as suspects.

The only fly in the ointment had been not retrieving his envelope. In the forty-eight hours following the murder, the mountain had been swarming with police, and there had been no opportunity for Henry to return to camp. Now, of course, the box was gone – the key in his pocket completely useless. He had resolved to hold his nerve and hide in plain sight. He would be identified as Miles's murderer at some point, but he has worked on enough investigative stories to know how slowly the police cogs turn. He gambled on it being days – maybe even weeks – before some IT geek happened upon the doctored sound clip. Longer still before anyone worked out what it meant. By that time, Henry planned to have melted away, assuming one of the many identities under which he works. In the meantime, he has been a model witness; helpful, compliant and unremarkable.

But he can't stick around now. The other detectives will be looking for DC Morgan and, eventually, they'll come up to the camp and they'll find her.

Drowned.

Henry shivers. His phobia of water was one of the few truths he shared with his fellow contestants, caught off guard by Aliyah's own fear, and by his own creeping sense of unease. Miles knew Henry had a weakness.

'I was crabbing from the pier,' he'd told Miles over dinner. They'd been talking about holidays – Miles's grandparents had

330

had a house in Abersoch – and Henry was explaining why he only ever vacations inland. 'I leaned too far forward and . . .' He made a dive motion with his hand, feeling – as he always did – the same clutch of terror in his stomach at the memory.

'Great!' Miles's eyes lit up. 'We can use that as your fear – it'll add a bit of authenticity.'

Henry stared at him. 'I'm not going in the confession pod, though; we don't need—'

'Relax – I'm just setting it up, that's all. I can't have the crew wondering why we've only prepped for six confessions, can I?'

A voice in Henry's head had told him he should be careful; that Miles wasn't to be trusted.

If only he'd listened to it.

Henry pauses outside the *Exposure* camp, deciding on his next move. He can't take the same route back down, not when Carreg Plas could be swarming with cops. He heads up, towards the summit. He'll go up a little further, then look for a path down on the eastern side of the mountain.

A few minutes later, Henry rounds a bend and sees a woman coming towards him. He looks for an escape route, but then he sees she has trekking poles and stout boots, a map tucked into the side of her rucksack. He carries on walking, his eyes fixed on the ground.

'Lovely day for it,' the woman says, as she draws near.

'Sure is,' Henry says, just as a faint scream drifts towards them.

'Did you hear that?' The woman stops walking. 'I thought I heard someone screaming earlier, and now—'

'They're filming.' Henry points, which has the added benefit of making the woman look towards camp, instead of at Henry's face. 'I saw a camera crew just now.'

'Ah, that's alright, then. Mind how you go – it's a little loose on the final ascent.'

'Thanks.' Henry keeps walking, fighting the urge to look back to see if the woman's looking at him, if she's pulled out a mobile phone. As soon as he's far enough away from her, he breaks into a jog.

It was on the second day of filming that Henry began to feel unsettled. He had successfully positioned himself as a good-natured, easygoing guy. Confident yet not alpha-male; supportive of the ladies but not sleazy (Miles was reserving that particular role for Jason, and would be shaping the edits accordingly). Henry almost began to relax. This was going to be the easiest sixty grand he'd ever earned.

'I'm so scared,' Aliyah said. They were all searching for Ryan, walking around the enclosure, calling his name.

'I'm sure the confession pod won't be as bad as you think.' Henry knew it would be worse – he'd seen the crates of spiders being shipped in. All different sizes, from furry fat-legged tarantulas to quick-paced gossamer-thin creatures capable of crossing a room in a heartbeat.

'It's not just that, it's not knowing who to trust.' Aliyah looked at Henry. 'I can trust you, of course—'

'Hundred per cent.'

'—but do you think there's something creepy about Lucas?'

'But he's a vicar,' Henry said.

'Exactly.' Aliyah stopped walking and lowered her voice, even though there were no cameras around. 'I overheard Roxy telling Owen there was a #MeToo contestant.'

'A what?' Henry feigned ignorance to buy himself time. He knew the other six secrets in that box, and none of them related

332

to the #MeToo movement. While he'd been researching the other contestants, had Miles been researching Henry?

'You know, like a predator.'

What had Miles found out? Henry wasn't sure what to do. If he dismissed Aliyah's concerns, would that throw her off the scent or make her more suspicious?

'Now that you mention it,' he said, deciding it was safer to throw someone else under a bus then risk falling himself, 'Lucas does have that look about him.' He turned concerned eyes on Aliyah. 'Be careful around him, won't you?'

She nodded, then threw her arms around Henry. 'Thanks for the chat. You're one of the good ones, you know?'

The following day, after the live segment had finished, Henry went to speak to Owen, who was packing away his camera.

'Is he okay?' Henry gestured towards a furious Jason, who was being escorted out of camp by Dario.

'I can't talk to you once we've finished shooting,' Owen said immediately. 'You know the rules.'

'I'm just concerned, that's—'

'Look, mate, Miles has clearly stated you're to have no communication from the outside world.' Owen heaved his bag on to his shoulder. 'And I don't blame him. I wouldn't want to lose five million quid either.'

'Five million quid?' Henry followed him.

'In sponsorship.' Owen flapped his arms as though Henry were a cat. 'Scram – you can get binned if you want, but I'm not risking my job by fraternising with contestants.'

Henry stared after him. Miles had never mentioned a five-million-pound sponsorship deal. The show was being filmed on a budget – *the concept will carry it*, had been the arrogant declaration – and although Miles had told Henry he'd secured financial backing, he'd given him the impression the numbers barely added up. 'It'll just about keep the wolf from the door,' he had said. Five million? That was one hungry wolf.

Meanwhile, Henry was the one risking his reputation for a measly sixty grand.

On day four of filming, Henry waited by the perimeter fence. He knew Miles's running route – had joined him for a couple of runs while they were working together – and he knew how the producer liked to adhere to a regime. Sure enough, at ten-fifteen, Henry saw a flash of fluorescent.

'Miles!'

The producer slowed his pace. He glanced at Henry and did a double-take, looking around before cautiously approaching the fence. 'What are you doing? We can't be seen together.'

'Why does Roxy think there's a #MeToo predator on the show?' Henry was wasting no time.

Miles blinked. 'I don't know.'

'Look into my eyes and tell me you're not going to fuck me over.'

'What are you talking about? We're a team.'

'The sort of team that shares the five million you're getting in sponsorship?'

'Production costs are escalating and—'

'Bullshit. I want more money.'

'We agreed sixty.'

'I want more.'

'I haven't got more.'

'Bullshit! You put an envelope with my name on it in the box of secrets.'

'So no one gets suspicious – mate, you're behaving most oddly.'

'What does the card say?'

'That you're a secret alcoholic, as we agreed,' Miles said, but his gaze slid away. He was lying. 'But that's irrelevant, because you're not going to be exposed. You'll be the last man standing. The winner of a cool hundred—' Miles corrected himself, '—sixty thousand pounds.'

'I want half a million.'

'That's not possible.'

'Half a million, or I expose this whole—'

Miles's hand shot out, darting through the wire fence and twisting the neck of Henry's sweater. His knuckles pressed into Henry's windpipe, sending the edges of Henry's vision black. 'Do you think I don't know your own secrets? Do you think I can't carry out a little investigative work of my own?' He gripped harder and pushed his fist sharply into Henry's neck. 'Stick to the agreement.'

Miles released Henry's fleece and turned, sprinting back into the woods. Henry put his hands to his throat, gulping in air. Miles was playing a dangerous game, but he'd underestimated his opponent.

Henry had led a life which might charitably be referred to as 'colourful'. He had a history of dubious journalistic methods, often involving young, vulnerable women already embroiled in the seedier side of life. Had Miles uncovered some of these murky moments? Impossible. But it was clear Miles had something, and now Henry would have to take action.

It took Henry several days to execute his plan, knowing that – at any moment – Miles might decide to expose him. Would Miles send him to the confession pod? Or perhaps he would feed information to another contestant, the way he had agreed he would do with Henry.

The group tasks proceeded as Henry and Miles had rehearsed, and Henry breathed a sigh of relief each time he realised he hadn't been double-crossed a second time. The first, just a few hours after their conversation, was the ridiculous lie detector test Miles had concocted, and despite his concerns he couldn't help being amused at the way he 'passed'. 'My name's Henry, I have brown hair and blue eyes,' he'd given as his three 'control truths', before the interrogation began. It didn't occur to any of his competitors that all three statements might themselves be lies.

None of them suspected him. Not the contestants, not the police. Until now.

Henry can't hear the detective's screams any more. Has he run too far to hear it? Or has enough water flooded in to fill that tiny room? Is she even now floating underwater, fingertips bloodied from clawing at the door, hair tangled around her staring eyes?

Henry smiles and keeps running.

FORTY-SIX

TUESDAY | FFION

Ffion can't hear the water coming in now. She can only feel it, swirling around the chair on which she has climbed to escape the rising flood. Only there's nowhere to go. Despite the extra height, the water is at her chest, the cold pressing her tight till her lungs are too small to take anything but small, panicked breaths. She stamps her feet up and down, keeping the blood flowing to her toes, which are so cold she can no longer feel them.

The door will not give. The confession pod is lined with something smooth, on which Ffion's raw and stinging fingers can't get a purchase. There is no escape.

Earlier, when the water was a metre or so deep, she'd tried to stem the flow of water. She'd taken off her jumper and rolled it into a tight ball, wadding it into the pipe. It had held for a while, but then the force of the water had propelled it out. Now, Ffion shivers in her wet clothes. She's going to drown.

When Ffion was five, Mam taught her to swim. With the lake just minutes from their house, it was non-negotiable; Ffion wasn't allowed near the water until she could swim a hundred metres without floats.

'*Mae dûr yn beryglys*,' Mam reminded her constantly. *Water is dangerous.*

Ffion chokes back a sob. Years later, it was Ffion who gave lessons in the lake, teaching a stubborn Seren first to float, then to swim. Is it really possible she won't see Seren again? She might be seventeen, but Ffion's only just begun to be her mother – surely life can't be so unfair as to separate them now?

The water is up to her chest. Ffion stretches her arms to the ceiling, desperately reaching for something – anything – she can hold on to. She loses her balance and tips forward, and, when she moves her foot to correct herself, she steps into nothing.

The water is ice cold. It pulls Ffion down and suddenly she's on the floor of the confession pod, water swirling violently around her. She opens her eyes, sees the maelstrom of bubbles around the inlet pipe, water gushing relentlessly into the room, roaring in her ears. She scrabbles at the chair, tries to pull herself up, but the force of the water throws her aside and for a second she's not sure which way is up. She wants to breathe out – the smallest of breaths, just to ease the pressure in her chest – but it escapes in a single, violent stream of precious air which shoots to a surface Ffion can't even see because her vision is blurred and her limbs aren't working and this is it, she thinks. This is how it ends.

FORTY-SEVEN

TUESDAY | LEO

What Dave lacks in speed and grace, he makes up for with sheer determination. Leo has never really thought about where the word 'dogged' comes from, but as he watches Dave plough through the undergrowth it makes perfect sense. Every few hundred metres, Dave stops dead and howls, before pushing on, barking furiously.

Behind him, the quad bike – still with its *Exposure* decals – bounces over the rough terrain with Huw at the helm. The bike is designed for one. Behind the seat is a metal rack, to which one might strap a bale of hay or a barrel of water, and it is to this rack that Leo and George are clinging. Leo's calves burn from the effort of stopping his feet from sliding off the wheel arches.

'*Iawn?*' Huw yells over his shoulder.

Leo is far from being *iawn*, but now is not the time to be a back-seat driver. 'We're fine,' he shouts back, realising as he does so that he hardly registered Huw asking in Welsh.

'Speak. For. Your. Self,' George says, each word punctuated by bumps in the path that send them flying. Leo tightens his grip on the rail and contemplates putting an arm around Huw's waist.

The helicopter is circling above them, and there's a crackle of activity across Leo's radio. *Possible sighting of the suspect on the eastern aspect.* The noise of the blades pulses through the commentary. *White male, dark hair – he's just looked up and now he's running.*

'It's him,' George says. 'It has to be him.'

Current location is above the scree, approximately two hundred metres from the summit.

'He'll be on the ridge.' Huw slows the quad bike and indicates up the mountain. 'But it looks like Dave's heading for the *Exposure* camp.' He twists around to see the others. 'That's good, right? If Ffion's in camp and Henry's up there, she's not in danger.'

'Right,' Leo says, because it's what Huw wants to hear and what Leo wants to believe, but he knows it's not as simple as that. The danger might already have happened.

The *chop chop* of the helicopter comes across the radio again. *Suspect is heading down, repeat heading down, still on the eastern ascent.*

Sending officers towards his location now, comes the response from Control Room.

'He's looped back,' Huw says. 'He'll be looking to come down on the horseshoe pass into the next village.' They're still following Dave, and now they can see the wire fence that marks the edge of the *Exposure* camp, and Huw twists around again. 'What do you want to do?'

'You find Ffion,' George says. 'I'll go after Henry. How easy is this thing to drive?'

'I've been using one since I was eight.' Huw brings the bike to a standstill, the engine idling. 'Go easy on the gas till you're used to it, though, or you'll end up under it.'

340

'Reassuring.'

Leo jumps off the bike. The Control Room operator is orchestrating the approach of a dozen officers, with the help of footage streamed directly from the helicopter. Huw's already running after Dave. Leo looks at George. 'I should—'

'Find Ffion,' she says firmly. 'Yes, you should.' She throws a leg over the quad bike and presses down her foot. The bike shoots off, its front wheels off the ground, and Leo hears a *Fuuuck* before it crashes back down. 'I'm fine!' George cries, as she bounces up the track. 'Totally fine!'

Leo runs after Huw and Dave. He's praying George won't come off; partly because he doesn't want her hurt, but mostly because he's fairly certain he should have done some kind of risk assessment before letting a DC engage in a foot pursuit on a quad bike.

Everything seems to happen at once.

A burst of noise from the radio: *twenty metres to your left; the two officers by the stile, turn ninety degrees to your right; suspect running towards you.*

Leo and Huw: tearing through the *Exposure* camp, throwing open the abandoned bell tents, shouting Ffion's name.

Dave: his barks even louder, even more intense.

Suspect in sight, Leo hears over the radio. Not from the helicopter, this time, but a male officer, breath laboured, boots pounding.

'Over there!' Huw shouts, pointing to where Dave is running in circles, barking at the peculiar structure he's found, half buried in the ground.

The confession pod.

Zero nine with – stop resisting! George's voice, cutting off her own update to take control of her suspect, and Leo keeps his hand on the radio as he and Huw run to the confession pod, as

341

though by being connected he can somehow help. But she and the others don't need his help, because when George speaks again – *Zero nine with one* – she's calmer and the shouting in the background has ceased.

Henry's under arrest. They've got him.

FORTY-EIGHT

TUESDAY | FFION

Ffion's hand hits the chair. Her fingers grasp it and something about the solidity of it grounds her enough to plant her feet, to pull herself up against the drag of the water and climb on to the seat and then the arms and then the high back, where she clings tight and gasps again and again until the burn in her chest subsides.

'Shit, shit, shit,' she says out loud, because it's weirdly reassuring to hear her own voice over the rush of the water and the—

She stops. What was that noise?

The water laps at her chin. In another minute or two, she'll have to tip back her head to keep her mouth out of water. And then . . .

There it is again.

Barking.

'Dave!' Ffion tries to shout, but her lips are numb with cold and her throat tight with fear. The barking is close, and now she hears Leo's voice too, and she calls again, and this time it doesn't matter that no sound comes out, because the door to the confession pod is being wrenched open. The water knocks Ffion off her perch and she's tumbling again, but this time she feels strong hands hauling her upright.

Two thousand litres of water rush out of the confession pod, and Ffion finds herself standing in a river along with Leo, Huw and Dave.

'*Ti'n* fucking idiot, Ffi,' Huw says. His eyes are glistening.

Leo takes off his jacket and drapes it around her trembling shoulders. 'Are you okay?'

Ffion tries to nod, but it turns into a shiver. Dave is trying to climb into her arms, and she crouches so she can thank him properly for finding her, but also because her legs won't support her much longer. 'Henry . . .' she starts, but her brain is running at half-speed. She isn't sure she can explain how she discovered it was Henry who killed Miles, but it seems she doesn't need to.

'He's been arrested,' Leo says. 'George is en route to Bryndare with him now.'

Ffion manages a tight nod. She doesn't trust herself to speak. Leo puts his arm around her, and she lets him guide her through the camp. 'I thought I was going to . . .' She can't finish.

'So did I.'

'I'm glad you found me.'

Leo turns to face her. He runs his hand down her shoulder and takes her hand, squeezing it tight. 'So am I.'

FORTY-NINE

WEDNESDAY | LEO

Henry Moore (or, more accurately, Clive Manning) rests his hands on the interview room table, his gaze low. Next to him is a solicitor, a woman in her fifties who occasionally interjects with reminders to Leo and George that her client has already answered that, or to ask Henry if he would like a break.

Leo and George sit opposite them. Ffion attempted to argue her case, but even she had to concede that she couldn't carry out an impartial interview of a man who, a few hours ago, had tried to kill her.

'It's a conflict of interest,' Leo said.

Ffion's expression darkened. 'You'd know all about that, I suppose.'

'What's that supposed to mean?'

But Ffion had turned away, and with Henry ready for interview there was no time to drag an explanation out of her.

'Why the fake name?' Leo says, when Henry has finished giving an account of his movements over the last few days.

'I never use my real one.' Henry shrugs, as though assuming a pseudonym is a perfectly normal thing to do. 'I'm an investigative reporter, often working with insalubrious characters. Not this time, of course.' He smiles and looks around, perhaps in the mistaken belief that he is warming up the crowd. Leo stares back at him, and Henry's smile fades.

'And you were employed as a researcher?'

'I was freelance, technically. But yes, Miles contracted me to hunt out secrets. I'm rather good at it, you see.' Another smile stretches across his face.

'I wouldn't know where to start,' George says. 'It's hard enough digging into people's lives when you have access to police databases, but . . .' She blows out her cheeks. Leo suppresses a laugh at her attempts to flatter Henry into a confession. As if he'd be taken in by—

'I've been doing this a long time,' Henry says. 'Although I have to confess, I made a few false starts – some secrets are too well hidden even for me.'

'Maybe they didn't exist,' Leo says. 'Not everyone has secrets.'

Henry smiles at him. 'Everyone has secrets.'

Leo says nothing. Partly because this is a police interview, not a game of truth or dare in the *Exposure* camp, but mostly because he realises his automatic response – I don't have secrets – isn't entirely true. Otherwise he'd tell Ffion how he feels.

'Reverend Lucas was just good old-fashioned surveillance work.' Henry directs his response to George. 'I went to a Sunday service with the intention of speaking to some of the congregation – finding out a bit more about him. Then I saw the way the organist's wife was looking at him, and . . .' Henry presses his palms together and touches his fingertips to his mouth.

'How about Aliyah?' George asks.

'Google images. She's on an archived site called Rate My Date.' Henry glances at Leo. 'Eight and a half, if you were wondering.'

'I wasn't,' Leo says, with barely contained disgust. 'And how did you discover Jason had been married twice?'

'That was a happy accident. His Facebook page had old photos from Australia and I thought I'd see if he'd racked up any drugs charges during his gap year. I tapped up a colleague who lives there, and they ran a register office check too – found the marriage listing. No death or divorce. Jackpot.'

One by one, Henry takes them through the methods he used to trace his fellow contestants' secrets, while Leo tries to work out what additional offences they might add to Henry's charge sheet. It turns out there was gossip on a local parenting site about Pam's openness to bribes, but Henry admits to hacking Ceri's emails and to stealing receipts from specialist shoe shops from Ryan's recycling bin. Indisputably crimes, albeit petty ones when compared to murder and attempted murder.

'And of course, there was your own secret,' George says.

For the first time since the interview began, Henry's face tightens a little. 'Miles said I had to have one in the box, in case someone tried to expose me and Roxy had to open the envelope. We agreed we would say I was an alcoholic.'

Leo leans back in his chair. 'Pretty tame, compared to everyone else's.'

'*Exposure* was all about the personal cost of secrets. I had a story ready, in case I was confronted. How I'd lose my job, how relationships were hanging by a thread, that sort of thing.'

'But it was all a lie,' George says. 'In fact, your entire presence in the show was a lie.'

'Might I remind you that lying is not in itself a crime, detective?' the solicitor says.

'But Miles didn't put that in the envelope, did he? He found something a little juicier.' Leo holds Henry's gaze, certain he detects a tremor of nerves about the man. He pulls a document from a file and reads aloud the photocopied secret. '*Henry has refused to pay child support for three years.*'

Henry's lips part. He stares at Leo without saying a word. Then his lips curve into a small smile and he leans back against his chair. 'Is that it?'

'That's it.' Leo views Henry's relaxed expression with interest, thinking of the anxious faces of the other contestants when their secrets were revealed.

'Miles got the wrong end of the stick,' Henry says smoothly. 'I – foolishly, as it turns out – mentioned an issue I had with an ex-partner. There's no evidence the child is mine, you see, and I move around a lot, so—'

'Not a problem,' George says. 'We'll let the Child Maintenance Service know where to find you. Something tells me you won't be sending a change-of-address card for a few years.'

'If I can recap on what you've told us . . .' Leo says. This is his favourite moment in an interview: the part where the suspect puts the rope around his own neck. 'You didn't leave the *Exposure* camp on Sunday, and the closest you've been to Miles's editing studio is when you walked past it—'

'On the way to my own room,' Henry finishes helpfully.

'Right. You've told us that on the morning of the murder you spent an hour asleep in the woods—'

'Approximately.' Henry accompanies his interruption with an apologetic smile. 'We weren't allowed to wear watches in camp.'

'You spent *approximately* an hour asleep in the woods, before returning to camp, when you went to the confession pod.' Leo looks at Henry for confirmation.

'For the benefit of the tape,' George says, 'the suspect is nodding.'

The solicitor closes her notebook with a snap. 'Is this really

348

necessary? My client has already given a full account of his where-abouts on Sunday *and* yesterday.'

'Ah yes, yesterday . . .' George flicks back through her own book. 'Yesterday you went for a walk up Pen y Ddraig mountain. You became disorientated when the police helicopter flew over-head, and you started running . . .' George pauses and consults her notes. '"In case you were in the way".'

'I don't appreciate your sarcasm, DC Kent, and neither does my client.'

'I thought the helicopter might be looking for someone,' Henry says.

'How very perceptive of you.'

'DC Kent, I must insist—'

George ignores the solicitor's protestations. 'When we found DC Morgan, she was locked in the confession pod.'

'I was shocked when I heard that.'

'Indeed.'

'DC Kent!'

'Someone had barricaded the door and turned on the flood tap.'

'Appalling.'

'But that wasn't you,' Leo says.

'It most certainly wasn't.'

'Because if it was, you'd be looking at a charge of attempted murder,' George says. 'In addition to the murder you say you didn't commit.'

'I had no involvement in either of those things,' Henry says.

'Officers, do you actually have a question for my client, or do you simply intend to keep going over the – frankly, very expansive – account he has already given you?'

'We just want to make sure we haven't missed anything,' George says. 'It's important your client has every opportunity to tell us what happened.'

'I appreciate that,' Henry says smoothly. 'But I have nothing else to say. Everything I've told you is the truth. I didn't kill Miles, and I was nowhere near your colleague today, at the time of her unfortunate accident.'

Leo places a clear plastic evidence bag on the table. 'What's this, Henry?'

'I've got no idea, I'm afraid.' Henry's voice is confident, but there's a faint tremor by his left eye.

By the time Jim and his dog Foster came free from their previous job, Henry was in custody and Ffion had been found. Foster was put to work anyway, leading Jim to a rabbit hole, where he began digging furiously.

'It's Miles's running jacket, beanie and sunglasses, and a pair of pink socks,' Leo says now.

'If you say so.'

'I do. But to be doubly certain, we've fast-tracked forensics, and sure enough—' Leo pats the bag '—Miles's DNA is on all of the items except the socks.'

George leans across the table. 'Guess whose DNA is also on them.'

Henry blinks. 'I'm sure I don't—'

'Yours, Henry.' Leo folds his arms. 'Why would your DNA be on Miles's jacket?'

'I – I might have borrowed it. Now that I think about it, I did ask him if—'

'Don't bullshit me,' Leo says, his voice growing louder. 'Your DNA is on there because you disguised yourself as Miles after you climbed in through his window wearing the socks on your hands – which, by the way, happen to match marks found on the window frame – and strangled him with this.' Leo reaches into his bag and produces a smaller exhibit bag containing a single shoelace. 'This was seized from the trainers you were wearing when you were arrested. A forensic pathologist has confirmed the pattern and size match the ligature marks on Miles's neck, and I have no doubt we'll find both his DNA and yours when we submit it for analysis. So . . .' Leo leans forward. 'Are you quite certain you've told us everything? Because remember: it may harm your defence if you do not mention now something you later rely on in court.'

'I'm quite certain.' Henry smiles apologetically. 'I'm sorry I can't be more helpful.'

'Oh, wait.' George produces a third bag, as though she's only just remembered she had it. 'And of course there's this, which was in your pocket when you were brought into custody.' She slides it along the table. 'It's the key to the box of secrets.'

There's a long pause.

Henry isn't smiling now.

FIFTY

WEDNESDAY | FFION

'And he still won't admit it?' Ffion has bitten her nails to the quick, waiting for Leo and George to come out of interview.

'His solicitor stopped the interview to "consult with her client" and, when they came back, he went no comment. Not that it matters – he's bang to rights.' George grins at Leo, still on a high, and Ffion feels a lurch of something she isn't ready to acknowledge.

'Thanks to you.' Leo looks at Ffion. 'Piecing together those film clips was an outstanding piece of work.'

'Someone in the tech team would have found them at some point,' Ffion says, ignoring the warmth that spreads through her at the praise.

'By which time, we'd have released the witnesses and Henry – I mean Clive – would have disappeared.' Leo's jacket rides up as he stretches out his arms. 'DCI Boccacci's on the phone with the CPS now,' he says through a yawn. 'She's proposing an alternative charge of false imprisonment, in case the attempted murder doesn't stick.'

If Clive Manning enters a not guilty plea, it will be months before they're all called to give evidence. Ffion thinks about standing in the witness box as a victim, not only as an officer; imagines her testimony torn apart by the defence. 'Are you staying on the investigation?' she asks Leo, then curses herself for sounding as if she wants him to. 'You're Boccacci's star pupil, after all.' It comes out sharper than she means.

'No, I'm done. Heading back to Cheshire now.' He turns to George. 'You'll follow up with the Child Maintenance Service?'

'Too right I will.' George looks at Ffion. 'You should have seen his face when Leo read out his secret. Like he didn't give a shit.'

'I guess it's the least of his worries now,' Ffion says.

'Take care.' Leo extends a hand to George. 'Great job in there.'

'Great job yourself.' She reaches up and hugs him instead, and Ffion stares out of the window into the back yard, where two uniformed officers are washing down a patrol car.

'It was good to work with you again,' Leo says, and Ffion realises he's talking to her.

'You too.' She snaps her gaze back and pastes on a smile. 'See you on the next one!' She laughs, but it sounds false, even to her.

'Bye, then.' Leo takes a half-step forward. He holds up a hand in an awkward wave. Then he leaves.

Outside, the uniformed officers are packing away the pressure washer. A few seconds later, Leo crosses the yard and gets into his car. Ffion can feel George's gaze on her.

'You're a fucking idiot, Ffion Morgan.'

'You're the second person to tell me that in as many days.'

'Do you know how often decent men come along?'

'I'll let you know when I meet one.' Ffion tries for a laugh, but her face won't comply.

'It's obvious you like him, and he clearly adores you, although God knows why – you treat him like shit.'

'Sure. He's such a fan, he grassed me up to Malik, who gave me a lecture on conflicts of interest, then took me off the job.' Ffion walks away.

'That was Alun, you idiot,' George calls after her. 'And – much as I hate to admit it – he had a point. You should have disclosed the fact that Caleb's in a relationship with your sister. He might not have been a prime suspect, but—'

'Caleb?' Ffion stops abruptly.

'Alun spoke to Seren at the farmhouse. You'd been arguing about something? She spilled her guts, apparently, and you know what Alun's like – total jobsworth. Any opportunity to make someone else look bad.'

Leo didn't tell DI Malik that Ffion had withheld Ceri's envelope.

Leo didn't tell Malik anything.

Ffion looks out of the window, but Leo's car has gone. What would Ffion say to him, anyway? *Sorry I was a dick? Any chance we can start over? I think I might be in love with you?*

She lets out a long breath.

Ffion can count on one hand the times she's said *I love you.* The words seem to get stuck somewhere between her head and her mouth, the weight of them too much to vocalise. She marvels at the ease with which other women say it – to each other, to siblings, to boyfriends they've known all of five minutes – and thinks she must be wired differently.

You don't have to say the words, Ffion always reasons, for people to know it's true. Mam and Seren know Ffion loves them fiercely, and when Ffion married Huw he'd known she loved him, in her own way.

But Leo doesn't know.

Ffion pushes the voice aside.

'Just tell him how you feel,' George says.

'I don't know what you're talking about.' Ffion starts walking again.

354

'Maybe if you loosened up a bit, you might feel—'

'Loosened up?' Ffion spins around. 'Oh, you're a fine one to talk! I've never met anyone more buttoned-up. You never come to the canteen, you never go for drinks after work, you hardly ever—'

'I'm an introvert,' George says. 'Like you.'

'I'm not an introvert,' Ffion snaps. 'I just don't like people. I don't turn down an invitation to drinks as though my colleagues have leprosy.'

'I wasn't aware socialising was compulsory.' There's an icy undercurrent to George's tone.

'You're basically dead inside,' Ffion snaps. 'So don't try to give me advice about relationships.'

She stalks down the corridor and around the corner to where Malik's office is, leaving George standing by the window. The DI is on the phone, and Ffion hovers by the door, still seething from George's unsolicited advice.

'How long till we have that confirmed?' Malik signals for Ffion to come in and take a seat. 'And you'll interview him in the meantime?'

Ffion checks her phone for messages. There are several emails in her inbox, including one from Alun reminding Ffion that, since she hasn't put a pound in the kitchen jar *for several weeks*, she should not under any circumstances make herself a drink until she does. Word of Ffion's confession pod ordeal has clearly spread around Cwm Coed, as she's had several concerned WhatsApps from friends, and even Mam – who hates technology – has messaged her. **Be oedd ar dy ben di???** *What was going on in your head???*

Ffion sends a quick response. **I'm fine, don't flap.**

Dwi ddim yn fflapio!!! comes the indignant response.

Malik finishes his call, and Ffion switches her phone to silent and puts it in her pocket.

'DCI Boccacci says she's very impressed with you,' Malik says, just as Ffion starts speaking.

'I came to say I'm sorry.'

Malik tries – and fails – to hide his surprise. 'That's a first.'

'Funnily enough, that's what I was going to say.' Ffion gives a weak smile. 'People aren't often impressed with me.'

'Well, the DCI is. A young woman has come forward with an allegation against Clive Manning. It seems he was working under-cover on a story about unscrupulous landlords demanding sex in exchange for reduced rent, and he blackmailed one of the contrib-utors. Said he'd only keep her identity a secret if she was "nice" to him.' Malik's distaste is palpable.

'That's vile.'

'She never knew his real name, and when the story broke, the paper refused to reveal their source.'

'Was she watching *Exposure*?'

'She recognised him immediately, but she doubted herself, because he seemed so charming and inoffensive.'

'So much for *the camera never lies*,' Ffion says. 'Miles orches-trated every fucking second of that show.' The DI winces. 'Every flipping second of it. Sorry about the swearing. I am trying.'

Malik sighs. 'You are indeed. Manning's real name won't be released to the press until he's charged, but the young woman read some rather damning tweets by a YouTuber . . .' Malik looks down at his blotter, where he has jotted down a name.

'Zee Hart?'

'That's the one. She's been told to delete them or face charges

– we don't want the trial collapsing before it's started – but it does seem to have flushed out a victim. One wonders how many others there are.'

So Henry had been the *#MeToo* contestant all along. Miles clearly hadn't found enough dirt to put into the box of secrets, but whatever he'd dug up had been enough for him to warn Roxy. *You can sue the ass off a production company if they don't protect staff from harassment*, she'd told Leo.

And now Henry-aka-Clive would be brought to justice. Murder, attempted murder, and now sexual assault. There's a certain irony, Ffion thinks, that, in attempting to protect one relatively small secret, he would now face far greater accusations. He'd tried to beat Miles at his own game, but in the end, there were no winners.

'But I've interrupted your apology,' Malik says. 'The floor is yours.'

'It was poor judgement not to have told you Seren was going out with Caleb.'

'Yes. It was.' Malik leans back in his chair. 'There's no reason you couldn't have stayed on the case – but when you're found to be withholding something like that, it gives rise to—'

'Also, I kept something out of the evidential chain.' Ffion says it quickly, before she changes her mind. 'It turned out not to be significant – and I'd put it back by then anyway – but for a few hours I . . .' Ffion sighs. 'You were right, boss. I'm too close. Investigating people I've grown up with . . . it's hard.'

'No one ever said the job was easy.'

'I know.'

'What you're admitting is more than a disciplinary offence, Ffion. It's a job-loser.' Malik rubs his brow. 'Why are you telling me this now?'

'Because I want to do better.' Ffion keeps her gaze level. 'Because not telling you makes it a secret, and if I've learned anything over the last two weeks, it's not to keep secrets.'

Malik nods slowly.

'I also came to ask for a fortnight's leave,' Ffion says. 'Starting today. I'm taking Dave to the rescue centre tomorrow and I'm going to need some time to—'

'Take as much as you need. I hear the mutt was quite the hero.'

Ffion swallows hard. 'Thanks, boss.' She stands. 'And if you need to file a report with Professional Standards, I understand.'

'How many final warnings have I given you, Ffion?'

'Um . . . three?'

Malik scrutinises her. 'Consider this your *final* final warning.'

'Thank you.' Ffion feels a rush of relief.

'And, Ffion?'

'Yes?'

'While you're on leave, have a good long think about what's more important: your friends or your job.' He fixes her with a stern gaze. 'Play by the rules, or find yourself out of the game. Understood?'

'Loud and clear,' Ffion says, as she leaves the DI's office. Of course she understands. What she has to figure out is whether she wants to be in the game at all.

FIFTY-ONE

THURSDAY | DC GEORGE KENT

DI Malik's door has been closed all morning, which is a sure sign that something's going on. George feels a prickle of apprehension as she takes the seat he offers her. Ffion's on leave for two weeks (*I need to see a man about a dog*, read her email to George) and this morning, Alun was only in the office for five minutes to pick up his notebook before heading to the training block, muttering darkly about 'diversity bollocks'.

'So.' Malik rests his forearms on his desk. 'How have you been?'

'Good,' George says. The DI's head tilts to one side, and she realises what he's really asking. 'Mostly. It comes in waves.'

'I understand. It's not the same, I know, but I lost my mother last year. It's very hard.'

George counts to ten in her head, a polite smile on her face to hide the scream inside. It isn't remotely the same. It never is, and yet George has lost count of the number of people who have offered up their grief for comparison. Grandparents, neighbours, even a guinea pig called Fluffy. *He had such a dear little face*, the woman in the post office said, and George had left without buying the stamps she'd gone in for.

George had met Spencer at the start of secondary school. Not that they spoke to each other then – twelve-year-old girls want little to do with boys, and the feeling is mostly reciprocal. She and Spencer started going out at sixteen, were engaged by eighteen and married by twenty-one, and, despite all the *it'll never last*s from their families and friends, they remained married until eighteen months ago, when Spencer went down to the garage at three in the morning and hanged himself from the rafters.

'I wondered if you'd spoken about it to anyone in the office,' Malik says.

'No.'

'It might help. On days when you're feeling particularly—'

'No.' George is adamant. She does not want Ffion to know. She doesn't want anyone to know. She finds grief exhausting; finds talking about it even more exhausting. There are too many questions and not enough answers, and God knows George asks herself enough questions as it is. Why did a seemingly contented man take his own life? Why didn't she see it coming? Why, when George heard Spencer stir that night, didn't she go downstairs to see what was keeping him?

She swallows. Blinks hard. 'I'd rather focus on the job.'

Malik looks at her. 'Understood. You know where I am if—'

'Thanks. Is that all you wanted to see me about, boss?' George feels the pressure subsiding. If she doesn't talk about it – doesn't think about it – it's manageable.

'Actually, no.' Malik hesitates. 'How did you find working with Ffion? I know she can be a little . . .' He doesn't finish his sentence, and George has the distinct impression he doesn't know how.

It's George's turn to hesitate. She hasn't seen Ffion since their confrontation in the corridor, and when she'd heard Ffion had taken leave there was a bit of her that had worried it was her fault. Because, contrary to the accusation Ffion flung at her, George is not 'dead inside'.

Years ago, George watched a documentary about a man with locked-in syndrome. His cognitive function was intact, but every muscle in his body was paralysed except for his eyelids, which he used to communicate. George feels the opposite. Her body continues to function, but inside she feels numb. Her outburst with Ffion took her by surprise, but there is something of Spencer in Leo, and George finds Ffion's dismissive attitude infuriating. Doesn't she know how fragile life is?

'Working with Ffion can be . . .' George searches for the right word. 'Challenging.' She wonders how many of her predecessors were tasked with working with Ffion, and how many complained about it. Ffion is frequently enraging. Occasionally insufferable. 'But . . .' She hesitates again. When she was standing in the corridor arguing with Ffion, she hadn't felt numb. She'd felt anger coursing through her veins, and after eighteen months of numbness that feels like a step in the right direction.

'But?' Malik says hopefully.

'I don't mind working with her,' George says.

'Really?' Malik fails to hide the surprise in his voice. He coughs. 'Excellent. In that case, I'd like to keep the two of you together on a permanent basis. Let me know if you encounter any more . . . er . . . challenges.'

'Will do,' George says, although she has no intention of running to the DI every time she crosses swords with Ffion. In fact, she realises she's looking forward to the next job that comes their way. Working with Ffion might not be easy, but it certainly isn't boring.

FIFTY-TWO

THURSDAY | FFION

A light drizzle mists the air as Ffion, Mam and Seren walk up Pen y Ddraig. They're following the footpath from the village, having tacitly agreed on a route that will take them nowhere near the *Exposure* camp. Automatically, Ffion looks around for Dave, then remembers he isn't there. She imagines him crying for her at the rescue centre, then forces the image out of her head. It's in Dave's best interests, she tells herself. She's doing the right thing.

Carreg Plas is out of sight in a fold of the mountain. Already Ffion feels detached from everything that happened there. DCI Boccacci's team are dotting *is* and crossing *ts*, but Ffion's part is done. It feels strange to be doing nothing, after the adrenaline of the last two weeks, and she's almost regretting asking Malik for leave.

It will be a while before the aftermath of *Exposure* settles. More complaints have been made to the communications regulator about the programme than about any other television show ever. There will be no second series. Nobody from Young Productions has arranged for Dario's caravan to be collected, so he is still living in it, pondering his next move. Zee Hart packed up her tent after being threatened with contempt of court. Ffion keeps seeing her pop up on social media, trumpeting another video or blog post.

Roxy Wilde intends to set up a new production company, employing only women. She wants Aliyah to be her co-presenter. Jason is not being prosecuted for bigamy. His divorce from Addison is in progress and he is tentatively building bridges with Kat, who was somewhat appeased by the unedited footage of Jason waxing lyrical about her. Pam's Board of Governors have informed her there is a necessary process to go through, but that they are fully supportive of reinstating her. Lucas has gone on a religious retreat, after which he has promised to return home and face the (organ) music.

When Ffion, Elen and Seren reach the summit of Pen y Ddraig, they collapse on to the grass. What an odd thing it is, Ffion thinks, this compulsion to climb mountains, only to walk back down them. She feels it every time she sees a peak, as though it's an itch that demands a scratching. She smiles at nothing – at the view, at being here with Mam and Seren. At everything.

'I'm not going to Bangor Uni,' Seren says suddenly.

Ffion stops smiling. 'We've been through this a million times! You're going—'

'I'm going to uni in London.' Seren picks at the grass. 'Caleb wants to work in TV, and he's got more chance of finding something there, and I don't want to travel to Bangor every day, Ffi, I don't want to live in Cwm Coed, I want—' She breaks off, then turns to look at Ffion. 'I want more,' she says softly.

'More than what?'

'More than this.' Seren sweeps an arm across their view: the mountain they've climbed, the lake deep in the valley. 'I'm suffocating here.'

Ffion turns to Mam. 'Did you know about this?'

'I did.'

'So I'm the last to know, am I?'

'She tried to tell you, Ffi,' Elen says gently.

Ffion colours, because she knows it's true. 'And you're okay with it?'

'She's nearly eighteen.'

'Eighteen's nothing,' Ffion says. 'Anything could happen to her in London.'

Mam puts an arm around Ffion and draws her close. She presses a kiss on to the top of Ffion's head. 'Things happen in Cwm Coed too,' she murmurs.

Ffion can't argue with that. She reaches for Seren's hand, and the three women sit in silence as the early evening sun streaks the valley with gold.

'I get it,' Ffion says at last. 'Small towns can be claustrophobic.' It's why Ffion spends so much time outdoors – at the lake, or up a mountain. Sometimes she feels as though she only breathes properly when she's away from Cwm Coed.

'I think it's a good thing,' Mam says. She nudges Ffion. 'Maybe it would be good for you, too.'

'London?' Ffion makes a face.

'Anywhere. You don't have to stay in Cwm Coed just because I'm here.'

'I'm not,' Ffion says. 'I stay because . . .' Why does she stay? Because she's always been here, she supposes. Because she tried leaving once before and she didn't like it.

Because Seren was here.

As they walk back down, Ffion's head is rattling. Malik thinks she's too closely entwined with everyone here, yet when Seren wanted to talk to her Ffion had been too focused on work to listen. Should she move away from Cwm Coed? She imagines speaking to people without the shadow of her childhood – without the hangover of her wild teenage years. She imagines responding to jobs without the worry of finding an ex-boyfriend or a best friend at the scene; imagines how easy it would be to simply do her job and do it well. Cwm Coed isn't going anywhere, after all: Ffion can come home whenever she wants, and when she does, she won't be distracted by work.

And yet.

Moving away means leaving Mam. It means walking down a street without a dozen *Ti'n iawn*s from people Ffion's known all her life. It means leaving Pen y Ddraig and the shimmering waters of Llyn Drych. No more jobs that cross the border of England and Wales, with all the challenges they bring.

No more Leo.

Maybe that's a good thing?

By the time they reach the village, Ffion knows what she has to do.

The hardest thing in the world.

FIFTY-THREE

SATURDAY | LEO

Leo has been for a run, had breakfast and cleaned the kitchen, and it isn't yet ten o'clock. It's Allie's turn to have Harris, and Leo knows he should be making the most of an empty weekend, but he finds himself drifting about the house, missing his little buddy. Being a detective sergeant is so demanding – the job spilling into evenings and weekends – that it always makes Leo feel his life is bursting at the seams. Then they wrap up a big case and there's finally space to breathe, and life should feel good, but instead it feels empty.

Last night, Leo called Gayle.

'It's been really lovely getting to know you,' he said, because sometimes lies are kinder than the truth. 'But I don't think it's going to work between us.'

'I know, you're a busy man. Hard to pin down!' Gayle laughed. 'How about breakfast tomorrow? I'll come to yours, and we can take it back to bed.'

'I don't think so.'

'Sunday?'

The hints weren't working. Leo briefly contemplated giving an alternative reason – he was gay, he'd met someone, he had a terminal illness – before opting for the truth. 'Gayle, I don't want to see you again. I'm sorry,' he added.

'At all?'

Leo took a deep breath. 'At all.'

There was a long and painful pause, before Gayle said, 'Well, why didn't you say so?'

Why indeed? Leo thought, as they ended the call.

Henry had appeared at Magistrates' Court on Thursday, where he'd indicated that he intended to enter a guilty plea to murder and attempted murder. He was remanded in custody, awaiting sentencing at a Crown Court. At Angharad's insistence – and because the CPS considered it would not be in the public interest to prosecute – all charges against Ryan Francis have been dropped. Ryan is recovering as a voluntary inpatient in a private psychiatric unit, paid for by the income generated by the viewer calls to *Exposure*. An investigation into Ceri's thefts is being carried out internally by Royal Mail, who will subsequently decide whether to refer the investigation to the police.

Leo re-reads the reply he's just typed. DCI Boccacci's email was brief but flattering. Would Leo consider a transfer? North Wales Major Crime Unit is based in Bryndare, but several officers work flexibly from other stations. There are excellent career prospects.

Leo presses *send*. His response is longer and more detailed, but the sentiment is succinct.

Thank you. But no.

Some of the lads from the office are meeting up for a pint tonight, and Leo will probably join them, but the hours in between seem endless. He makes himself a coffee he doesn't want. Maybe he should get himself a hobby. What do middle-aged men do with their days off, if they don't want to squeeze themselves into Lycra and spend six months' salary on a bike? Leo has promised Harris they'll go paddle-boarding this summer, so perhaps he'll take a drive to Cwm Coed and line up a hire for next weekend.

Maybe bump into Ffion, says the voice in his head. Leo ignores it. Mirror Lake is the best place for water sports within driving distance, it has nothing to do with Ffion Morgan. He puts milk in his coffee and stirs more vigorously than is necessary.

Ffion hasn't been in touch.

Leo hasn't messaged her – he's not going down that road again – and he has deleted her number once again. Ffion is incredible. She makes him feel alive in a way no one but his son has ever done. But she's also infuriating, impossible to read, and totally . . .

The doorbell rings, and Leo takes his coffee with him to open the door.

. . . totally unpredictable.

'Are you busy?' Ffion says. Dave's with her, his lead wound tightly around Ffion's hand.

Leo considers the question. 'Pretty busy. Why?'

'I'm . . .' Ffion takes a breath. 'I'm not good at messaging people.'

'No shit,' Leo says mildly. He watches Ffion pick at the cracked paint on the doorframe. He's been meaning to rub it down and repaint it. He could do it this weekend, he supposes, before work takes over again.

'I overthink things.' A flake of red paint floats to the ground. 'I write a message, then I delete it, then I write it again and delete it again and . . .' Ffion frowns at the doorframe, levering off a larger slice of paint. Underneath, the woodwork is a garish lime green. Leo's hands twitch.

'Um, would you mind not—'

'I thought it would be easier in person.'

Leo stands very still. Ffion's still frowning, and Leo realises she's about to draw a line under whatever it is that's been simmering beneath the surface. She couldn't find the right words to break it to him by text; feels she owes it to him to tell him face to face.

'But it isn't.' Ffion screws her eyes shut, then opens them and looks directly at him. 'What's wrong with me, Leo?'

'Nothing's wrong with you, Ffi.' Leo has an ache in his chest.

'I can't say it.'

'Say what?' Leo is definitely going to meet his mates for a pint tonight. In fact, he's going to get blind drunk, in a way he rarely does.

'I took some leave.'

'You came here to tell me you're on leave?'

'Dave spent the day with a dog trainer at the rescue centre on Thursday. We've got a lot of homework to do, so I took some holiday. I've still got ten days left and I thought . . .' Ffion chews the inside of her cheek. 'I thought I might spend them here.'

Leo blinks.

'With you.'

She has a bag with her, Leo realises, dumped behind Dave.

'But you're busy.'

'I'm not really that busy, actually.'

'So . . .' Ffion picks up her bag.

'You'd like to be with me for ten whole days?' Leo wants to be absolutely certain he understands what Ffion is saying. He has a strong feeling this is a pivotal moment in their – can he call it a relationship? Fuck it, he's going to. A pivotal moment in their relationship.

'Yes.' Ffion exhales.

'Just ten days?' Leo says.

A slow smile spreads across Ffion's face. 'For now.' She picks up her bag and pulls the strap over one shoulder. Automatically, Leo steps back to let her inside, then he stops.

'No.'

'What?' The colour seeps from Ffion's face.

'No,' Leo says quietly. There's a beat, as he tries to marshal his thoughts into something that will make sense for them both. 'I can't do this.'

'Do what?'

'Let you into my life, only for you to run out again because you're scared.'

Ffion laughs. 'I'm not—'

'Yes, you are. Scared of getting close to anyone. Scared of saying how you feel. And I get that, I do, but it isn't fair, Ffi. I'm not putting myself through that.'

'Why are you being like this?' Ffion blinks rapidly. 'This isn't you.'

Leo leaves a beat. 'I guess I grew that spine you said I needed.'

Ffion opens her mouth to say something, then closes it again. She gives a curt nod, then turns and walks away. Every fibre of Leo wants to call out to her, but he makes himself close the door and he presses his palms to the wall until he trusts himself not to open it again. He's done the right thing, he knows he has, so why does he feel so shit?

He goes to the bathroom and washes his face, then gets changed and puts on his trainers. He'll go to the gym and punch the fuck out of a bag, then he'll shower and meet the lads for beers, and he'll get so wasted he won't think about Ffion Morgan or the fact that he just let her walk out of his life.

When Leo opens the front door a few minutes later, he sees Ffion's car parked on the road. He can't see Ffion herself, because Dave

370

is sitting upright on the passenger seat with one paw on the dashboard, looking like he's about to break out a picnic.

Leo walks past the Triumph, his gym bag over one shoulder. He hears the car door open, hears footsteps running after him, but he keeps walking. He's done the right thing. He's been pushed around in relationships before, and if Ffion can't even say how she feels, then—

'I love you.'

Leo stops. His heart's pounding faster than it does in any workout, and he wonders if it would be safer to keep walking. He wonders if he misheard, because it didn't even sound like Ffion; it's not something he ever imagined her saying.

She says it again. Louder, this time.

Leo turns around.

ACKNOWLEDGEMENTS

It turns out that writing a series is very different from writing standalone novels. It has felt at times as though I were a beginner writer all over again, and I'm grateful to the wisdom and patience of my publisher, Lucy Malagoni, for steering me through a few rocky months (and even rockier early drafts). My thanks to Lucy and her fellow editor Tilda Key for their editorial brilliance. This book really is a team effort.

On that note, a huge thank you to everyone at Sphere, and within the wider Little, Brown team, who work so hard to put my books in the hands of readers. Thank you to Laura Sherlock for PR; to Gemma Shelley, Brionee Fenlon, Fergus Edmondson and Emily Cox for marketing; to Hannah Methuen and her sales team; and to Rebecca Folland, Jessica Purdue, Helena Doree, Louise Henderson and Zoe King for looking after my international rights. Thank you to copy-editor extraordinaire Linda McQueen; to desk editor Jon Appleton; and to Hannah Wood, for another stunning cover.

Thank you to freelance editor Nia Roberts, for reading the manuscript and checking my Welsh; to Ella Chapman, Sam Sutcliffe and Siobhan Graham for keeping on top of my newsletter and social media channels; to Tim Marchant for web work; and to Lynda Tunnicliffe, Sarah Clayton and Huw McKee for being admins of my Facebook group, *The Clare Mackintosh Book Club*.

Thank you to Colin Scott. You know what for.

Lucia Boccacci made a generous bid in a *Books for Ukraine* auction, and I'm delighted to honour her beloved mother by naming a character after her.

Thank you to my agent, Sheila Crowley, who always has my back; to Tanja Goossens for her attention to detail; and to the wider team at Curtis Brown Literary and Talent Agency.

Thank you to my husband Rob, and to Josh, Evie and George, who are probably all very relieved this book is finally finished. (Guess what, though? I have to do it all again now . . .)

Thank you to my friends for indulging my authorly ways and for being so generous with your support; and to beautiful North Wales, for continuing to inspire me.

Finally, and most importantly, my thanks to you. Thank you for picking up this book, for investing your time in it, for reviewing or sharing it. Thank you for being the reason I get to write stories for a living.